I stopped the tape at counter zero where I'd reset it after its last recording, and pressed Play.

I heard the monitors beeping, a gasp and grunt that must have been me from the kitchen, distant sounds of traffic, the thudding run and squeak of my bare feet, silence, my expletive, "Fuck!" a grunt and thwacking clatter as I destroyed an expensive digital camera, a sob, stumbling, breathing. Just me. As usual. Just—

"Daddy? I'm right here. Where's Mommy?"

It came from the tape. Because there was my voice too, right after it: "Birdy?"

More footsteps. The sound of the camcorder being rewound and played.

Audio recording ends.

Oh, *shit*.

OTHER WORKS BY
JAMES KINSAK

Driven
Mind Games (collection)
More Mind Games (collection)
Mind Games Deluxe (collection)

JAMES KINSAK

DESPERATE

fiero
PUBLISHING

For my dad, a dynamic guy who still found the time to give his best to his family, and exemplified the motto: *Never say die.*

DESPERATE

1

As if summoned, the pre-dawn mists rolled over the Bay and hissed around the buildings of downtown San Francisco. They piled and spread, and piled again, working their way inwards.

As they rolled over a crumbling tenement just west of Market Street, a young man in a third-floor room pushed himself to his feet and staggered one last time around the circle of guttering candles and improvised smoke pots.

He collapsed to his bare knees.

His lean brown body was stripped to a pair of sweat-soaked boxer shorts. His feet were wrapped with tough green ti leaves tied with butcher's twine. The black smoke that sputtered from the cut-off soup-cans filled with kerosene-soaked balls of hemp made his eyes sting and head buzz. His back wept from wounds caused by the razor edged pandanus leaves he'd whipped himself with.

"Weki!" he croaked.

The other man in the room, an old Hawaiian kahuna who'd been sitting, rocking and chanting, in the center of the candles and soup cans, stopped but didn't turn his face. And for a moment the young man wondered if the old man was still with it. The kahuna's cotton trousers, stained from food and urine, bunched up on his stick legs. His tee-shirt stretched limply around the bloat of his belly. Scabs from his picking fingernails and burns from his crack pipe ran through his grizzled chin and scalp.

Then he slowly turned his head. His eyes were too black to be real.

"It's time," the young man croaked. "I can feel the desolate ones, the *Au-Kuewa*. They are with us."

The kahuna blinked, the blackness of his eyes lightening just a little. "You still got more purify, *pi kai*."

"More?"

"For what you do, yeh, brah. Chant you family now, all you mother and you father lines."

Grunting, the young man gripped the pandanus switch again, stood, almost fell as his legs buckled, then recommenced staggering about the room, muttering the names of his cursed lineage as he hit himself with the leaves.

He saw the kahuna shuffle his pile of stones, *pohaku kapuha*, on the floor in front of him and raise his chin.

"*Ike!*" the old man called out. *The world as you believe it to be.*

"*Kala!*" *There are no limits to what you can be.*

"*Makia!*" *You control where your energy goes.*

"*Manawa!*" *The power is right now.*

"*Mana!*" *The power is in you.*

The young man felt a shock thud through him, as if someone had slammed a door beside his head. He stumbled and fell to his knees in front of Kahuna Weki Naea Kapu, momentarily blind.

"I feel it," he said and all at once could see again.

The old man raised his black eyes again, all weakness and need gone from the ravaged face, his being rippling with the power of magic, his connection to the dead a visible thing. *Lanikâula*—dark magician of Molokai.

The young man felt his gut tighten in fear even as his heart sped with excitement. Rain began spattering the window.

The *lanikâula* struck him hard on both shoulders, then reached back and retrieved a small wooden bowl. Holding the bowl in front of him, he mumbled another chant, but to the young man everything sounded like buzzing flies.

Until the *lanikâula* held the bowl towards him and ordered, "Drink!"

The young man took the bowl. He put it to his lips. The liquid slipped across his tongue dark and soapy and bittersweet. Kava kava. His lips and tongue went numb as he gulped it down. The buzzing in his head increased.

Throwing down the bowl so it clattered across the floor, he pushed himself to standing.

"Now!" he said. He ripped the ti leaves from his feet, found his pants, his shirt and hooded black sweatshirt. Dressed spastically. His sandals. The knife? He needed the knife.

"You see the child?" asked the *lanikâula*.

The young man nodded, staggering, his vision swimming. The old man was holding something up to him. A crack pipe. "Now?"

"No! Must be perfect time."

The young man fumbled a cigarette lighter out of his jeans pocket and held it under the bulb of the other's crack pipe. "Now!" He waved the flame back and forth. "Now!" A plea.

"No second chance."

"NOW!" Agony.

The *lanikâula* who was also a crack addict, a slave, a nothing, held up the boar knife. "Go."

The young man grabbed the knife and howled as he flung himself at the door, wrenched it open, and threw himself into the piss-soaked hallway, down the stairwell, past a Latina hooker pushing last night's john from her room, through the front door and out into the fog and rumbling traffic.

End of the world, he laughed as he ran.

2

YOU CAN LIVE YOUR WHOLE LIFE watching for the bogeyman and still not recognize him when he appears. All it takes is a distraction.

In this case it was a marital spat with Sherry, with our three children right there.

We stood in a long, blowy line-up of hundreds waiting for the doors to open on Mad Music's fall sale. It had been spattering rain all morning. Cars rumbled by slowly on the two-lane street. Everyone pressed back on the narrow sidewalk, shivering and mumbling in their clammy rain gear. While Sherry and I went at it.

"You'd rather I was still back at Cisco," I snapped *sotto voce*. "That's what you're saying?"

"No!" A violent shake of her red hair under her hood.

"Then—"

"But if you're going to run this thing from home—"

"So *you* can go back to work."

"—you could set some hours! The kids need you."

"And I'm here"

"Half here."

"Oh, Jesus..."

"David!"

Sherry reached down and covered the ears of six-year-old son. Not that Josh would have heard anything. He was one of the whuffling-wind miserable. He'd huddled in between Sherry's legs and tried to pull the bottom flaps of her rain coat around him.

And ahead of us in line, our twelve-year-old Martha had almost certainly heard nothing. Her own rain hood was up and she was absorbed in her usual mix of hormones, punk hair, and whatever was blasting through the ear buds of her MP3 player. The only other person she'd even acknowledge these days was her younger sister, Birdy.

Because how could you not? Birdy, our seven-year-old, had a sunshine smile you couldn't ignore. Right now she was tugging on Martha's hand and pointing to some bird flying through the rain. Laughing. Martha looking. It had almost brought me out of my blackness before Sherry snapped me back.

"So *will* you?" she pressed.

"What?" I ground my teeth. "You want me to cut back on the business just when it's critical Raj and I give it feet, right? That's really smart."

"You give it feet while you lose your heart. I want *you*, David. It's not just for the kids. I want you to find yourself again."

"Mys— Oh. Right. Painting." I gave an ugly laugh to mask the fear response that shot through me.

"Why not?"

"It's not even—"

"You could do it part-time."

"Get off it, Sher! What? Like you'll do ballet part-time? Maybe you can dance while Martha plays sax."

Sherry's face flamed the color of her hair and even though I was feeling hot too, I kicked myself hard. Stupid. My fear made me stupid. Ballet had been Sherry's childhood dream, derailed at fourteen when she'd grown her Marilyn Monroe figure. Something I loved and she bemoaned.

I swallowed hard, fighting to clear my bile. "Sorry, Sher. Look..."

It died as I saw the guy about ten people back in the line-up, watching us.

He looked like a drifter with dark Asian features, shaggy black hair, chin bristle, squinting through the downpour at us. He caught my eye then looked away, burying his nose and chin down into the neck of his soaked hoodie. Without putting the hood up. His hands in the front pocket pulled the front taut so I could read the logo there–*Dias de los Muertos*, San Francisco. Day of the Dead.

Despite the heat of my argument with Sherry, I shivered. Then I shook it off. This was 10:30 a.m., a few blocks south of the SF Museum of Modern Art, not some late-night deserted alley.

I shut the creep out and turned back to see Sherry looking down, stroking Joshie's head now as he clung to her.

"Sher?"

She looked up and I saw she was crying. And just like that I was sorry for everything. Sorry for not making more money sooner somehow so I didn't *have* to run this business. Sorry for not being stronger for her, for needing security like I did. Sorry most of all for reflexively striking back at her when all she wanted was...was what? To make me different than what I was?

"Sher, you have to understand this is important. I can't afford to fail."

"You're already failing. You just don't see it."

That shut my mouth in a thin line. But I also stupidly let my eyes drop to Sherry's magnificent chest. Her hard breathing had popped the top button of her raincoat and even in my anger, or because of it, my eyes stayed fixed there.

Sherry saw my look and went ballistic. Tearing Josh off her leg, she pushed him towards me, and stepped forward to stand with our daughters.

"Dad?" Josh whimpered into his soccer jacket. "Is Mom okay?"

For a second I couldn't answer. Jesus, when had everything gotten so fucked up? I cleared the lump in my throat. "She's...fine."

Probably true, now that she was away from me. She'd wrapped her arm around our eyebrow-pierced eldest daughter and leaned in, smiling.

She was probably telling Martha about Mad Music's incredible demo booths on the third floor, sound rooms to try out instruments, karaoke machines, a first floor with every piece of sheet music known to man.

"Daddy?"

Birdy, no longer holding Martha's attention, had jumped back to talk to me. Despite everything, I smiled. Like I said, she had that effect. White-blond hair under her rain hat, her mother's generous features, and the cheerful disposition of a cherub.

"What is it, hon?" I asked.

"Someone's watching us."

I jerked up straighter. The guy in the hoodie? *Dias de los Muertos.* I couldn't see him. "You sure?"

"Uh-hunh. Ask Joshie."

I looked and suddenly wondered if Josh's pained expression wasn't just from cold and his parents fighting. Before I could ask, he shrank back.

Martha had been watching over her mother's shoulder and now rolled her eyes. "Jesus."

"That's swearing!" Birdy sang.

Martha mouthed what looked like "Fuck you" and turned back towards Mad Music.

As she did, my peripheral vision caught the hoodie guy again. He was standing just far enough out of the line-up to ensure I saw him. The wind whipped the rain around him like he was calling it there. He looked early twenties, maybe six feet tall but cadaverous. His hair straggled thickly to his shoulders in the rain. Prominent cheekbones glittered over a sharp, hard jaw.

When I looked directly at him, he gave a mean smile.

Birdy and Joshie, Sherry and Martha—no one else saw him. Like he and I were in this frozen world apart with wet wind rushing, all the people in the line-up frozen statues.

"Sherry?" I said. I turned towards her. "Sherry!"

She bit her lips before answering, "What?"

"I'm thinking that maybe we should go and do something else for awhile. Maybe come back here when—"

"No!" Her face blazed. "No way, David. Not this time. We're here. We're going in. They're just opening the doors." She whirled back to Martha, the matter closed.

And when I looked back for Mr. *Dias de los Muertos*, he was gone. I stepped out of the line a bit as it began to move and scanned each miserable soaked head, each shuffling body.

Truly gone. Tired of waiting, maybe. Split. Gone.

Please.

~~~~

"David?"

It was almost two hours later and I barely heard Sherry's question because I felt sick. My head hurt and my stomach gurgled like I was one piece of undigested crud getting shoved and squeezed by a packed bellyful of us. Already beaten down by my fight with Sherry, I'd just gone along for the whole ride, but there was a limit to how much dank perfume and halitosis I could take. And the noise! Over all the mumbles and coughs, some teen behind us played a thrumming wail on an electric keyboard.

"Hello-o?" Sherry tried again.

While in front of me, mimicking the abomination in Seattle's EMP, Mad Music had installed a twenty foot high cyclone of instruments—guitars, cellos, keyboards, banjos. It stretched from the just inside the front entrance up through an opening in the second floor. In response to an interactive computer screen against the second floor railing, tiny robot digits plucked strings or plunked keys in something that sounded like Bach.

"*Hey.*" Sherry bumped me from the left. I turned towards her, ready for another assault, but she just pointed. "Martha."

Our little punk queen had shoved her way up to the railing and stood dumbstruck by the music tree. Her eyes darted around, following

8

the instruments which played. You could see the music clicking across her face, sorting notes, what *should* be playing, the way only a true musician could.

Good. Okay. If this trip reawakened Martha's love of classical music, got her off the goth and punk stuff, it was well worth a throbbing headache, a churning stomach.

But now I had to pee as well. Major pressure.

As I stood on tiptoes to look for a washroom sign, I noticed Josh pressed back against the wall to our left His elfin face twitched back and forth like he was trying to hear something through the cacophony. Birdy stood right beside him, watching his face with interest.

"Josh?" I called.

He didn't seem to hear me. Sherry indicated she was joining Martha, so I pushed my way over to Josh and Birdy.

"Josh?" Still no answer.

I turned to Birdy. "What's he listening to?"

"One person," she said. "He's good at that."

I looked around. The dull roar of a hundred conversations mixed with a plinking, plonking, moaning wail of Johann Sebastian Bach, and he listened to one person?

Frowning, I touched him on the shoulder and he jumped.

"What do you hear?" I asked.

He shot Birdy a look, shook his head hard, and skipped through the crowd to where Martha was still staring up at the frozen cyclone. Birdy shrugged. "He gets scared by it," she said. "Like you."

"Like me."

"It's okay, Dad. It's mostly just lonelies."

I narrowed my eyes at that one, not wanting it to mean what I feared. Birdy was just seven years old; Josh, six. How old had I been...?

"Birdy, when you—"

Martha interrupted by suddenly appearing and grabbing Birdy by the arm. "This is *bo*-ring. Let's see what else they got."

Without waiting for me, she tugged Birdy after her to the stairs up where Sherry and Josh stood waiting. I rubbed my head, watched them head up. It was the wrong direction. A little tingle at the base of my scalp told me we should all be heading down. Heading *out*.

Shaking it off, I searched the second floor and finally went down to ground level, found the washroom there.

But even with a now-bursting need, I cringed as I pushed through the scarred wooden door. Along with my other fears, I'd always had a shy bladder. Me, Joshie, and seventeen million other Americans had trouble peeing when anyone else was in the room, okay? In extreme mode, it's called paruresis, a social anxiety disorder. And even though my problem wasn't that bad, going into a washroom at a public event where people line up and *wait* for you to pee is just masochistic.

Except this time I'd lucked out. Despite the lone toilet stall having an "Out of Order" sign, and the three wall-hung porcelain urinals had no dividers between them, the men's room was empty.

I hurried to the urinal furthest from the sinks, unzipped, let the pressure descend, then sighed as it let out in—

The men's room door opened and my flow choked off.

It was the *Dias de los Muertos* creep. He ambled to the pair of sinks. Leaned onto the counter with both hands, flipped back his still-damp hair, then brought his face close to the mirror. He drew back his lips like he was checking for something between his teeth. He had the flat nose and square face of a...Japanese? Skinny arms and legs. Ropy. His jeans and dark navy hoodie looked dirty and slept in. A thin bristle darkened his square chin and upper lip. Leather sandals on tough-looking feet. And his eyes... This close, I could see the pupils were dilated, strange looking. He was on something.

Great.

He turned and looked at me. I still held my penis. I quickly turned and looked back to the wall in front of me, my face burning.

At that point I could have just zipped up, flushed, and walked out. But damn it, I wasn't done. And I was *not* a paruretic. If I just focused, imagined I was all by myself on a mountaintop or deserted island, or if

10

I waited patiently until he left...

There was a scuffling sound and the guy was right beside me at the urinals, unzipping.

I swallowed and almost zipped up again.

The thing is, nine times out of ten, when there's more than one free urinal in a men's room, the next man up will take the one furthest away from the current pisser. It's respect. Probably a bit of homophobia.

But here there were two more urinals to the right of the guy and he'd chosen to stand hip-to-my-hip. Humming. Staring at his stream. At the wall. Glancing down sideways at my equipment?

He was smiling too, because by now I'd waited too long to zip up. If I did it now, I couldn't pretend I'd just finished. I'd be admitting he'd scared off my flow. He'd beaten me. This long-haired creep, who looked no older than twenty-two or three, had humiliated me and knew it.

His flow stopped.

He didn't zip up. He kept humming. Waiting for me to run first.

Swallowing a sour taste, I mentally measured his frame against mine. He was an inch taller but I had a thicker chest and shoulders. I probably outweighed and out-muscled him if I had to fight. Not that I'd ever learned to fight, but if I *had* to...

With fear tingling my limbs, I shook myself, zipped, flushed my urinal, and stepped back, turned.

And he was directly in front of me, facing me as he slowly zipped up his fly. He hadn't bothered flushing.

"David, me name's Luka," he said in a sing song accent I'd heard before. *Day*-vid. *Mi name's Loo-kah.* Hawaiian, that was it. Not Japanese. He extended his hand. Ropy forearms, the muscles popping.

Oh God. My breath rose in my chest, headache and nausea forgotten. How crazy was he? *Just step around him.*

I stepped sideways and he mirrored it so he was still in front of me, his callused hand still out. My hands sweated, muscles tensed.

From outside the washroom came a frightened cry. "Daddy? *Daddy?*"

"That you boy, Josh," Luka said.

The words sent a chill of unreasoning panic through me. With a grunt I pushed past Luka, jerked open the bathroom door, and ran out.

3

*D*ADDY!"

  I followed the voice left and found Joshua huddled beside a wall rack of heavy metal rock CDs. His eyes were closed, his arms outstretched and pressed back against the wall behind him, his face white.

"Josh!" I said. "I'm right here."

I crouched before him and put my hands on his shoulders. When he felt my touch, his eyes opened wide and he flung his skinny arms around my neck. He still smelled like cherry shampoo, sweet and soft, and so tiny. Jeez. When he was younger I'd hugged him like this all the time. Then his hyper-sensitivity had started to trigger all my own insecurities and...I'd gotten busy.

Now I scooped him up and he wrapped his legs around my waist. His chest jumped up and down, the tears coming.

"It's okay, Joshie. It's okay."

"I was scared for you, Daddy," he said into my neck. "I came looking and I couldn't find you. And the man came by."

"I was just in the bathroom," I said. And with that, his words sunk in. *The man came by.* I spun back towards the washroom, half-expecting to face the rush of my long-haired pee partner.

There was no one.

And here again, the feeling in my scalp told me to round up my family and retreat. But instead I found myself taking a deep breath and gritting my teeth self-righteously. How dare this jerk threaten me, my family, like this? Except...he'd known my name. He'd known Josh's name.

And Josh had said *I was scared for you.*

With Josh still in my arms and a blind mix of panic and rage, I strode back to the bathroom with a half-formed intent of confronting "Luka", or delaying him while Josh called Security.

The washroom was empty.

I stepped out again with Josh still clinging tightly to my neck and saw Sherry with Birdy in tow. Sherry's face was tight the way she got only when she was very scared. We were down two levels. How had Josh even found me here?

Birdy saw us and pointed. Even through the crowd I felt Sherry's instant relief roll from her like a wave.

Then she was to us, taking Josh from me, kissing and hugging and telling him he must never ever wander off. Her trembling voice and hands, her spontaneous, charismatic love spread around her like a living thing— her special gift. And I remembered all at once why I loved her deep down in the core of my being. Because she had chosen me, when she could have had anyone, when she saw all my fears and never demanded I explain them to her. She had chosen *me.*

"Where's Martha?" I said suddenly.

"Still up in one of the private demo booths," Sherry said.

"Alone?"

"She's twelve, David. What exactly—?"

But I had already started pushing past other shoppers, reaching the stairs and leaping up them two at a time. And the second flight. I took a wrong turn at the top, swore and backtracked to find the row of five music booths. Barging into one after the other, not bothering to excuse myself, I finally burst in on Martha. She spun with a shriek, then leaned down to her karaoke mike and croaked with the music, "My man—he—look look *look*—like a brick!"

She had the reverb control cranked so the echoes words splashed and crashed wildly around the tiny space.

Then she flipped off all the switches and turned and beamed at me. And even with her cheeks too plump, hair all short and colored purple, nose and eyebrow metal flashing, she was my little girl again. The little girl I'd been so reluctant for Sherry to have, whom I'd fallen hopelessly in love with, and, for a crazy five minutes just now, whom I'd been scared out of my mind about losing.

I cleared my throat. "You okay?"

"Dad, this is so *mangy*," she squeaked. "But I was just coming out anyway. I have to go to the bathroom."

She brushed past me, but I caught her arm. "It's down on the ground level. You wait for me and you take your mother in with you."

"Da-a-ad." She shot me a withering look.

"I mean it. There are some strange people here. You take your mother with you to the washroom."

She rolled her eyes at me, but finally sighed and went out with me to meet Sherry halfway up the stairs. We all went down to ground level. Then, while Sherry and Martha hit the ladies' room, I wandered with Birdy and Josh to the bottom of the guitar cyclone and scanned the press of people around us and around the second floor opening.

No sign of the pervert.

I still had a chill up the back of my neck, though, like he was watching us. I think I might have stood right outside the women's washroom like a sentry if I hadn't worried about scaring Joshua more than he already was.

When I looked down at him, I saw he was holding Birdy's hand. Happier for it. But when Josh looked up at me, his big eyes were worried. "He's still here, Dad."

"What? Who?"

"The bad guy."

"What bad guy?" Birdy said. She shook his hand to make him explain, as if annoyed he hadn't told her this earlier.

"Did you see him?" I said.

Joshua sniffed and shook his head.

I leaned down. "Did he stop and talk with you earlier?"

He shook his head again.

"Follow you around? Point to you? Do anything to make you look at him?"

Another head shake. "But he's bad and...he wants something."

I straightened. Stood on my tiptoes and scanned the crowd around us. They'd blocked the door now, only letting people in when an equal number of people left. A trio of girls were jamming towards the entrance playing air guitar. Nowhere did I see a man with long black hair, dark blue hoodie, sandals and—

Wait. There.

Over by the cardboard cutout of Beyonce Knowles. A flash of black hair and over-dilated eyes. I came down on my heels and took a step in that direction.

One step. That was all the risk I could muster. Then my mind, well-trained as a child to cower, got stuck whirring. I considered Josh and Birdy, the risks of leaving them alone, the chances of a chase, a confrontation, getting hurt, leaving them fatherless.

And again Luka was gone.

It was a sign of my state that I looked down to my six-year-old son for answers. Josh smiled nervously and took my hand.

"Maybe we should leave, Dad," Birdy said.

I wanted to nod, but then Sherry and Martha were back, all smiles and eagerness, and yet another chance to run just...passed.

It took us another full forty-five minutes to get out of the store, Martha with a classical guitar in a case under her arm, a book of beginner's sheet music, and a commitment to practice at least fifteen minutes a day. I'd seen nothing more of Luka. The rain had stopped. It was easy to just write it off as one of those downtown *things* that happen.

Until we began walking south. It was enough into the afternoon that Sherry was determined to stretch this into a dinner out too. "Hamburger Mary's!" Martha said. "Yeah!" said Birdy.

I shook my head and pulled out my cell phone. I remembered I'd said I'd call Rajiv to—

"Daddy!"

It was Josh, tugging on my hand and pointing across the street. Sherry and I both looked. My heart skipped.

Luka.

He slouched on the far sidewalk, staring at us across the street. A truck moved between us and him. Passed by. Luka was gone.

Josh whimpered and hid behind my legs. Sherry laughed. "It's okay, Joshie. It was just a recent client of mine. Probably as surprised to see me here as I was to see him."

"A client?" I said. "At social services? What's his name? What are you helping him with?"

"Luka Keawe." She pronounced it *Kee*-ah-*way*. "He's a displaced Hawaiian. Down on his luck. Lives down in the Tenderloin district. Trying to get out." She saw my look. "What?"

"Is he mad at you for something? Likely to want revenge?"

"No. Why would—?"

"Does he have a crush on you?"

She colored and shook her head angrily, but her eyes said yes.

For an involuntary second I gloated, getting some of my own back from the argument I thought I'd left behind. I might work too hard, but Sherry, with her flaming red hair and lush body that just got better with having kids, always looked a bit too ready to play. With Luka? The thought blasted an instinctive fury through me.

"You told him about your family," I said. "Us."

"A little. You know. Sometimes it helps to break the ice if—"

"He knows all our names?"

"So?"

"Where are the girls?" I whipped my head back their way and saw them ready to cross the street. I grabbed Sherry's arm and Josh's hand and set off after them at a run.

4

Yet still my family's inertia, something I think I'd treasured up until that day, held us downtown.

Hamburger Mary's had an hour-plus wait list. As did the next two places we tried. So here we were on our fun Saturday out, dinner time, dead tired, starving for a real meal, inside a frigging shopping mall.

And because the kids couldn't wait in the bar, we stood outside the door of the eatery we'd chosen, in the atrium of that shut-down mall with a skylight arching two stories overhead and shops shut tight and dark all up and down the concourse. No one else but us, yet I kept thinking I saw moving reflections in the storefront glass.

I'd been thinking that all afternoon. Luka—here, there, everywhere.

Josh, Birdy, and Martha played tag around a fountain that gurgled hollowly in the middle of the concourse.

Sherry brushed back her hair with her hands and turned to me. "Your turn," she said and sucked in her lips expectantly.

"Tell me about this Luka Yowee guy," I said.

"Kee-ah-way," said Sherry.

"Luka," I said.

She sighed and shrugged off her raincoat, probably trusting it make her look more vulnerable. Bad choice. It just emphasized how sexy she was. How every guy she worked with probably saw her. How Luka must have seen her.

"I helped him get his welfare set up. I set up job interviews for him."

"What kind of jobs?"

"Waiting tables, greeting people. He's good with people."

"I bet."

She stared at me for a long moment. "Are you going to tell me what this is about or do I have to guess?"

I told her about the washroom incident and spotting him in the crowd after. "So when he stared at us across the street, it wasn't the first time. He was following us."

A shape in the windows again. Gone.

"It makes sense," Sherry said.

I looked sharply at her.

She shrugged. "Luka saw us in Mad Music and wanted to say hi."

"So he approached me. In the washroom."

"You're cute. Maybe he has a thing for cute guys."

"I thought we'd established he has the hots for you."

"No, you established that in your own mind. Which is what I suspect this is really all about."

"What?"

"My working. My getting back out into the world of people and mixing with them. Doing something I love. Not locking myself away in our house with our kids."

"That's what you think I'm doing?" I said.

"You didn't want me to go back to work."

"I mean me. Do you think I've been hiding out at home?"

She pursed her lips and before I could press her further, our hostess came out to tell us our table was ready.

So in we went to an upscale burger joint that was Denny's meets Casablanca. Wood floors ran under fifties-style booths that buzzed with conversation. Teak ceiling fans lazily spun the smell of meat and sizzling grease around. All of which I actually appreciated. It helped fill the huge gulf I felt growing between me and Sherry.

When the hostess led us to a booth near the back, Sherry put the girls on either side of her and ordered a beer for herself like a challenge. I ignored it and took Josh with me to the washroom to wash hands.

But as I splashed cold water over my face at the single sink and mirror, my insides twisted. *Was* I hiding? Was that the real reason I'd left Cisco? So I could go home and build up the barricades against my childhood? If so, it was pathetic, Sherry was right, and I had to change somehow.

I stepped back, grabbed some paper towels to dry my hands, and watched Josh wash his. For him, for Birdy, for Martha, for Sherry—I'd do whatever it took.

Josh finished. I reached for the door to go out but Josh grabbed my shirt.

"Don't, Dad!" His face was pale.

"What?"

"He's there again."

"Who?" I said, but I knew. I felt a shot of fear that soured to anger in my gut. My problems with my family I could deal with, but not if an outsider kept sticking his nose in. Client of Sherry's? Fine. But he had to learn that there were boundaries.

I squeezed Josh's shoulder. "Stay behind me. It'll be okay."

We went out and stopped. There he was, sitting in my seat, his elbows on the table, leaning forward toward Sherry like he was her date. Smiling.

And this time I was able to notice that underneath the tangled black hair and stubble, Luka was actually good looking. His teeth were white and straight. His clothes might have been rumpled, but his slender hands looked manicured. Worse, he projected sex as strongly as Sherry did when she was turned on. You could see it from here. You could see it in the way Sherry unconsciously leaned towards him, laughing at whatever he was saying. Martha too. She was barely pubescent but her eyes shone as she tried to include herself. Her round face flushed red.

Even Birdy—*seven years old*—looked excited and eager. She'd climbed up on her knees and now bounced her bum up and down on her heels.

Josh swung himself behind me and grabbed my pant legs. I reached back and stroked his head. Then I whispered, "Come on." I took his hand, and walked back to the table.

But despite my determined anger, I found myself doing nothing when we arrived, just standing there, trembling inside like a little boy who has to face up to a bully. I smelled his ripe b.o., sensed him laughing at me, and I couldn't think what the hell to say.

Sherry looked up, embarrassed. "David! This is Luka Keawe. I guess you two have already met!"

I made myself lock eyes with him. "We have."

Luka grinned back at me until I was forced to look away. Then he looked down to Joshua, hiding behind my legs again. "Me seen your boy also." The voice chuckled with a false sing-song of friendliness. All-*so*.

"Sherry says you've been out of work for awhile," I said. I didn't move to sit.

Luka didn't move either, but his eyes glittered. He suddenly bobbed his head down like a fawning servant and sang a kind of pidgin English. "Oh, yeah, brah. All da kine was junk. I wen see da offer man down San Jose this morning. He lolo."

Lolo? As in crazy? He was laughing at me now. Pushing.

"But you had enough money to...what?" I said. "Catch a bus down there and back?"

"Jump da cars."

"You stole a car?"

"No, brah. Hitchhike." He waggled up a thumb. I saw Martha's imagination going into overdrive, but Birdy's brow wrinkled like she was starting to feel something wasn't right here after all. It bolstered me.

"Then you followed us to Mad Music, and here."

"You got chicken skin, brah?"

"You followed us?" I pressed.

"You give me stink eye?"

"You *followed* us?"

"What doing?!" He exploded out of his seat towards me. I took three quick steps back from the table, pulling Josh back with me. Luka stopped, laughed like it was a all a joke, and eased back to sitting. He winked at Sherry, Martha, and Birdy. Sherry and Martha smiled back like they'd been hypnotized. All a game, their faces said. All pretend. Birdy bit her lips and frowned. She looked at Josh, me, then Luka.

Luka saw it and dropped back to normal English, his voice still sing-songy. "It was just coincidence, brah. I was at the store to see what they got on the king. You know, Elvis Presley? *Blue Hawaii. Blue Suede Shoes.*"

"Ohhh," said Martha with an eyebrow raise that said, *Of course.* That *king.*

"And it was co-in-*see*-dence," I mimicked him bravely, "that you saw us on the street later? And that you met us here?"

"David," Sherry scolded.

"S'okay, Sher," he said, and made it sound like the French *cher,* beloved. He gave me an injured smile. "You husband don't know me and me go breaking in. Right, Davie?"

"It's David," I said. "Her name's Sherry. And that's right. We were about to eat."

Sherry blanched with embarrassment. Josh hid deeper in my pant legs. Martha glared at me. But Birdy nodded like she approved of my stand. Then Sherry turned to Luka and said as if she'd just thought of it, "Would you like to join us for dinner?"

"Well..." he began. Josh's fingers clawed desperately into the back of my legs.

"No," I said.

"David, it's late. He's got no money. What were you going to do for dinner, Luka?"

Luka shrugged.

"See? We can't very well—"

"Excuse me," said our waitress. "Is he joining you?"

"Yes," said Sherry.

"No!" I said. And with an over-the-top forcefulness I slammed my hand down on the table. The waitress jumped back but it still felt like too little too late somehow. I straightened and took a deep breath. "He's leaving now. Aren't you."

Luka's upper lip curled, his eyes flicked to the concerned waitress who was looking around like she might call for help, and he nodded. But he glared at me as I stood back and let him slide out. My guts twisted up inside. My hands went clammy. Getting ready...

Luka slid out so he was standing nose to nose with me. Then he turned to Sherry and the girls with a broad smile, gleaming teeth. "Next time, mebbe."

"Or not," I blurted.

He turned back to me and said, "Next time, mebbe you gon' fine you maki."

"What?"

"I said," he articulated carefully, "the next time maybe you can't stop me."

"Get out of here."

"Try move. I mean, *please* move out the way."

I did and he slipped past me. Out the door of the restaurant. Gone.

I turned back to my family, my insides rattling, and tried to ignore the dagger looks from Sherry and Martha. They didn't see the threat he posed to this family and I couldn't blame them; even I couldn't pin it down. All I knew was he was pushy, dirty, and he'd been doing some sort of drugs earlier. And Josh didn't trust him. Still...

Josh edged out from behind my legs and Birdy caught my eyes. For them I found the spine to not back down.

"We'll eat," I said as I pointed Josh into the booth. "Then we go home. No movie. No wandering. No nothing else."

Which should have ended it.

5

WE FINALLY WALKED under the shelter of our peaked roof by seven p.m. Neither Sherry nor Martha were talking or looking at me. The minute we arrived home, Martha phoned up her best friend and arranged a sleepover.

Josh heard and got so scared he'd be left the buffer between his mom and dad that, even though he'd only recently learned how to use the phone, he managed to call three friends in ten minutes. The third said they'd take him. It was only Josh's third sleepover, but Sherry and I each agreed with little more than a grunt. I pulled out his sleeping bag. Sherry got his pajamas and toothbrush, stuffed them in a bag, and drove him there.

When she got back it was almost nine and Martha had left—walked to her best friend's house just down the block.

Sherry stalked into the kitchen where I was cleaning out the cooler we'd brought along on the trip. "Birdy?" she asked.

"Right here, Mom," Birdy said, popping in from the family room.

Sherry turned and pursed her lips. "Daddy's going to get you ready for bed," she said, and walked out. To the living room, I guessed. If she didn't want to see me, it was either there or hide downstairs where my office, testing room, and equipment storage had sucked up all our former family room space.

I poured out the water I'd been slopping around in the cooler, set the cooler on the counter, then turned to Birdy. Her open innocence was like turning from a blazing furnace to a cool breeze. "Did you want to call any of your friends for a sleepover?"

She shook her head.

"Too tired?"

"Uh-unh. I figured you and Mom wanted me home right now."

"You figured."

"Uh-hunh."

And the thoughts I'd had at Mad Music tumbled back again. Not only was Birdy sensitive, she was a Sensitive. Josh too, probably. They could both see/hear/feel more than what was visible to most people's eyes. Like Josh could tell when people were lying. Like my dad thought he could see ghosts. Like I once thought I could talk to them.

Welcome to Crazyville.

"Honey," I said, "that man in the restaurant today, the Hawaiian guy who knew Mommy—what did you think about him?"

Birdy sucked in her lips like her mother and lowered her head a little so she had to look up at me. "You don't like him. Josh doesn't either."

I smiled. "But maybe we're being silly. What do you think?"

She shook her head.

"What?"

"At first he was nice. But you and Josh came back and *pp-fff*. He got all mean inside and talked funny. Specially to you. How comes he hates you?"

Hates me? I pulled out a kitchen chair and sat, my legs a little weak. "I...don't know. Could you tell how he feels about Mommy? Or Martha or you?"

"He likes Mommy. *Really* a lot. Me too. He doesn't care about Martha."

"What about what he wants to do? Did you—?"

We were interrupted by Sherry stomping back into the kitchen. "Are you going to put her to bed? Or is that a Mommy job too? You bark the orders and I do the work?"

"We were just talking."

Sherry's face was flushed and tight. She shoved her fingers back through her hair, hard, and I could feel her anger like a twist in my gut. "It's past her bedtime. She's been out all day. It's not a time for talk."

"Okay, I'll—"

"No, you won't. You blew it."

Now my own face burned. I stood up. "That's enough."

"You're going to get tough again. This is a new thing with you, right? Want to slap the table?"

"*Later.*"

"*Your* timetable again."

Suddenly Birdy was standing between us, smiling up at Sherry and reaching out to her. "Mommy? I love you and Daddy too. Please don't fight. Fighting doesn't solve anything."

Sherry looked down at her little girl parroting Sherry's own homilies back at her. Her grimace visibly dissolved. "Come here, little button," she whispered. Birdy did and Sherry scooped her up, turned to go to the front hall and upstairs.

"Daddy too," Birdy said.

So Sherry waited awkwardly as I joined them and the three of us made our way up. Sherry suggested we skip the bath because it was late and Birdy had been mostly sitting all day. I agreed. Birdy was ready for bed five minutes later and we said prayers and sat on her bed, side by side, Sherry closest to Birdy's head.

"Daddy's just scared of that guy," Birdy said as she held Sherry's hand.

Surprised, Sherry looked back at me. I grimaced and shrugged, my face hot.

"He can't get us here, though, can he, Mom?" Anxious.

"He never wanted to get you, button," Sherry said. "He was just lonely."

Birdy's eyes went wide like she'd just understood something important. "*Yes.* He's lonely, Dad."

"Ah." I walked around Sherry and leaned down to give my little angel a kiss. "Love you, honey."

"I love you too, Daddy."

Then I was out and retreating quickly to our bedroom, not sure whether Sherry would follow me here or pick some other spot in the house to sleep. Martha's bedroom maybe. But by the time I was crawling into bed in my boxers and tee-shirt, she'd entered too. Silently she lay her summer nightie on the bed. She turned from me to pull off her top and unclip her brassiere.

But even her back, the scent of her, the sound of her fingers on the snap, the straps against her skin, spoke of sex to me. As if the meeting tonight with Luka Keawe had fired her up. Or me?

As she pulled on her cotton nightie, exposing a quick flash of her right breast, I pulled up the sheet to cover my swelling penis. This was absurd.

Sherry turned to catch me watching her.

"You could have made it as an artist," she said.

I laughed roughly.

"I mean it, David. You were so good."

"We couldn't have had kids. Maybe never married."

"I would have worked."

"Leaving me with the kids. Oh, that would have worked."

My voice had gone ragged. Because I knew—*knew*—that if I'd been the one raising the kids all these years, I'd have wrecked them. That was one of the fears that getting a steady job in computer networks was supposed to have fixed. It focused me and provided enough stability for Sherry to be the one raising the kids. Because, for all her fiery outbursts and tears, Sherry never sank into existential despair like I did. Like I used to.

Sherry and the kids had quite literally saved me from myself. They were the best things in my life and I was doing my absolute best to protect them. Why in hell could Sherry not see that?

I became aware that the bedroom had grown silent and looked over to see Sherry still standing by her side of the bed, staring at me with her lips drawn in. She'd crossed her arms over her chest, squeezing her breasts into attractive mounds I knew I wasn't supposed to look at. Her eyes were wet. Pain, frustration, bitterness rolled off her like scalding pitch. I had to steel myself to not roll out of the bed and retreat.

She shook back her hair. "Do you even care?"

"About what?"

"About what..." Her lips came in again and she shook her head like I was stupid.

I sat up, my anger flaring. "Tell you what I do care about. I care that some whacko creep you work with downtown thinks he can—"

"Oh, stop it, David."

"—muscle into our family. Kick me out."

"Grow up."

"Oh!" I held my hands up to my chest. "Funny, that's what I thought I'd done. Got married, got a degree, got a job, had kids, bought a house, established a business. What am I missing here, Sherry? Tell me. I'll do that next!"

"A heart!" she said. "Humor. Imagination. Courage. All the things that made me love you!"

"Ah," I said, rolling out of bed to stand on the carpet barefoot, breathing down on it. Chinese brocade over hardwood. Matching ones on either side of the bed with a sponged-on red-earth lacquer on the walls to give our bedroom that designer finish. "Meaning you don't love me anymore. Because I have no heart, no humor, no imagination, no courage."

"David..."

"Forget it." My gut was tight as I walked to the chair where I'd thrown my pants, picked them up, and pulled them on. "You know, one of the advantages of not having a heart or imagination is that I can just turn away right now and go downstairs to work."

Her face and body changed instantly, unlocking, opening, her arms reaching for me, her heart suddenly open and needy in a way that usually made me rush to her and wrap her up in my arms. Protect her. Love her.

But not now, goddamnit. She'd just told me what she really felt. That I was a failure. That everything I did, all the sacrifices I'd made—they just made me soulless.

"I'll be up in an hour or three," I said and stalked out.

I made it as far as the third step down the stairs before I heard, "Daddy?"

I turned. Birdy was standing in the door of her room. She looked half asleep, but her heart called out to me as clearly as her mother's. And how do you refuse a seven-year-old daughter?

"What is it, honey?" I whispered.

"I'm scary."

I smiled in pain. "You mean scared?"

She nodded and yawned.

I hesitated, then walked back up the stairs and to her doorway, picked her up, and carried her back to bed. When I'd tucked her in again and checked her window was closed, I sat on the edge of her bed. "Now just what was it that scared you?"

She'd heard us fighting?

"That man we saw. And...you love Mommy, right?"

I smoothed back her hair, held my hand against her soft, warm cheek. "That man is hundreds of miles away for a few days at least. And yes, I love Mommy. And I love all my kids. I love you."

"You love me best?" Her face squinched as if she wasn't sure she wanted me to say yes.

I took a deep breath to clear out all the shit with Sherry for just a minute. "That's the great thing about love, honey. There doesn't have to be a best. I love each one of you so much I can't measure it."

"Past the moon!" Birdy giggled. It made me uneasy but in my revved state I couldn't say exactly why.

"And around the sun and out to the stars," I responded, pulling the other lines from the book Birdy was quoting from. Rote. Couldn't get such creativity from me, after all. According to Sherry I didn't have any.

I stroked her hair back again with my hand and murmured a bunch of comforts I only half-heard myself because my mind was out in the hall, at the door to our bedroom. Sherry inside it. Passionate. Loving. Volatile. Smart. Jesus, what she did to me. Made me so angry. Made me so desperate to please. So miserable. So everything.

"Daddy?"

The sudden fear in Birdy's voice snapped me back to her. "What, hon?"

"I hear something."

I raised my eyebrows and cocked my ears. Nothing unusual. The dim sounds of people in the restaurants two blocks behind us. Some teens skateboarding on the street. We shouldn't have even heard those because I'd double-glazed all our windows last year, but Sherry liked the windows open at night. Security hazard, I'd complained. She'd said I could put alarms on the basement and all my stuff down there. She wasn't going to live in fear upstairs.

I could hear Birdy's breathing. The tick of her kitty clock.

A creak.

"Probably just Mommy," I whispered and kissed Birdy's forehead. "But I'll go check. You go to sleep."

I stood before she could object and slipped out her door, closing it behind me. The light in our bedroom had gone off but I heard rustling from inside. Sherry still awake. Probably all unsettled. I'd have to talk with her, work this thing out. But first a quick check downstairs.

Worried that turning on the hall light would disturb either Sherry or Birdy, I left it off and crept to the top of the stairs in just the green glow from the bathroom nightlight. No sound, but I thought I felt a breeze on my bare feet. Sherry must have opened a window downstairs. I needed to close that.

I made it as far as the bottom step when a shuffling sound stopped me. Looking back up, I saw Birdy's face. *Bed*, I mouthed. Pointed. She retreated. A moment later her door clicked closed.

And Luka sprang.

6

IN THE SAME INSTANT OF KNOWING you'd get stepping onto a train tracks to find a train rushing at you, I knew everything at once—who it was, what he was doing, that I was about to be hurt real bad.

I froze.

He hit me from left side, drove me against the bottom of the stair railing then spun me backwards and down with his bare hand clapped over my mouth.

We thudded onto the entry carpet but Luka kept me rolling until he was on top of me, hand still clutching my mouth. His other hand grabbed my left arm and jerked it up behind my back. Pain shot through my front shoulder like someone had stabbed in a knife.

"You scream, I kill you now," he grunted in my ear, breath hot and fast. "Understand? You get it?"

Fighting the pain and gag reflex, I did, and saw Sherry's face in my mind. Birdy's. If I died here and now...

I swallowed the chunky bile in my mouth and nodded.

"Good, Davie. You keep shushy and I talk just to you. Give me trouble, make sound, and I kill you, then go upstairs. Understand?" He jerked my twisted-back arm.

I squealed into his hand but nodded again.

"Okay," he said and suddenly rolled off me. But before my freedom could register, he was on me again, jerking my other arm behind my back too, tying something stretchy around my wrists. Even then, maybe I could have jackknifed him off me, freed my hands and fought, or at least screamed a warning, but my brain had never worked that way. Never had to.

He jerked the bindings tight so they cut into my skin, then turned around on me, his boot clopping the side of my face as he did. "Bend feet up," he hissed and jerked at the arms tied behind my back.

I lifted my feet and felt the same slippery material wrapping around my bare ankles, jerking them as tight as my wrists, then tugging them upwards so I was bent backwards like a bow. When Luka jumped off, I fell over sideways, my back and arms stabbing again with pain, my forehead beaded in sweat. He'd tied my bare ankles and wrists so I was stuck in the painful backwards arch with my boxers bunched up around my crotch inside my pants. Helpless in too many ways.

"Luka," I gasped. "Look, if you want—"

"Shut it! I said no sound. Look me." Luka suddenly jumped onto his knees in front of me and brandished a large knife with an elaborate bone handle he'd pulled from somewhere. And Luka's eyes—the pupils looked wide and distended again. He was on his drugs again. Crazy. Still wearing the dark blue hoodie. Still wet.

"You talk again, *mahu*, and I will cut off your dick, then cut up your wife, yeh? And your little girl."

Little girl, singular. He knew Martha wasn't in the house. He hadn't mentioned Josh because he knew Josh was out. He'd been watching. How long? And what should I do now?

Luka snapped his fingers in front of my face. "You still don't listen, yeh. You think too much, Davie."

His knife was down and he had a black sock in his hand. And even as I decided I had to scream, he'd pried open my mouth and jammed it in. I gagged, but now Luka had more of the slippery material—pantyhose?—wrapped twice around my mouth and head, tied tight, holding the cloth in. More bile came up, choking me, making me panic that I'd drown. I convulsed and tried to swallow it back, suck in air through my nose, couldn't get enough, choking on my own vomit. Swallow! *Swallow goddamnit fuck!*

Fifteen seconds and the panic eased back enough that I could see again, that I could feel the water in my eyes, the pain in my ribs where I'd hit the stair rails, a hard ache in both my shoulders. But I was breathing at least, and...

Luka was gone.

Upstairs? Oh God. Upstairs?

I heard the click of a bedroom door and began to thrash and grunt. "Ehhh!" I managed. "Eh-eeeeee!"

I paused and saw light coming from somewhere upstairs. *No!* I wanted to yell. *Sherry just call the cops!*

A door kicked open upstairs. Sherry screamed. A struggle. "David! Da—"

Whap! Crashing glass. Thuds.

And again I lost it. I grunted and thrashed, mashing my toes as I finally tried to roll to the phone in the kitchen. But the entry carpet bunched up under me and rolled me back. I'd made barely ten feet before I heard tumbling thumps on the stair and jerked around, red-faced.

Luka stood at the bottom with Sherry. She was still dressed in her cotton nightie. Luka's left arm was clutched tightly around her waist so that her nipples showed rigid through the cotton as her chest heaved. Her face was bruised purple on one side.

Luka's knife pressed flat against her neck. His eyes glittered black. "Hey, lolo," he said.

I gagged and swallowed. My neck strained. My eyes filled with tears, trying to find Sherry's eyes, apologize, tell her everything about my love now, ask her about Birdy.

I don't know, she mouthed, and I understood she meant Birdy.

Luka didn't catch it. "I don't kill neither one you if you don't do nothing to *fuck—it—up*. Understand?"

Sherry nodded. So did I. Had Birdy hidden? I tried again and again to swallow. *Swallow.* Sherry and Birdy needed me! I had to save them!

"Luka," Sherry said slowly and evenly. I could feel her forcibly exuding her calm over herself, me, Luka. "If what you want is money, it's all upstairs. David can give you the access code to go down to the basement for any computer equipment you want to resell."

Luka said nothing, but his mouth kept working soundlessly and his knife hand jiggled like his body didn't like staying still.

"If...if you want...me," Sherry said, "then I'll go with you. We'll just walk out of here. Or we can take our car. You just let me get the keys and we'll..."

She let it trail off as Luka began to giggle. Then he looked at me, at her, jerked his arm up under Sherry's breasts to make them jiggle, and whinnied high in his nose. "Oh, yeah, me going have you, Ms. Friesen. Cherry, yeh? Going have you, fuck you, all that kine. But we going do it right here where Davie can watch. Cause that be part of the *fun*."

I could hardly see. My blurry vision went red. My throat convulsed and my head shook off its pain. As part of me watched Luka make Sherry raise her arms and rip Sherry's nightie over her head, the rest of me pumped with blood. My arms were pistons; my thighs and calves, pile drivers. Sherry needed me. Birdy needed me. And I was a man. This was *my* cave. *My* family. Don't you dare mess with *me!*

With a massive grunt, I wrenched my arms sideways behind my back while driving my bare legs straight back behind me. The bonds tightened like razor wires that might cut through my popped-out veins. But they stretched. Stretched. My muscles shook.

Luka laughed and kneaded Sherry's breasts now, her big soft tits that I'd lost myself in so many times. Mine. *Mine.*

And the bonds, stretched to their limits, cut deep, shook as my arms spasmed, and...held.

My breath exploded from my nose in a snotty burst and I sucked it back hard, choking again as my body collapsed in on itself. Adrenaline-backlash made me shiver.

But I still *saw.*

Luka shoved Sherry back against the wall at the bottom of the stairs and made her stand still while he shakily cut off her panties. Then he fumbled down his own pants and underwear. Motioned for her to go down on him.

God.

Sherry whimpered and shook her head. Cried out when Luka's grabbed up her red hair and dotted the knife down the back of her neck, scraping the skin, drawing blood. Until she finally sobbed and slid down the wall to her knees.

Luka turned sideways to me to I could watch, his penis jutting out from his dark thatch of hair like something in a medieval woodcut. Pan. The devil. He murmured his commands to Sherry.

I tried to look away and block it out. If I could just go somewhere in my head, come up with a plan...

Sherry met my eyes. Luka ordered and pressed the knife on her neck again. Pointed it at me. Crying, Sherry took his erection with her hands, stroked him, desperately worked saliva into her mouth, guided him in. Watching me.

And my vision went red again. My body thrashed without any conscious decision, bruising my knees, my feet, my hips, my forehead.

Somewhere in there I became aware that Luka had thrown Sherry off him and onto the wooden floor in the door to the living room. He dropped down on top of her, wrenched her knees apart, grabbed his hardness, and thrust into her. Sherry cried out in pain. *Pain*. It rolled off her like a physical wave as Luka drove into her again and again. Then he drew back up to his feet, pulled her up, and shoved her farther into the living room, throwing her face-first over the coffee table I could just see through the door. That table—picked up in Thailand on the one long vacation we ever had, shipped back here with no contract or bill of sale, but still made it and became a symbol of our love— magical and protected.

Luka grunted and stabbed the butcher's knife into it.

Stabbed himself into Sherry.

Then he drew back and slapped her off the table. Glass broke. I couldn't see the two them anymore. Just heard the thumping, Sherry's cry, Luka's grunts. Occasionally Sherry's bare legs stumbled past the living room door like she was blind and trying to find her way out.

And I was in hell. Dead. No! Fuck. Tears. It went on and on.

Stopped.

The silence slammed through the house and left me breathless. I blinked. Listened. Terror shot through me as profound as anything I'd ever felt as a child.

Was Sherry dead?

Luka?

And Birdy upstairs—was she still alive, hiding and listening? Would she try to come down?

I was about to grunt and begin a systematic roll towards the stairs when Luka emerged soundlessly from the living room, carrying a rucksack. He'd done his pants up but removed his hoodie and whatever had been beneath it. His naked torso was slick with sweat and blood. He looked at me with a glazed smile, brushed back his stringy black hair with both hands, then turned and ran upstairs.

"Aughhh!" I shouted through my gag.

An unsteady *slap, slap, thump...slap*, jerked my focus back to the living room door. Sherry appeared from the shadows. She held onto the walls with her left hand, the bloody bone-handle knife with the other. Her bare feet slapped forward, then she tripped and fell awkwardly to her knees beside my chest. Her face was cut in some kind of bloody pattern, her body smeared with blood, sweat, semen, black hair.

I gagged then nodded her to hurry as she fumbled the knife up to cut the pantyhose cord binding my wrists. She moved it to my feet. Slow! I grabbed the knife and cut the bands off my feet. Leapt up.

And almost fell. My legs had cramped. My feet had gone to sleep on me so I couldn't even feel my mashed toes.

I ran for the stairs anyway. Up.

Our little night light was out at the top, smashed or removed I couldn't see. My eyes were still adjusting.

My heart pounded so hard I was sure Luka could hear me coming, but I held my breath and crept forward. I had his *knife*. To *stab* with.

Birdy's room was the second last one at the end of the hall, the smallest room, but with the best view of the Japanese elm we had in our little back yard.

The door was open.

Shaking and keeping my mouth wide, my breath silent, I listened.

Nothing. Not a sound. Then I thought I heard a little shuffle or squeak. Birdy in hiding? Or Luka?

I stepped to the door, listened harder, pushed it open, holding my knife up. The lights were out, but light from some neighbor's house gave everything a surreal glow. Nothing moved.

"Birdy," I whispered. "Birdy? Come out. It's Daddy. Come on, honeybun."

Nothing. Just my heart beating faster. Prickles forming on the back of my neck. Sweat trickling down my underarms.

"*Birdy*. Come on, honey. Please."

Absolutely nothing. Except...I finally saw the window, our beautiful sliding new double-pane style window, was wide open and the cold air blowing in. Sounds of distant traffic and honking came with it. This window looked out on our back lawn and all the houses were built tight on narrow properties around us, all sloped roofs with overhanging eves, two street over from the commercial restaurant area.

Wide open.

I stumbled to it and looked at the sill stupidly as if I'd see something there, some proof of passage. There was nothing visible in the dark. A thought, a wildly impossible hope suddenly flitted through my mind that maybe Birdy had heard Luka coming and climbed out the window herself?

Luka laughed.

It came from above me, a reptilian cackle, harsh and sibilant. Maybe not him? Some neighborhood kid? A trick echo? I whipped my head around and up the eves. He couldn't possibly have...

"Up here, brah," came his voice from the roof. "Got you little girl. Come get me."

I swallowed harshly. He could have. He had. He'd half-climbed out this window, pulled Birdy out behind him, then either flung her up there or had her hold onto his neck while he climbed up.

Grabbing onto what? There was no trellis or drainpipe here. The house had overlapping metal siding, a straight drop from the sloped roof. There was only...

I looked up and even in the overcast darkness I could see the gutter was bent down now, half torn off.

"You coming, you daddy? Ain't going wait much longer."

Swallowing again and not thinking how I was almost forty, barefoot and old and heavy, I pulled back inside the window, took a deep breath, dropped the knife, put my right foot up on the sill and pulled myself up and out, twisting wildly and grabbing the bent gutter so I didn't plunge to the stone patio.

The gutter screeched and the three foot section I was holding pulled free of the roofline. I scrabbled my hands sideways along it, kicking back at the house in a vain attempt to find a foothold. My feet found nothing, but my hands got some gutter that was bending down but holding.

Fingers and forearms shaking, I pulled for my life, grunting and cursing under my breath—"Mother*fucker*"—until my stomach cleared the gutter and I scraped my arms and feet all to hell scrabbling up.

It was only when I was fully on that I looked up to scan the rest of the roof. My muscles went so weak I almost rolled off again.

Luka was a few body lengths away, backlit by the dizzy glitter of northern streets, the Golden Gate, the pinpricks of Sausalito as he stood up the slope of the roof at the very end of the house, just down from where it peaked at the chimney. It was a three-story drop onto the patio stones that ran around that side of the house. Luka held Birdy wrapped in his arms in front of him, facing away from him. He'd completely trapped her arms as if she'd been fighting him. He swayed back and forth like he was listening to some kind of music in his head.

"Daddy?" Birdy squeaked.

"It's okay, sweetie," I said.

"He s-said be quiet or...or...he'd hurt you."

"You didn't do anything wrong, honey."

Between his neck and the chimney, and Birdy's neck and the chimney, were two thin lines that drooped to the rooftop and up again. More pantyhose? Rope? Luka's rucksack lay in a formless heap near his feet.

"Hey, you daddy," he said suddenly, his voice musical and happy. "I need you here see me, yeh? This been too long search. Then too long watching all you. But I get finally close today, yeh?"

I licked my cracked lips. "Luka, don't. Please. I don't know what the problem is, what you've been looking for, but...this won't solve it. *Please*. Put my daughter down."

"Daddy," Birdy whimpered.

"Hang on, hon."

I tried to project the calm in the way I'd seen Sherry do so often. I held up my hands, open and empty to show Luka he could trust me. Then I put them back onto the shingles and began, very slowly, to raise myself up.

Something like triumph and fear flashed across Luka's face in the dark as he stepped up the slope of the roof a little, right to the edge. Then, still clutching Birdy with his left arm, he muttered something I couldn't follow, used his right to crane her tiny face back so he could press his mouth obscenely onto hers, and threw himself and her backwards off the edge.

I screamed and scrambled forward, heard, *ker-thud-thud*. Then an awful gargling sound.

I dove flat to the shingles and looked over. Two bodies jerked on the end of their nylon rope lines, still a good fifteen feet above ground. I tugged at one of the lines. Too heavy. Luka. Grabbed the other line and saw my little girl's body weave left.

Then I paused, desperate, my mouth working soundlessly. Pull her up and snap her neck? Leave her to suffocate? Try to untie the cord and let her drop? "Oh, please," I said and began hauling her up, hand over hand. "Please."

Luka's body had stopped twitching. Birdy's body bumped the end of the house as it rose.

She reached the roof line. I held the rope to the roof with one hand and reached over and down with the other. Grabbed her little arm. Pulled her limp form up and over.

"Oh, my little girl. Birdy, it's all right. It's all right. It's okay."

My fingers fumbled with the cord around her neck as I refused to look at her face or acknowledge her still chest. The rope was tied at the back. In frustration I rolled her over on my lap and went at the knot with my teeth. "I'll geh thih. I'll geh ih."

I did. The knot moved. Tugged. I had one part of it free. Then another. Then the knot was undone, the rope was off.

But the marks all over the neck. The floppy head. The lack of movement.

I very tenderly turned Birdy's body back over on my lap, looked at her face, and smoothed back her hair. Blinking very fast because I could hardly see, I put my ear down to her nose and mouth to listen for breathing. I moved down to her chest to listen for a heartbeat. Then I drew my head up and just stared down at her. Her eyes were still open as if they were looking into a great, terrifying beyond.

I couldn't breathe. Couldn't move.

The clouds swung around in the sky above me, holding back the rain, not even giving me that.

Couldn't.

Time slowed to a crawl. Stopped.

Then somehow I'd laid her out flat on the shingles and crossed my palms over her sternum. Not too hard, I remembered. Can't press too hard. Just enough to restart the heart. Intermix mouth to mouth, but mostly restart the heart.

Come on!
Push...one...two...three.
She will live.
Push...one...two...
She. Will. Live.
Push...

FIND ME

(eight months later)

7

WHEN SHE WAS SIX, Special Agent Alizia Nightingale Sweetness had been pulled from her crowded bed around three a.m. one summer night and jerked down the back stairs of their New York tenement by her daddy. He dragged her out the back door, mumbling that 'Lizia never spoke to no one but her white bitch mama. Probably wa'nt even his. He was crying as he said it.

In the black hush of the quadrangle between wings of their building, made her stand upright in her pajamas and bare feet. Stumbling, he backed off about eight feet, turned and faced her.

He was drunk. That much little Sweetness knew. He wove like a coal-black god of anger before her, stinking of cigarettes and alcohol. His face was covered with sweat. But now, in the sludgy darkness that usually saw kids riding their bikes on makeshift ramps over the discarded concrete, and drug dealers spilling in around the far corner to finish their business away from the street, he went quiet. His clothes and skin smudged so into the night she could just make out the whites of his eyes.

There were no lights on anywhere. No moon. No sound but the skittering of some cat or rat somewhere. No breeze even. The air was too thick. And her daddy was blinking at her, hard.

Still Sweetness didn't say anything. A determined, deliberate child by temperament, she'd learned to be as still as a mouse around him. But her skinny brown legs were ready to run. Itching to run. Her gaze twitched back and forth around the lot, trying to make the shadows and shapes fit with the place she knew in the daylight. Nothing looked right. Her tongue was dry in her mouth.

"Ready?" he finally growled at her. He shifted closer. "Gotta fight. Find somep'n."

For a few seconds Sweetness froze just like her mama did before she got beaten. Then she understood that *Find somep'n* was a command and she dropped to her knees on the hard dirt, frantically darting her hands through dry grass, grit, stones little and big, then glass. Sharp—ouch. Part of some broken bottle. Paper still on it. Big as her hand. If she could wrap the paper around one side, maybe...

Her daddy's shoe caught her in the shoulder and sent her sprawling backwards.

"Firss lesson," he said. "Don' take your eyes off th'enemy."

Then he rushed after her and kicked her again, his big clumping shoes catching her ribs so her chest exploded in pain. Again, in the legs. She rolled over to get away from him and caught it in her shins. Dirt in her nose. Swallowing grit. She curled up and the hard toe of his shoe cracked her forearms, flipped her right over so she felt her teeth rattle in her head.

For a second she couldn't hear anything. Then there was that scratching sound from somewhere—the cat? Rat?—and the intermittent sobbing of her daddy.

Little Sweetness herself made no sound.

He took her out once a week after that, always in the middle of the night when everyone else was sleeping. Alizia learned to never sleep completely. She began wearing her shoes to bed—her mother let her, as if she knew—and memorized every door and hiding place of the quadrangle. She learned its shape, its stoniest parts, hollows, the brick walls and low window ledges you could scramble up and jump off, places where the dealers left needles and, once, a knife.

Her daddy always caught her, disarmed her, ended up kicking her on the ground. But Sweetness got better at twisting away, at kicking and hitting *him* too, gashing his face, using weapons like rocks and old pipes, heavy enough to kill if she'd been stronger.

One night she knocked him unconscious with a tire iron and stood over him, gaping. By that point in her training, it never occurred to her to run away. She'd figured out that running away did no good if your enemy still lived, and she could see her daddy's big chest rise and fall, rise and fall. Like a shot black bear. Like a wounded bogey man. She shifted the tire iron back and forth in her little hands for almost a minute, trying to figure what to do. What her daddy would have *wanted* her to do.

Then he woke up, snatched away the tire iron, and shoved her across the lot to the door to their building. "Go *on!*"

The next week she had her seventh birthday party in the hospital where her mama lay with a broken arm and concussion she told the doctors she'd gotten from falling down the stairs. Alizia rocked her baby sister, Thea, and crooned "Happy Birthday" to herself while she watched the machine hooked up to her mama beep its bouncing green line of light.

Her daddy showed up at dinnertime with a Big Mac for her and new bottle for Thea. He gave her a present, her first ever book for just her—Machiavelli's *The Prince*. She stared at it silently. He kissed her on the forehead and left.

She never saw him again.

Twenty-two years later, now, she remembered her daddy again. Not that her boss behind the desk resembled him much. Special-Agent-in-Charge Daryl Hinkson was a perspiring white, balding, flabby bureaucrat with a sly manner and sweat-stained armpits that would be with him all summer. But he had her daddy's same streak of dissatisfied meanness. Particularly where Sweetness was concerned.

"Motherfucker," Hinkson muttered now to the file he was reviewing. He smoothed back his thin gray hair and sank his chin into his chest. It made him look like an overweight rat. His office was filled with filing cabinets and pictures of gray-haired, blue-suited men. Like them, he guarded his turf from everything female, black, and/or uppity. That's why Sweetness was still GS-13, and should have been soothing and groveling like she'd learned to do at times with her father.

But she was no longer a skinny six-year-old. She was twenty-nine, with a master's degree in criminology and a 2nd degree black belt in *wado ryu* karate. She'd gotten her father's height, five-eleven, with café-au-lait skin and a hard-muscled body that wore its regulation navy pantsuit like a karate fighter's *gi*. Her high cheekbones were shields, her brown eyes cold. Even the broad curving lips were only enticing until you saw the fine network of scars around them, as well as around her jaw and unplucked brows.

She didn't grovel.

Hinkson finally cleared his throat, reached for a second folder in front of him, opened it, and slid an eight-by-ten photograph towards her.

Frowning, Sweetness glanced at it. It was a corpse, a body on a beach. Lacerations and abrasions covered every inch of exposed skin and they'd all gone puffy, bluish white, as if the body had been in the water some time before it had washed up on shore or been dragged out.

"It happened at night," Hinkson said, templing his fingers. "Huntingdon Beach. Witnesses didn't call anyone until late the next day."

"Because?"

Hinkson smiled, doling it out bit by bit. "They were out there doing some kind of séance. Trying to contact dead surfers. This goon apparently jumped up in the middle of the ceremony like he'd been bitten and started screaming someone was trying to kill him. Three of the others claim they saw flashes of two ghosts attacking him."

"Drugs."

Hinkson said nothing, but smiled and pulled a second eight-by-ten from the folder in front of him and slid it over beside the first one. This one showed a corpse, female this time, slumped over the steering wheel of a car. Her forehead was bloody from where it had smashed against the front windshield, her head at an unnatural angle.

"Highway 1, near San Simeon," Hinkson said. "Her companion, wearing her seatbelt, survived this one. Claimed the woman was attacked by ghosts and drove off the road."

Hinkson pulled a third picture out and laid it beside the other two. This one was clearly a murder. Multiple stab wounds. The victim was an African American male in his fifties or sixties, lying on his back, wearing the bloodied uniform of a short-order cook.

"Let me guess. Ghosts."

"Pac Bell Stadium in San Francisco last night. Derby Grill restaurant. Stabbing was done by a fellow cook. He claims he was possessed."

"Bullshit. Sir."

Hinkson's smile took over his whole face. Evil. "The stabber," he said, "claims he and the corpse were both 'sensitives.' Same thing the people on the pier said. And the survivor from the car crash."

"So?"

"They all gave solid descriptions of the ghosts who attacked them."

Sweetness frowned. "Solid how?"

"Enough to match the descriptors to each other. Some keener in the LAPD who saw the Huntingdon case, heard about the others and followed up with a call to a guy he knows who's going through Quantico. This guy ran it through NCIC. Got an easy positive on one of the two descriptions."

He waited, but Sweetness didn't bite, so Hinkson said, "Luka Keawe."

Sweetness shook her head. The name meant nothing.

"He's a dead drug dealer," Hinkson said. "Hawaiian. Killed himself in a suicide up in San Francisco last November. Took a little girl with him after he raped her mother. Guess who the second, smaller ghost described by the witnesses matched up with? The girl."

Sweetness narrowed her eyes. "So?"

"I want you to look into it."

"Why?" She said it without blinking, still not sure if Hinkson was serious or just using this to jerk her chain about her mother. Ghost murders. Ha-ha. Why don't we call in Sweetness? It wasn't the first time Hinkson had tried pushing that button, using what he could to rile her, to give him a reason to give her beach time.

Hinkson collected the pictures, stuck them back in the file, and pushed it across the desk towards her. "The LAPD and the SFPD have requested our help."

"For some perp who looks like Luka Keawe, or a bunch of crackheads hallucinating."

"Probably. I don't care. It's possibly drug related. Maybe a serial killer. Official request for assistance. I'm sending you. The Quantico guy who dug up the pattern is your new partner."

It hit like a gut punch. "I'm working with the DEA on the Carano Felix fallout."

"I gave it to Richards and Brown."

"You bastard." Sweetness took one step towards him and Hinkson scooted back, his eyes narrowing.

"What did you just say?"

Sweetness set her jaw. "I said you might have asked me." She held his eyes. "What do you think I said?"

Hinkson's beady eyes had sunk back deep in his face now and for a moment Sweetness wondered if maybe it really was her fault she'd been passed over this last round. Except...she would eat shit before she'd kiss this fat man's ass.

And a new partner? Some dickhead first office agent? He expected her to just—

Hinkson cut off the thought, his voice was cold and precise. "The victims were all 'sensitives' so it's possible your mother knew them. So why don't you start up with the Pac Bell case. Take your mom out to the game there the day after tomorrow—Giants and Cardinals. You like baseball, right?"

"You want me to go up to San Francisco, see my mother, take in a baseball game."

"You and your partner, yes. It's a murder scene. It's the city where Luka Keawe supposedly killed the little girl and himself. And..."

Sweetness frowned at her S-A-C's hesitation. Like something had probed through that fatty chest to touch his heart somehow.

"What?" she said.

"The father of the little girl who was killed—he's still up there too. You should go talk to him."

8

KAHUNA WEKI NAEA KAPU DROVE SOUTHWEST along the 101 with the top of his Miata down. His long, steel-gray hair flapped up and down on the collar of his jean jacket. His old legs, looking somehow strong in his faded jeans, sprawled as wide as the seat let them, like he was a free man who could be going anywhere at all.

But you know where going, his croaky little mind voice told him. *Going for three little white rocks. Mebbe got enough for a forty-rock? Twenty hits.*

No! *Kapu!* He must forget everything of the old life.

Shutting off the voice like the counselors had taught him, he thought of other things—the job teaching Hawaiian culture that he started tomorrow, the pale blue of the sky above the L.A. smog, being clean inside himself. No more mistakes.

Sure, the voice hummed, crouching down like a torpid lizard inside his gut and rocking back and forth. Weki had kept it caged there for almost six months now, first with help at St. Jude's, then on his own, staying with a detox friend who owned a health club until Weki was strong enough to go to his own new house, the house left to him by Luka Keawe. And today he felt strong enough to go driving alone in this car that had also been left to him by Luka Keawe.

"Heyah!"

He'd just turned down Cahuenga Boulevard without thinking, and could not turn back because of the traffic.

He began to sweat, his foot jerking on and off the brake. Because that left turn ahead–that was Universal Studios Boulevard, leading to the City Walk. To his past. If he could just drive by it...

He turned left and the lizard bobbed happily in his gut.

Weki's mind began to rationalize wildly. This was a necessary test. He needed it to prove to himself that he was free.

He found a parking space just steps from the outdoor mall. Two minutes later he staggered with the crowds through the silver and primary colors, his blood rushing, his nostrils wide. Sketchers and Gladstones clinked glasses at him and blew out smells of fried food. The giant blue ape of Sam Goody's seemed to roar and wave. Movie theaters beckoned. Left and ahead, behind, stores waved their trinkets and laughed: Go on. Go.

Which he did, every sight, sound, and smell a mental trigger for those like him who *knew*.

They knew that behind the clean shimmer and flash, the Universal City Walk was a free-trade zone for drugs. Unlike most L.A. blocks and neighborhoods where one gang or another owned the street traffic, the Walk was so heavily policed to protect the tourists that no one gang could hold it. As a result, dealers of every color just picked a corner, a doorway, an alley.

Weki slipped his right hand into the pocket of his jeans as he reached the main food court and gripped the long loop of *hei* string he kept there for small magics and comfort. This, more than the mind tricks of St. Jude's would keep him safe. "*Ua mau ke ea o ka ʻaina i ka pono*," he whispered. *The life of the land is preserved in righteousness.* He silently added the Christian prayer that his counselor Chris had taught him—"Yea, though I walk through the valley of the shadow of death..."

But Weki's running shoes slowed of their own accord. His gut lizard knew this piece of City Walk.

Someone whistled and Weki jerked his gaze up to search the area near the giant electric guitar of the Hard Rock Café. That had to have been a spotter's whistle. It signaled an all clear—that the cops had moved up the block.

Weki looked left, right, and his eyes locked onto the grinning welcome of Merco.

The Mexican lounged against the white stucco building just right of the Hard Rock with his hands in the pockets of his baggy shorts like he was waiting for someone. His Hawaiian shirt offset skin the color of a macadamia nut. Merco's hair was short and neat like a tour guide, always smooth, always smiling.

Now he winked liked Weki had been here only yesterday, and spat four pea-sized plastic baggies out of his cheeks. He held them out casually for Weki to see.

Weki's knees went weak and he found his hand coming out of his pocket as he walked over. But still he managed to shake his head—*No.* Merco shrugged, made the spitty bags vanish, and pushed away from the wall.

"Ho, Naea. Long time. Howzit," Merco said, drawing out Weki's last name—*Nah-ayyy-ah*—like Merco was Hawaiian himself. Like he could be anything you wanted him to be. Your best friend.

"I'm..." Weki cleared his throat and forced himself to articulate. He had never liked Merco. "I am trying to get clean."

"Oh, brah. Truly?"

The expression of sympathy seemed so real that Weki, despite his dislike of Merco, found himself spilling it all—Saint Jude's, his struggles there, what the counselors told him, how they helped him. Merco nodded sympathetically, listening without interruption even when the whistlers signaled cops-approaching and signaled again all-clear. Until Weki felt like Merco truly understood and approved. Despite his profession. Despite his loss of Weki as a customer.

"And you?" Weki asked when he was done. "What happens now Luka is gone?"

Merco shrugged and fingered back his short oiled hair. "Ray stepped in. You know how it is."

Ray Aznar. A dangerous, acne-scarred hothead, a Mexican graduate of the Crazy Riders who had pushed Luka repeatedly to reveal his drug connections. Weki was comforted that Merco would share this news with him. Merco had dropped his Hawaiian act and was being honest. "Business," Weki said. "It does not stop."

"Too true, man. But I heard rumors, you know? Bout Luka. People saying they'd seen him around. Like he faked his death, you know? Ray was wondering."

Weki's gut went so cold the lizard there stopped bobbing. "I hear nothing bout that," he said.

"Yeah?" Merco smiled at him.

"Truly. I been locked away. Learning to live again."

"Yeah, man. Very cool. Very good. Proud of you, man. But you know, if you hear something, if Luka calls you or whatever, you tell me. Ray don't want to walk on nobody's toes, right? Right? Now get out of here before someone who don't care about you grabs you, man. You ain't made of steel."

So saying, he clapped a hand around Weki's stooped shoulders, turned him around, and gave him a push back in the direction he'd come.

But even as Weki stumbled off, his brain registered the feel of Merco's hand stuffing something into the right front pocket of Luka's jean jacket, and it was like Luka all over again, taking control.

No.

Weki made himself walk all the way back past the storefronts and cafes, down the side block, and right up to his Miata, the car that Luka had bought for him.

Then he could not stop himself. Weki reached his trembling fingers into the pocket where Merco's hand had gone. There, in the tangle of some old facial tissue, he felt a slimy wet plastic bag, no bigger than a pea, something hard inside.

A rock. Base. Crack cocaine. A free little $10 reminder of heaven and where to get it. And a reminder of *everything* from his old life, the crazy thing he did that last night for Luka. The unforgivable.

Fingers shaking, Weki pulled the spitty bag slowly from his pocket. He stared at it and felt the adrenaline rush through his veins, the blood rush from his head like he was going to faint. His wrinkled hands both shook now like he was ninety.

The lizard inside bobbed eagerly.

Breathing hard, Weki gnashed his teeth and cursed Merco. He tried to throw down the little spitty bag. Luka was gone. Weki had a new life.

He tried again to throw the baggy down.

On the third try he succeeded and quickly stepped onto it, grinding it into a plastic paste with his shoe. Then, knowing even that would not stop him from trying to retrieve it, he climbed quickly into his car and roared wildly out of there.

But the thought that Luka might still exist in the world, and what that meant, he could not leave behind. He needed to find a public library or newspaper shop with back issues.

He knew what stories to look for.

9

*B*AREFOOT, IN DIRTY JEANS I stumbled out of the living room where the morning show had just run highlights of last night's baseball game on TV.—Giants versus Cards. I'd watched not for enjoyment, but as another way to call Birdy to me. Another try.

You see, Birdy used to snuggle down on the couch there with me to watch Barry Bonds. We'd even gone to a game at the Pacific Bell last year, walked the concourse around the infield, cruised the overpriced food stands, finally chosen garlic fries, of course. Just the two of us. No one else in the family "got" baseball.

"Come on, Birdy," I whispered hoarsely, knowing it sounded like calling a cat. *Here, ghostie ghostie.*

Stopping in the front hall, I hovered over the latest digital camcorder I'd set up. Then I wove a bit to my right and had to grab the wall to steady myself. I noticed I was salivating. That memory of garlic fries.

When had I last eaten? Yesterday? Two days ago? Nothing since.

I dragged my hand over my mouth and half-beard and tried to shake my head clear. Not good. Saliva or not, my stomach felt leaden. Still, I should make myself eat. If I collapsed I might miss something.

And poof, there would go my chance to get Birdy back. And Sherry, Martha, Josh.

Turning from the boot room/laundry room where I had the camcorder aimed, I fumbled my way to the kitchen, careful not to trip

56

over the wires of the camcorders, tape recorders, EMF meters, air ion detectors, and night vision cameras set up there and in the kitchen. Also in the living room, the top of the stairs, each of the bedrooms and bathrooms upstairs, the basement. The place had become an obstacle course, dangerous in the dark.

I wove around the two filing cabinets of stored media by the door and made it to the fridge. Opened it. All the condiments and a few pickle jars from six months ago were still there because I couldn't stand pickles. The salsa jars had been cleaned out. The margarine tubs were gone. No eggs or meat, fruit or vegetables. So I had to have eaten lately because I'd bought groceries just...last week?

The remains of a giant block of cheese sat lonely on the top shelf along with half a loaf of stale bread and a carton of suspicious-smelling milk. I threw the cheese and bread on the kitchen table and grabbed the carton of milk. It glopped. I went to chuck it out but found the garbage bag under the sink was overflowing. Throwing the carton in with the sink's crusty dishes instead, I pulled a small butcher's knife out of the mess and rinsed it clean. Took it back to the cheese and bread. Sat down.

While I pulled the rubber band off the cheese, I contemplated the blinking light of the answering machine. There were so many messages the blinks all ran together.

I looked at the calendar on the wall. July. All I had marked were my weekly times to visit Sherry in the hospital, and a forced appointment to renegotiate my partnership agreement with Raj.

Raj. Bastard.

It had been only what? Five months since I'd given up work to bring Sherry home from the hospital. And Raj couldn't have expected me to work after we had to take her back again. Not after the way that happened, after the kids had to leave, after there was just me to prove Sherry wasn't crazy. That Birdy was still with us.

Wasn't.

Was?

The absurdity of that made my mouth twitch a little. I stared at the butcher's knife I'd unconsciously picked up. Even as my mouth filled with saliva over the feel and smell of the cheese I'd positioned with my other hand, my gaze wandered from the cheese to my wrist. The pale flesh was exposed because I'd undone the button on my cuff for something and hadn't bothered doing it up again. I could see the thready pounding of my pulse. *Thump...thump...thump...* Cut it and it would go *splash... splash...splash...*

Just a little movement. Lift the knife, drag it across in a nice diagonal. And everyone would stop blaming me for Birdy's death. Even me.

I moved the knife above my bare wrist and watched it hover there, begin to quiver.

Then I moved it back and set it down. I couldn't, of course. I couldn't leave Sherry alone, with everyone thinking she was crazy. And Martha and Josh—they needed me even if they didn't live with me anymore. Even if they were scared of what I'd become.

A low beeping sounded.

My head jerked up. One of my EMF machines, specially rigged to work unattended, 24-7, had detected unusual electromagnetic activity, a signature of ghosts. Or not. Could just be one of my computers downstairs humming to life for a scheduled virus check. Could be a passing cell phone outside.

A second beeping, higher-pitched, began. One of the air ion detectors. Something was happening. Birdy! Maybe called by the baseball game on TV after all.

I dropped the knife and clattered my chair over backwards to leap for the door of the kitchen. The hall camcorder was recording. The camera had started clicking pictures. I stumbled to the center of the hall and stopped dead, curled my bare toes against the wood, breathed deeply, tried to feel the presence.

Hear it.

Touch it, goddamn it.

I waited.

But the tingle I felt was probably just my starvation dizziness. There was nothing else.

Despite the sounds I thought I heard at night. Despite the digital photos I'd collected of little balls of light. And the mumbling recordings I got on my tape recordings—roars, whispers, possibly a voice saying my name.

They all meant nothing.

"Fuck!" I ran over and cracked my fist into the still-clicking camera, sending it and the tripod flying into the lintel post at the bottom of the stairs. It crashed down, the back spun off, and electronic pieces chittered across the floor, the first time the camera had been without power in months.

And who cared? Who *cared*?

How many photos or videos of floating lights and luminous threads did it take? Orbs, ghost hunters called them. Dust specks? Mold? Light flares? Real ghosts? Who knew? If they weren't Birdy in some form I could identify and talk with, get proof of, then who–the fuck–cared!

Choking, I staggered back to the middle of the front hallway, overcome with a flood of physical memories. I remembered the feel of Keawe hitting me from the side, tying me, gagging me. I remembered choking while he brought down Sherry, hurt her. Most of all I remember how helpless I felt when Keawe ran upstairs again, going for Birdy...

Oh, God.

I collapsed to my knees on the floor. Sherry! Birdy! Josh and Martha. If I could tell you how sorry...

Daddy?

I coughed and steadied myself with my hands on the wood. That had been a distinct word in my head, clear and precise. Not an illusion. I swear.

I closed my eyes and stilled my breathing. Listened like I used to as a kid, with my whole body.

There was the electric hum from all the monitoring devices I had set up all over the house to catch ghost activity. And...a dripping somewhere—some tap I hadn't turned all the way off. A bird outside. The occasional thrum of distant traffic. I could smell the dust in my nose from the wood and front door carpet not swept or vacuumed in ages. I could smell...myself. Feel the itch of my beard and underarms, the lank greasiness of my hair.

Then, maybe, just at the edges of my mind, like the sense you get of someone watching you, I thought I felt a presence. No sound, but a feeling of someone...little? Afraid? Of what?

I raised my head and opened my eyes slowly. I saw just the front hall. All done in white ivory wood. Elaborate cove moldings around the ceiling. Beautifully strip oak flooring. Heavy front door. A gilt mirror to the right as you came in. A visual representation of my struggle to do well for my family.

Birdy?

I suddenly felt the presence again, like a sigh running through me, the feeling I remembered when she sat beside me or touched my face with her little hands, smiling.

"Birdy," I said out loud.

Nothing.

But she'd been there. Just like I'd dreamt of her. Like I I'd felt her sometimes in her bedroom with its boarded-over window. Like her mother screamed she'd seen her that day home from the hospital.

Birdy was here somewhere. She was.

Pushing myself up to my feet again, I staggered over to the digital camcorder that had been recording from the time the EMF meter and ion sensors had beeped. I stopped it, rewound, then played the tape as I watched in the little window on back.

Camcorders, six different types, had been my first exploration into trying to mechanically detect Birdy's ghost. The ghost hunters I'd contacted online had said video results were sporadic, but I'd set them up all over the house anyway, had them record all night, moved them around. Then, on the suggestion of my contacts, I'd added EMF and ion meters, cameras, audio recorders. Finally networked them all using old Pentium III computer boxes and routers, got very scientific.

The result was the sort of stuff I was watching now—nothing.

Actually, sometimes there were orbs or streaks of light that the ghost hunters online whom I sent the clips to assured me were ghosts. Nothing that I could hold up to the few people who still worried about us and say, *Look! I'm not crazy! Sherry's not crazy!*

I shut the camcorder off and sucked in a long breath. Enough of these. They didn't work. I'd take them out tonight.

But the sound recordings? I bit my lips and hit rewind on the old-fashioned Panasonic cassette recorder I'd picked up at Target.

Trying to record ghost voices was called hunting EVP or "Electronic Voice Phenomena." It had gone in and out of fashion over the decades. In Luxemburg in the late 1980's, a husband-wife team had even claimed to contact a group of EVP researchers who'd formed up on the "other side" to work the contact from that end. For me, it was the one mechanical thing I'd tried that suggested true communication with things I couldn't see or hear. Not that the garbled sounds I got were definitively words, but they often came right after I asked a question to the air. Even after I'd accounted for all other noise sources. Even when, despite the loud roars I recorded, my naked ear had heard nothing at all.

So now?

I stopped the tape at counter zero where I'd reset it after its last recording, and pressed Play.

I heard the monitors beeping, a gasp and grunt that must have been me from the kitchen, distant sounds of traffic, the thudding run and squeak of my bare feet, silence, my expletive, "Fuck!" a grunt and thwacking clatter as I destroyed an expensive digital camera, a sob, stumbling, breathing. Just me. As usual. Just—

"Daddy? I'm right here. Where's Mommy?"

It came from the tape. Because there was my voice too, right after it: "Birdy?"

More footsteps. The sound of the camcorder being rewound and played.

Audio recording ends.

Oh, *shit*.

~~~~

Just northeast of Berkeley, my brother-in-law had found a "retreat center" for Sherry and forced the Department of Social Services to pay for it. That's where Sherry was now. That's where, showered, shaved, and wearing my one clean shirt and pair of Dockers, I now drove in the family station wagon.

On the seat beside me was a satchel with a cassette player and Birdy's tape.

I cleared the Oakland Bridge and approached Berkeley as the sun finally broke through the haze of morning fog over the bay. The air smelled thick and sweet with spring. New green on the trees. Sweatshirt weather. Like when I, Sherry, and the kids had driven this highway out to Grizzly Bay. Martha had just finished grade five; Birdy and Josh, their different pre-schools. Sherry hadn't started her job with the San Francisco's Department of Social Services yet, and—

"Shit!" I jerked the steering wheel as a Grand Am almost cut me off.

Thankfully I had to turn off the highway anyway. Minutes later I was driving, jittery, through the winding canopy of trees that led to what looked like a transplanted British estate—a hulking, two-story stone mansion with a high sloping red-tile roof, a circular front drive, and gardens out back. The White Pines Retreat.

I parked, secreted the cassette recorder in my windbreaker, and loped into the building. As always, the lobby made my nerves worse. The walls were pink, with climbing ivies, patterned Mikwok Indian baskets, security cameras. But at least the young receptionist knew me by now and smiled from behind her desk. "Hello, Mr. Friesen."

It gave me another memory flash—the first time I painted Sherry. She was nude, in love with me, and sexy as hell. We kept interrupting the painting to make love on the mattress on the floor.

I shook it off as the girl pressed a button to release the lock on the oak door leading into the patients' hallways. Inside, I climbed the worn stone stairs immediately to my left. The second floor housed the women. It had another security doorway and camera. Someone buzzed me through and I walked the smooth stone corridor to Sherry's room, second-to-last door on the right, a room with a view out to the gardens.

But she wasn't there. Nor was she in the day room on the on the other side of the corridor. And the door at the end of the hall that I knew led up to the roof was unlatched. Alarmed, I stepped towards it. The sound of scuffling fee coming down stopped me. I stepped back from the door as a white-suited orderly named Dave burst though, slipping and swearing, dragging down the last stairs an elderly male patient in just his underwear. Mr. Augusto, I remembered, an Italian man prone to violent outbursts.

"I'm-a gonna fly!" Mr. Seta yelled.

"One of these days, Alice!" Dave yelled back. Then he saw me, apologized for the security lapse as he kicked the door to the roof closed, and said he'd seen Sherry from up there. She was out in the gardens.

I found Sherry beside a pond ringed with blossoming yellow tulips. Someone had obviously helped her dress today, because everything was coordinated—tan slacks, a white blouse that looked too light for the weather. But as she shuffled, I noticed that her glorious red hair was tied back in severe ponytail and streaked with gray. She wore no makeup. The weak sun washed out her complexion, eyebrows and eyelashes.

I swallowed a hard lump in my throat. "Sherry?"

She didn't respond so I stepped directly in front of her. She stopped. Her eyes flickered just a little, but I might otherwise have not been there.

"Sherry, honey, I...um...brought you something you have to listen to. I was watching baseball on TV.. You remember how Birdy used to like watching baseball with me?"

Her eyes stared through me.

"Listen to what I recorded just after."

Fumbling the tape recorder out of my jacket, I held it up and pressed play. As the hissing of the background noise began, with the monitors beeping and my running and thumping, Sherry's head bobbed forward slightly, registering something familiar. I realized you could hear the dim *tick...tick...tick...* of our living room clock on the tape in the background. Maybe the last backgrounds sounds Sherry had heard that night with Luka. Maybe just that she recognized it as being ours, from our house.

As I yelled *Fuck!* on the tape, her nostrils flared and her breathing quickened. Then Birdy's voice came out of the machine and Sherry's eyes jerked up, wide and aware, looking straight into mine.

"Birdy?" she asked like a little girl.

"Yes!" I wanted to grab her by the arms, jump up and down with her there on the dirt path. This was the first time since her brief visit home that she'd actually *seen* me. And to share with her what I'd been doing, for her, for me...

I jabbed a finger onto the recorder's buttons to stop the tape and rewound it, watching the counter. Then I pressed Play again.

But I was so excited by this that I hadn't been watching Sherry. Now, as the tape began running again, she shook her head back and forth in short, jerky movements and her body trembled. "Birdy *no* Birdy Birdy *no no* don't don't Birdy..."

Birdy's voice on the tape came out again before I could stop it— *"Daddy? I'm right here. Where's Mommy?"*—and Sherry suddenly raised up her hands in tight fists and screamed so hard her body shook. Even the leaves on the trees around us seemed to shake. The tulip leaves fell off. My own heart stopped beating.

She screamed again and I was dimly aware of running feet—two men in orderly outfits, running down the garden paths, coming to take me away. One grabbed my cassette recorder. The other jerked me back, saw my face, and pulled me more gently, leading me out of the garden.

While Sherry screamed and shook like she was dying.

~~~~

Dr. Morry Brandeis sat across his desk from me in his stiff white doctor's coat. His office was equally severe, bare-walled but for the psychiatrist's degrees (all from back east, I noted). One tall skinny window rose behind the desk and flickered with trees and sunlight, maybe to distract supplicants from the fact that Brandeis himself was short, squat, bearded, and almost bald. All he needed to complete the stereotype was a pair of horn-rims. Except, of course, this was the west coast. He'd probably had laser eye surgery.

"Did you hire someone to do this?" he huffed now, nodding at the cassette recorder in my lap with which I'd just played him the Birdy tape. His lasered eyes were beady, his lips pursed. I resented the way he made my face flush.

"I told you how I recorded it."

Brandeis sat back, playing with a fat black pen. "What did you hope to gain?"

"A reaction."

"Like this?"

"A...communication," I blurted, instinctively knowing even as I said that this man had never been happily married and couldn't understand what it was like to share everything with someone, to validate your feelings and opinions through that sharing, then to have your partner suddenly gone. He was listening, though, so I plunged on.

"I wanted to show Sherry that I believed her, that she wasn't crazy, that Birdy is still...with us."

"Your business partner told me what you've been doing," he said. I looked up, surprised, and he continued. "Mr. Rajiv Singh. He was in here last week, checking on Sherry himself. He wanted my expert opinion on whether you were delusional."

"What?"

"Whether you'd gone crazy."

His eyes flashed with amusement, a moment of true sympathy perhaps, but all I could think of was the timing of Rajiv's request. It was probably just before he forced his way in to demand a meeting to renegotiate our partnership agreement. My shirt started feeling tight around my chest, the air in the office harder to breathe. "What did you tell him?"

"That grieving takes a long time. That you have been hit not only with the loss of your daughter, but with the loss of your wife, perhaps with the loss of your other children as well."

I was about to protest that I hadn't lost my wife *or* my other children—they were all just away for awhile—but the words got stuck in the dryness of my mouth. I coughed. "I'm okay."

Brandeis tilted his thick head forward and tapped his pen on his desk. "Are you really, David?"

For a moment I almost bought it. I'd fought most of my life to shove my father's terrifying realities and those of my own younger years into a locked closet. The final step had been marrying Sherry, a woman so sunny and practical that thoughts of ghosts shrivelled before her light. And now Brandeis was challenging me to make that choice again—cast away the spirits and I'd get my wife and living children back. All I had to do was erase this little tape recording, remove all the ghost hunting equipment from our home, go back to smiling at everyone, work hard with Rajiv, gently persuade the kids to come home, be patient with Sherry...

A black rage swept through me. *No way!*

Birdy was dead and Sherry in here because I'd blinded myself to what I and Josh and Birdy had felt. What we'd *known*. And Birdy was still—in—our—house.

I jerked up the recorder, rewound, and played it again. *"Daddy? I'm right here. Where's Mommy?"*

"That's real!" I said. "That's our little girl. She's in our house. I'm not making that up!"

Brandeis grimaced with a mask of professional pity. I imagined his fat little fingers were itching to dump the pen and buzz an attendant to drag me away. Instead he said, "I think you believe that."

"Because I'm crazy!"

"Because you're grieving. Perhaps dealing with post-traumatic stress disorder. I think this process plays many kinds of merry hell with our emotions, our perceptions, what we'll do to deal with others."

I stared at down at the tape recorder in my lap, my lips pressed together so tight they were shaking, my eyes watering. Fighting it. "I'm not making this up."

"This isn't really about helping your wife, is it, David. You couldn't save her from Luka. You couldn't save Birdy, either. This is hard to deal with. The guilt. Trying to change things."

"Shut up." I said it so softly I barely heard it myself.

"You know what you have to do to move on, David, don't you? To help Sherry get better?"

My mouth was fixed shut, my eyes locked onto my knees.

"You have to clean your house. Sell it. Start a new life somewhere else. If Sherry knows you are doing this, she may eventually want to join you in it."

He said nothing more, waiting for a response. But I could barely breathe, as if the impulses in my body were so strong in opposite directions that it had simply frozen, locked up like a glitchy computer.

"David?"

Then I remembered what Sherry had kept telling me that day we'd gone to Mad Music. *I want you, David. It's not just for the kids. I want you to find yourself again.* And it tipped me just enough in one direction that I answered, "I can't sell the house."

"Because why? Because you want your little girl's ghost to still be there? Don't you see what this is driving you to do? To fabricate?" He held up a hand to stop my objection. "If her ghost were there, David, it would surely know how you feel. There's nothing more you can do for her. But your wife and your other two children, you can. Life is for the living. If you truly want to get your family back, sell the house and move on. Do it."

I raised my eyes just enough to see he had been stabbing the air at me with his pen. Now he dropped it and I saw again the glint of real compassion in his eyes. As if he reserved it only for the most hopeless and lost. Like me.

Creakily, like I was breaking the seal on something rusted shut, I forced myself upright in my chair, each vertebra popping, and shook my head. "No." Then I stood, stiffly holding my cassette recorder with its recorded electronic voice phenomenon, and walked to the door.

As I left, Brandeis called after me, "This is not good, David! You are failing this test!"

10

*H*E STILL COULD NOT ACTUALLY TOUCH THE WORLD. *Sight, sound, taste—they were all blurry and inconstant. But slowly, with the thrill of each unconscious possession and the death it caused, he felt his desire sharper in him. It was the hard little nut of his being, from which he reached out...*

One hand grasping.

The other hand holding tight to the web of his companion guide. Girl.

One eye seeking.

But it was the guide who jerked them about. She was in control as she too reached for a sticking place, didn't find it, and moved on.

Or flew away in fear when the place asked too much.

~~~~

In the secure women's room of the White Pines, Sherry Friesen jerked up on her bed and threw herself flat against the wall, cheek pressed to the cold paint. Her whole body thrummed, from the tip of her toes, her shoes and socks removed, to the tip of her ponytail.

"No," she moaned. "No-o-o-o... Birdy, come back."

Sherry waited, her eyes sightless to the room but staring into the mist that rolled around her and through her. It came to her unexpectedly now, ever since that visit home, ever since she'd seen a flash of Birdy and understood the other world was there.

Her little girl was there. Wanted her. Needed her. But kept running away.

Sherry licked her dry, cracked lips and felt the other, darker presence that followed Birdy around. The demon reached through the mists as if trying to touch Sherry again.

It took all her strength to not scream as she called past him, "Birdy! I'm here for you. Please come to Mommy and...leave Daddy alone. He's not strong enough, do you understand? Leave Daddy alone..."

~~~~

I drove into the lane to the rear of our house, screeched the Volvo station wagon to a stop in our little garage, climbed out, and slammed the door. I stamped my foot for good measure before I entered through the kitchen door.

Something felt wrong.

Forcing myself out of the White Pines funk, I shuffled to the middle of the kitchen and did a slow 360. I cocked my head and listened. It was what *wasn't* there.

Shaking my head, I hurried into the hall, checking doors and windows as I went. Then the living room, upstairs, into the washroom, each bedroom there. I finally stopped beside the video camera setup in Birdy's old room with my mouth dry and heart beating hard.

All the digital clocks showed there'd been no power outages while I'd been gone. None of the windows or doors had been unlocked or tampered with. No one else had a key to get in.

Yet here, as in every other area I'd carefully rigged in the house, my carefully networked ghost-hunting equipment that I'd once again considered shutting down and removing...had been turned off.

11

2:00 PM. San Francisco, Tenderloin district, Ellis Street.
The drifting sheets of fog and smell of garbage made it harder, as did the navy trench coat and suit, but Sweetness pushed her *chi* low in her belly and sank into a natural stance, *no kamae*, to find her center.

She looked across the traffic at the brownstone where Keawe had lived the last week of his life.

Slumming tourists and locals wove together along the sidewalks; the sharks on the corner only attacked the locals. A kid went running by to another building, in and up. All too familiar. Sweetness's mother might have fled New York with her girls and pushed herself and them through school, but Sweetness and Thea both eventually found their way back to the street.

Thea had died there by hanging out with the wrong people.

Sweetness stayed alive by trying to put those wrong people away.

Not that it mattered. Anyone who saw her now, black and proud, probably didn't see college and post-grad and federal agent. They saw "hooker."

Fuck.

It made a cold sweat break out on her scalp and she instinctively sank her weight onto her left leg, *neko ashi dachi*, so she could kick someone. Like the SFPD liaison officer she'd met this morning. "Forget Friesen," he'd grunted. "Open and shut." The file? Shredded. Coroner's

71

findings? Murder-suicide. Spinal trauma and asphyxiation for both. (She already had that report.) Bodies? Cremated.

Fuck.

The scratchy sound of running steps made her turn. Her new partner, Francisco Ramirez, came puffing up like he'd just run a marathon.

"Sorry," the twenty-three-year-old wheezed and planted his hands on his knees. "Parking. Jesus. Blocks away. Just...let me...catch...my breath."

She cut him off. "The Yellow Brick Road."

"Wha—?"

"6.1 mile obstacle course at Quantico. Woods, climbing walls, ropes, cargo netting, windows. You had a top ten percent time."

"Uh..." He glanced up. "Yeah."

"So why are you breathing hard?"

Ramirez's heavy breathing stopped, he paused, then he suddenly popped up straight with a smirk on his pretty, too-small mouth. "Didn't want to intimidate you, Ma'am."

"The male-female thing?"

He shrugged.

"Or is it the beaner-nigger thing?"

"Hey, I got no quarrel how you got through."

"And I don't give a fuck how you got through either, Ramirez. Just don't bullshit me."

"Sure. Ma'am."

"Sure?"

"Yeah."

"Okay."

She stuck out her hand and he grinned and took it. When their hands gripped, Sweetness jerked him forward against her outstretched leg, simultaneously executing *kokuto*, wrist lock, and folding his thumb inwards on its natural fold. The pain folded Ramirez's legs under him and Sweetness drove him face-down to the wet sidewalk, his held hand twisted up behind his back. Pedestrians on their side of the street crossed over to avoid them.

"Now," she said, not releasing her hold, "I've been giving you rope the last two days because you're a first office agent, but you know what? Your people skills are shit and that's dangerous."

"Fuck you," he said, his face white.

Sweetness smiled nastily and ground her knee into his kidneys. "Ahhh!"

"Let's try that again," she said. "You and me—equal partners?"

He tried to throw her off and she let him roll, but pushed his thumb in more until he cried out and stopped jerking.

"Equal?" she repeated.

Ramirez spat sidewalk grit from his mouth and said, "Equal."

She lowered her head so it was almost beside his ear. "Wrong answer."

Before she could crack his thumb, though, her jerked his head up. "I meant no! You lead! Ma'am!"

Sweetness stepped off him and stood, waiting. She knew he wasn't convinced any more than the other two male partners she'd worked with had been. Or her DEA partners. Or Hinkson. Or the Mick SFPD liaison officer. Like her father had taught her—expect crap. Deal with it.

Sure enough, a second after he'd rose and gently worked his abused thumb, Ramirez jabbed at her gut...

...and missed as Sweetness turned to the side, wrapped Ramirez's outstretched arm in her trench coat, gave him a quick elbow strike to the nerve cluster at the base of his neck, a backhand whack to his right ear, and a foot sweep that dropped him once more to the sidewalk.

He half-lay there, stunned. Sweetness looked down at him. "Whatever you've heard about me, whatever Hinkson told you, I don't give a shit. Just remember that at the end of your time with me, I write your eval. Got it?"

"Yes...Ma'am."

"Now get up and act professional for the audience. We're FBI."

He straightened himself out, glancing red-faced at the gawkers who'd formed, both across the street and ten yards back in either direction. Ramirez snarled at them, but no one backed off. Finally he ignored them and Sweetness ran through her memory of his report out loud.

How Keawe had moved to S.F. and within a month got himself onto the social services list with GAAP, the General Assistance Advocacy Program, assigned to the very building where the Department of Social Services General Assistance sent Sherry Friesen.

It took a beat, then Ramirez nodded. "Yeah."

"So Keawe just hangs around, connects up with her, decides to rape her and kill her kid?"

"Uh...no?"

Sweetness looked at him. He could not possibly be as dumb as he seemed.

"Before I got yanked for this investigation," she said, "I was working with the DEA on Mexican drug pipelines. I tapped my contacts there and they told me Keawe wasn't a two-bit dealer. He had major connections and no gang affiliation. Freelance. Four dealers under him. Cleared maybe eight hundred grand a month. You think that sounds like someone who plays homeless for kicks, then randomly chooses someone to follow and rape, murder-suicide?"

"So..."

"So I think whoever investigated this case completely missed what went down. Why did Keawe go after the Friesens?"

"Drug deal gone bad?" Ramirez said.

"Maybe."

"So how's it connected to the ghost murders?"

"Deaths," Sweetness corrected him. "Only one clear homicide. And it's not connected."

"But the descriptions..."

"Of ghosts? What are you thinking? Luka faked his death? Copycat killer? Or did you figure this was the X-Files?"

Ramirez blinked but stuck out his chin. "The descriptions match."

"Suggestible witnesses. The Friesen murder was big news, Keawe was Hawaiian, and there's a big ghost culture in Hawaii. I'm betting ghost hunters everywhere lapped it up."

"But..."

"Yes?"

Ramirez ducked his head, rubbing furiously at the scrapes there. Finally he looked up and blurted, "If you don't buy the descriptions match, why am I here?"

"Because," Sweetness said with a cold smile, "you gave my SAC a chance to fuck with me. He gives me a case where there's nothing to find but just investigating it makes me looks stupid. You, rookie, are just collateral damage."

Ramirez stared, his jaw open and working slowly back and forth. For once he had nothing to say.

"But like you guessed," Sweetness said, "there may have been a drug connection with Friesen. Still a chance for a good bust if we look sharp."

"I can do that," Ramirez said quickly. "Ma'am."

She smiled at him. He grinned back. As she turned to cross the street, he suddenly shot an elbow at her head. She caught it, twisted it, and ended up behind him, his arm up his back and her arm around his neck.

"Just...checking," he gagged.

~~~~

The front door of the brownstone sported graffiti-covered mailbox slots, one of which still had Keawe's name, printed in pencil on a slip of paper and taped on. No superintendent. No security on the front door.

Sweetness and Ramirez went door to door, banging, trying handles. They found an old man and a roomful of underage Chicanos on the first floor. Someone had plugged the toilet; it had overflowed into the main room. One kid was trying to mop it up with a disposable diaper.

On the second floor, there were two women/girls who hung in their doorway so scagged and hollow-eyed that Sweetness wondered how they could see straight to guide their johns up here. Thea had looked like this the last time Sweetness had seen her. It almost made Sweetness step in.

But Ramirez had moved on, already addressing a third woman, in the apartment next door, who seemed normal but knew nothing about Keawe. Ramirez pressed. A smelly guy in nothing but a jock strap appeared behind the woman with a baseball bat, and Sweetness strode over before things escalated.

The rest of the floor was a washout, but the on the third floor, right beside Luka's old room that still had yellow police tape across the door, they hit gold.

He was a ferret-like white guy named Jack. Maybe thirty, he had blackened teeth and shaky hands, but also a threadbare, button-down shirt and broad-striped tie which were both tucked crookedly into his pants. He waved them into a bare room that had a dirty mattress and sheet on the floor, surrounded by ripped magazines, and empty fast food containers. Twitching his hands around, he said, "Heard you out there, questioning everyone bout Luka Kiwi, right? Right?"

"Keawe," Sweetness said. "Yes."

"Mr. Fucking King of the World!"

"What?"

"Like just stay out of his way. Don't say nothing. But then all these people show up, kay? Day or night like we don't deserve no fucking sleep."

"What sort of people?" asked Sweetness. She gestured for Ramirez to take notes.

"Heads, hookers, suits, musicians. Coupla mean fuckers who thought they could take on Kiwi." Jack gave a snorting laugh.

"Because?" blurted Ramirez.

"Drugs," Sweetness said. To Ramirez: "Keep writing."

The ferret bobbed his head and Ramirez scribbled.

"Setting up contacts? A network?"

Jack shrugged and picked at this cheeks. "Kiwi had a cell phone on all night, kay? Talk and talk, Jesus. Right through the wall. Guys named Aznar and Merco. Shouting, right? 'Check it the fuck out!' Right? And 'No can! No can!' Like some big kind of threat. Right to the end, dude. Right to the fucking end."

"You told this to the cops?" said Ramirez, frustrated, no doubt that it wasn't in his reports.

"They didn't fucking *ask*. They bang round Kiwi's room, find baggies, guns, pipes—*whoah!* Like they got the whole deal. Woo! Drug dealer! Dick-wads! Never—fucking—asked—*me!*"

Ramirez was about to speak but Sweetness held up her hand. She stared hard at Jack and waited.

He jiggled his head sideways at her with a big smile like he had something dying to burst out. The licked his lips and held out his palm. He opened and closed his hand spastically. "He was looking for a woman." Then he squinched his eyes closed and shook his head and whole body, keeping his hand out, trembling.

Sweetness waited, then had another flash of Thea and she pulled a five dollar bill from the wallet in her pocket and pressed it into his hand. He opened his eyes to look, looked disgusted, and Sweetness reached to take it back.

Jack jerked it away. "Came here to get Cherry," he said. "Mother fucking sonofabitch." Jack suddenly had his head down, chewing on his lips and shaking his head side to side. But he kept going. "Nicest fucking lady. Made you feel...like could of change, kay? Special kinda feeling."

"Cherry. You mean Sherry Friesen?"

Jack nodded, his body shaking harder now. "She had this big hair, right? Bright red. Big boobs. Total MILF. And she talked... And listened. You know where she ended up? Know what the fucker did to her? Cops told me. Know where she ended up?" For a moment, Jack's face collapsed in a kind of wistful pain.

"Why'd he want her?" Sweetness asked.

Jack shook his head.

"Did he ever mention Sherry's husband, David Friesen? Or a drug deal connected with either of them? Payoffs? Anything?"

"Fuh-fuh-fuh-fuh-fuh-fuh-fuh...*k!*" Jack said, shaking his head hard. "He just wanted to *fuck* her, man. That's all. Totally wasted. Screwy-dewy. Went for the little girl too, right? Wasted!"

"So he never mentioned the husband?"

Jack looked at her funny and his right eye began twitching. She tried another tack.

"After he got Sherry calling on him, anyone else ever come by?"

For a second Jack held his stare. Then he snapped his head sideways. "You know she—Sherry—tells me once I could do radio? Cause I used to be in sales. Stereo stuff. Big bass, tweeters?" He tugged on his tie and looked back and forth at nothing.

Then he twitched, began pacing, and babbled about some "Old Kahuna guy" that Keawe kept with him, a crackhead. Maybe his lover, maybe his father. Treated him with respect some days, kicked him around others.

Ramirez cut in to ask where the old guy was now. Jack turned and blinked at him and Sweetness, looked down like he had to see the question written on the floor, then shook his head. "Don't know. Fuck. Gone. I don't know."

"Great," Ramirez said, stepping forward when Sweetness didn't seem to be stopping him.

But Jack's brain had shut off. His twitchy eyes turned long and sallow. Every motion looked suddenly painful and he kept shifting back and forth like he had to pee.

Sweetness finally pulled Ramirez back, threw her contact card on Jack's bed, and dragged Ramirez out. A minute later they were standing in front of Keawe's old room, 306, tugging off the dusty police tape that had crisscrossed the door for eight months now because the local law hadn't bothered coming back after they'd closed the file. Odd that not even the landlord had disturbed it in all that time. Had been afraid to?

"Think I heard something in there," Sweetness said.

"What?"

Sweetness rolled her eyes, pushed open the unlocked door, and walked in.

It was empty but for an unmade bed against the wall and a collection of what looked like cut-apart soup or bean cans littering the floor. The can were blackened inside as if they'd been used as crude candle holders and the room still smelled of smoke. Sweetness looked at the empty light socket in the ceiling. Had the cans been the only source of light?

Ramirez was shuffling. Sweetness looked at him. "Something to contribute?"

"You were right," he mumbled.

"About what?"

"Doesn't add up that he was just here for the woman or kid. Not if he was still running things by phone."

"But Jack says he never mentioned David Friesen."

"So, like, we interview Friesen, right?" He looked at his notes. "And this 'Merco' and 'Aznar' in L.A. Maybe Friesen's still doing business with them."

Sweetness nodded. She continued checking around the bed, lightly thumping the walls.

"The police would have been all through here."

"They were looking for the wrong things."

"Yeah?"

"They assumed Keawe was crazy and suicidal. I'm thinking he wasn't."

Sweetness was on her knees now, scanning under the bed, the ratty armchair, and the only other piece of furniture, a lopsided chest of drawers, one short leg stepping down on what looked like a few pages of yellow newspaper, folded over and over into a little square. Sweetness went to it, tugged out the furniture leveler, and unfolded it. She looked through the pages then handed them to Ramirez.

"The yellow pages. Associations. The Hawaiian clubs of San Francisco?"

Sweetness nodded. "We're going to call and find out which ones Keawe spoke to. And for what."

Ramirez's lower lip stuck out. "Now?"

She shook her head. "No. Now it's time we paid David Friesen a visit."

12

OKAY, THIS WAS STUPID.

Standing by the profusion of cables and wires by the stairs in the front hall, I stabbed my finger down again on the Play button of the Panasonic tape recorder I'd taken with me to White Pines. Nothing. Like every other electronic recording device in this house.

Okay, maybe I'd banged the Panasonic or drained its batteries on my trip, but the rest? Every connection on every recording device in the house was secure. The surge suppressors had recorded no spikes. Pacific Gas and Electric said there'd been no power outage. There was nothing. No explanation for all my recording devices being fried. *Nada.*

Short of some massive electromagnetic pulse sweeping through the house and somehow shorting everything out—and even that wasn't consistent, because my computers downstairs still worked, as did the fridge, my clocks, the lights, the microwave—I was at a loss. This was a targeted disabling of my ghost-sensing equipment.

Which meant what? Birdy's ghost had somehow overloaded everything? Nothing I'd read about ghosts so far said they could do that.

Break in? No signs of forced entry.

I dragged my hands down over my face, trying to clear the cobwebs. It had to be someone with a key, someone...

The kids!

I felt a flare of anger. Could it really have been Martha and Josh acting out some of their frustration? Or maybe it had even been their current guardians—Sherry's sister and her husband. Maybe Dr. Brandeis had called them from the White Pines and suggested it.

My angry energy drove me back to the rear door, where I realized I wasn't wearing any shoes. Where had I taken them off? When? God, I needed sleep.

But first, the kids. I needed to talk with them.

~~~~

I stopped the Volvo in front of Sherry's sister's house in Sausalito. Rose. Rose and her good German husband, Gunther. I wobbled out of the car, slammed the door behind me, and walked up to the covered front porch.

It wasn't my usual visiting day, but I rarely made those these days so I had to have some extra ones coming, didn't I?

I shakily batted back my hair, tucked in my shirt, and rang the doorbell. Waited. Looked around. The gentrified little neighborhood was quiet for a Saturday afternoon. No kids around. Gunther and Rose were old.

A screen door slammed somewhere and I heard a scuffling inside the house. A second later the front door opened to reveal Gunther standing there in a brown cardigan, his reading glasses perched on the end of his nose, a pair of soiled gardener's gloves in his left hand.

"David? What is it?" He sounded like a German concentration camp guard who'd just caught me tunneling under a wire. Amazed that I could be so stupid.

"I want to see my kids."

"I don't think that would be a good idea right now."

"I want to see them anyway."

"Look at you." He gestured at my face and clothes. "Do you want them to see you like this?"

No! I wanted to shout. *I want them to see me healthy and whole, but that's not possible these days, is it?* Instead I said, "I just need to ask them something."

A shadow loomed behind Gunther and Rose was there in a gray cotton dress, like an older darker version of Sherry with all the sex and life drained out of her. The sight of her usually made the guilt meter jump inside me so much I sometimes wanted to vomit. This time I steeled myself.

"Rose!" I said. "Where are Martha and Josh?"

Gunther stepped back so that Rose could take his place. She held sharp little garden shears, spring loaded, and spoke in a patronizingly voice. "They're playing with friends today, David."

"Where?"

"I don't think I'll tell you that."

"I'm their father!"

"Yes," she said.

"You don't have a court order, you know. You've got them strictly on sufferance. Because I let you. Because I've been having...trouble. But if you start trying to hide them, or keep them from me..."

"We're not hiding them, David." I could see Gunther in the shadows behind her, shaking his head. It made my own face grow hot, the back of my head tight and pounding.

"Then tell me where they are, damn it! I have a question to ask them!"

Rose didn't even flinch. She just stood staring at me, the cold bitch. Holding her sharp garden shears. A wall of ice between me and my remaining children. No, she was a Valhalla prison guard, only I was somehow the prisoner and she was making sure I didn't mess with the living. I wanted to lunge at her, disarm her and break her away so that I could run inside to my family, to Martha, Josh, and Birdy. To Sherry.

Instead, I started crumbling inside, wishing I could curl into a fetal position on their porch. Like Sherry had said on her last healthy day, I was nothing. When I'd run from my painting, I'd given up my life, devoted everything to building useless firewalls around the family.

You're failing the test.

"I...just had to ask them a question," I said.

"What?" Ice cold.

"Someone...came into our house this afternoon. Without breaking in. I wondered if the kids...or you or Gunther..."

"Martha and Josh have been with friends since lunch. Gunther and I have been gardening. None of us has been to your house."

"My house..."

"Go home, David. Sober up. Get some sleep."

I ran a hand shakily back through my hair. *My house.* Not the children's house, not Sherry's any longer. *My* house. Brick house. Just me and a ghost. And it struck me that of course the kids hadn't gone back there, *would* never go back there.

Nodding stupidly, I backed up all the way to the car, managed to climb in and drive back across the Golden Gate Bridge with the fog, to Balboa, to our back alley and garage.

I shut off the Volvo, and shlumped in the back door. The boot room was clear of most of the kids' boots and shoes now, though Sherry's were still there. And mine. A pile of dirty laundry lay on the floor from last Tuesday when I'd actually thought I might do a wash.

Daddy.

I snapped my chin up.

That had been a clear voice in my head. Birdy.

I looked back and forth, and somehow knew the call had come from further inside the house. I staggered onwards, forcing myself to open my senses up.

A tug inside made me look up. Maybe it was just my memory of that night, but I could swear I sensed someone upstairs. I grabbed the banister and clumped up beside the string of networking cables stapled against the wall.

"Birdy?" I whispered at the top. "Where are you?"

Daddy.

It was almost a sigh, but it was coming from behind the closed door of her room, straight ahead of me at the end of the hall. I swallowed and began walking slowly towards it, my head pounding. I could *feel* her in there, waiting and...scared? Something was jangling inside me like my nerves being scraped.

I reached for the doorknob and paused. My nostrils flared. It smelled like someone had burned garbage in there. Not possible. An olfactory illusion. If there was one place I kept clean in the house, it was Birdy's room.

Still my forehead broke out in a clammy sweat as I reached for the knob again.

The doorbell rang downstairs.

My head twitched. Who? What? *Rajiv?* Was it three-thirty already? Could I just ignore him?

The doorbell rang again, followed by hard knocking on the door. Not Raj. When he really wanted in these days, he went for the hidden key out back.

I swallowed and looked back to Birdy's door. The sense of someone there, the smell of burnt garbage—they were both gone. I twisted the knob and threw the door open.

Nothing.

Birdy's perfect bed with its neatly-arranged stuffed animals, her closet, her short dresser, her bookshelf, dead camcorders and cameras on tripods, a silent ion and EMF sensor.

Nothing.

Stepping back, I turned and stumbled down the hall and stairs to the insistent knocking at the front door.

When I threw it open, it took me a second to process the trench-coated government types standing there, a man and a woman. The dark-skinned woman looked like some kind of Amazon princess, with short-cropped hair, full-but-scarred lips, and a solid stance that made her look like a jut of rock in a crashing ocean. I had an embarrassing urge to fling my arms around her and just hang on.

She held up an FBI badge.

"David Friesen? We've got some questions to ask you about what happened to your wife and daughter."

13

*A*BOUT...WHAT HAPPENED?" I said. "And about Luka Keawe."

"Luka..."

The spike in my heartbeat only got worse as the woman extended her hand and I took it. Calluses along the edge spoke of hardness. Coldness. And those scars on her lips? My crazy urge to hold onto her flashed to a fantasy of kissing her, then to a wild kind of masochistic despair, imagining her throwing me back to the floor and demanding I call out my shortcomings.

"My name's Gale Sweetness," she said. "Special Agent with the Crimes Investigation Division of the FBI." She withdrew her hand and pointed behind her. "My partner, Special Agent Francisco Ramirez."

I swallowed. Was this about me going after my Martha and Josh? No. Of course not. It was about Luka and the night. A part of me leapt with hope that they'd discovered something. That Birdy had somehow miraculously survived. That everything was a big mistake and...

I shut my eyes hard. They stung with pain. I opened them again and the two feds were still there.

The woman tried a half smile that somehow rocketed my attentions back to her lips, the smoothness of her skin, the straightness of her broad nose. "Can we come in?"

"Have you found something new?"

The two feds shot looks at one another, the woman said, "Possibly," and my earlier foolish hope jumped again. Not really that Birdy had survived (not her physical body, anyway), but that they actually knew *why* the night had happened. Even that, some reason for it all, would be something.

"Does Detective Reichert know?"

Another quick look between the woman and her partner. "I believe Detective Reichert was transferred. There was apparently a legal wrangle involving the D.A.'s office, advocates for the homeless, and the lawyer for Mr. Keawe's 'business interests.' After the coroner's office filed their report on the methamphetamine in Mr. Keawe's blood, the case was closed."

My head jerked. "What?"

Sweetness held up a hand. "My partner and I believe the investigation was incomplete. Luka Keawe was not an addict. Nor was he a resident of San Francisco, poor, or in need of social services. In fact his only apparent reason for being here had to do with your wife and child. Or you."

"Me..." *He hates you, Daddy.* Birdy had said that.

"May we come in?"

"Uh...yeah. Yes." I stepped back and waved them past me, then closed the front door and followed them to the middle of the front hall. "The...uh...place isn't very clean..."

But it wasn't the filth in the kitchen drawing Agent Sweetness's eyes. I saw her studying the spaghetti of wires running everywhere, from the basement door through the hall to the kitchen, the living room, up the stairs. And the ion sensors, the smashed video camera I'd left lying by the stairs, all the other cameras you could see from here.

They made me look crazy. Well, I felt crazy. No sleep, my life a shambles, and now, suddenly, Luka had come here because of me?

"Drugs," Sweetness said and turned to me. "Did you or your wife buy narcotics?"

"I...not in...when we were both young... No."

"You'd be willing to take a medical exam to check that out?"

"Yeah. I guess."

"What about your children?" She pulled out a flip-pad and glanced at it. "Martha? Does she use drugs?"

"No!"

"Did your wife go on business trips often?"

"No."

"Sometimes?"

"Never."

"Old boyfriends down in L.A.?"

"They'd have been a bunch older than Luka Keawe."

"And might have business dealings with him."

"No old boyfriends," I said. "No drugs. No secret meetings. Her parents live in San Rafael. We've been down there *as a family*."

"But you're not one now. Your kids are with your sister-in-law. Your wife's in the hospital?"

"For now."

"Did your wife ever cheat on you?"

"Jesus Christ."

"That's a yes?"

"That's a no." I glared at her, changing my mind about this woman's sexual attraction. Her eyes were cold as slate, her face stone.

When the partner, Ramirez, came clumping up from the basement, I realized I hadn't even seen him vanish.

"You, like, expecting a major drug raid or something here," he said. "You're wired like the CIA."

I spun towards him angrily. "Don't you need a warrant?"

"You invited us in," he said.

"Not into my basement!"

"There something you're hiding there?"

"I'm not—"

Agent Sweetness raised a hand to cut me off and shot her partner a look that made him shut his mouth. "Are those ion sensors?" she asked, pointing.

I nodded.

"Ghost hunting equipment," she said. "All of this."

I tried to read her face but it was still blank. Fine. Screw it. "Yes."

"Ohhhh," her partner said. "Right. Why doesn't any of it work?"

"You tell me," I shot back and suddenly just wanted them *out*. They had nothing to offer. They just had more scorn and questions to pick with. Disassembling my past since there was so little of the present worth touching.

I started swaying towards the door, planning to open it and bum rush them out. But Agent Sweetness was walking in the other direction, the stairs going up. I fought an involuntary surge of panic. Birdy's room! But as my legs tensed to spring, she stopped. It wasn't the upstairs she wanted, it was the pictures on the walls leading up—family photos.

"You've been to Huntingdon Beach," she said, studying the first one.

I swallowed, dry mouthed in the after-effects of the adrenaline rush. "As a family. No drug buying."

She half-smiled at that then looked at her partner. He looked back, clueless. "The file pictures," she said.

"But—" he started.

"Just get them."

He nodded and jogged out the front door, presumably going to their vehicle. A minute later he was back with a briefcase and a colored plastic envelope big enough for eight-by-tens.

Sweetness took the envelope from him. "I have some photographs I want to show you," she said.

~~~~

Picture one was a dead body fished out from below the pier at Huntingdon Beach.

It's March, 2004. Birdy is four years old. We've just taken our first family trip to Disneyland and are decompressing by taking a side trip to

Huntingdon Beach before getting on the I-5 to drive home.

There's a fierce wind blowing in off the Pacific. Big waves. Lots of surfers riding.

We walk out on the pier and I slip my hand around Sherry's waist. She smiles up at me, hair whipping about. Martha runs against the wind with her arms out like she's Superman. Joshie runs after her.

Then we're at the end of the pier, walking around the big gazebo thing and suddenly I can't see Birdy anywhere. My heart leaps to my throat. All the benches along the edge of the pier! She could have climbed up, toppled over...

I feel a warm little hand slip into mine and I look down to see Birdy smile up at me like her mother. Her face is bright with the sun.

"I like this place, Dad," she says.

~~~~

Picture two—a dead woman crushed between a snapped steering wheel and crushed car roof, the car half-full of ocean water. The note on the back said the car went off Highway 1, about 26 miles north of San Simeon, and tumbled down a steep embankment.

March, the same Disneyland trip. Sherry has persuaded me to drive back by Highway 1 versus the I-5 because the weather's so beautiful, the kids are so happy, and she wants to stretch out this perfect time.

I pull us over south of a jutting cliff called Ragged Point because all three kids are pointing to the hundred foot drop to the ocean. This is what Highway 1 is all about. Sherry leads them in scrambling out of the car.

"You watch the kids!" I call out after her.

She laughs. By the time I catch up to them, they're all standing so close to the drop that my own stomach is in knots. Despite growing up by the mountains, I have an intense fear of heights. I want to grab all three kids, pull them back to the car, roar straight back to the I-5 at the earliest opportunity.

"Hey! Hey!" calls Martha. "What if you drove the car over the cliff here?"

"Yeah! Full speed!" says Josh.

"It would fly-y-y-y," Birdy says dreamily.

~~~~

I didn't recognize anything about the third picture—some stabbed black man on the floor of a restaurant kitchen—until I turned it over and read where it was taken.

Birdy is more hyped than I've ever seen her. She and I are at a real live baseball game, she keeps telling me. Pac Bell Stadium! Just the two of us! Forget the slides through the giant latticed coke bottle up behind our bleacher seats. Barry Bonds and JR Snow are playing! Maybe next inning Barry will hit one into China Basin!

I laugh and drag her with me down to the Field Club level where I've heard the food is better. Need to get something to ward off the chill from the water.

A minute later she's calling, "Daddy? Here!" and pointing at the front of the Derby Grill, where a black guy is waving at her from behind the counter.

I order garlic fries. When they're served, they're perfect—crisp, hot and golden, seasoned with bits of real garlic and plenty of salt. "Now this is as good as it gets," I tell her. I pay and turn to leave.

The black guy waves at us. "You two come back now, awright?"

~~~~

"What is it, Mr. Friesen?"

I looked up from where I'd sat on the stairs. Agent Sweetness watched me closely.

"We...visited those places," I said. "But lots of families have. What am I supposed to be seeing?"

Sweetness shot a *Shut up* glance at her partner, then considered for a moment and said, "Each of these deaths happened in the last three months. In each, witnesses claimed that either the deceased, or the person

92

who killed them, was possessed by ghosts. They even gave descriptions of two ghosts they claimed to have seen. Those descriptions were remarkably consistent between witnesses of the different events."

I felt a prickle of panic in my gut, suddenly knowing what she was about to say.

"The descriptions," she said, "were of your daughter and the man who kille d her, Luka Keawe."

I stared, the prickle turning to nausea and a clenching feeling even though I kept my face blank. I remembered Sherry on her abortive trip back from the hospital, suddenly screaming over and over from upstairs somewhere. I tore up there to find attic stairs pulled down from the ceiling of the upper hallway. I climbed up. Sherry huddled in the dark, pointing and crying that she'd seen Birdy, that Keawe still had her, that I had to save Birdy! *Save* her!

I physically dragged Sherry down from the attic and walked her around for over an hour as she sobbed and shook. Finally, when it was clear I didn't believe what she'd seen, she went as blank as she had been in the month right after the rape and murder. I sat her in the kitchen and hugged and smoothed back her red hair. Martha ran out to call her aunt. I told Sherry that what she'd seen wasn't real. The attic light was playing tricks.

Now I wasn't so sure. That horrible smell I'd gotten from Birdy's room. Maybe it wasn't just Birdy who was still here.

I took a deep breath and said, "You believe this?"

Sweetness said nothing. Just watched me. But her partner twitched impatiently and said, "You'd like us too, right?"

Special Agent Sweetness collected the pictures from me, looked them over again, then put them away. "Truthfully, Mr. Friesen, I don't believe in ghosts. But I'm still looking for why Luka Keawe came after your wife and daughter. If he truly had no business dealings with you, what was there?"

I shook my head vigorously.

Sweetness's partner stepped forward. "You say no extramarital affairs, but sometimes the husband doesn't know, right? Maybe Keawe was her boyfriend. Maybe they met on the sly. People saw them together. Good looking guy. Cute little girl."

I launched myself up from the stairs and would have got him if he hadn't jumped backwards, smiling, raising his hands. As I stumbled, he stepped forward.

"Stop it!" Sweetness snapped.

Her partner dropped his hands and stepped back with an innocent shrug. I turned, still fuming.

"I'm sorry," Sweetness said. "Do you carry a cell phone? When you go out?"

It caught me by surprise. "Usually."

"Show it to me."

Fumbling it out of my shirt pocket, I handed it to her. It was a little Samsung folding model, barely as long as my fingers.

"Scotch Tape?"

With one more snarl at the Latino partner, I walked to the kitchen. When I came back with the tape, Agent Sweetness pulled out her business card, tore it down to a smaller size, and fitted it across the back of my cell phone. She took the tape from me, taped it into place, and handed back the tape and cell phone.

"You think of anything, any way Keawe would have known your wife before coming to San Francisco, call me."

She turned and left with her partner.

~~~~

Outside, climbing into the rented Corolla, Ramirez said, "Did you believe that shithead? 'What am I supposed to be seeing?' No wonder the wife screwed around on him."

"You think she did?" Sweetness said.

"You saw the pictures in the house. You think a number like that's going to stick with a dud like Friesen?"

Sweetness considered that. Truth be told, she'd found David Friesen quite compelling. Handsome, intelligent. He was obviously a bit unstable since his wife was raped and daughter murdered, but she would have wondered about him if he hadn't been. No, her gut told her the man was innocent. Not strong, not resourceful, but innocent. There was a lot to be said for that kind of man.

"Hey," Ramirez interrupted her thoughts. "Friesen's got a visitor."

She looked. A man with East Indian features knocked on the front door, and again. When the door swung reluctantly open, he entered.

"The business partner," Ramirez said. "What do you bet he's in there to end it? I give Friesen three months before he loses the house. Less if he flips and goes after his kids. Probably already maxed out his credit. Loser is going down."

"Ramirez," Sweetness said without looking at him.

"What?"

"You talk too much."

She started the car, drove a hundred yards up the street, did a U-turn and cruised to a stop where they could watch Friesen's house. Ramirez did an exaggerated *What?* without opening his mouth.

"I want to question the business partner when he comes out," Sweetness said. "Get us a different take on this 'loser.'"

14

*T*HE SEATTLE TIMES ARTICLE about the killing in the Pac Bell stadium was five days old when Weki found it in the library. He stared at it for a minute, then, breathing quickly, ripped it out and stuffed it into the breast pocket of his jean jacket along with the others from today.

He stood and walked to the exit. Paused. The girl named Paula at the checkout desk elbowed her friend and called out. "Hey, Weki! Got that low-hipped, Hawaiian Willie Nelson Thing going!" Then the two girls giggled and smiled at him.

And Weki understood. He had the power of the *kumu*, the teacher, stamped on him from all his years on Molokai. The boy who had cultivated man-sized taro, yearning for adventure, had become the kahuna who controlled the ghosts around him, good and evil, ancestor and demon, as none before him. So much power.

So much.

Now, when he shook back his long silver hair and raised his hand to wave back to these girls—"Goodbye!"—it was like waving an old stick. A stick tied together with other old sticks in the form of an old man. Moment to moment wiry, but any time he could fall apart.

No longer *kumu*. No longer anything.

"*Onip'a*," he whispered as his legs wobbled and he clutched the doors and pushed through them. In the humid heat outside, he reached into his pants pocket and clutched the tangled loop of *hei* string, ran it through his fingers.

"*Onip'a*," he said again. *Stand firm.*

And somehow he had the strength to set off up the hill for the fifteen minute walk home.

His bungalow was twelfth on a small Santa Monica cul-de-sac, a conch-like exterior of pink and green stucco, sighing with cool tile within. It was, along with the rehab, a death gift from Luka.

When Weki reached it, he went straight to the room he had been planning to set up for meditation and token offerings to his *ao-aumakuas*, the spirits of his ancestors. The entire south wall was covered with newspaper articles.

At the center, the older yellowing articles were pinned like butterflies, dug up from newspapers almost a year old and clipped from every newspaper Weki had been able to find that ran stories of Luka's atrocity.

Shooting out from these, like blown spawns of evil, fluttered two clusters of clippings, grouped by date, each with their own color of pins. The first cluster: "Pair of ghosts kills surfer." "Friends deny suicide pact." "Battered body at Huntingdon." "Foul Play at Huntingdon." "Surfing drugs." "The killer Pier." Beside them on the wall was a large *1* in red marker.

The second cluster: "Driving to hell—a car possessed." "Ragged Point crash." "Plunge to ocean kills one." Others. They had a large red *2* beside them.

With shaking hands, Weki fished his most recent clippings from his pocket, added one to *2* and two to *1*, then grabbed a purple stickpin for the Seattle Times addition. "Possessed man murders chef."

He grabbed a marker and wrote a *3* beside the last one.

Then he shuffled backwards and stared, trembling, long and hard. Yes, he could deny it no longer. This was Luka. Which meant that everything Weki had foolishly promised was happening.

A sudden sick taste of horror filled his mouth and he could not swallow it away. And with it came the horrible need again, the lizard that bobbed over and over, *Escape this world. You know how.*

"*Ua mau ke ea o ka 'aina i ka pono!*" Weki cried. *The life of the land is preserved in righteousness.*

It did not help.

And though he'd hidden his car keys from himself the second he'd come home from his last Universal City Walk, removing temptation, he somehow went straight for them now.

The lizard inside him bobbed happily. *Yessss.*

15

WHEN RAJ LEFT OUR LONG MEETING, I stood in the front hall of my house and half-heartedly pumped my left fist in the air.

My right hand held an agreement of dissolution of partnership. It said Raj would deposit in my personal account a check for $350,000, a very generous buyout. All I had to give up in return was my half of the business I'd sweated blood over for the last three years, including all the used computer and routing equipment downstairs that had been used to coordinate my ghost detection equipment the last four months.

So no more work. No more ghost hunting.

I lifted my copy of the agreement and watched it begin to shake. Would Sherry like or fear this development? Gone was the job she hated. Gone too was our last chance to find Birdy.

I dropped the paper and watched it flutter to the floor.

Reality time. When Sherry had seen Birdy being chased by Luka, it had just been her nightmare continuing. When I sensed Birdy still in the house, that was my festering guilt. Time to move on.

Except...that voice on the tape recorder. How had I managed that? Unconscious ventriloquism? Was I that delusional?

"Birdy?" I called out to the empty house, then shouted as loud as I could, "BIRDY!"

Here, kitty, kitty.

Nothing.

And it was time to move on. I bent over stiffly, retrieved the dissolution agreement, and folded it, stuffed it into the pocket of my pants. Then I walked to the downed video camera, lifted it up and began unplugging the network cables from the back. All these cables and the piles of dishes in the sink, the overflowing trash can. If I started now, I could—

Daddy.

I spun around. Martha? No. Not Josh either. I knew the voice. Birdy. Which meant a delusion. A tricky one—crystal clear and scared.

"Damn it," I said, breathing hard.

Daddy.

Just as clear but further away this time. From upstairs. And the smell of burnt garbage suddenly wafted down like a fog.

With a cry of defeat, I dropped the network cables and sprinted up. If Birdy had truly been in her room just before the feds had shown up, maybe their coming had scared her away. And the smell? Luka?

Puffing, and shaking from more than just fatigue, I stalked down the hallway to Birdy's bedroom, gripped the knob, and threw the door open.

Nothing. Not even the smell of garbage.

At least...not from here.

My face broke out in a sudden sweat and I jerked my head around. I still smelled it. From where? Eight months ago I'd run up here and been too late. I'd failed. Three months later I'd run up again for Sherry, again too late.

To the attic!

I looked up and licked my lips. "Honey? Birdy? Are you here?"

What might have been a bump sounded from beyond the ceiling and I ran for the hallway. Filled with manic certainty, I jumped into my and Sherry's bedroom, grabbed a flashlight, then dashed back out to creak down the attic door and stairs from the middle of the hallway ceiling. I climbed up.

It was as dank as I remembered. The only stuff we stored up here were Christmas decorations we never used, our old rug, out-of-fashion clothes, boxes of old books and memorabilia, a broken sled.

My eyes followed my flashlight beam to the far corner by the chimney where I'd found Sherry that night, wailing in her nightgown between the chimney bricks and our half-crunched boxes of baby clothes, her hands clutching the frame of one of the last ever paintings I'd done—abstract of a fisherman.

I shone my flashlight up at the brick of the chimney to where it met the inside frame of the roof. On the other side of that framing, plywood, and shingle, Luka had tied his nylon ropes, one for him and one for Birdy, then...

My flashlight beam dropped unsteadily down the brick. Stopped.

Asphyxiation. Severe shock to the third and fourth vertebrae. Near instant death. That's what they said. *Near.* Her neck hadn't been cleanly broken. Which meant she might have been alive before I pulled her up. Which meant I might have killed her.

Might have.

And even if not then, by not listening to her and Josh sooner. By not fighting Luka harder. By not rushing upstairs faster.

I swallowed and dropped to my knees, hung my head and shut off my flashlight. The afternoon light, a somber silver with the afternoon fog, shone through the soffits and the attic opening behind me to make the attic junk look like hunched monsters from my conscience. Waiting.

Then, suddenly, she was there. I could feel her like a cool wind on my cheek. I spun on my knees but saw nothing. Scrabbling, I found the switch on my flashlight and turned it on. Shone it around. Piles of boxes beside me. Nothing but boxes. I turned it off again and squinted through the dark at the boxes, urging Birdy to be there.

I blinked and she was. She looked exactly like she had the day she'd died—bunny pajamas, face freshly scrubbed for bed. And if this was a delusion, some kind of psychotic break that meant I was going to be joining Sherry in White Pines after today, I didn't care. It just must not end.

"Daddy?" She said it wistfully, like she didn't believe I could hear her.

When I nodded, she blinked and chewed her lips in and out, like she suddenly didn't know where she was. Her form grew faint.

"Birdy!" I choked out. "Stay here. Please!"

She stabilized and looked curiously at me.

"Yes, honey. Stay with me. Talk to me. Please. Come on. You can do it."

Birdy's ghost stood still and seemed to dart back and forth like a shadow at the same time. "I...go to the park with you," she said, her voice reverting to toddler speech for some reason. "You throw me...a ball."

"The park. The Pacific Bell ball park? Did you go there?"

"'You can do it.' I can do it. I try." She reached up her hands then dropped them and looked frustrated that there was nothing there.

"What is it? You want to catch a ball? You want to see them catch a ball?"

Her eyes had drifted away from me, as if seeing something at a great distance. "Park," she said simply and suddenly merged with the shadows of the boxes behind her.

I was about to shout out to her, order her back, when I caught a whiff of garbage rot and something stirred in the shadows beside where she'd been—a second form, darker, taller, malevolent. It seemed to uncurl from where it had been perched to watch. But I could not see it, exactly. It was more an impression of form—dark burning eyes, lean fingers, overwhelming stench. It now reached those lean fingers into the place where Birdy had vanished as if to hitch onto something. It smiled quickly and seemed to draw the rest of itself after the hand until it too faded into the shadows.

I cried out and leapt forward, slamming into the space where the two forms had disappeared. I shoved the boxes aside and beat at the wall.

"Keawe! Stay away from her, you sonofabitch! Stay away! You fungus! You fly shit! Stay *away* from her!"

And more, shouting and whispering, pleading, and finally sobbing until I collapsed in a wussy heap on the attic floor.

But even as I let myself go pathetic, a small inner core of me churned through the actual words Birdy's ghost had said. *I go to park with you. You throw me a ball.* This was no delusion; this was a clue. Like she was trying to tell me something.

After ten minutes or so, I thought I had it. I wiped my face on my sleeve and dragged myself up to stagger to the attic stairs leading down.

I knew where Birdy was going next.

16

H^{*AI!*}" Clad in just tee-shirt and panties, Special Agent Sweetness finished the last lunge of her *kata*, then slowly drew herself up to neutral and folded her hands together. She took a deep breath and tried to clear her mind.

No bitches here, white or otherwise. No weakness.

Just strength. Just her. Partnerless. And antsy as hell.

She'd hustled Ramirez onto a plane that morning to go check out the drug angle back in L.A. that she'd come up with but only he still committed to. And now, with the sun low in the sky but still bright through the window of her hotel bedroom, she had to do the one thing in this investigation that she'd been dreading. She had to call her mother. Hinkson has as much as demanded it.

But what was Sweetness going to say? That she was investigating a serial ghost killer? She wasn't. She'd mention the witness statements, of course. And David Friesen? A guy who'd obviously gone a bit nuts with everything that had happened, but who still somehow came off as deep-down solid. Compassionate even. It was enough of a contradiction that Sweetness hadn't been able to stop thinking about him.

Oh, yeah. Her mother would love that. Replacement father figure, she'd say. Mixed with wounded bird. Perfect for you, dah-ling.

She'd laugh herself silly.

Taking a deep breath, Sweetness dove for the bed, grabbed the phone as she rolled over it, and came to rest on the floor on the far side of the bed in a sage seat position—cross-legged, heels drawn under her perineum.

Another huff, then she dialed her mother's home phone number, waited, got the answering machine, and hung up. Stupid. Just because it was Saturday night, why would her mother be anywhere but her laboratory?

Sweetness was about to dial there when the phone rang under her fingers.

Startled, she picked it up and heard Ramirez on the other end. She could hardly hear him through the static and music and people jabbering in the background. Some complaint about his flight back. She cut it off. "Well?"

Ramirez audibly shifted gears. "I'm at Universal's City Walk. Hit Keawe's main dealer, hood named Merco. Claims everyone here's independent, no one working for anyone else. But when I suggest he's working for an old buddy of Luka Keawe, he hints maybe Ray Aznar and Keawe were never friendly. And he's never heard of David, Sherry, or Martha Friesen before the murder-suicide. Wondered if I actually saw Keawe's body, though."

"What?"

"I think he's scared Keawe faked his suicide."

"And?"

"I told him we were looking for Keawe's buddy, an old Hawaiian probably. Kahuna guy. Merco's face got mean and he took off."

"To warn Aznar?"

"Maybe," Ramirez said. "Or maybe he knows where the kahuna guy is. You want me to ask around?"

"Yeah. If the kahuna's in L.A., find him fast. Check with Richards and Brown and see if the DEA people know anything. I'm checking the S.F. field office too up here. Maybe nose out Friesen's background some more too."

"Sure you don't want me back up there?"

Sweetness heard the animosity and suddenly realized it might be some kind of jealousy. Wonderful. Her sole romantic prospects this year? A despairing married man and a none-to-bright, hotheaded, rookie partner. "Just do your bit in L.A., Ramirez. I'll probably join you tomorrow night."

She hung up, started to dial her mother's lab number, couldn't summon the emotional energy. Besides, she could smell herself. How could she speak to her mother smelling like a gym locker?

Jumping up, she padded to the bathroom, cranked the water on high, ripped off her clothes, and stepped into the spray. As she began lathering, she tried to work out what to say to her mother. But thoughts of David Friesen kept getting in the way. Despairing but sexy, in a wasted kind of hollow-eyed way. She closed her eyes and imagined it was *his* hands running this bar of soap all over her body.

She breathed faster and focused her rubbing where it counted. Tingling.

Okay, she gulped and sinking back against the wall of the shower, putting the shower head on pulse and raising her center up to meet the spray. *Just a fantasy. It means nothing.*

~~~~

Los Angeles, Universal City Walk.

Less than five yards from where Special Agent Francisco Ramirez pocketed his cell phone, Weki Naea Kapu stepped back and weakly grabbed the railing around the Hard Rock Cafe patio. Only a few minutes ago he'd been hurrying to Merco for the pellets that would calm his panic and make everything right.

Then this FBI man had appeared from nowhere. He'd grabbed Merco before Weki could reach him, and questioned the dealer. No, the FBI man said. He hadn't seen Luka's body. But where was "the old Hawaiian kahuna?"

And Merco had left.

Onip'a. Onip'a. Now Ray Aznar would be after Weki, thinking Weki knew something, thinking maybe he must shut Weki up.

Weki gulped and his old heart raced wildly. He clutched his bony chest through his shirt, trying to massage the tight feeling away. Maybe he should go to this federal agent? Claim sanctuary? But what if the agent knew about him? Knew that Weki had drugged up Luka that night, had sent him wailing out the door to stalk and kill a little girl?

Weki remembered so little from that period. For all he knew, everyone in that awful building had heard and witnessed everything. And claiming he was not in his right mind at the time, that he did not believe any of his magic would work, did not change what Weki had done.

He was an accomplice to murder. He was condemned to wander the earth when he died.

But...not yet.

In a gasp of selfish desire, Weki sank back against the patio railing and held himself there. How he wished he had gotten to Merco first. Then he would have a 40-rock. He'd scam a Pyrex pipe somewhere, a piece of Brillo pad shoved in one end as a filter, then fade behind the Hard Rock Café for a hit. He'd collapse until this all went away.

"Hey!"

Weki snapped his head up and around to see the federal agent looking straight at him.

"Hey, you!" the man called again and took a step his way.

Weki was at once over the railing and stumbling through the people at the tables. Then he was into the restaurant, through its kitchens, pushing past shouting young waiters and cooks, and out the back door, hurrying down the familiar alleyway. He heard the crashing sounds of the FBI man pursuing him.

And from an instinct not completely dead inside him, Weki reached into his front pants pocket and pulled out his *hei* string.

Twisting and hooking the string automatically between his hands as he puffed along, Weki imbued it with it primal purpose—to ensnare, entangle, catch in a net. Simple magic. No ghosts. And he knew this alley well. He took a side alley that wove out to a support street lined with cars but little foot traffic.

Chanting and reforming his *hei*, Weki slowed to a walk and stepped into the doorway of a meat shop. From there he watched the alley opening.

A moment later the young FBI agent stumbled out, confused, blinking hard against the low sun. After a second the young man cursed loudly and went back the way he'd come.

Weki leaned against painted wood of the entryway, shakily stuffed his *hei* back into his pants pocket, and wiped his lips with the back of his hand. He felt every one of his seventy-six years.

Muttering a guilty thank-you to the *ao-aumakuas*, the spirit ancestors who watched over him, Weki hurried to find his car.

Now everyone was after him. He had to run for true.

~~~~

Still tingling with the pleasant surprise she'd given herself in the shower, Sweetness wrapped her towel around herself and went for the phone.

She took a deep breath, dialed, and her mother picked up.

"Hi, Mom."

"Do you know," said her mother without missing a beat, "how many messages I've left on your answering machine, young lady?"

Seventeen, thought Sweetness but said nothing. She let the silence draw out to make her point, because Angela didn't take subtle hints. When Sweetness's father had left them, her mother had retaken her maiden name, Angela MacPhail, and otherwise remade herself with a single-mindedness that made Sweetness's own seem trivial by comparison. Ironically, she now studied stuff that wasn't there, and didn't know how to handle stuff that was, like Sweetness.

"The thing is, Galey," her mother said at last, "I've had not one, but three of my psychics tell me you're in danger. Some kind of nasty spirit has seen you. And this is not the time to have a nasty spirit on your tail. Do you understand? Something is happening in the spirit world that's got half of my ghost people calling in sick. Those still active walk around like they haven't slept in weeks. They're afraid. Are you listening to me? Do you hear me?"

"Mama," Sweetness said, "just what do you want me to do?"

After the briefest pause, almost as if undecided whether to say this, Angela blurted, "I want you stay away from psychics, medium, or sensitives. Anyone who thinks they can sense ghosts—you stay away from them."

This was so contrary to what she'd expected that Sweetness had to ask, "Why?"

There was another pause, longer this time. "You're doing the ghost murders, aren't you?"

Sweetness quirked up one corner of her mouth. "That's what I was assigned to do, but—"

"You've read who it was that got attacked?"

"People who thought they could sense ghosts." Sweetness didn't bother to hide the sarcasm.

"The paper's only reported the cases where people died."

"Pardon me?"

"You heard. And the ghosts attacking the others were the same as the ones who killed the three."

Sweetness felt a lump settle in her stomach but she shook her head angrily. It was unnerving to think there were more supposed ghost attacks, but the very fact that her mother's psychic network knew all about them meant they were sharing information. Hence the similarity of the "ghost" descriptions. At least this was one part of this investigation she could wrap up.

"You have any of your psychics or 'sensitives' who claim this stuff available for interview?"

"I can get them here," Angela said carefully. "If you come out tonight. Right now."

Sweetness glanced at her watch. 8:15 pm. Too late to drop in on David Friesen again anyway. "I'm on my way," she said.

17

THE PARKING LOT AT LINCOLN PARK was almost empty when I walked back to where I'd parked. The dying light shone golden through the spruce and pine trees. Most of the golfers at the eighteen-hole course were wrapping things up. Most of the families were long gone. The playground I'd hung around like some kind of pedophile had emptied over forty minutes ago.

And I'd seen nothing. Felt no presence. All that had come with the twilight was a growing sense of unreality.

Only...

I sagged against the side of the Volvo as I watched a family of four climb into their SUV and pull out. *You throw me a ball. I try.* At a park. With babyish words. It had to mean here. This was where we'd come when the kids were younger—Martha eight, Josh a baby, Birdy just two years old. I'd remembered the playground and assumed we'd spent our time there, but had we?

I ground my fist into my forehead as if I could pull out the memory by force. Amazingly, it came. The place we'd gone, the place that had made this trip special to Birdy, had been the cliffs. Like Ragged Point. Cliffs and water and ocean winds. The scariness of the heights mixed with a sense of freedom—that's what I got from them. Birdy had seemed to get some of the same.

Worried I was now too late, I hurried for the paths to my left. As I ran past the bottom of the golf course and plunged into a veritable cave of long-trunked Sitka spruce trees, everything got dark. I was stumbling along almost blind, hearing the ocean to my right. Finally, though, the path wound back that way and opened up so the ocean and its setting sun shone now on my left. Twisted branches and calla lily plants carpeted the slope. And spiders. I remembered that Martha had found bevies of spiders somewhere around here the first time.

I shuddered and picked up my pace to reach Land's End. As the path climbed, the ground cover became rock and gravel across thin scrub and the cliffs to my left became scarier. The wind picked up too, buffeting me, filling my nose with a dank salty roar of the waves and seaweed.

That car crash in the rocks at Ragged Point—something had caused the driver to veer off the cliff.

Through the fog in the distance, I caught sight of the Golden Gate bridge, and remembered we'd gone to a beach around here, nestled down among the cliffs. We'd waded into the icy water. Was that where Birdy had been going?

No. *You throw me a ball. I try.*

We *hadn't* done that. Because Birdy wanted me to throw her a ball when we were on top of these very cliffs. She and Martha and Joshie had danced along them, making my heart almost stop.

The sun was now half down into the ocean. I could almost feel the day sputtering. Two hikers passed me, looking worried about the coming dusk.

Out of morbid curiosity, I walked over to the cliff edge, inching the last three feet, and looked down. I swayed dizzily in the wind. The drop had to be over a hundred feet. The waves smashed the dark rocks down there like grinding teeth.

A burst of laughter behind me made me start. My right foot slipped on some loose sand, my arms windmilled, my heart roared with adrenaline.

Then I was stumbling back from the edge. Safe. Breathing hard.

I turned to locate the source of the laughter and saw nothing. The last tip of sun disappeared into the ocean and the light dropped to twilight.

"Hello?" I called. There was only wind.

My memory told me that if I kept going on this path, it looped back to the parking lot. I had to get there before it got too dark to see. I turned and began walking quickly.

Another burst of laughter. Jerking my head back and forth, I could make out voices, whispers and giggling, little snaps and popping sounds all coming from off the trail to the right. A small group obviously hid in the thicket of trees and salal bushes.

I picked my way through the undergrowth and crouched as I saw a clearing. A gathering of seven teens, four boys and three girls, sat around a mini-campfire. They'd dug a shallow pit for it. I looked up to follow the thin trail of smoke and sparks into the sky. Did they think no one would see them? And the fire hazard...

"Saying *honesty*, you know?" one of the boys said.

The others giggled, raised their beer bottles, and drank. Two of them, a boy and a girl, looked only about a year older than Martha. Maybe fourteen. The others about eighteen.

"You get down right to the end, like, nobody cares," the boy speaker went on. He was a blond boy, handsome, clean face, lanky and dressed in what looked like a nouveau brat ensemble of baggy jeans and button-down shirt open to the navel.

"Not about your lily ass," cut in the girl beside him. Moon face. Haunted eyes.

The others laughed but the blond boy went on, obviously drunk, very intense. "I'm talking death, man. The end. The zip. Only it's not. Cause you come back."

Everyone in the circle held their breaths. I held mine, too.

Then moon face reached behind her and brought forward a quart-sized squeeze bottle of something. "No ghost crap, Foley, okay?" She squirted liquid onto the fire. Flames whoofed upwards.

It broke the seriousness of the circle and the other kids giggled again. Some of them rolled backwards and shrieked out ghost sounds and barks.

But the intense kid, Foley, was already on his feet. He grabbed the squirt bottle from the moon-faced girl, then a burning branch from the fire. "Foley, what the fuck?" muttered moon-faced girl as Foley stumbled out of the circle, coming my way.

I faded quickly sideways, filled with dread. Should I step forward? Say something? Risk attack? A year ago I would have just hid, but now I knew hiding didn't stop the bad from coming.

Before I could commit, Foley reached the cliff edge, the moon-faced girl right behind him, the other teens straggling along. Foley wobbled for a second on the edge, then took a step away from it and turned. Though the sun had set, he was backlit by the lights of the city. I could smell a garbage stink blowing in, thick and foul.

"Ghosts go west!" Foley shouted. "Don't you get it?! That's where my brother is! That's where..."

The moon-faced girl was close to him. "Graham, come on. Let's go home."

She reached a hand forward but he waved her back with the branch that still sputtered with a little fire. "I'm gonna... I'm gonna... throw him some light."

Weaving drunkenly, he managed to spray some of the starter fluid he held in his left hand onto the branch. It flared up. Foley turned and drew back the hand holding the burning brand like he was about to throw it out to sea.

Except he couldn't. He struggled like something was holding his arm. He howled.

"Hey, come on, dude," murmured some of the kids. But not the moon-faced girl. She was clenching her fists and staring wide-eyed.

Then Foley, the hand holding the stick still pulled back behind his head, spun around. With a desperate look on his face, he jerked up the squeeze-bottle of starter fluid and squirted it all down the front of his shirt. Then both legs, over and over, and back up his shirt to his shoulders and hair. And I suddenly knew the smell that was choked me wasn't from the city at all. It was Luka! He was here. With the kid.

I surged up from my hiding place at last, again too late.

The girl, cried, "Graham, don't!" and tried to grab him. Foley slammed her back. She screamed, "*Let go of him!*" The others muttered, "What?" "What the fuck?" "Dude's crazy!" "Shit, man!" "Bone *me*."

And Foley brought the flickering branch in towards his body.

I was halfway to him when that tiny flame bit into Foley's chest like a ravenous beast. It exploded down his front and up to his hair, and when his mouth opened to scream, the fire dove in there as well.

The smell of cooking flesh hit me as I ran, making me suddenly gag and trip. As I hit the ground, I felt something familiar slide out of the boy, something with burning dark eyes and a foul stink. It paused just long enough to twitch its victim towards the cliff like a dog shakes off water.

"No," I groaned.

Foley, stumbling in a flaming circle by the edge while his friends screamed around him, stepped off the edge.

"Graha-a-a-m!"

The girl's scream snapped me back to myself, nauseated and clammy. The thing I'd felt slide out of the boy—I knew it. The girl, I was sure, had actually seen it. Him. Luka Keawe. He'd somehow just murdered that boy. Which meant that all those other murders Special Agent Sweetness had told me about, the "ghost murders", might well have been him too.

And Birdy? Was the bastard somehow making her watch?

Shaking and sick, I pushed to my hands and knees to see the aftermath. Most of the kids had taken off. I saw two of them disappear up the path on the right. The moon-faced girl and one other boy were sitting by the cliff edge. The boy was dialing a cell phone. The girl stared at me accusingly.

Helplessly, I fumbled my own cell out of my pocket, turned it over and held it up to catch just enough glow from the city to make out the number on the business card taped there.

I dialed.

18

SWEETNESS WAS HALFWAY UP TO BERKELEY when her cell phone rang. At first she didn't recognize the ragged voice on the other end. Then she did and it made her swerve off into an Arby's parking lot, turn around, and head back into San Francisco with her cell phone still pressed to her ear.

"Tell me exactly what happened."

Her heart, pumping hard because the man of her recent fantasy was in trouble, calmed as she pieced together what had happened. It was suggestibility, plain and simple. David Friesen hears about a ghost killing and promptly sees one.

Yet he said their were other witnesses. And why was he on the scene this time? Was he not so innocent after all?

Her hands were dry and focused as she wove in and out of traffic one-handed.

"Listen, Mr. Friesen," she said. "Can I call you David? You stay exactly where you are. When the police show up, you just tell them what you saw. Don't elaborate and don't let them take you from the scene. Stall. I'll be there in twenty minutes."

~~~~

When Sweetness reached Lincoln Park, the sun was fully down.

Two SFPD cars, a SFPD van, and an ambulance lit the parking lot. The ambulance still flashed its lights. A pair of officers had strung police tape blocking off the end of the parking lot and all paths leading from it.

Sweetness used her badge to get escorted to the actual site. There they'd set up string of pole lamps running from the cliff edge to a copse of trees to the west of the path. Sounds and lights beyond the cliff told her they had people down where the boy who'd torched himself had come to rest.

Friesen was being questioned apart from the two huddled teens he'd told her about, but he could have been their twin. He looked just as haunted, dressed in a light gray sweatshirt, his arms wrapped around himself like it was too light for the weather. A need to run and comfort him threatened, but she clamped the feeling down.

"David!" she called and walked over. She flipped her badge for the older cop who'd been questioning him.

"You know him?" said the cop.

"I do. My mother works with a lot of bereaved parents who think they've seen the ghost of their loved one." She turned towards Friesen. "Is that why you were out here, David? Seeing if you could contact the ghost of your little girl again?"

He looked at her with pain and confusion, then slow understanding. No doubt the biggest sticking point for the police had been why he'd been out on these cliffs alone. It probably hadn't occurred to him to simply tell the truth. If what Sweetness had suggested was, indeed, the truth.

He nodded now. "We...used to come out here as a family." The break in his voice was real.

The police officer, a good ten or fifteen year veteran from the stress lines and gray hair, looked from her and Friesen to the two teens who were being questioned a few yards away.

"Girl who called this in says a ghost attacked the kid who torched himself. It grabbed him, then slid inside him. Claims there was a second ghost here too. A little girl."

Friesen looked like he was going to lose it. Sweetness quickly put a hand on his arm, squeezing hard. "You believe in ghosts, officer?"

The man gave her a hard look that she guessed was enough to make a lot of witnesses or criminals say more than they wanted to.

Sweetness gave him the look back. "Well?"

"I read about two other murders where the witnesses say ghosts did it. You wouldn't be looking into those would you?"

"I told you. My mother works with bereaved parents. And I don't believe in ghosts. Are we done here, detective?"

The policeman looked from her to Friesen and back again. "You got a card?" She gave him one. "L.A. office? Far from home."

"Visiting my mother here."

"He doesn't leave town."

"Of course."

And they were away, Sweetness half dragging Friesen after her even as she questioned all the quick decisions she'd just made back there. She hadn't lied, exactly. But if the cop ever checked out her story, she could say goodbye to any future cooperation with the SFPD. Like they'd been so helpful so far. A bigger loss was not getting to question the kids, though she figured she'd get the same thing from them she'd found in the witnesses to the *three* other ghost killings—ingenuous wacked-out beliefs.

When they were back to the parking lot, Sweetness talked the police into releasing Friesen's car and followed him back to his house. There she got out and followed him to the door. The front light shone, presumably on a timer. She could hear city sound spilling in from the surrounding blocks, but this street of mostly nineteenth century houses, many three stories with gables and stucco, others shorter with shingled sides and wooden porches. An enclave of suburbia. Supposed to be safe.

Friesen seemed to be thinking the same thing. He stood on the front step and stared at the door like he was afraid to go in.

"Thank you," he said suddenly.

"For what?"

"For coming to get me when I called. I...don't know if I could have gone through more questioning. That boy..."

She went to put a comforting hand on his arm, but stopped herself. With children and frightened witnesses, she'd often played the comforter. But with this man, she was concerned that the touch would mean something different. To her, if not to him.

"I'll be by in the morning," she said. "Get some rest, eat breakfast."

He dropped his head without saying anything and she turned to go.

"Wait," he said.

She turned back.

"Could you..." He cleared his throat and she saw fear in his posture and face. "I don't sleep well. Pace the house. See things. Hear things. After tonight..." He looked at his feet. "Could you maybe sleep in the house? Just for tonight."

Sweetness wavered. This was crossing way over the procedural line here, particularly given her admitted attraction to this witness. On the other hand, playing by the FBI rule book had never been her strong suit. And gut instincts which she refused to attribute to sexual attraction told her this man was both harmless and somehow key to this investigation. It was worth bending the rules for.

"All right," she said. "Downstairs. On the couch."

He breathed out in relief and nodded, keyed open the lock, and led her in.

~~~~

The next morning I awoke with sunlight filling my room. Time? Almost eleven a.m..

Wha—?

I rolled stiffly out of bed and blinked my eyes. I'd slept. Despite the awfulness of last night, of all of yesterday, my fears for Birdy, for my own sanity, I'd actually slept through the night. No insomnia, no pacing, no hearing things, no night sweats and nightmares. It was almost as if, for the first time in many months, I'd momentarily felt…safe.

Then I remembered why and ran my fingers through my hair in disbelief.

Had I actually done that? Seen a teenager off himself, then invited a beautiful, ultra-cold federal officer to spend the night in my house? Hoo! Rose and Gunther would have loved that one. First David comes looking for the kids, talking crazy, then he gets mixed up with both the federal and local cops.

The thought sobered me and my stomach gave a long, squealing grumble. After my first good night's sleep in months, my body decided it was hungry. I showered, shaved, and dressed in fresh jeans and blue-and-green rugby shirt.

Downstairs I had another shock. The federal officer was still there.

She was sitting cross-legged and straight-backed on the wood floor just beside the ion sensor in the living room archway. Cables ran in a curve around her. Her feet were bare, her torso covered only with a body-hugging tee-shirt that was damp under the arms and showed the strap lines of her bra, the bumps of hard nipples on smallish breasts. Her bare arms rested easily in front of her with their hands upturned in her lap in some kind of meditation.

Her eyes blinked open. She watched me descend.

As I did, I was struck not so much by her cold stillness as by her animal energy. Sherry's sexuality had been—*was*—all about sex. You felt it every time she moved or smiled at you. You longed to stroke her curves, melt her lips into yours. And you knew—*I* knew—she was always open to it. It was a basic generosity and enjoyment in her life.

This woman's energy was different. Darker like her skin. Hard and aggressive like the set of her jaw, the striated lines of her shoulder muscles, the clean line of her short, tight hair. It all said *Don't fuck with me.* But it also hinted that if you did literally *fuck* with her, it would be with the kind of wild ferocity that drove you both to screaming abandon.

My foot hit the bottom stair and I snapped out of it. Sex? With this woman? Even if I weren't married, that had to be about the last thing I was fit for. I was awash in murder and mysticism and personal failure.

Seeming to sense the turn in my mood, Special Agent Sweetness reached for her button-down white shirt sitting behind her on the floor and tugged it on. When it was buttoned and tucked into her regulation-blue slacks, she pulled on her knee-highs and shoes, the large gun harness I hadn't consciously noted before, and a navy blue business jacket that matched her slacks.

This done in silence with me watching, she now turned, looking again the cold professional, and gave me a slight nod of her head. "Apologies for my appearance. It helped me think."

I shrugged. "Okay."

"I bought you some food. Let me make you some breakfast." She glanced at her watch. "Lunch."

"That's kind, but—"

"You're going to need your strength," she said and led me to the kitchen.

I shrugged and followed to find out that, without touching any of the dead ghost-sensing equipment, she'd cleaned the room of all its refuse. She'd washed and put away the dishes. She'd totally restocked my fridge with eggs, bacon, milk, cheese, bread, oranges, apples, lettuce, broccoli. A bunch of bananas sat on the counter beside a box of Shredded Wheat and one of Total.

For some reason this unexpected kindness made me turn weak inside and I had to grab the table and sit down.

She cleared her throat. "You want me to make you some bacon and eggs?"

I shook my head.

"Soup?" Another shake. "Cereal?" I nodded.

She crunched up a biscuit of Shredded Wheat in a bowl, poured some Total on top, doused it with milk, and served me. She'd obviously explored the kitchen at length. She'd pulled out the bowl and spoon without hesitation.

I forced myself to eat slowly as she watched. When I was done, I considered a second bowl but decided my stomach couldn't handle it. I pushed the bowl away and looked at her.

"Thank you," I said.

"Your partner bought you out."

"Pardon?"

"Your business. Wiring up new LAN systems out of second-hand parts. Your partner bought you out. You have no job now. No income."

It felt like she'd just taken a pitcher of ice water and poured it down the front of my pants. "That's right," I said.

"So this obsession with your daughter's ghost—that's all you do."

I nodded with an ironic smile.

"Okay." She sat at the table kitty-corner to me and swung up an inexpensive ghetto blaster she must have picked up that morning. It had a cassette tape in it. She pressed play and I heard the recording I'd made yesterday morning.

"Daddy? I'm right here. Where's Mommy?"

It sent shivers down my spine again. More so with Sweetness watching me.

She hit the OFF button. "EVP," she said. "The cassette's the one you were carrying in your dead cassette recorder yesterday."

I nodded. Electronic Voice Production—EVP. Had I told her and her partner about that?

"And the boy who killed himself last night—do you believe you saw a ghost enter his body?"

I shook my head. "I felt it, though. Felt him. Luka Keawe."

"What about your daughter?"

"I didn't sense her there. Everything happened too fast. But she's why I went. It was another of our special places. Like the pier at Huntingdon Beach, Ragged Point on Highway One, the Derby Grill at the Pac Bell Stadium."

It came out hard and firm. Despite the treatment I'd received from everyone else regarding my beliefs, I somehow needed *this* person to believe me. I stabbed a finger at the tape. "You heard it. You think I faked that? That's my daughter's voice. Take it to a tape expert. Verify it wasn't dubbed or doctored or whatever."

"We might just do that." She removed the tape, pulled out a plastic evidence bag she was carrying in one of her suit jacket pockets, and bagged the cassette. "It's remarkably clear for an EVP recording."

"How do you know that?"

"That's why I wanted you to eat. I'm driving you out with me to visit someone I have to speak with at Berkeley this morning. A professor who done more studying of supposed psychics and ghosts, ectoplasm, cross-dimensional contacts, whatever, than just about any person working in America today."

Her grimace made her skepticism clear. But then why was she even bothering?

"Who is this person?" I asked.

"Go brush your teeth," she said.

19

*M*OMMY?

Right here, Sweetie. I'm right here. Come to me.

I want to. I want to.

Then just come, Sweetie. Leave that bad man and come to me.

I can't, Mom. He...follows me. And...and...I think it's my fault.

Oh, it's not, Sweetie. Birdy, listen to me. It's not your fault, Sweetie. Just come to me. I'll help you. I won't be scared this time. Come to me, please.

I can't, Mom. Tell Daddy.

What?

Not to...

What? Sweetie? Birdy?

Sherry woke up shaking violently in her bed only to find they'd strapped her down again. She screamed David's name over and over.

~~~~

Luka.

That was his name. Yes. Time slipped through him like he'd slipped through the boy and *controlled* him. Yes. Control. Like he needed to control himself.

The girl he held onto kept trying to break free of him, but he wouldn't let her. And every time he *controlled* someone living, his hold on the girl was stronger.

Like he grew stronger or she grew weaker. Or both.

He understood how it worked now.

Oh, yes...

20

*A*LIZIA! I was beginning to wonder if you'd forgotten where I work."
Sweetness and I were in a hallway in a building on the edge
of the Berkeley campus. The speaker was a white woman in her late
forties who'd just stepped out of one of the side offices. She'd arched her
eyebrows under the frosted blond hair. Her hands were in the pockets
of her lab coat as if she wasn't entirely sure what to do with them.

When Sweetness didn't move, she pulled her hands from her lab
coat pockets, walked straight to her, and attempted an awkward embrace
and kiss. Sweetness remained stiff as a statue.

The older woman pulled back. Looking at me with an ironic twist
on her lips, she said, "She and I are very close." She held out her hand
to me and studied me as we shook.

"David," Sweetness said coldly, "this is Dr. Angela MacPhail, professor
of abnormal psychology and parapsychology. My mother."

"Dr. MacPhail," I said.

"Call me Angela, David." She gave my hand a squeeze, and smiled
at me until her daughter's stony gaze made her release it with a sigh.
Then she waved for us to follow and set off down the hall without looking back.

Sweetness watched her with eyes narrowed to slits. "She was born
and raised in Vegas. Met my father there when she was sixteen. He was
on a winning streak that ended shortly after she ran away with him.

They had me nine months later."

I waited for the story of how Angela had ended up with a doctorate, but Sweetness was done. As Angela turned the corner, Sweetness strode brusquely after her and I jogged to keep up.

Angela led us through a maze to end up in a small room with a wall-to-wall desk-height counter along one wall. Everything above the counter was what I assumed to be two-way glass. On the other side of it was a blank white room with two chairs. In those chairs sat a set of homely female twins in their twenties, waiting. They had broad foreheads, close-set eyes, intense expressions.

Angela pressed a button on the countertop. "Gudrun? Nanna? I want you to concentrate. I have some guests here who will pick up some cards with pictures and concentrate on them. You will tell them what is on each card. Do you understand?"

The twins nodded. Angela turned towards me and nodded to the stack of three-by-five cards lying face down on the desk. I reached down and slid one out from the middle of the pack. A purple triangle.

Almost immediately, the twin on the right said, "Triangle." Her sister chimed in, "Purple."

I took another card, then another, and another. Some of the descriptions the twins gave were confusing—a mother suckling her baby was alternately described as a mother and kitten or "mousie"— but the differences were insignificant. They had a hit rate near one hundred percent. Too high.

"It's rigged," I said as I put the last card down.

Angela was looking at me, fascinated. "It is not. But I've never seen the twins this accurate. Follow me, please."

I looked to Sweetness but she merely shrugged so I followed her mother out. We entered the room we'd just been observing. The twins jumped up. Gudrun smiled shyly at me. Her sister nudged her with a frown.

"Nanna doesn't trust you," Angela said. I noticed she slowed her speech to speak with these two. "Why is that, Nanna?"

The scowling twin hesitated, then said with a conviction that sent shivers through me, "He twist-up inside. Fill with *vanskelighet*. Bad."

"*Nae nae*," said the cheerier Gudrun. "*Luremus*. A trick-mouse, yes?"

"But nothing more? No one is following him?"

Both twins shook their head and I looked questioningly at Sweetness. She sighed and looked away. Angela took the twins to one side for a debrief, then walked Sweetness and I down the hall to an immaculate office. Her name on the door. The blinds on a tall, open window were up and I could hear traffic but smell forest.

Angela had gone straight to the credenza behind her desk and opened one of its doors. She drew out a cheap photo album and thumped it onto her desk. Then she looked at me.

"You're the father of the dead girl."

"Excuse me?" I looked at Sweetness who'd retreated to a corner.

"Oh, she didn't tell me, David," said Angela. "Remember that I work with mediums, psychics, ghost hunters, sensitives. It's a tight community out here, if a bit competitive. They fight over coverage in the *Enquirer* and who gets to read for Demi Moore." She made a dismissive gesture. "A few told me my daughter was looking into the ghost murders."

She'd opened the album now and I saw it was the kind where you peeled the plastic up from the sticky page, placed your picture, then rolled the plastic down again. Except here someone had placed newspaper clippings. The first story was the *Examiner* article from ten months ago that had a grainy picture of our house and a story of Birdy's murder.

Angela picked it up and walked to the front of her desk, sitting on the corner nearest me and crossing what I noted were still shapely legs under her above-the-knee skirt. "The father's name was David Friesen," she said. "You, I assume. And the little girl ghost that keeps turning up at these ghost attacks, that's your daughter Caroline, isn't it."

"Birdy," I said, fighting a swell of emotion. "No one called her Caroline but her grandparents. Maternal grandparents."

"This adult ghost she's with, that's the man who killed her?"

"Luka Keawe. A client of my wife's. According to your daughter, he was also a drug dealer."

Angela shot Sweetness a look that was half question, half accusation. Sweetness ignored it walked to the window, staring out. Angela turned back to me, unconsciously tugging back her lab coat from her plain white blouse as she arched her back. Her own figure was still trim, her bust larger than her daughter's.

"Have you contacted your daughter? Spoken with her? Is she with this man by choice?"

The directness of the questions, the subtle flirting, and Sweetness's antipathy all unnerved me so much that I found myself stepping back. But then I spilled it all out again, as stupidly as I done with Sherry's psychiatrist, then Sweetness and her partner.

But this time the reaction was sincere interest. Angela looked to her daughter by the window. "Anything to add, Ali?"

"That your own psychic sleuths haven't dug up?" Sweetness twisted her lips in a bitter smile. For just a second I saw the mother-daughter resemblance. "We've learned that there's maybe a Hawaiian medicine man involved. And that Keawe was pumped full of methamphetamine when he killed David's little girl."

Was that an offering to me? *Keawe killed your little girl. You didn't.*

Angela said, "Hawaiian magic. I'll have to look into that."

"You believe that my daughter's a ghost, though," I blurted. "Could the ghost of the man who killed her be controlling her now?"

"Possibly," Angela said.

She put down the album and slid off the desk. She went to the credenza again and returned with a sheet of paper. It had a list of places and dates that included, I saw, Huntingdon Beach, Highway One, and the Pacific Bell Stadium. But before them were four places noted as "non-fatals"— Sleeping Beauty's castle in Disneyland, the Japanese Tea Gardens in the Golden Gate Park, and a street address in Outer Richmond.

Angela pointed to that last one. "You recognize this place?"

"Sherry and my first house," I said, keeping my eyes on the paper. "We half-raised Martha there. We moved when Birdy was three."

Angela nodded in satisfaction. "And you'd visited each of the other places, I'm guessing. They were all special to your daughter?"

"Yes."

"Good. The public places, Disneyland and such, could be coincidence. They're special to lots of people. But this last one, it says your ghosts are following your daughter's agenda, not this man's." She looked at her daughter, who was frowning hard, thinking about what her mother said.

"Why?" I asked. "And how do I get him to stop?"

Angela turned back to me with a hard smile on her face. "That is the million dollar question, isn't it. The reason you're here. The reason my daughter was willing to brave the ridicule of her peers to come up for this consult."

Sweetness shook her head. "I'm only here because I was ordered to come," Sweetness said. "I brought David because he believes."

"And you still don't."

Sweetness tapped on the window sill. "It doesn't matter what I believe. People are dying and the people around them think it's ghosts killing them. I need to understand the reasoning. So tell me—how do these 'ghosts' do it? And how do we make this stop?"

Angela smiled tightly. "You want results. Scientifically provable hypotheses about ghosts and how they work."

"That would be nice."

"Then, dear daughter and handsome man,"—she stood up and strode to the door of her office—"you must again follow me."

~~~~

Room 116A was another observation room, evidenced by the large mirror on the right wall as we entered. It smelled of disinfectant and plastic. The twins from before, Gudrun and Nanna, were there.

131

But this time the focus of the room was a La-Z-Boy recliner surrounded by what looked to my eyes like a full array of life monitoring equipment sounding a steady *beep...beep..beep...*A shirtless, hollow-eyed man in his twenties sat on the recliner as we entered. His arms and legs were strapped down. He was so thin and sick-looking he reminded me of pictures I'd seen of concentration camp survivors.

Even more striking was the elaborate shower cap of electrodes that covered his entire head and much of his face, the skein of wires from the electrodes trailing out behind his head to come together in a rope as thick as the man's arm. He also had sensors taped onto neck, chest, and back, with the wires running out from them to the same computer array recording things to the man's left. I.V. tubes ran into his left arm.

Sweat trickled from his forehead and underarms.

Opposite him in two chairs were the intense, staring, twin sisters, Gudrun and Nanna.

"Carl," Angela said softly as she stopped us a few feet back.

The man's eyes, closed tightly as we entered, flickered open for a second. Then they closed again and his teeth re-clenched as if he was in considerable pain or concentrating hard or both.

"Anything yet?" Angela said to the twins as we stopped.

Gudrun and Nanna shook their heads.

"He's trying to call his ghost," Angela whispered to me.

"Pardon?" I'd tried calling Birdy, but I hadn't thought her appearance was related to my will at all. If anything, it had been the baseball game that had called her.

"Certain highly sensitive people seem to be able to call ghosts to them. Personal ghosts that is, ones who need to be near that person for some reason or other. Then there are séances, of course. Mostly nonsense."

"What's with all the Frankenstein equipment?" I said. "Is the guy going to have a seizure?"

"Those are EMF and ion sensors," she said, pointing to the small boxes immediately behind the La-Z-Boy's head.

Oh. Right. Duh.

"The mini-bath to Carl's left is a type of mass spectrometer, essentially a hyper-sensitive ion sensor sampling the wider electromagnetic spectrum around Carl. Most of the sensors on Carl's abdomen are measuring his galvonic skin response, heart rate, etc.. The head web is a Geodesic Sensor Net with 512 miniature electrodes," Angela said, tugging my sleeve to pull me right over to the subject on the chair. Whispering now, she said, "It measures EEG data, electroencephalograms—brain waves."

I looked closely and saw the head electrodes didn't seem to be taped onto 'Carl's' head but rather held in place by the tension of their own geodesic net. "What's it supposed to show you?" I whispered back, uncomfortable talking as if Carl were not there at all. I could smell his sweat. He was scared.

"What I've been researching for the last two years," Angela said. "The physical signatures of ghosts." Sweetness shifted impatiently behind me, but when Angela saw that I was actually listening, she continued, striding over as she did to check the three monitors on her computer array.

"My daughter tells me you tried detecting ghosts with EMF meters, ion sensors, and voice and video recording, correct?" I nodded. "Well there's a reason why these things sometimes get results. I believe, and am accumulating evidence for, the proposition that ghosts are a form of electromagnetic energy that are generated by the synaptic processes of living beings. While the creators of this energy live, the bundle is a unique signature for that individual that is present at all times, though hard to detect using normal EEGs. It's not affected by the ongoing flux of wave cycle change you get with sleep or excitement or focus or whatever, though it does change somewhat as the host grows, feels, and thinks. When the host dies, the signature energy usually dissipates with its generator, the brain. If the death is somehow sudden, traumatic, or unusually disturbing to the host, however, the signature energy somehow detaches from its host and continues in a coherent or semi-coherent state for some time after the organism's death.

"Are you with me so far?"

I nodded, a little dazed by the surreal nature of her discussion. "You're saying that our thoughts *generate*...what? A physical soul? That can continue on after we die."

Angela frowned. "I claim nothing about souls. That's religion. This is science, a provable hypothesis."

Sweetness snorted but I ignored her. "Provable how?"

With a swift glance at her daughter, Angela said, "We've managed permission from two terminally ill patients and their hospitals to run setups much like these on them the days they died. The GSN showed a lingering coherent brain signature, completely separate from the subjects' normal readings, that continued almost two hours after all normal heart and brain activity had ceased."

"What?" Sweetness looked furious. "Normal body functions ceased, but they were still producing brain waves. That just means their brains weren't fully dead. So?"

Angela shook her head. "We've managed to isolate such electro-magnetic signatures in rooms where sensitives have detected ghosts."

"Random noise," said Sweetness.

"Coherent noise. Continuing and repeatable."

"Repeatable because it came from some source you didn't identify."

"In a form that mimicked exactly the sort of wave forms we've only found previously in human beings? Come on, Ali."

But the twisted resentment in Sweetness's face told me she wasn't buying it. This was a personal battle, about much more than a dispute over her mother's research. Her pacing had taken her right beside me and the Carl, still concentrating furiously in his chair and apparently oblivious to the argument in progress behind him. Without thinking, I reached sideways to touch Sweetness's arm and she reacted like I'd shocked her, looking back at me with wide, hurt eyes.

Angela broke the moment by walking to stand face to face with her daughter so I could look past the difference in skin color and see the similarities in the fine nose and lips. Sweetness's chin was squarer and it should have made her extra three or four inches of height that much more imposing but for the fire in Angela's eyes. It made me wonder for the first time about Sweetness's father, what Sweetness looked for (or didn't) in a man.

"You think we're not working for more proof?" the mother said. "This is going to be a fully laid out, quantified, repeatable—"

Carl jerked on his chair beside me and Nanna spoke in her deep voice. "Ghost is here."

Angela hurried to the monitors on her bank of computers and I was vaguely aware of the screens showing spikes and jumps of lines dancing across, but it was Carl's face and body that kept me riveted.

Every muscle in his body had gone taut, straining against his restraints. Then his face, which would have looked like a pug-nosed schoolboy's without all the electrodes sprouting from the chin, cheeks, and forehead, changed. His straining jaw dropped, his nose twitched, his clenched-closed eyes loosened, his entire body sank back into its chair.

I expected him to suddenly open his eyes, look at me, and speak in a rasping demon voice to tell me something about Birdy or my long-dead mother. But all he did was relax in his chair, his breathing evening out, his face looking peaceful.

"It is same ghost as before," said Nanna from her chair.

"Yes," chimed in Gudrun. "The old man. He not find his brother. Is crushed by the van. Is die all alone. Very sad."

Nanna spoke again, echoing, expanding, then Gudrun, and I realized Angela must be recording it. An audiotape somewhere. Maybe hoping for some EVP results too. Before I could ask, Angela was waving Sweetness and me over to the first of the three computer screens.

We joined her and I saw the screen had two windows. The lower one ran multiple streams of changing numbers. The top one showed what looked like a simple wave graph with numbers from zero to forty above and below a baseline. Clusters of bars were bunched and jagged all along the bar, with a dramatic shrinkage about forty clicks back. The history of Carl's thoughts, I presumed.

Angela confirmed it, pointing. "You see up to here you get mostly Beta 2s and 3s, 18-23 cycles per second, intense focus bordering on panic. Then it spikes as the ghost arrives and drops down to mostly Alpha waves, 8-12 cycles per second. Interesting to see exactly where the main wave production was,"—she waved a finger at the scrolling numbers on the bottom window—"but not that important."

Before Sweetness could interject, Angela waved us to the second monitor. This one was more complicated, with four different boxes, each holding dancing wave forms in multiple colors.

"This is the key recorder," Angela said. Her fingers flew over the keyboard below the screen and the images on the four screens momentarily froze, three of the color shades becoming brighter while the other shade dimmed. "This is Carl's brain wave signature. It's usually detected around the hypothalamus, but it moves around. It's unique to him. Unchanging year to year barring major life developments. If you hooked up twenty different subjects and ran their results to me long distance, I could tell you which one was Carl."

"You've—" Sweetness began.

"We've done that," Angela snapped. "And yet, if you look at the point from just two minutes ago, when Nanna signaled the arrival of our ghost—the ghost's name is Mazor Feineman, by the way, Carl's gay lover..." Her fingers flew over the keyboard again and the first color waves dimmed so that a second set could brighten. These had a definite starting position at about what I gathered was two minutes before on the graphs. And their shape and colors, while meaningless to me, were noticeably different from the supposed brain wave signature we'd just seen.

"This is Mazor's signature," Angela said proudly. "Again, I'd recognize it anywhere. We have almost two hours worth of it recorded from sessions like these. It's priceless because Mazor is one of those rare ghosts who actually possess their attachment person, become one with them. That's let us map him using the GSN and work out corollaries with the ion sensors."

"So you can detect him even without the electrode hookup," I said, catching on.

"Exactly! Something the normal terminal patients never gave us—a brain wave that ceases then returns."

"You map him out before he dies and hope he returns as a ghost, with the same signature."

Beaming at me like I was a star pupil, Angela took my hands forcefully and I had the disconcerting sense she'd have kissed me if her daughter hadn't been standing at her right elbow, fuming.

Angela turned to her. "We can't predict who will leave a ghost behind, but Carl is dying, as you've guessed, and his AIDS seems to have made him more susceptible to Mazor's visits. It's one of the reasons he came to me. One of the reasons he begged to be part of this. He, like many of us working here, wants to *understand*, not bury his head in the sands of cynicism.

"Which brings us," Angela said before Sweetness could respond, "to your little girl. She and this Keawe ghost have got my people scared," Angela said.

We still stood by the computer array, watching the Carl's calm Alpha waves on one monitor and the eerie double brain wave signature on the other. Gudrun and Nanna were droning on for the record about Mazor Feineman's ghost—what he liked, what he felt, what he heard, what he wanted. My attention was riveted to Sweetness's mother.

"My hypoteses of ghost existence fit the experience and recorded tales (accounting for exaggeration) of known ghost encounters. Consider lingering brain wave signatures, shaped into coherent energy bundles. Most are no stronger nor more organized than balls of light—'orbs' as they're normally described when caught on film. Some are so highly charged that they produce unstable air pressure changes—poltergeists. More tightly preserved signatures carry memories with them and sometimes even thought patterns, residual self-image, even awareness of others. These impress those who encounter them as true personalities, sometimes even imparting the illusion of shape—the 'man in the black hat' or 'the weeping woman'—though most ghost sightings are no doubt imagined.

"But all of these ghosts, if you study the literature, fade with time. Something in a place or event has triggered the energy signature to cling. Eventually it's not enough and the signature fades away, becomes absorbed by the greater universe."

I nodded. "The second law of thermodynamics: entropy increases; organized energy tends towards disorganization; order towards chaos."

Angela smiled at me. "This is why your two ghosts have scared every psychic and sensitive who's seen them. Not to mention a few ghosts who seem to have brushed their paths."

"What?"

"The organization and power of your little girl and tagalong adult are *increasing*."

17

*I*SHOOK MY HEAD at Angela's words. The rational life I'd pursued ever since deciding to have a family with Sherry clutched at Angela's version of ghost existence, but my childhood-artistic side had been screaming she was all wrong. And here was the proof. Birdy's ghost was getting stronger. Or at least my perceptions of it were. They'd started with whispers and sounds. Then, yesterday, I'd seen her. She'd talked to me. I couldn't believe she'd been just a lingering brain wave signature.

"Even if she is," I said, "I don't see what—"

"David Frie...sen."

I spun around. The voice hadn't come from Angela or Sweetness, but from Carl in the chair. And his voice, weird like he was speaking in some foreign accent, struck though me like a knife.

"David. I met your daugh...ter. Innocent. She won't stay that way."

I was on him before he finished, grabbing his bare, bony shoulders. "Where is she? What do you mean? Is it Keawe? Are you Keawe?"

"You must stop...Birdy." He grinned like a death mask.

I shook him. "What do you mean? Leave her alone, you son of a bitch! Just leave her alone!"

Angela and Sweetness were both suddenly behind me, pulling me back and off in a quick wrenching motion. But I freed myself again and went for the freak in the chair. Gudrun screamed and Nanna barked, "No! He gone!"

I faltered, spun towards the sisters.

"Look at the monitors," Angela panted behind me. "His wave signature is gone. You apparently scared him away."

"Where?" I said, rocking on the balls of my feet. Struggling. "Was that Luka Keawe? Was it?" But I knew even as I asked that it wasn't. There was no rotting smell.

Nanna looked at me with distaste but Gudrun said, "Mazor. He scared. We all scared."

"I think," said Angela coldly, "that we're done for today."

"*Done?* You show me all this, tell me my daughter's some kind of freak superghost, then tell me we're *done?*"

"Come on, David." Sweetness's iron grip on my arm guided me to the door.

~~~~

Back at my house, Sweetness stopped the car out front and looked across the seat at me. "You want me to come in?"

In another time and place I would have taken it for a sexual overture. But after my behavior at Berkeley and from the look in her eyes, I suspected she just wanted to keep me from doing something stupid.

Like what? Running away? Driving to every place I thought I might be able to commune with Birdy? Dr. Angela MacPhail wanted to meet us again tomorrow to help guide me in contacting Birdy's ghost. If we helped this "residual brainwave signature" gain greater self-awareness, Angela thought, we might help it separate from Keawe's "residual brainwave signature."

And then what? It would dissipate? Vanish forever? Was that what I really wanted?

The best I could hope for, right?

"So?" Sweetness said.

I shook my head and climbed out, shut the door behind me, and went to my front door without looking back. Inside, I began pulling plugs and connections, wrapping up extension cables and activator boxes, bringing them to the front hall and dumping them in a heap. Proceeded to the living room.

Don't, Daddy, sounded in my head like a phantom voice as I worked.

Don't. Don't. I need you.

I shut it out furiously. I couldn't give her what she needed. No one could. She was dead. So I kept going, yanking and wrapping, going for boxes, telling myself not to cry. Just put the equipment away. All junk that looked for something it couldn't find. Couldn't help. I discovered the stereo system in the living room was working and put on an alternative rock CD of Martha's. It was loud and incomprehensible, rattling the windows and my nerves. Perfect.

By seven o'clock, I'd cleaned out most of the downstairs and filled the front hall with boxes. Martha's "music" was still screaming but quieter because the neighbors had come by, threatening to call the police. Going to the kitchen, I made myself eat a ham sandwich, sat, and chewed it one bite at a time. I could actually make out most of the words on Martha's CD now. I could predict the simplistic riffs too, the crashing progressions.

One bite at a time.

I finished dinner, climbed the stairs, stopped for just a second to stare down the hall at the closed door of Birdy's bedroom, then began disassembling stuff in the hallway.

I was done everything at half-past midnight. After double-checking every door and window lock in the house, I lay down in Josh's bedroom and stared at the collection of Star Wars toys he hadn't taken with him when he'd moved out.

Left behind. Helpless. Like me.

When the phone rang two hours later, it took me so long to wake up that I heard it six times before I understood what it was.

~~~~

"Yeah?" I rolled sideways off Josh's bed and thumped onto the floor.

His bedside light was on because I'd been too afraid to turn it off, but it still took me a moment to figure out where I was.

The phone rang twice more in that time and the answering machine picked it up. I ran, stumbling, from Josh's room to my and Sherry's bedroom and jerked the phone off the hook. The answering machine made the line echo hollowly as it kept recording.

"D-Daddy?"

Birdy? No. I shook my head to clear it. "Josh?"

"Daddy..." His voice was tiny, whispering, afraid, and all at once the loss of him and Martha welled up in me so strongly I curled in pain, my fingers growing white on the phone handset.

"I'm right here, Josh." I cleared the froggy sound from my throat and flicked my gaze to the glowing red numbers of the clock by the bed. 2:38 a.m.. "What's happening? Are you okay? Is Martha okay?"

"Uh-hunh." Uncertain.

"Did Rose or Gunther do something? Do you need me to come?"

"Daddy...um..." I waited because I could hear in his voice he was struggling to say something. And then he did and my world shook. "Birdy was here."

I sat down on the bed, my hands suddenly shaking. In all their time at home here since Birdy's death, Josh had never once seen Birdy or even felt her presence. It was that fact as much as anything that had made me doubt my own feelings. Josh was twice the sensitive I'd ever been.

"Tell me," I said weakly.

"I...thought I was having this dream. That guy, the bad guy, told me to get up, like out of bed. And I was going to, but then Birdy said no, he *couldn't.*"

"Couldn't?" I said, trying to bring down Josh's rising voice even as my own insides were tightening towards hysteria. "Couldn't what?"

There was a rustling sound of the phone changing hands and I heard Martha's voice. "He thinks Luka's ghost tried to possess him. And that Birdy saved him."

There was anger in her voice. Coldness. It would have felt like a dagger had I not already been careening inside over the fact that Luka would not *let* me be willfully blind and give up. He was attacking my children, both dead and living. I forced myself to clear my throat.

"Hi, hon. Did you see what happened?"

There was a long pause. "I saw something."

I wished I could reach through the telephone wires and put my shaking hands on her shoulders, tell her it was all right. Whatever she saw, it was all right. It didn't mean she was going crazy like her mother and father. It was all right.

"Martha..."

"Whatever was going on, it's over. They...it...left, but Joshie's still freaking."

Another scuffling sound and muted, "I am not!" Then hard breathing and Josh was on the phone again, trying hard to be as collected as his sister. "Birdy said Mom told her to stay away from you, Daddy, but she was scared. I think she needs help. She kept thinking pictures of a trip we did."

"Disneyland?"

"Nuh-unh."

"Lincoln Park? The coast?"

"Nuh-unh."

Another scuffle and Martha was back on. "Jesus, Dad. It was that trip out to Grandpa's when we stopped at that ranch where Josh got sick. Josh says Birdy flashes that ranch, the road, Grandpa's house, all freaky, like she can't really help herself. And going, 'Don't tell Daddy. He won't let you. No Daddy.' So, like, of course Josh has to call you right away."

She was trying for world-weary cynicism, but I could hear the fear in her voice and felt an unexpected surge of pride for her courage. What must it have been like to wake up in the middle of the night, in a house not really your own, to find your brother crying out one door down? To run over there, feeling responsible somehow now that your parents were both gone, and find him terrified, fighting off...what? What exactly had Martha seen? Enough to let Josh call. Enough to actually admit she'd seen something.

There were more scuffling sounds and Martha must have put her hand over the receiver as I heard a muted, "Shut up! You just shut up and sit down! You want to wake up Rose?" A crying sound from Josh. Heavy swearing from Martha. And I reminded myself that this was the girl who'd called Rose and Gunther in the first place to take her and Josh away from me.

I waited for a minute, then said carefully, "Martha? Are you there? Martha?"

After a pause and heavy breathing, she said, "Yeah. Jesus, Dad. Josh is just so freaked. Like I can't calm him down. And all white like. He just...wants you."

Like that admission hurt seven ways to Sunday.

"Okay, look. Tell Joshie that I'll be over there in fifteen minutes, okay?"

"Middle of the night, Dad."

"Fifteen minutes. You don't have to wake up Rose or Gunther. Just sneak Josh down to the front door. I'll talk to him, okay? We'll work something out."

"Dad..."

Oh, jeez, had I so messed up that my little girl wouldn't even let me see her little brother? Was I that far gone? "Please, Martha. We'll keep it simple. Short. I'll bring along one of his toys he left here or something. Okay?"

There was a long pause, then Martha's voice, very small. "Okay."

~~~~

It took me sixteen minutes, clocking over seventy through most of the deserted downtown streets and over the Golden Gate. It was pure luck that I didn't roar past any cruisers on the way.

144

When I pulled up in front of Rose and Gunther's, however, I got a sinking feeling in my gut. All the lights were on and Rose herself stepped out on the chill front porch as I climbed out of the car. She was dressed in her bathrobe and slippers, her hair in curlers and a net. Her shifting weight creaked the porch floorboards like an accusation.

"I...um...," I mumbled as I walked up.

"They're right here." Rose's voice could have stopped a charging bull in its tracks. I halted at the bottom of the porch steps, looking past her to see Martha and Josh carrying out a packed suitcase apiece. Both kids were dressed for traveling, with jeans, runners, spring jackets. Gunther was following them out worriedly, fully dressed himself and wagging his head like he was going to grab them at any second and pull them back in.

"I could call the police, you know," Rose said bitterly.

Totally perplexed, I turned to Martha. She looked hollow-cheeked. Catching my eye, she shook her head hard as she passed me. She'd clearly fill me in later. Josh, behind her made it just past me with his suitcase, then dropped it, turned, and flung himself around my legs, crying hard and pulling on my corduroys like he wanted to pull himself inside me. My own eyes welled up and I reached down to pick him up and hug him to me, murmuring it would be okay. Everything was all right.

Holding him with one arm, I reached down with the other and scooped up his small suitcase. Light. Obviously not heavily packed.

"You call us en route," Rose commanded harshly as if I knew what she was talking about. I nodded.

"Please," said Gunther. "Please...be careful with them."

I looked into his eyes and even in the dark could see the honest concern. This for children not even his own blood. A good man. Strong and sure. The type of man my children deserved.

Instead they had me.

I swallowed and nodded and backed away to the car, throwing Josh's suitcase in beside where Martha had already placed hers. She'd slid into the backseat, whether to avoid me or to be there for Josh, I wasn't sure, but I slid her brother in beside her. I paused there for a minute as I buckled Josh in and held Martha's eyes.

"Head for Utah," she said, not looking at me.

I nodded. Of course. To protect by running in place didn't work. Nor had giving up. Whatever had to be done, it was out there, waiting for us.

So I went for the driver's seat, both giddy and scared. It was going to be Josh and Martha with me, looking for Birdy together.

The chase was on for real.

18

WEKI NAEA WOKE UP with a crack addict's spinning depression, and for a almost a full minute couldn't recognize where he was. Finally the pale green light outside the windows and the babbling from the television made everything tumble back into place.

A Motel 6 north of L.A..

He groaned up to his feet and scuffled around for his baggy shorts, polo shirt, and sandals. Fighting the overwhelming sense that Ray Aznar was just outside his door, about to burst in, he pulled on his clothes and went to the bathroom. After a fifteen minute session of straining to clear his bowel and bladder, he used his *hei* string to tie his hair back in a ponytail and shuffled out.

The woman on TV. was talking about a boy who'd lit himself on fire and thrown himself off a cliff in San Francisco. His friends claimed he was possessed. Weki stopped dead and watched.

Number four.

Licking dry lips, Weki shut off the TV.

So, then. Luka. The victims were coming closer together as Weki had told Luka they would. Did that mean the rest of it was true also? That once Luka had eight he could do what they had planned together? What Weki had only imagined from legends and stories. A horror of power Luka must not have.

Would not. Could not.

But if he could?

The face of one of the counselors from St. Jude's appeared in Weki's mind as Weki shuffled out to the car. Chris. Brother Chris. He'd talked of how antisocial crack addiction was, how it made a person totally selfish and heedless of others. Weki had to change that, Chris had said, connect to others, rediscover what it was like to care about others.

No! Too much guilt.

The sky was gray overhead and starting to spit. Weki raised the top of the Miata and climbed in. As he drove out of the motel lot, he tried to pretend he still didn't know where he was going. He was merely running from L.A. and Ray Aznar. The fact that the I-5 ran straight to San Francisco was a coincidence.

You have make Luka come back, you kolohe. *Now you must do what can.*

Because I am so noble? Yes, ho ho. But I can do nothing. No way to stop what is coming.

Some way. Some one. You know.

Yes. Yes. Scared by what it would ask, but he knew.

The father.

Weki pressed his foot to the gas and sped faster through the rain.

19

THE NEXT MORNING began badly for Special Agent Sweetness.

She did a twenty-minute hard run, kata practice, and swim cool-down and still wasn't able to expel her frustration at how badly her trip to her mother's had gone. David Friesen, who had just started turning to Sweetness for stability and strength, now thought she was a bitch who had a flake for a mother.

It got worse when she called his house and he didn't answer. Swearing, she drove to his house and found it empty, his car gone, the door unlocked. His answering machine had a conversation recorded near midnight that sent Sweetness to David's sister-in-law. That woman, a veritable chunk of ice, said she only knew David had showed up and taken his children with him for some sort of trip. The children had not told her where they were going.

"Their grandfather's," Sweetness supplied. "Do you know where he lives?"

"David's father? No."

As she'd driven away, Sweetness had churned through her options. One, she could spend the day tracking down David's grandfather, even though he could live almost anywhere. Two, she could trust that David getting away from his house was best for everyone and trust him to call her if anything happened.

Trust him. An interesting concept. He hadn't exactly proven himself the most dependable of men so far. But she *wanted* to trust him. To spite Ramirez, if nothing else.

Meanwhile, all her searching through the Hawaiian groups in S.F. had turned up only one dubious connection—a seedy old Hawaiian man who'd purchased a number of Hawaiian plants and trinkets, most significantly a ritual knife made with a boar tusk handle. Had it been the same old Hawaiian whom Ramirez had seen hanging around Keawe's old drug grounds? Nothing on any security cameras. Poor physical descriptions.

The knife was a problem too. Given that the evidence from the rape/murder/suicide night had all been disposed of and the records she'd seen of it were cursory at best, there was no way to confirm the knife was the same one that had been used on Sherry Friesen. Her doctor wasn't letting her see anyone at the moment and the hospital records were unhelpful.

Temporarily stymied, Sweetness wrote up her incident reports, went to the airport, and by noon had joined Ramirez in Los Angeles to do a heavy search through the City Walk for Aznar or the old Hawaiian who might somehow be the link between Luka Keawe's dealings in L.A. and his time in S.F..

~~~~

At 1:30 p.m., Weki Naea turned the doorknob, then crouched his way beneath the dusty police tape strung across the door to Luka Keawe's filthy San Francisco launch point.

He expected the smell of vomit or evil, or maybe just smoke. But none of these remained, even though the soup-can lanterns still described a holy circle on the ground and Luka's bed still lay pushed against the wall, unmade just as it had been that night eight months ago.

Walking with painful deliberation, Weki went to that bed and sat. And finally the sense memories flooded over him—bliss and craving, a tunnel of need and the exhilaration of telling Luka what he must do, making Luka dance and sweat in an elaborate ritual Weki had created out of his own fevered mind.

Something shuffled in the next room but Weki ignored it as he sank into the memory of that night. Luka staggering, whipping himself with pandanus leaves. Weki chanting and rocking. Yes, he had made it up to satisfy Luka, but it was good huna. It drew on the lore of the *kahuna 'ana'ana* who could pray people to death, and it used the spirit of Aloha to pull energy from the Ao-Aukmakuas, the ghost-gods. It was something new that Weki did.

And it created a monster.

Someone banged on the door, jolting Weki back to the present.

"Ka-hoo-oo-na," someone called through the door. "Ka-hoo-oo-na."

Weki swallowed. Who knew he was here? Aznar! No. He could not. Was it some local dealer or addict, then? Someone Weki had once shared a crack pipe with?

Shaking in advance over the call of the cocaine, Weki pushed himself to his feet and made himself shuffle to the door. Opened it.

There, rocking back and forth outside, was a man who could have been Weki a year ago. Grizzled and withered, the skin around the visitor's bones stretched like plastic wrap. The man grinned and his twisted-tooth smile seemed to fill half his face. He looked vaguely familiar.

"I know you?" Weki said.

"Motherfucker, yeah. Jack Jack, watch your back Jack. Don't remember me. Okay, okay. Cause you're different now, right? The clothes. Clean. Shit fuck look at you, Weki-eki kahoo-oo-na."

"Who—?"

The man prowled in around him, went to the bed and touched it, looked under it, under the mattress, went to the dresser and pawed through it too. "No one come in here since you left, okay? All scared of the Kiwi and you and your mumbo-kajumbo. Just the fibbie and partner. They come in a few days ago, okay. Oh yeah, oh yeah."

"The FBI come here?"

"Yup. Did." The man was patting himself all over and the action twigged a foggy memory in Weki's head. This addict had been there back then. In this building. Staggering around like Weki had once staggered. Banging into walls as Weki had done. Needing. Desperate. Obviously tough to still be alive.

"Here!" the man crowed and pulled out a business card to wave in the air. He finally calmed enough to hold it in front of his face. "Special Agent Gale Sweetness," he read slowly, articulating. "Felatio and handjobs. S&M. Anal on request."

Weki stepped to him and snatched the card and stuffed it into his front pants pocket. "Jack," Weki said, pulling the name from somewhere. "You tell me about her. Everything you know." And without waiting to be asked, he pulled out a twenty dollar bill to slap into the man's still-grasping hand.

Jack held it and froze for a second, staring. Then he grinned and started to babble. Twenty minutes later Weki was driving to Berkeley.

~~~~

Down in Santa Monica, 278 Los Cabos Way, Nightingale Sweetness and Ramirez had little trouble entering Naeae's private residence. The local authorities were already on the scene when they arrived.

This was because the entire front side of the house, entering into what appeared to be a living room and kitchen, had literally been blown open, apparently by a rocket launcher. Major shit. It still stank of burnt gas. The interior walls were chunked through by what the detective on site said were 12-guage shotgun slugs. No bodies, apparently, though one of the cops stretching police tape said some neighbors had suffered injuries from flying bits of mortar and wood.

"He wasn't home," Sweetness said to Ramirez as they did a slow perimeter walk.

She didn't need to ask who had done this, only why it was done. She and Sweetness had come straight here from the Universal City Walk, where Ray Aznar and company had vanished this morning. A runner Sweetness knew from the 18th Street gang figured Aznar was after Luka Keawe's crack-bitch. Even had an address. The reason? Apparently the guy had ratted Aznar to the feds the day before.

"What was there to rat?" Ramirez said now.

"And who uses a rocket launcher to make the point? It's not even in the 'hood.'"

"So?"

Sweetness shrugged and Ramirez picked his way into the back of the blown-out house. Sweetness walked to the detective on site, a hulking bruiser named Ross. He was finishing up with the neighbors, taking notes, giving them directions to be available for later questioning. They moved away and Sweetness moved in with questions.

Ross sighed. "Neighbors said Naea ain't even lived here the last six months," he said. "Was at a clinic somewheres. Comes back clean and sober. Says he got a job. Then he roars off last night in his red Miata. Don't come back. Must have known they was coming for him."

"Why?"

"Why'd he know?"

She inclined her head. Before Ross could answer, though, Ramirez came out of the house and signaled her. "You gotta see this."

Sweetness thanked Ross and followed Ramirez into what looked like a second bedroom in the back. Its front wall had been shredded from the opposite side with shotgun slugs, but the room itself was fairly intact. One couch, a desk, cheap wood paneling on two of the walls, one of those paneled walls covered with pinned-up news articles in the shape of a middle lump and spun-out pieces.

Sweetness read the articles then stepped back while Ramirez pulled out his little digital and snapped some photos of it.

"This is him, isn't it?" said Ramirez. "The old guy who was with Luka just before it happened. You think he knows something?"

Sweetness nodded at the wall. "Maybe." She hesitated a second, then pulled her notebook from her pocket and handed it to her partner. "Flip back a few pages. You'll find a list of things someone matching Naea's description bought from two Hawaiian distributors in San Francisco, June and July of last year. Ti leaves, taro, kava kava, the knife. They all have innocent uses, but they're also used in traditional ceremonies."

Ramirez studied the list and nodded like he was trying to keep an open mind. "Like what?"

"You remember crackhead Jack, the guy who lived beside Keawe's room? And what he called the old Hawaiian who visited a lot?"

"Kahuna."

"Good memory. You know what that is in Hawaiian?"

"Big shot, right? Frankie Avalon and his pals were always worshiping the 'big Kahuna' who was this great surfer." Ramirez shrugged. "My mother loved old movies."

"Okay." Sweetness caught herself smiling at one of the first signs he'd seen her partner had a tender side. "Simply—Kahuna means expert. You can be an expert in surfing, in carving..."

"In magic?"

"According to the guys and woman I talked to, no educated person in Hawaii believes in 'magic' anymore, but *historically* you've got your good priests, like the *kahuna makani*, who can cure a person by possessing them with spirits then driving those spirits out; and you've got your bad priests, like the *kahuna 'ana'ana*, who pray people to death."

"Voodoo." Ramirez's small lips were twisting again.

"If you like. But if Weki Naea was a *kahuna 'ana'ana*, maybe he was the one who doped up Keawe and sent him out with some delusion of magical protection."

"To do *what?*" Ramirez said. "Wait. Let me guess. Pull off a body-switch—and where did he get the corpse to replace himself with?—or to give him some special route into a life after death?"

Sweetness retrieved her book. "You're assuming Naea was just the henchman in all this."

"'Crack bitch.' That's what they called him."

"A crack bitch who owns his own house and has people gunning for him with rocket launchers." With her finger she ran an imaginary line around the secondary groups of clippings. "What do you make of the numbers?"

Ramirez looked and shrugged. Each secondary group had a red number marked on the wall beside it—one, two, three. "Guy's keeping score. So?"

"I don't think the man's stupid or just a watcher. He's involved. The counting means something."

Ramirez stuck out his lower lip. "You say so."

"I also say we need to find this Weki Naea before Aznar does and ask him about it."

"How?"

"First," Sweetness said, "I visit our boss and give him a shitload of paperwork, get clearance for more travel. Then we start thinking like a *kahuna 'ana'ana*."

~~~~

Weki staggered out of the White Pines Retreat.

Sherry Friesen raped and cut. The signs of Luka all over her still. Weki was responsible for this, he knew. *The mother's blood shall be the lure.*

He bent over in the parking lot, his fingers still looped tightly into the intricate concealment web he'd made with his *hei* string, and vomited onto the pavement. Then he took a gasping breath and thought hard.

Sherry Friesen confirmed all that Luka had done. Even more, she had cried that her child still lived as a ghost and that Luka's ghost was attached to her, hurting her, changing her.

All as Weki and Luka had planned.

But what they had not planned was that the ghost girl's father, David Friesen, followed her as she quested along old journeys. That Sherry Friesen could know all this in her ravings, that David Friesen was also a reader of spirits—these things did not surprise Weki. For who else could have produced the great *'i ane* that was "Birdy" Friesen?

Weki sucked one more rattling breath before wiping his mouth and walking his tired old body to his car. Soon they would know that

Weki had left the building. Someone might come to find him.

He opened the Miata's door, took the *hei* string from his quavering fingers to bind up his in a ponytail, then he climbed in. Even without looking at a map, he knew he would have to drive fast and long to catch David Friesen and the unholy duo before they reached where Sherry Friesen said they were going. Maybe...maybe he should score some crack first. Fortify himself.

And a sudden vision gripped him—Luka as he would be if Weki did not show David Friesen how to fight him. Then no crack would be enough. Nothing would be enough. There would be no escape.

With a shaking hand, Weki fumbled his key into the ignition and roared the dusty little sports car to life. Then he paused. His hand went down to touch the pocket where he had put the business card of Special Agent Nightingale Sweetness. Should he, like they said on American cop shows, call for backup?

He laughed a crazy laugh. His actions eight months ago made him part of a rape and murder. No. He and David Friesen were the ones who must do this. Just the two of them. His hand moved from his pocket to the gear shift and slammed his car into forward.

He got almost as far as the end of the White Pines drive before an oncoming purple Mercury Grand Marquis with tinted windows slammed on its brakes and fishtailed sideways to block the road. Weki stomped on his own brakes, stopping just five feet short of hitting it.

The Grand Marquis's two rear doors popped open. Out of the one nearest Weki, Merco climbed out, holding a machine gun which he and the man behind him aimed casually at Weki.

"Hello, old man," said Merco with a smile. "Ray wants to see you."

20

WE'D BEEN ON THE ROAD almost thirteen hours, stopping at a dusty waypoint between San Francisco and Elko, Nevada that looked familiar to the kids, when Josh suddenly popped up in the back seat and pointed.

"Skeeth!"

I slammed on the brakes so hard that the station wagon, fishtailed to the right on the highway and back again before I regained control and pulled over. Luckily we hadn't seen a car for thirty miles, but my hands still shook as I pushed up my sunglasses and turned off the engine.

"Jesus!" Martha gasped beside me in the front. She wrapped her bare arms around her chest and dug her chin down, angry that she'd been afraid enough to speak.

My heart pounded too. Both from the stop and because the cries from Josh and Martha were the first sounds they'd uttered in hours. It was like they'd made a pact not to speak. I'd pushed and probed after we stopped for a McDonald's breakfast, wanting to catch up on who they were, what they'd become in the last six months. Because Josh was pale now, like he hadn't been sleeping well. Martha had lost weight. Her eyebrow/nose piercings were gone, along with, apparently, any residual respect she might have had for me.

Now this.

I stared out over the same endless desert flats that early settlers passing through would have seen—low hills in the distance (always in the distance), eggshell sky, dry heat, dust. And a ceaseless wind. Over the sound of the idling engine, you could hear the wind moan around us like it wanted to suck out our lives and leave just our husks in the car.

Josh cleared his throat and ran his hand nervously over the buzz cut he'd gotten at Rose and Gunther's. "You gotta turn off here, Dad."

He meant the sign ahead. A little green patch with Skeeth written on it. One of the many exits-to-nowhere that popped up from time to time. They all had names like Rye Patch Reservoir or Puckerbush. Often as not they led to nothing but a truck stop or gravel road through the desert. And I didn't remember this exit. "This was the one she...?"

"Jesus," Martha said. "Don't we have anything to drink up here?"

"Don't swear." I took off my sunglasses. The cooler, water jugs, fruit, cheese, lettuce, bread, and peanut butter I'd bought there were all packed in the trunk, out of sight, invisible, like my pride and sense of parental control. "But at least you're both talking to me."

Josh's eyes dropped down and he sucked in his lips. He looked like he was going to cry.

"We stayed in Skeeth," Martha said quickly. "That time we came out for Thanksgiving. Last time we came out. Some kind of ranch."

I looked at her. "You're the mouthpiece, hunh?"

She glared at me.

I held the look, suddenly wanting to shake her and break down crying myself. Finally I said, "She hasn't been at any of the other stops. Why would she choose this one?"

Martha furrowed her brow and looked back over the seat at Josh.

"It was special to her," he squeaked.

"How?"

Josh shook his head, so Martha said, "It had horses and railroad tracks. I remember."

"And you think Birdy's ghost is attracted to horses and railroad tracks."

"Fine!" Martha threw herself back against the seat and crossed her arms tightly over her chest again. "Just drive on! You never cared about anything we said or thought anyway! Fuck!"

Josh gave a little gasp from the back seat and a shiver of ice ran through me. All this profanity was just a signal, a tail light receding in my rear view as she mentally drove away from me. In fact I suspected the only reason she was physically here was because she was scared Josh would go back to me without her playing reality check. The minute we'd done this trip and satisfied Josh that Birdy was truly gone, she'd drag Josh back to Rose and Gunther's. Maybe convince them to file for custody in court.

First I'd lost Birdy. Now I was losing Martha and Josh and Sherry. And there was nothing I could do or say to stop it happening.

I turned back to the sign, shoved my sunglasses back on, and drove forward.

Five minutes later we were driving south past abandoned houses and struggling of ranches, long lines of fencing so dusty and dry they looked like they'd blow away. I took the first road forking left from the rail line, vaguely recalling where we'd stayed that time three years ago. With Fletcher Harbell and his wife Sue. Fletcher had worked the mines with my dad in Utah before moving west, coming to Skeeth for the cheap land and starting a horse ranch. But even then Skeeth was struggling. No town center as such. There'd been talk of closing the old railway depot that acted as—

"That's the one," Martha said.

I slowed at the two-storey weathervane on our left and turned down the drive. The weathervane looked rusty but functional. Their was a gate across the drive and a fence extending off a mile in either direction. Josh pointed to three horses off in the distance by a copse of trees.

With the kids' help, I opened the gate, drove through and closed it again. Five minutes later we were unloading at the two-story ranch house with wraparound porch, dusty, but as sound as I remembered. Sue met us joyfully despite our unannounced arrival and wouldn't hear a word about just "dropping by." Two laconic-looking cowboys were exercising horses in the nearby paddock. As Sue took our bags out of the car, the door of one of the two large stables that butted up against a training paddock, opened and Fletcher came ambling out. He squinted at me through the smoke curling up from his cigarette, then took it from his mouth and broke into a grin.

"Well I'll be hanged," he said and walked to me with his right hand stretched out.

"Fletch," I nodded, shaking. His grip was rough but strong, the way I remembered my father's. His clothes reeked of cigarette smoke and horses.

"Y'know I was just talking about your pa to Sue. Thinking I should bring him out here to live with us. Could use a good full-time man." He took a long drag on his smoke, then took it out again and looked at Martha and Josh. "Where's the wife and your other little one?"

Sue cleared her throat in warning, making Fletcher look at her. It was hard to imagine he didn't know. Our house had been swamped with reporters right after the crime and again when Sherry returned to White Pines and the kids moved out.

Now Fletcher's mouth dropped half-open. He remembered.

"It's okay," I said. "We're dealing with it."

"Yeah," said Martha over by the porch rail and curled back her lip.

The rancher's face had gone a bright scarlet. "Well, hell," he said. "Your gonna come in and stay the night, I hope."

Sue gave him the eyes again, pointing to the bags she'd already unloaded, and Fletcher laughed at himself. He puffed and shuffled his leather-tough self back and forth like a gawky teen.

"Well okay, then. You kids want to come see the new colt we got in the barn? Got a bad leg. Cute as a button, though."

Martha shrugged, but Josh nodded quickly, eager to be away from the uneasiness.

~~~~

That evening, after I'd had a long jaw with Fletcher about the state of horse ranching, the trouble with day workers, and the nature of scraping along, Josh timidly asked to sleep with me. With a lump in my throat, I agreed. Martha shot me an angry look and huffed off.

At half-past-midnight, I was still awake, moving groggily around the room while Josh slept soundly in the double bed I'd left. I stopped at the window in just my pajama bottoms, a dormer with one of those old windows that slid up and down. Thick wood. It was open a few inches but I grabbed it, shuddered it up, and stuck my head out.

The cold desert night swept over me. A quarter moon. Far from the city. And my chest still clenched tight, my mind just this side of panic. Far off, a howl rose from the hills.

"Dad?"

I jerked back, banging my head. Martha stood at the door of the room in her nightgown, an old white shift that Sue had dug up from her. It hung low at the neck, drooped below the armpits, and for a second I saw my little girl as a young woman in her mother's image. With the spiky hair and piercings gone, a slimmer face, and the beginnings of a bust, she looked almost grown. And I hardly knew her.

"What is it?" I said.

"Did you...um...see anything?"

"No. Did you? Did Birdy show up in your room? Did you feel her presence? Hear something?"

Martha looked down and I realized how I sounded.

"No," I repeated. "Nothing."

Her eyes flicked to the sleeping form of her brother in the double bed. "Is he going to be okay?"

"I think so."

"Okay then." She hovered at my door for a moment, then just as I thought I should go to her or say something more, she slipped away, closing the door behind her.

There was a slam from downstairs.

Josh jerked upright in his bed and Martha shot back into the room as I ran to the window. In the pale moonlight, I saw a thick-boned figure running from the house like he was being chased. Fletcher! Fully dressed. A pungent smell drifted up.

Fletcher stopped just outside the nearer stables and spun around in a circle like he was trying to brush off a swarm of bees. I'd seen this before. That kid at Lincoln Park. It meant—

"Luka!" Josh gasped.

I jerked around eyes wide. I hadn't said a thing about Luka to either of Martha or Josh; we were just on this trip to find Birdy. Then a thump dragged my focus back to the stables. Strong rotting smell now. Fletcher had thrown back the bar on the stable door. He ran inside and pulled the door closed after him. There was an instant uproar of shrieks and whinnies, thumping and crashing. Sue ran outside in the yard now, still in her nightgown, calling for Fletcher.

Josh was almost hyperventilating, too terrified to even get off his bed. "Dad—Dad—*Dad?*"

I tore myself from the window to go to him and Martha took my place, sticking her head out for a better view. As I cradled Josh, Martha jerked back inside, turned, and ran for the door.

"Martha!" I called. "Stay here!"

She spun, her face twisted like I remember Sherry's being the night she said she'd seen Birdy's ghost. "Birdy's out there!"

"Don't," Josh whimpered.

Martha was already gone.

I stood up, picking Josh up with me, his arms and legs wrapped around me like a baby chimp, and thumped downstairs. At the front door I jammed my feet into my shoes and ran outside.

I knew the air outside was cool, but it felt hot on my bare back and face, blazing with the screams of terrified horses and women, the incoherent shouts of Fletcher. I smelled smoke, and fire shot up the right side of the stable Fletcher was in. Where was Martha?

Still clutching Josh to me, I ran for the stable doors.

I reached them just as they burst backwards and a panic of horses exploded out, mouths flecked, eyes wild, galloping towards the house, veering west.

I staggered back against the stable front until the horses passed, feeling the heat from inside scorch my back. Where was Martha?! I peeled off the wall and ran to the side just as Martha and Sue came staggering out, coughing and spitting, their faces black, their eyes streaming. Sue's arms looked like they'd been shoved into a furnace, their skin bright pink and black and pealing. Both her and Martha's bare feet looked burned.

"Dad, he's still in there!" Martha coughed.

I pulled Josh into Martha's arms and pushed them and Sue towards the house. Then I ran into the stable.

Heat pounded into me. A burning coal dropped into my running shoe and I hopped sideways, brushing it out frantically. The fire roared up the walls. The stalls were all open, the hay burning or gone. Above me, a booming crack said the structural beams were giving way. A monster of flame crashed down and cut the place in half.

I thought I saw Fletcher's body on the far side of it.

Squinting against the terrifying heat, I dashed forward, twitched at another crack and boom above me, and jumped aside as something tumbled to my left. Sparks bit my chest. Two burning timbers blocked my way, but I could finally see Fletcher.

There was no point trying to reach him. His charred body lay still like only the dead can. The arms and legs jointed and twisted at unnatural angles. His abdomen spilled across the dirt like a crushed milk container. His face spread around his mashed skull in a jaggy pulp. It was as if thirty horses, 120 sharp hoofs, had done everything they could to obliterate the evil Fletch had carried inside him.

I turned to puke and stagger out, but discovered I couldn't move. Even as my body heaved in panic, a presence inside me pinned my feet to the spot. The smell of rot filled my nose.

No!

The skin on my shoulders and neck began to blister. My pajamas smoldered. The ceiling above me crackled.

Move!

Suddenly the thing in my mind jerked back with a hate that made my eyes blur as crazy sounds rocked through my head. I wavered, staggered, then my bare feet on embers snapped me back and I jumped out of the way of another crashing timber.

I ran.

~~~~

By six a.m., the fire had finally burned itself out and the heap that was once stables sat like a black series of lumps in the pre-dawn twilight, still smoking. No fire trucks had ever shown up, the nearest being over in Elko and going through some labor troubles. The two day-worker cowboys had arrived about thirty minutes before the Nevada state police. They were out rounding up the runaway horses while the cops started the interviews of the aloe-smeared Sue and Martha inside the house. Josh and I would be next.

"Daddy?" said Josh.

I turned my face down to where he snuggled into me. My own back was to the wall, sitting on the wraparound porch. Josh had a blanket wrapped around him and hadn't taken his face out of it to speak. He hadn't looked at me much in the last hour or so, pulling back into his shell. Shaking him or ordering him out of it had never done much good in the best of times. Which this wasn't. I was frankly surprised he'd surfaced so quickly.

"What is it, Joshie?"

"Luka...said he didn't want to hurt Fletcher and the others. Who are the others?"

I frowned. "What?"

"Who are the others that Luka hurt?"

"How...? Josh, how did Luka talk to you?"

"After the horse came running out, and you were still in there, I... called him to me."

I stared at him, horrified. "You did what?"

Josh swallowed and his little hands closed and opened on my shirt. "He was mad at you. I tried to pull him off."

The presence in my mind. The garbage smell. Luka. Inside me, pinning me inside the barn, until...I stared at my little boy and felt sweat break out all over my body. What had I done, dragging him and Martha out here with me? Not that they'd been safer by themselves, but...

My God, what had I done?

Josh looked scared and rushed through the next bit. "I didn't, like, see him. He just kind of, you know... I knew right away it was him. He's a ghost now too, right? And it was like I could hear his thoughts. Sort of."

I gulped and pulled Josh hard against me with both arms then eased off a bit when I realized he couldn't breathe. "Did he try to make you do anything?"

"Uh-unh," said Josh, scared now by my intensity. "But he kept picturing Grandpa's place and said Birdy's taking him. He said he wants us there too. To forgive him. So he can leave."

Forgive? "Josh," I said after a beat. "Do you believe what he told you?"

There was an even longer pause, then a movement of Josh's head which I thought was a shake. "He's lying, Daddy."

I nodded. "And you know you can't tell the policemen any of this when you go inside, right?" I whispered.

"But Martha..."

"I don't think she'll be saying anything about it."

I shut up as Sue walked out the front door of the house. She looked shell-shocked. She must have believed that the hand of God had just come down and zapped her with misfortune. *Act of God*, after all, was how the local police were going to write this up. Fletcher went into the barn to check on the horses. Must have lit a cigarette and dropped the match.

Sue drew up one of the two wicker chairs and sat. She stared out at the smoke.

One part of me wanted to hug her and sympathize with her loss. Also to run inside and protect my brave thirteen-year-old who'd been through just as much shock, and now had to cope with the fact that no one but her crazy father and baby brother knew there was more going on here than met the eye.

Oh yeah.

Like the fact that Luka truly was still with us somehow and still killing people? Martha might not believe it yet—believing in Birdy's ghost was already shaking up everything she knew—but she was going to have to deal with it sooner than later. Luka had already come after Josh. Now me. Would he come after Martha next?

Why should he? What was he after? Why did he want us to follow him and Birdy to my father's house? Why didn't he just kill us here? Or ignore us completely. What did he...?

The knot of fear in my stomach suddenly ballooned upwards. I knew. Somehow, like I'd just had my last grip on normal perception ripped away, I *knew*.

Luka was doing it all for Birdy's benefit. The murders, the invitation to us, the possessions. It was all to change her somehow. To dirty her, kill her innocence.

Because that presence I'd felt in my mind in the barn? That hadn't been Luka alone. Birdy had been with him, almost *part* of him. And I could remember now that as they'd let me go to fly out to Joshie, the crazy sounds that had rocked through my head. I knew what they were.

Birdy. Laughing.

21

9:30 A.M.
Weki Naea woke with a blistering headache, his blood-crusted nose pushed into a scratchy pillowcase. When he groaned and tried to roll over, rough hands jerked him upright on the bed. Motel bed. Cheap room. Old orange carpet with cigarette burns and stale smell.

And bad people. Over by the door was the man-mountain named Jose Fidel. Like Weki, his hair was pulled back in a ponytail. But for Jose Fidel, whose hair was a greased black and whose arms were chiseled boulders, the ponytail was in imitation of his movie star hero, Steve Segal. Beside him, lounging in the door of the washroom, was Pedro Amerigo, Merco's understudy. Pedro spent more time researching and playing with guns than learning the business of dealing drugs.

Finally, hauling Weki to his feet was that smiling alligator, Merco.

"Ray has arrived. Flew all the way here to see you, Weki. You should be honored."

"Oh yeh," Weki muttered, feeling the honor already of having his face smashed around, every rib and internal organ bruised, his toes mashed, his skin pinched and slapped everywhere until his whole body stung. And this was just for running away, he believed, for Merco had asked him no questions during any of it. He had been waiting for Ray Aznar.

Jose Fidel clumped out the motel room door and Merco shoved

167

Weki out after him. Beside the purple Grand Marquis was a forest green Cadillac with darkened windows. Its left rear door was open and a thin trail of pungent smoke trailing out.

Merco pushed Weki that way, shoving his head down and into the Caddy.

~~~~

In the security office of the White Pines Retreat, Dr. Morry Brandeis, who'd been *incommunicado* when Weki Naea had broken in the previous afternoon, sat in the guardroom's lone swivel chair and watched the videotaped meeting between his patient Sherry Friesen and the ponytailed Hawaiian who'd called himself Kahuna Weki Naea Kapu. It was Brandeis's second viewing and it made no more sense to him than the first time.

Kahuna. Kapu.

Brandeis stroked his beard and tapped his pen on his guard's desk. He reached forward and turned the volume down to focus on the interpersonal dynamics. From his four visits to Maui—twice with his first wife, once alone, once with his current wife, Sheila—he knew "kahuna" meant priest and "kapu" meant forbidden. So...this *goy* was Priest Weki Naea Forbidden? Not a real name. More likely a coded personal disclosure, a trait Brandeis found pervasive among religious schizophrenics. Put it together with the ponytail, cowboy boots, jeans, and jean jacket, and Brandeis diagnosed a cross-cultural shaman identification, possibly—

"Hem." The guard, who'd stood through the entire first viewing, couldn't take it any longer. "I don't know how he got in, Sir. Joyce...ah, Ms. Coolidge...says she remembers him coming in, then there's this like haze. And me, Sir, I was—"

"Ssst!"

There. That was what he was looking for. The old man had casually drawn out some sort of string from his pants pocket and was twisting it lazily between his fingers like a cat's cradle. Sherry kept on humming and nodding her head, but her eyes, Brandeis saw, were following the old man's fingers. The string figure operated much as a hypnotist's swinging watch—a focus of attention.

Brandeis turned the volume back up as the Kahuna Weki snapped the string figure tight between his fingers and realized the old man's chants, which Brandeis had wondered over before, came to an abrupt end. Then the amazing question and answer started:

"Your daughter, Birdy, where she be?"

"With him."

"Who?"

"Luka," Sherry said. *"She's with Luka. He's holding onto her. Very angry. He's very very angry. Pretending not to be."*

"They be alive?"

"They're...no, yes, they're...not dead...they're here in the world. I can feel them." Sherry Friesen bobbed her head down, grabbing her hair.

"It is okay. Tell me what he doing."

"You're as bad as him! You caused this."

"Mebbe yes. You tell me what he doing."

"He's..." Sherry Friesen's words trailed off like she'd seen something awful.

"Tell me."

"He's trying to make her...go somewhere else, to try again. He needs to keep pushing her, trying to make her...edible."

"Is working?

Sherry Friesen neither shook nor nodded her head. She just stared straight ahead, trembling, her face pale and sweating.

Edible? Was this a sexual reference?

On the tape now were sounds of feet thumping down the corridor. That would have been the orderlies looking for Weki Naea. The old man raised his head at the sound and then raised the raised one finger to lightly touch Sherry Friesen's face. She instantly stilled and looked at him. What Brandeis would have given for that kind of magic with his patients.

"Don't worry what he be trying to do," Weki Naea said on the security tape. *"You tell me where they going."*

Sherry Friesen murmured out a name, her father-in-law's name. Then she jerked up her head and yelled, *"You think you can stop him! David thinks he can stop him! But you can't! He's too strong! He's almost got her! You understand? She's too far gone!"*

Brandeis froze the tape.

"Sir?" said the guard.

"Can you enlarge this part of the frame?" He pointed to Weki Naea's face, fully facing the security camera as Sherry Friesen screamed.

"Yes, sir," said the guard and waited for Brandeis to move. When he did, the guard sat and took a screen capture, then began enlarging and sharpening Naea's face.

"Good. Print copies and circulate it. The man's to be detained if he ever shows up here again."

"But...shouldn't we be notifying that man she mentioned, sir?"

"What? That ghosts are coming?" Brandeis let scorn drip from his words, then reached over and took the security tape.

"Um...Sir? Procedure...um..."

Brandeis stared him scornfully then turned with the tape and walked out.

~~~~

The lime green Cadillac cruised slowly through the industrial lakeshore of Oakland with its tinted windows rolled up. Its passengers were all but invisible.

One of those passengers, Weki Naea, was so soaked with sweat that his underwear squished when he moved. And the smell of it was sharp and sour because it was filled with the juice of his fear.

To Weki's left sat Merco, waving another syringe of acid like the two he'd already used on Weki, injecting them just under the skin of his groin and armpit so that Weki had felt like those parts of him were being scorched off his body. The pain was worse than the beatings. Almost too much.

Merco brought the needle just under Weki's left eye. It was all Weki could do not to scream like a wahine. His bladder released, and the warmth of his urine spread across his thighs. He saw Merco wrinkle back his nose.

To Naea's right, the short Mexican named Ray Aznar who'd taken over all Luka's suppliers and real estate to build himself a cartel based in Alhambra, muttered, "Fuck," and ordered the driver to stop. When the driver did, Aznar made a sign and Merco pulled Weki out, slinging him around to the trunk. There Merco slammed Weki down, back first so he was spread-eagled over the metal. From this position, Weki watched Aznar's acne-pitted face walk around to him. The hulkingly stupid Jose Fidel followed.

Aznar batted away Merco's hand holding the syringe and grabbed Weki's hair near its roots. "You run away from me, you tell me garbage about ghosts, then you piss in my car. I think we should dump you into the harbor. What do you think? Or maybe take this string you always carry"—he pulled Weki's *lei* string from his pocket—"wrap it around your balls, and squeeze them off."

Merco said something in a low voice that Weki didn't hear and Aznar jerked away from Weki to reach out and grab Merco by the smaller man's shirt front. He shook him and began screaming at him in Spanish so that flecks of spittle sprayed Merco's face. Weki thought about running, but Jose Fidel just then thumped one of his large hands onto Weki's chest. Aznar finally dropped Merco onto the concrete and turned back to his prisoner.

"Merco says," said Aznar, drawing it out like a piece of disgusting slime, "that you might tell us more if we offered you something you want."

He waved his fingers. Merco, who'd risen from the ground, handed him a Zippo lighter and filled glass crack pipe.

"Sit up." Aznar grabbed Weki's hair again and yanked him to sitting on the hood, his feet splayed wide, his bones sore and right thigh cramping.

But the pain in legs was nothing like what was happening in his head and rest of him. Because as Aznar flipped the lighter and began melting the little ball of crystal in the crack pipe's sealed end, everything in Weki wanted to dance and leap. Then the smell of the smoke curling up the tube hit him, the sickly sweet smell like pure car exhaust, like fermenting corn and burnt rubber. The wasted muscles of Weki's arms and legs strained. *No can. No can!* said his mind. For though he'd told them already that Luka was a ghost who was killing people, he hadn't told them why. How it all had to do with winning the soul of the dead girl away from her family. Aznar would not believe, of course, but he might go after the rest of the Friesens just to be sure. And that would be the final straw of guilt that would break Weki forever.

Forever.

Which mattered not a bit the instant Aznar swirled the lit crack pipe under his nose. "Oh, brah!" Weki cried.

Aznar pulled the pipe away and Jose Fidel's big hands held Weki solidly on the car trunk. "Now you tell me," said Aznar, "where Luka is staying."

"He dead! He dead!" Weki babbled. "He be nowhere and anywhere. Girl take him. He just goes, yeh. Follow follow give me a hit, brah. Just one."

And he kept babbling like he couldn't help himself, dimly aware that Aznar and Merco were standing back, Merco mumbling something in Aznar's ear. Then Aznar was holding the smoking crack pipe up to Weki's mouth, the hot glass to Weki's dry lips, and Weki was puckering those lips forward trying to close on the retreating teat, suck in its gift.

Aznar pulled it back and shoved his scarred brown face right up to Weki's so the Mexican's eyes filled Weki's whole view. "So where's Luka now, *brah*? You tell me, and you smoke."

Weki's shook his head back and forth in a sudden paroxysm as he remembered the surf of Molokai where he'd grown up. He remembered his counselors in St. Jude's. He remembered what it was like to wake up in the morning and not need a fix. And the horrible pictures of the Friesen family after their little girl was killed. He could not give them up and say where they were, but surely he must give Aznar something, someone. *Manawa.* Now is the moment of power. He gasped for breath.

"No...can," he grunted.

Aznar hissed and looked at Jose Fidel. Fidel produced some silver duct tape from somewhere and bound Weki's wrists together. Then he lifted him all the way onto the trunk lid, taped his ankles, and hauled him off again. The trunk opened before Weki's nose like a black pit.

~~~~

In his spare little office, Dr. Morry Brandeis frowned down at his speakerphone. Two FBI agents were waiting for him in the lobby. They wanted to speak to him about Sherry Friesen.

"Tell them five minutes," he ordered Joyce and punched the disconnect. He touched his beard lightly. He had to figure out what, exactly, he was going to say.

Point one: David Friesen was no longer at his home and his answering machine was filled to capacity.

Point two: his sister-in-law had answered Brandeis's phone queries by reporting that Friesen had come for his children last night. At the children's request, supposedly. Friesen hadn't said where he was taking them.

Point three: this security tape in his pocket.

It was the sticking point. Not only did the tape show the White Pines' security in a bad light, but revealing the tape was potentially a breach of patient-doctor responsibility.

And yet if it showed a clear threat to someone's safety...

Brandeis picked up his "thinking pen", a black Montblanc that was thick, rounded at both ends, and undeniably phallic. His Duke colleagues would have identified his pen fondling as a sex substitute, but Brandeis didn't care. It helped him sort through difficult issues.

To show the tape or not to show the tape?

He set down his pen and pulled the security tape from his pocket, stuck it in his office machine, and sat back to watch the last few minutes of Naea's visit, the ones he hadn't wanted the already-jumpy guard to watch a second time.

"—*too far gone!*" Sherry Friesen shouted at Weki Naea as the tape started up a second or two back. *"They'll go to David's father in Utah. David will figure he has to confront Luka there!"* Then the upsetting capper. *"And Luka will kill David! He has to!"*

Brandeis stopped the machine and pulled out the videocassette. Clearly Sherry Friesen was delusional. And even if David Friesen shared her delusions, tried to "confront Luka", it could only be a positive step. For David had given no indications of being a violent man. Therefore the confrontation would be strictly emotional, a way for the man to move on.

And the threat from "Luka" himself? There was none. Luka lived only in the Friesens' minds. Ghosts did not exist.

Brandeis put the videocassette in his top desk drawer and strode out to meet the FBI.

22

*I*T'S A TRAP.

The words kept whispering in my head as we cruised slowly into my home town of Morris, Utah. I'd pushed hard with that Nevada police sheriff to let us leave his jurisdiction and he'd finally relented after getting my cell number and other contact info. But should I have kept driving us here? Ignoring my children's insistence we keep on, did it make any sense at all?

And the answer came back again that *I* had to go on, and I didn't trust that anyone else had the necessary understanding and commitment to keep Josh and Martha safe. Or maybe it was just that now that I had them back with me I couldn't bear to let them go again.

But that creepy laugh of Birdy's after the fire...

Josh and Martha distracted me by powering down their windows and sticking their heads out like dogs, panting in the dry heat and laughing. The resiliency of children. The instinct to survive.

Even I found myself smiling as the kids pointed to one piece of Midwestern Americana after another—the dusty barber shop with its candy stripe pole; a Thrifty drug store; the Stone Cinema, running a Mel Gibson festival, with two of the movie titles spelled incorrectly; a Pick-a-Part Auto store with a lime green junker hoisted on a pole on top. It was like the outside world—war, technology, race and abortion debates, AIDS, SARS—never touched it.

Yet under my smile I also felt the upswell of fear. Life here. Death here. In my memories they ran together way too tightly, cutting schizophrenically from maudlin joy.to terror in the dark. It's what I'd run from all those years ago. What I'd married Sherry to make dead and buried. Why I'd buried my painting and it's route to my subconscious.

It had followed me anyway, so I might as well face it head on.

That steeled my jaw a bit as we passed the town boundary and turned onto Stickney Road, its pavement rutted and crumbling on either side, heading out to my dad's. Smells of the Wasatch mountains blew into the car—aspens and evergreens, meadows, dirt, Jumper's Creek. Also the acrid smog from the potash mine along the ridge, still belching after all these years.

Past the eastern windbreak (and privacy shield) of poplars, I turned down the long gravel driveway to my dad's acreage and pulled up to the left of his pickup. The worn stencil on the truck's passenger door said, "Friesen's Stone Cutting: patios, walls, ponds, decoration" and a phone number. My dad's line of work after the potash mine laid off two-thirds of its workforce.

The stencil should have included "tombstones."

For there to our right, in front of the two stories of rotting white board and batten, under a green-shingled roof that sagged near one end, was a weedy lawn of squared-off tombstones. Three years ago, the one time I'd brought my family back here, the one time *I* had been back, it was only the back yard that was filled with tombstones. The front had been reserved for only two—that of my mother, and of my big brother, Tim.

Now my mother's was lost among dozens just like it. Tim's, though, was easy to pick out. It still lay where my father had smashed it over with the crazy strength of guilt and alcohol on the night I left home for good.

Josh jumped out of the Volvo first and of course went directly to Tim's stone. He stared at it as if trying to remember it from our one long-ago journey here, then knelt and touched it. "Why's this one—?"

A snarling bark cut him off as a brown-and-black beast suddenly shot from the side of the house and straight for him.

"Dead-eye!" shouted Martha. "Here, boy!"

My father's mutt, mostly Labrador and the kids' constant companion the last time we were here, turned mid-rush and tumbled sideways. Not the most graceful of dogs. Blind on his left side from some accident he'd had before my dad got him, but friendly, thank goodness. And he seemed to remember Martha. His tongue lolled out of his mouth, dripping slobber, as he trotted over to her.

Josh had seen none of this. With an intensity that scared me, my six-year-old had curled his fingers under the top edge of the Tim's tombstone and was trying to lift it upright. Josh's scrawny arms and back strained. His face turned red. For one terrifying second I thought he was going to budge it. Then reality kicked in. This was eight-inch-thick granite and taller than all the others. Josh fell back in the weeds, panting.

The front screen door banged open and I looked to see the intimidating bulk of my dad in blue overalls. His short white hair was wild on his head. His thick arms held a slide-action shotgun up by his cheek. It was aimed at Joshie's head.

"Get *off!*" he roared.

"No!" I leapt forward between my dad and my son, arms spread wide. "Dad! It's us! Hey!"

Dead-eye barked and yowled in Martha's hug.

The shotgun wavered a second as my dad's heavy eyebrows twitched. The blue sky seemed to swing overhead. Then he lowered the gun and his thick jaw fell open in a look of such bewilderment that he looked the same age as Josh. Because of course I hadn't called ahead to warn him we were coming. Not just because of our rush, but because I'd been afraid to. I'd brought my family here only once, three years ago, and that time only because Sherry had made me. And Sherry had run everything from the moment we'd arrived. She'd charmed my father, directed the kids, cleaned the house, seen to the meals...

My dad's eyes swept the yard. They rested on Martha with Dead-eye beside the Volvo, went back to Josh scrambling quickly off my brother's gravestone, then out to the road, to the neighbor's place beyond the windbreak. He didn't look at me.

"Caught kinda cornered," he muttered at last. "Where's Sherry? And the bird?"

For a second I wondered if this was a deliberate stab, but I shook it off. His blank look said he truly did not know.

"Sherry's sick, Dad," I said. "Birdy's dead."

"What's on my head?" he said and touched his wild hair.

"Dead," I said louder. "Birdy is *dead*."

The dumbfounded look lifted just long enough for fear to flash across, then he tossed his head with an inappropriate laugh that made him look like a bear chuffing a challenge. Still not looking at me, he said, "How'd you get here?"

"How?" I stalled.

I was relieved from answering when Dead-eye chose that moment to squat and shit. Martha jumped back with a cry of disgust, but my dad laughed again and waved us all inside. I went back to the car for the bags then followed, careful to step around Dead-eye's little welcome near the car.

The inside of the house wasn't the shock it had been on that visit three years ago. That time the smell of stale rot and disintegration had nearly choked me. Formless junk had lain everywhere, the second-floor ceilings had rotted from water damage, the upstairs toilet and sink had been crusted with rust and looked like they hadn't worked in years. All this after Sherry had called my father six months ahead of time to let him know we were coming to visit.

This time the house stank of sweat and mold, but at least it was only three years of build-up; Sherry had spent much of our one visit cleaning. She'd made me carry out endless boxes of old newspapers, magazines, cardboard, grimy glass jars, empty cans. A truck had hauled it all away.

My dad and the kids were upstairs. I could hear his heavy bulk creaking around. "Josh! Martha!" I called up. " Be careful where you walk. There could—"

A cracking sound made me drop our bags to sprint upstairs. At the top I froze. Martha and Dead-eye were in the doorway to Tim's and my bedroom watching Josh, who was nearer to me. He straddled the line under the linoleum between the original house where the front living room and stairs that had been inexpertly added on before I was born. Josh's face was a mask of concentration. He rocked back and forth between the sides of the join like he was determined to split the house apart. First the gravestone, now this.

My father suddenly pushed past Martha and Dead-eye with a rusty old machete in his right hand. Martha shrieked and Josh froze, staring at his grandfather with wide eyes.

The old man glared back. "Place is dusty," he said finally. "Have to shake out the spreads. Boys in here. Martha in there. 'Less you want to all sleep together."

"No way," said Martha behind him.

My dad blinked and shook himself. Still holding the machete, he nodded and creaked left around Josh to enter the added-on upstairs room that had once been my mom's sewing room.

I frowned uneasily at my kids, then went back downstairs for the bags. As I carried them up again, I paused on the narrow stairs and it was like I could feel the entire house lean, ready to fall over. Or maybe it was just me. The heat and dust pushed at me like it was trying to burrow its way in. Tear me and mine to pieces.

With a thump-thump, the bulk of my father was suddenly on the stairs above me, his rusty machete blade raised.

"Let's go outside and talk, Davie," he said.

~~~~

The kids stayed in the house and my father led me to a building out back. "Whole new batch showed up after you left last time," my father said as we entered it. "Drove me plumb crazy."

He switched on the lights and I blinked my eyes. The workshop was the size of a three-car garage with a high ceiling, everything thick dark wood, so it was gloomy even fully lit. Piles of stone and granite blocks filled one half, carefully separated by size and type by wooden skeleton frames. The half we were in had a long bench of tools and two huge tables butted with radial, diamond-blade saws and pneumatic tools for shaping and carving. Everything was swept clean and smelled of machine oil and gasoline. Almost professional.

"New batch of what?" I asked.

He didn't answer right away. Instead, he tugged out a smooth, dull slab of granite from the nearest stall and wrestled it up onto the saw table with an impressive show of strength for someone in his late sixties. He straightened the slab, pulled on a set of safety goggles, started the saw, and pushed the stone forward. The blade squealed as it bit through. Even with water spraying down on it, fine dust spat out on either side and I could feel the heat roll off. After the first pass, my dad pulled the two pieces away and lined them up again, sideways, to trim the height. Paused.

"Batch of ghosts," he said. "It was like you were this kind of honey they latched onto. Made them all crazy."

I swallowed. Was this some weird-ass way of telling me he himself missed me? I studied his set jaw as he aligned the cut slabs on the saw. No. He meant exactly what he said. I'd brought more ghosts down on him. My fault.

My father squealed the two granite pieces through, then rested, panting. "At least they ain't shy. Come down moaning their names. Let me pin them down."

"With tombstones."

"You got her."

My dad's solution to being haunted, discovered when I was six, I think—find the ghost's name, carve it on a tombstone, ram it into the earth. And damned if it hadn't seemed to work. How would Sweetness's mom explain that? It made the "persistent personality signature" realize it was dead?

My dad had shut off the saw and now slid one of the blocks to the side. He leaned over the other block with a pneumatic carving chisel in his hand. With a high-pitched whirr like a dentist's drill, he started the tool up and began the teeth-chattering process of doing a name. For all my snobbery over my dad's lack of education and his stupidities when I was growing up, I found myself admiring his work.

He lifted the chisel to say, "You still watch baseball?"

He'd carved an elaborate "B" in the stone, as fancy as anything the newer computer-laser cutting combos would have produced. Now he did an "i."

"You and the bird used to watch, Sherry said."

An "r" and my heart suddenly jerked upwards inside me.

"Dad. What're you...?"

"Josh told me!" he called over the chattering. "'Bout why you're here!"

A "d". A "y". Birdy. He pulled back and straightened. Turned off the chisel and set it down. When he saw my face, his grin faltered a bit, but he held out both hands to me, rough palms up, like he was offering the sweetest gift. Like I should recognize he loved me and always had. We were chasing down my little girl's restless spirit, see. So George-the-stone-mason Friesen, had set to work with a personalized solution. Still watching out for me.

The stupid bastard.

The big, stupid, goddamned, moronic bastard.

"Wipe it out," I said.

"Hunh?"

"It's not even her real name. Scratch it out. Blast it out. Get her name off that thing or I'll smash the whole stone to bits."

He moved his body in front of the carved stone and furrowed his brow at me like I was a little boy. "Davie, you can't hang onto the dead. You never got that."

I could feel my face flushed and my eyes watering. Always, even when I was seventeen and at last ran away from home, this man had scared the piss out of me. The size and strength of him were awesome. And while he was usually a good-natured clod, he'd become a drunk after Tim's death and pushed me and my mother around a lot. Never beat us, but still managed to give me bruises. He chased us into church once and, in front of everyone, dragged us out to shout that a ghost had said we were keeping money from him. I was, taking a portion of my weekly paycheck (Dad and I both worked for a regional contractor then) and socking it away. That was the money I used later to run away. After Dad had killed my mother.

Now I wasn't seventeen. I was thirty-nine and my dad was nearly seventy. Even if he could haul a granite block up onto the table, he wasn't going to tell me what to do about my own family.

"Get away from it, Dad."

His old eyes hardened and his lower lip stuck out. "No."

I stepped forward and he raised his hands to meet me like he was still a young tough in a bar or the red-necked farmer's son who'd left his own home in Kansas at age fifteen to travel west.

I stopped and glared into his eyes, so angry my ears were buzzing, my vision going red. But I was thinking also of Martha and Josh back in the house. If I struggled with my father and hurt him, *if* I could hurt him, what would they think? And could we still wait here in this house for Birdy to show?

The moment was decided for me by a scream and the sudden wild barking of Dead-eye. It jolted me back to myself and I turned with a icy rush in my veins. Birdy. Luka. They were here.

Forgetting my father, I sprinted for the house, crashed in through the back door and kitchen. The barking and screeching were coming from upstairs and I ran out through the living room and up three stairs at a time, crashed into Tim and my old room...and found Josh restraining Dead-eye while Martha rolled on the bed hugging herself and laughing so hard her eyes streamed. Martha saw my face and laughed even harder, while Josh suddenly burst into tears. Dead-eye stopped his own barking at once and turned to lick Josh's face.

I stepped to Josh, knelt, and pulled Dead-eye off him. "What did you do?" I asked Martha.

Then I saw the open door beside the bed Martha lay on. Just four feet high, that door led to a closet that ran behind that entire wall. My father had hidden there a few times when I was a kid and thumped and bumped late at night, moaning to scare Tim and me. Which was pure evil if you thought about it. He *knew* that ghosts existed.

And now had Martha done the same thing? She was quiet now, but defiantly sticking out her lower lip just like her grandfather had done minutes ago.

"She jumped out," Josh sniffed.

I looked from him to Martha, back to him, then off. In some families this would be innocent fun and I'd have chuckled along with Martha right then. Maybe should have. God knew we could have used a sense of humor. When was the last time I'd laughed? Or Josh?

"Let's just...be sensitive to each other's needs right now," I said. "Okay?"

It sounded so lame that I couldn't look at Martha as I said it. I could feel her chagrin turn to frustration and smoldering anger. Just like her mother would have done. And I had no answer to it. Somehow, with my timid refusal to face up to my fears all these years and *deal* with them, I suspected I'd brought this all upon us—Luka, the murder, the ghosts haunting us, desperately struggling among themselves.

But whether I had or not, all this shit was upon us and we had to deal with it. We had to rescue Birdy. We had to get rid of Luka. Survive.

"Reckon she'll show up here."

I turned to see my father standing at the doorway, wiping his hands on the front of his overalls, looking around the room. He meant here as in this room.

"Why?" I said.

"This is where she stayed when you come out last time. All three grandkids right here." His eyes grew suddenly moist.

Embarrassed for him and angry at the same time. Like he'd any right to care about his grandkids? He'd never tried once to find me in all my years in San Francisco.

But I nodded because when it came to Birdy's ghost, he was probably right. And maybe there was even a way he could help. I took a deep breath. "She might not show up alone, Dad. And the ghost following her... If there's any ghost we want to pin down with a tombstone, it's him."

My father nodded slowly. "Okay. Sure. What's the feller's name?"

I told him and spelled it for him a few times. He nodded and left. A minute later I heard the pneumatic chisel rattling away. I was amazed at how much it picked up my mood. Not only had I told my father what to do, but he was doing it. And it was the right thing to do. It might actually give us a weapon to use against Luka, something more than his supposedly-needed forgiveness.

Which is when I realized I'd made the shift into thinking of the coming encounter as a showdown. Up to now, I'd just been chasing Birdy, hoping somehow that simply communicating might give her a way out, and give me exoneration. But the incident at Fletcher's and Sue's ranch had finally drilled home that Luka wasn't just piggy-backing on Birdy. He was shaping her somehow, *using* her. Which meant he wasn't going to just give her up.

"Dad?" Josh asked suddenly.

I squeezed his shoulders. "What, Josh?"

"Do ghosts mostly come at night?"

"Seems that way, doesn't it."

"Are you gonna sleep in that bed?" He pointed to the bed where Martha still lay, the one with closet running behind its headboard.

"I am. And the closet door will be closed and blocked."

Martha rolled her eyes and hopped off the bed, shutting the door and pulling the heavy armchair from down the wall to block the door from opening again.

"Thank you, Martha," I said.

Like the ghosts who were coming would notice one way or the other.

23

4:30 P.M..

Sweetness saw Ramirez pause, frustrated, when she walked from the door of the White Pines to the driver's side of their rented Sunfire. Her partner apparently still felt it was the man's job to drive.

She was tempted to stop and flatten him on principle, except it wasn't really him bothering her. It was the prissy old Jew who was chief shrink of the White Pines—Dr. Brandeis. Even after she'd told him Weki Naea's vehicle had been found crashed in the woods close to here, he'd maintained that he couldn't tell them more than that the old Hawaiian had been here yesterday to speak to Sherry Friesen.

And? she'd pressed Brandeis.

Pardon me?

You didn't monitor it? Any security?

A videotape, but it's protected by doctor-patient privilege.

Someone's life is possibly at stake here. You want me to get a warrant?

Brandeis had turned a bit green at that but had kept stonewalling, stroking down his beard, refusing to even let them interview Sherry Friesen themselves, since she was heavily sedated.

Since her meeting with Weki Naea?

Privileged.

Privilege this, Sweetness had been tempted to say and grab him by one of twelve different pressure points she knew could cause exquisite pain.

185

"So we get a warrant?" It was Ramirez, holding up his hands in the passenger seat. Sweetness realized she'd just been sitting, glaring out the driver's-side windshield.

"Hell, yes. Something weird here. They just let an old Hawaiian man walk in to interview one of their patients? It may be the last info we get out of Naea."

"You think Aznar's got him."

Or Luka does. She didn't voice that thought out loud, though. Wasn't even sure what she meant by it, exactly. "Yeah," she said.

She pulled out her cell phone and handed it to Ramirez. "Flip through my stored numbers. Call Hugh Clarkson. He's with the D.E.A. and probably has some intel on where Aznar might be holing up here in S.F.. Try Richards and Brown in our offices if you can't reach Hugh. Also call Detective Ambrose, SFPD. He's the guy handling Naea's abandoned car. See if he can get the videotape for us."

Without waiting for a dumb-assed objection or questions, Sweetness put the car in gear and skidded out of the driveway.

~~~~

The hell inside the Cadillac's trunk smelled like carpet cleaner and Weki's urine. Every joint and bruise of him throbbed and he couldn't uncurl his body as the car bounced him along through what sounded like a place of heavy industry. Chugging ships. Steam blasts. Clanking and banging.

But even with all this, for the first time in many days, Weki was happy. He had not told Ray Aznar everything. Despite Weki's age and history of weakness, he had protected the remaining Friesens.

'Onipa'a. Stand firm. He had done the right thing.

His heart skipped as he felt the Cadillac pull to a stop. Its doors thumped open and closed. Steps. But they were not coming towards the back. They were thumping on a wooden door somewhere.

With grunting contortions, Weki managed to pull from his hair pocket the *hei* string Aznar had thrown back at him in disgust. Weki wrapped it around his fingers and began frantically mumbling a chant of protection, he heard muffled voices talking, rising to shouts, cries. There were thuds and two gunshots. The footsteps came back towards him.

A second later he was blinded as the trunk swung open, then a cloth bag was pulled over his bed and he was dragged out like a sack of potatoes. They dragged him into a darker place, pulled off his hood, and he saw he was in a small warehouse. A dead East Indian man lay on the cement floor, leaking blood. Jose Fidel dragged Weki to a metal chair alone in the middle of the floor and sat him down. There, Merco pulled the *hei* from Weki's fingers while Jose Fidel cut off Weki's jacket, shirt, and pants, and bound him to his seat.

With a cruel smile, Merco pulled out a switch-razor, held up Weki's *hei*, sliced the string into pieces, and flung the pieces to the cement.

Aznar, still sitting in the car, barked an order in Spanish. Merco nodded and, still smiling, advanced on Weki.

~~~~

"Aznar's a sick pscyho pussy," Ramirez said. He'd just disconnected from his sixth phone call, the last being the longest. It had lasted the whole way over the Oakland Bridge and downtown to where Sweetness was cruising them through Luka Keawe's old neighborhood.

Sweetness raised her eyebrows at him.

Ramirez shrugged. "That's what Clarkson called him. Illegal immigrant who got landed status by marrying a Valley girl, worked his way close to Keawe by doing crazy-Sadie stuff. But he's paranoid too. Clarkson's not surprised that he or his goons flew up here." The local Bureau office had confirmed that a Merco Juliannes had rented two cars at the airport, one yesterday and one that morning, presumably for Aznar and his boys. "If Aznar thinks somehow Luka Keawe's still alive, Aznar'll chase across the whole country to nail him."

"Preemptive strike."

"Basically."

"Which helps us how?"

Again the shrug. "Clarkson suggested Aznar wouldn't just pop Naea, not as long as he thinks the old guy might help him find Keawe."

"And where does he suggest we look?"

"Deserted buildings. Basements. Old warehouses. Seems the guy gets off on old-fashioned torture with knives. He likes to hear his victims scream."

"Oh, that's helpful." Sweetness swung the car over to the curb in frustration and jerked to a stop, shut the engine off, and hung her head forward against the steering wheel.

"What?"

"Crackhead Jack. If I were Aznar and trying to track down Naea, I would have come to Keawe's old digs first. If I had, I probably would have questioned his old neighbors just like we did. Maybe that's how Aznar knew to go to White Pines."

"Okay," said Ramirez. "So where's he go once he gets the man?"

"He's going to question him. But..."

"What?"

Sweetness raised up her head. "He's not going to stop looking while he questions Naea. Especially if the old man spouts some kind of Hawaiian ghost crap. So he's going to keep looking through Keawe's life. Everywhere he went. The people he knew. What sort of connections he might have had with Friesen's family."

"You got an idea," Ramirez said. "I can see from your eyes you got an idea."

"An intersection of information. Gut hunch, maybe."

"Hunch? Like a good guess? Logic maybe?"

Sweetness turned her head to smile as Ramirez as she slammed the car into gear. He was such a little boy, she saw, talking and blustering to cover up his incredible need to make the grade.

"Just thinking like the bad guy, Ramirez," she said, and roared the car back towards Oakland.

24

THE HEAT IN THE KITCHEN OF MY DAD'S HOUSE, the home where I grew up, had settled in dry and gritty. Breathe it in. *Tick-tick.* Blow it out. *Tick-tick.*

Not that my father or kids seemed to notice. As we ate dinner, my dad joked with them, telling them about the winters here, where the snow blew down so hard from the hills that you could get drifts clear up to the second story windows. Where one year he took Tim and me out snowshoeing to check the snares we'd set for rabbits and came across a mountain lion.

"What'd you do?" Josh asked, eyes wide.

My father mimed raising his shotgun, aiming, pulling the trigger. "Pow!"

Martha shrieked with delight.

Josh looked upset. "Did you kill him?"

My father lowered his arms. Sweaty. "He took off like bolt—zoom. Never kill nothing without a good reason, son."

I stared down at my hamburger hash. *Never kill nothing without good reason.*

When I was seven, my dad took me and Tim out in the middle of the night to hunt pocket gophers. They were called "pocket" gophers because they had pouches in their cheeks. It made them look awfully cute, with their dark brown fur and short hairless tails. I'd almost managed to coax a few up to the porch with some low talking. But Dad said they'd been eating up all of Mom's vegetable garden. Only years later did I realize the real reason Dad had it in for them. Their burrowing in our back yard had threatened to undermine Dad's growing tombstone collection.

I remember Tim telling me the proper way to deal with pocket gophers was to flood their tunnels and sic cats on them. Or slide traps into their holes, staked down so the little rodents didn't get one leg snapped and drag the trap deep into their tunnels. Tim said they could have as much as 200 yards of tunnels. You could also throw down poison bait or gas cartridges.

None of these methods interested Dad. Instead, we crept out in the middle of the night and staked down thin wire snares around the tops of five of the little mounds in the front yard that seemed to have the freshest dirt. Then Dad had me take a flashlight and hunker down about three feet from the holes, shining the light at each entrance in about fifteen second bursts.

When the curious little critters came up for a peep, Dad and Tim, their hands itching on their wires, would yank quickly and garrotte them.

One of the snares Dad pulled, I remember, snapped closed so hard that it snipped the gopher's head right off. Like a pair of scissors. Blood sprayed on our faces. Time howled with laughter. I wailed so loud Dad thought I'd wake the neighbors. And I didn't stop. I just kept right on wailing and sobbing and slapping at my face until my mother finally woke up and carried me inside.

The next day nobody said a thing about it. But it was the last time my father ever took me out at night. In fact it was the last time he ever tried to do anything he considered fun with me. I suspect if Tim hadn't died three years later, he might never have spoken to me again at all. He was embarrassed to be seen with me.

"Why don't you tell them about their grandma," I said, wiping my brow and standing to clear dishes.

Dad shot me a cautious look.

"How you met her," I said. "What she was like."

After a pause and cautious throat clearing, my father began.

I piled up the plates, glasses, and silverware and carried the lot quickly to the sink. I wanted the kids to hear the stories, but suddenly realized I myself couldn't listen. It would make me angry, then weepy, maudlin. Poor Davie. Lost his big brother, then his mommy. Ran away from home. Started his own family. Now he was losing that one too, one by one.

I clanked the plates *et al.* into the double sink, sprayed in some soap, and set the water running. As it filled, I looked through the window to the south side of the house and noticed my father had planted tombstones there as well. His neighbor, to the east was at the windbreak with a chainsaw, taking down a dead poplar. I could hear the muted buzz of his chainsaw as he made his last cut and toppled it, went for the branches.

It suddenly struck me that I hadn't bothered to search through and identify where Mom's tombstone was out front. If it was still there.

Suddenly claustrophobic, I reached forward and slid the right window open a bit to let some cooling afternoon breeze in through the screen. But all I got was the chainsaw buzz and a sudden stench like rotting garbage.

The *stench*. I grabbed the window and slammed it shut.

When I turned, everyone at the table was staring at me like I was crazy. "Bad smell," I said.

"Dad, the water," said Josh.

I looked down, blinked, and quickly shut off the water. It and the suds were overflowing, the water dripping in great pools on the floor. "Sorry," I said, not sure to whom.

Suddenly, from under the table where he'd been lying, Dead-eye began to whine and Martha slapped at her ear. "Mosquitoes!"

My father grinned and shook his head. "Hunh. Been awful dry. Not many places for them to hatch."

Then Josh shook his head hard and swatted at it like he too was being attacked, but by an entire swarm. Dead-eye scrambled out and began to growl at him, his hackles up.

Dad's face fell and he pushed himself out from the table. "We got company," he said. Dead-eye barked and pranced around Josh.

I jumped past Dead-eye and grabbed Josh by his waving hands. "Joshie," I said. "I want you to tell whoever's bothering you to just *go—away*. Can you do that?"

He nodded, but before he could even open his mouth, the mosquito ghost seemed to have gone from Josh to my father. Dead-eye whirled on him and my dad started shaking his head and roaring. The big man staggered to the kitchen door leading to the backyard and threw himself against the doorframe. *Wham! Wham!* The dusty picture of an Oriole came loose from the side wall and fell, its front glass tinkling across the linoleum.

Then my dad shuffled back into the middle of the kitchen with a look of triumph. "He's gone."

Everyone looked at me expectantly, even Dead-eye, his hackles still up, big feet still dancing. But though I held my breath, nothing happened. I walked to the window and slid it open. It still stank outside, coming from the direction of the neighbor's idling chainsaw—*spu-rut-put-put*. I closed it and looked around, but nothing more was happening here. So maybe I'd been wrong about the smell this time. Maybe Dad's neighbor was just burning garbage. They did that in the country.

"Was it him?" I heard Martha whisper to Josh.

He whispered back, "I don't know. But it's gone now. Can you feel it?"

Daddy? Just a sigh.

I jerked my chin around. "Did you hear that?" I asked Josh.

He looked at me, wide-eyed, and shook his head. That disturbed me almost more than the mosquito attacks. How could I have felt something Josh didn't? And if I hadn't, but only thought I had, how could I trust my feelings anymore?

I closed my eyes and reached out internally but felt and heard nothing now.

"Dad? You're freaking us out." It was Martha. "Whatever it was, it's gone, okay? And maybe it *was* just mosquitoes."

I opened my eyes and shook my head. "I think we're all going to sleep in the same room tonight after all. Dead-eye at the door."

"What? No way!"

"Yes way," I said with such tired conviction that Martha opened her mouth to speak but then shut it again.

"Daddy?"

It was Josh, but his voice was even tinier than usual. As tiny as it had been that time in San Francisco when he'd realized Luka was in the restaurant with us.

"What?" I said.

"Are we going to die?"

~~~~

Birdy, get away from there! Go somewhere else! Anywhere else! Daddy's not strong enough!

I can't, Mommy.

You have to!

Sherry rocked back and forth on her bed. They'd tied her down with straps, they'd drugged her, but they couldn't break the strange connection in her head with Birdy's ghost. This time it was like Sherry was right there. She'd been in Birdy's disjointed thoughts as she whirled through the dirty farmhouse, pushing Luka a*way* from her. Then they were in the kitchen, Luka gone. She saw David—he looked gaunt and pale, deathly troubled but committed; still foolishly trying to protect his children, both living and dead—and Martha and Josh and David's father, George Friesen.

Sherry had even tried to reach out and touch Martha, then Josh, then George. They'd felt her. Dead-eye had felt her.

But she couldn't touch David.

Because Birdy was now clinging so tightly to him herself, like she had as a baby, when she'd had bad dreams and David had been the only one who could rock her back to sleep.

Birdy had been protecting him before, but now she was just scared. She was growing stronger but less and less in control. As if something in her struggle with Luka built up power she didn't want, making her surge inside like a building energy ball, a nuclear core, a growing sun. Terrified.

Birdy, Luka's going to try to hurt Daddy. Do you understand?

H-he won't. I told him not to. I sent him away at that farm we were at.

He's going to try, honey. Do—you—understand?

You go away, Mommy.

Sherry's connection with her was abruptly cut, so her mind was floating in darkness. And again she wanted to cry out for help, but the drugs now asserted themselves and she could not.

~~~~

Ramirez drove slowly. Sweetness pointed to the third warehouse from the end.

They were a good three blocks back from the harbor and the buildings here illustrated the hard times that had hit Oakland's shipping center. It was 6:15 and this loading alley, coppery in the lowering sun, was nearly deserted. One truck loading back to their left. A few pickups and sedans sitting forlorn against shut warehouse doors.

"Wife said 15A, right?" said Ramirez. The "wife" was that of Friesen's now-*ex*-business partner, Rajiv Singh. She'd given them the exact address of the warehouse Re-Link rented space from, told them Rajiv rarely came home before seven.

Sweetness nodded then signaled him to slow down. She pointed to the two cars nosed against 15A's wooden walls. One was Singh's Sebring; she recognized it from the time she'd seen the man at Friesen's house. The other looked like a lime green pimpmobile, fitting the description of the Cadillac that had been rented at the airport that morning. Sweetness had no doubts it belonged to Ray Aznar.

"Tracking down everyone Luka's had contact with, I get," said Ramirez. "But—"

"Keawe attacked Friesen's family then committed suicide. Supposedly. But what if he was in league with Friesen?"

"That's what said!"

"Which shows you're as paranoid as a—what did you call Aznar?—'a sick psycho pussy?' I don't think for a second Friesen was in bed with Keawe, but Aznar might suspect it. Which means that Friesen and Friesen's business partner and warehouse are possible targets. Keep driving."

Ramirez ducked his head lower and drove past and pulled up on the far side of the last warehouse. Without a word, he shut the car down and pulled out his FBI-issued Springfield .45. Checked the clip.

Sweetness pulled out her own weapon-of-choice, a Desert Eagle .50 Magnum and did the same. She noticed Ramirez checking the weapon out. The Desert Eagle was a big gun. Not as good as a shotgun or high-powered rifle for taking someone down, but guaranteed penetration. With a snugged-down Jackass shoulder holster, she could wear it under her jacket without it being obvious to the average person. Those who would notice, well, it was probably a good thing if they were a little intimidated.

"I figured you for a .357 or 9 mm," Ramirez said.

"Because?"

"All that karate shit. I figured you liked to beat your guys up in close and personal."

"There are times when I can't get as close to them as I am to you." She leveled her gaze on him until he shrank back. "You ready?"

He nodded and they both climbed out.

~~~~

"We're not going to die, Josh," I said finally and looked around at the others. "No one's going to die."

"Fletch died," Martha said. "Mr. Harbell."

I shot her a dark look and she got up from the table to huff over to the door to the living room. She crossed her arms over her chest.

My father's hearing hadn't failed him on this one. He turned to gawk at Martha. "Fletch died? When?"

"Last night," I said and held my hands out. "Sorry, but with everything else that's been going on, I...forgot to tell you."

"Sue?"

"No. Just Fletch. A fire in the barn. Cops are blaming it on smoking."

My father rubbed his jaw and the doorjamb he'd been slamming himself against moments before. They were both rough and dirty. "What're *you* thinking happened?"

I shook my head. Martha pursed her lips but when her grandfather looked at her, she shook her head too.

"The guy who killed Birdy at our place," said Josh. "He's a ghost now, following Birdy's ghost around. Hurting people."

"The guy I did the name of?" my dad said. "Who else did he hurt?"

I looked at Josh, sighed, and gave them a carefully edited version of the other attacks that might have been caused by Luka Keawe.

Martha stared at me with her color high, eyes wide. The spitting image, for a second, of her mother. "And you brought us out here to chase this guy?"

"Not to chase him," I said, not pointing out that it had actually been *her* who'd sent us out here. "To get rid of him. Or at least separate him from Birdy."

"How?"

"I...don't know exactly." I looked to my father, then to Josh, but there were only questions and fear in their eyes. "Maybe Grandpa's tombstone..."

"What?" said Martha with rising hysteria.

"Pins them down," said my father.

"Or maybe just talking with Birdy. She's talked to me once. If I can actually get her to listen..."

Martha cut me off, flinging out her hands. "I can't believe it, Dad. I can't believe you'd *do* this. This is, like, so unfair to us. You know what it's like having a mom in a mental home and a berserko dad who chases ghosts? Jesus! You know what they call me at school? You want to know?"

Daddy.

I blinked, suddenly only half-listening to Martha's tirade. Had I imagined it? Then I saw Dead-eye skitter out from his place under the table to sniff at the back door near my father. That rotting garbage smell. A sputtering sound from somewhere.

Daddy, watch out.

"Dad?" Martha stamped her foot. "Hey! Are you even listening to me?"

Dead-eye was backing away from the back door now, his hackles rising. My dad, frowning, was watching him.

The back door.

I hesitated again. It nearly cost us our lives.

The sputtering sound was clearer now, just beyond the door. As the doorknob began to turn. I sprinted and lunged for the knob just as the latch released. My body slammed the door shut. Pain whacked through my shoulder and cheekbone. My hands, suddenly slick with sweat, fumbled the turn-lock below the handle. It spun uselessly, broken. I gripped the knob with both hands to keep it from turning again.

"Davie," said my father. "What...?"

He trailed off as he finally heard it. From the other side of the wood came the distinctive sound of a rough-idling motor.

Spr-ut-put-put.

The neighbor's chainsaw. The rotting stink.

"That's just Cam from next door," my dad said. "He...prob'ly..."

The chainsaw roared to life like a million angry bees and began to rattle against the top of the door. Martha screamed. From the corner of my eye I saw her run to the butcher's block beside the sink. My dad backed away, dumbfounded, then fled to his bedroom/downstairs washroom area. Josh huddled under the kitchen table. I jumped backwards as the wood near my head finally gave way and the tip of the saw burst through, clattering the entire door as it came down.

Then the saw drew back and the doorknob turned completely.

"Luka!" Joshie screamed.

With a sputtering roar, the door flung wide.

25

THROW DOWN YOUR WEAPONS AND FREEZE!" Sweetness shouted.
"FBI!"

She stood on a series of tall metal boxes, her Desert Eagle straight-armed in front of her, aimed at the man who looked like the leader of little torture group. The target was an acne-scarred, short Mexican (Ray Aznar?) who stood two feet back from the man (Weki Naea, she presumed) who was strapped to the chair.

She trusted Ramirez to cover the bodybuilder who stood to her short guy's right, but wished they had backups for the other two. One was a slick-looking, skinny guy who had obviously been having fun cutting up Naea. The other carried a submachine gun slung loosely down by his hip. He'd begun sauntering to his right, making it impossible to cover the whole group.

Fuck that.

Sweetness, swivelled, aimed, and fired. The Desert Eagle boomed like a canon in the large space and tore out a chunk of the sauntering man's leg. No major arteries, no vital organs, but thankfully Mr. Machine Gun belonged to that segment of the population who, when they get shot, are predisposed to fall down.

The other three Mexicans weren't predisposed to give up, though. They ran in three different directions, pulling out sidearms as they fled.

It looked like Ramirez got the big man with two shots of his .45

but it didn't slow him. The man fired back with two loud cracks as he ran, including one at her that made her drop down behind a box.

The slick Mexican and the acne-scarred one Sweetness had identified as the leader had similarly dived behind stacked boxes. Not computer stuff, Sweetness noted as she herself stepped sideways and dropped down to ground level behind the metal crates she and Ramirez had snuck in behind. A couple of fork lifts were parked near the window she could see up to her left. If things went to shit, climbing those and busting out through that window was the exit she and Ramirez had planned.

Right now—

She paused and finally registered a cloying metal tang that wafted up from below her. Scanning the shadows, she saw a dark shape snugged between two upright containers. Unconscious or dead. She dropped down, confirmed the body was dead and East Indian, well-dressed, and familiar. The guy who'd visited David just yesterday. Rajiv Singh. Okay, she thought grimly, as she leapt back up to higher ground. They'd have Aznar on murder charges as well as kidnapping, assault, and battery.

A loud *budda-budda-budda-budda* told her the scrawny guy she'd hit had revived enough to get his submachine gun going. Wonderful. Sweetness flowed two boxes along her little ridge and stuck out her head just in time to watch *budda-budda* go down a second time, this time from Ramirez's gun.

A retort from the far side located one of the shooters for her and she sighted and fired, splintering wood, not flesh. She turned as a bullet fired her way helped her pinpoint another of the shooter.

The bangs and clacks and percussive shots danced back and forth. Only the submachine gun guy went down. Then Sweetness realized that Weki Naea (*better* be goddamned Naea) had revived and was jerking his wrinkled face around in terror. Sweetness rubbed her nose with her gun butt. She thought hard. Any second, one of these shots was going to go wrong and take the old man out. Worse, Aznar might decide to use Naea's death as a distraction to cover his exit.

Sweetness couldn't let that happen. Naea had too many answers she needed.

Dumping her old clip and ramming home a new one—damn seven-shot wonders—she dropped down to ground level, leaned out, fixed her eyes on Weki Naea, and got ready to run.

~~~~

The roar of the chainsaw and stench of garbage battered me back.

Then I saw the torn look on the paunchy man wielding the saw. One second "Cam" looked bewildered about what he was doing there; the next, an evil grin slid across his face and he revved the saw harder, scanning the room, drinking in our fear.

I had no question that Josh was right. This was Luka in another man's skin. I also had no question that, Birdy's protection or not, Luka intended to kill us. But the man he possessed was an innocent, damn it. Even as Martha ran to me and slapped one of the two butcher's knives into my hand, I wavered.

Luka/Cam in his evil phase saw this, roared the chainsaw, and ran at me.

I saw it all in slow motion—the unsteady steps, the bounce up and down of the racing saw as he charged. But chainsaws that size were meant to be operated from a standing position, legs wide, so Cam couldn't stop as I lunged to the right and clipped his shoulder.

He spun, off-balance, the roaring blade doing a pirouette before it sliced through the kitchen wall over the table then kicked backwards as it hit something solid. The possessed man staggered and got his balance with a gnashing, hooting noise, stink rolling off him. He turned to look at me, then around the room.

Joshie was just under the table, inches from the madman's foot. *Don't look at him.* Don't *look.*

Cam refocused on me and gave the saw two quick revs.

"Dad!" Martha shouted from near the sink. I could see her holding up her own knife, hand shaking. "We gotta knife him!"

"Martha, stay back," I said. "No one's knifing anyone."

I hadn't taken my eyes off Cam's, and now the evil face broke into a strangled laugh. He braced the chain saw's body against his right hip, squeezed the throttle button, and began to *walk* forward, saw blade straight out and roaring, stench overpowering.

Six feet. Four feet. I could hardly breathe. The heat and sound battered me. I raised my knife. I couldn't do it. I could dodge or shove him maybe, but not stab him. Sweaty hands. Two feet. *Roaring saw.* I could feel the hot wind in my face as he raised it. My muscles tensed.

~~~~

Sweetness hit Naea at a run, grabbed him and toppled him over in his chair as bullets spat the concrete near her thigh. She rolled to her feet and shot back. She hit the slick Mexican who'd been torturing Naea when she came in. He'd jumped out to blast away and now got two .50s in the abdomen, jerked a little, but kept firing.

Suddenly the guy Sweetness had pegged as Aznar came running out with his gun pointing at her, firing and screaming, "*Ay, puta! Chupe leche del pene!*" until she rolled again. She grabbed Naea's toppled chair top as she did and heaved it around her as if playing snap the whip, so Naea went skidding behind the nearest crates while she still lay exposed.

~~~~

Luka/Cam stabbed the saw forward like a sword, but I was already moving, jumping away from Martha, into the corner. Nowhere to go now. I had to do something, dive, slash. Even then, I'd put myself in a place where he was going to cut me. The only question was how deep.

Luka/Cam had staggered to his feet again and turned towards me.

I saw Martha over his shoulder. Her face was pale, her knife-hand raised with knuckles mottled from gripping the weapon tight. She tensed to leap...

~~~~

"Don't!" Sweetness shouted to distract Aznar as she popped to her feet. She'd been bruised or knocked, though. She was having trouble standing. Aznar seemed to sense it and smiled as he took three steps forward, targeted her chest, and pulled the trigger.

But as he did, two things happened. Ramirez, who'd been watching the whole deal, ran yelling and shooting at Aznar with the submachine gun he grabbed from the first shooter's body. His blasts went wide but close enough to draw the Mexican's attention so his hand pulled slightly right as he fired.

At the same time, Sweetness dive-rolled after Weki Naea, coming up with her gun turned to get Aznar.

~~~~

"Don't!" I cried, but I lifted my own knife. If someone had to kill, it wasn't going to be my thirteen-year-old daughter.

"*Wahine!*" shouted Luka/Cam and waved the roaring chain saw blade at me. Back and forth. Back and forth. Closer. The ghost was obviously getting better control. He/it added, "T-t-told her."

He came at me then with his chain saw swinging to one side like he *wanted* me to stab him. I raised my knife hopelessly.

A sudden *CRACK!* sounded close in front of me and spatters of red gore suddenly shot from the top of Luka/Cam's head to my face.

Bullet to the brain. As he fell, my dad stepped out from the alcove, his slide-action Winchester still to his shoulder.

~~~~

As Aznar snarled and lunged sideways behind the crate where the slick Mexican had fallen, Sweetness boomed off two shots. Both went

203

wide, but it gave Ramirez a chance to get cover.

Then, as if Aznar had motioned for it somehow, the hulking Mexican stepped out from nearer the warehouse door with what looked like a rocket launcher. He aimed it at where Sweetness and Naea were hiding.

"Shit!" said Sweetness and dragged the semi-conscious Hawaiian after her through the stacks of metal and wooden crates. The front row, where she and Naea had just been, went up with a loud *foom*. By the time Sweetness recovered, rammed her last clip into her gun, and limped back to the front, she saw just the tail end of the three Mexicans leaving the warehouse.

A moment later their car engine roared to life and squealed off.

"Boss!" said Ramirez, suddenly at her side. "You're bleeding."

She looked down, saw the copious quantities of blood leaking from her left thigh, and finally understood the dizziness and lack of cooperation she'd been getting from her body.

"Give...unh." She slumped backwards and had to grab the crate behind her to keep from falling over. She sat. "Your handkerchief. Give it. Then confirm the downed Mexicans and call 9-1-1. Police. Ambulance for me and Naea. Give them a description of the Caddy. Ask for an all-points. You got the license plate when we came in?"

Ramirez nodded but had trouble pulling out his phone. She saw he looked pale and his hands shook badly.

"Exciting," Sweetness said.

"Yeah." He swallowed and turned away.

She let him go on that. He'd talk to her if he had to talk. Meantime she had to bandage her wound before she bled out right here on the concrete floor. Her head felt light. Everything smelled overripe, like how she remembered the fridge in their tenement apartment growing up. Mama always bought the old vegetables and fruit to save money. Apples and lettuce always half rotten. Always smelled bad. All this blood.

She gritted her teeth and had the handkerchief tight around the wound by the time Ramirez came back to say the ambulance would be here any minute. They'd be at the Highland General in ten.

"You gonna hang on?" Ramirez said. "Gonna be okay?"

"I'll be fine."

"Cause you know... Shit, you know? All the training you do, it's nothing like the real thing."

Sweetness looked up at him, seeing him as he was, barely out of his teens. "You had it soft growing up."

He ducked his head and looked like he was going to puke. "Bel Air. Shit. My dad did movies."

"But you wanted to be a cop."

He nodded and wiped his brow.

"You did fine. How's Naea?"

"He's...he says he didn't tell them, over and over. Crazy."

"Okay...ungh...come sit. I need you to hold my hand." Meaning she knew he needed her to hold his. He pulled himself together enough to look manly as he sat and took her hand. She wrapped her fingers around his and squeezed.

"It's going to be all right," she said. "It's all over."

~~~~

"S'okay, kids," my father said as he walked to his downed neighbor and kicked him. "It's all over."

I wanted to hit him for that. Or for shooting the poor man who's only real crime was being conveniently close to us and not on his guard.

But I bit my tongue and went for the chainsaw. Because Luka had made Cam swing it wide as he advanced, it had dropped harmlessly to the linoleum, the spin stopped the instant Cam's finger left the trigger. Now it sputtered on its side, leaking oil and gas fumes. The garbage stink had vanished.

I put the butcher's knife on the table and picked up the saw. It took me a minute to figure out how to shut it down. By then Josh had crawled out from under the table and Martha had returned her own knife to the butcher's block. My father had gone to the phone near the sink and dialed the local law.

"You kids...," I said slowly. But before I could finish, Josh had flung himself at my waist and wrapped his arms around me. So had Martha, smothering her brother and my chest with sobs and squeezing me tighter than I could remember her doing since she'd been six.

"Daddy?" she said through her sniffles. Then again, "Daddy." It was all she seemed to be able to manage.

"Yeah," I said and bent my head down to press my cheek to her hair, my hands rubbing her back and Josh's arm. "Me too."

What I didn't say was that inside my stomach was clenched up like a writhing caterpillar. The danger I'd put them in... Dad's possessed neighbor had been after *me*. The chainsaw, the madness, had been to get *me*. I'd seen it in the eyes. Was Luka playing out some sick kind of beyond-the-grave revenge? Or was I somehow his way to get to Birdy?

In either case, Martha and Josh were in more danger with me than apart. I had to get them to safety somehow. I had to face Luka alone.

I chewed my lips bloody at the thought of that, sending them away, splitting us apart again. But I forced myself to straighten up even as I hugged them and saw my father staring at us, ends of his mouth curled up, eyes watering. He'd gotten off the phone and again held his gun over the body of the man he'd killed.

After a moment more, I squeezed Martha's shoulder, combed back her thatch-like hair until she looked up at me.

"I have to make a phone call," I said.

"To the police?"

I shook my head. "Grandpa's done that. I'm calling someone back in Berkeley, a doctor of parapsychology, a ghost expert."

Now Josh looked up too.

"Tonight," I said, "if we're not all stuck in the police station, I'm going up to the room where you two and Birdy stayed the last time we were out here. I'm going to hold some kind of séance, call Birdy and Luka to me, and finish this off once and for all."

26

M<small>Y HUNCH THAT</small> A<small>NGELA WOULD STILL BE AT HER OFFICE</small> when I called was correct. In fact it took me an hour of repeated calls to get through her busy signal, interrupted by the arrival of the local county sheriff and yet another series of questions for me and my kids. At least they didn't have our names from what had happened in Nevada. There were only so many "wrong place, wrong time" stories I figure most cops would accept.

As it was, I got through to Angela around nine o'clock and was frustrated to find her reluctant to help. She grew even fussier when I told her what had happened in the last two days.

"Let me get this straight," she clipped out. "You've been actively seeking contact with your little girl and so far two more people have died."

"Yes."

"And you have your other two children with you."

"I said that."

"Put my daughter on the phone."

"She's not here, Angela. This doesn't really concern her. The local cops have ruled it clear self-defense. They're friends of my dad. Didn't even drag him back to town. Just took pictures and hauled away the body."

"The body?" I heard her let out a long breath. "All right, David, look. *Forgetting* for the moment that all these people are dying in the same manner as the ones my daughter was assigned to investigate, are you really so dense that you don't see how she feels about you?"

It was out of the blue and I was struck dumb for a second. A tumble of images burst through my mind—Sweetness writing her name on a paper and sticking it to my cell phone; her coming to rescue me out of Lincoln Park; staying the night and how I'd had my first good night's sleep in months; waking up to find her sitting half-naked in my living room, drenched in sweat; her almost-jealous behavior when her mother held my hand. And my response to her? Animal. Automatic. And strictly impossible. I wasn't some Lord Rochester who emotionally abandoned his crazy wife. I couldn't believe Sherry was lost to me. Not yet.

"You call her," I said. "Tell her what I've told you." I gave her the exact address and how to get here. "And tell her that she'll find my kids staying in the town's one hotel with my dad. The Hotel Astrid. You got that?"

"Pardon me?" said Angela.

"What?" said Martha and Josh at the same time as they hung near the phone. My father frowned with his lower lip so far out he looked like he was trying to dislocate his jaw.

"Like you implied," I said into the phone, "it's criminally irresponsible to have my children here with me for this. To have anyone near me, for that matter. So I'm sending them to safety."

The clamor that broke out around me made it impossible to hear the phone at all. Martha's "No fucking way, Dad!" stuck out gratingly. So did the scornful look on my father's face, a powerful flashback to that night when I'd broken down as a child, crying over a gopher with a severed head.

When they'd finally shouted enough for Joshie to break down crying, I got a second round of it from Angela by phone. "Are you insane, David?"

"*What?*" I snapped.

"Yes, you were stupid to drag your children into this, but you cannot send them away now."

I pictured her tossing her carefully coiffed hair. I ground my teeth together and glared at the shaking heads of Martha and my father. "Why," I said slowly, "can I not send them away now?"

"Because that's just what Luka wants you to do, to split up your family, split up your little girl's identity support."

"Her what?"

"David," Angela said, "I do not pretend to know exactly what your evil friend Luka is doing to your dead daughter, but it obviously involves shaking her up and severing her ties to you. You and your family are her identity, do you understand? You give her the persistent personality signature she has. If she loses that, then only he will be in control.

"Besides which"—she took a pause for an audible intake of courage—"you will need your children and father to properly perform a séance."

"No."

"Yes, David. You need a group, the four of you. Six is even better. If you wait until my daughter and her partner—"

"It doesn't work that way!" I said and wanted to smash the phone. "You talk about Luka getting more control? Well I can feel that, okay? I could see it today. If he somehow leaves here before I deal with him..."

"He won't leave, David," said Angela. "He wants to deal with you too. But you need to do it right. Wait for Gale and her partner."

"No."

There was a silence like we were facing off over the phone line. She broke first. "All right. I'll tell you how to proceed, but only if you promise to follow my instructions down to the letter. Understood?"

I nodded and closed my eyes. "Go ahead."

"No, you have to write this down. Do you have a pen and paper?"

I opened my eyes to find my father and two children still watching me, Josh sniffling. Looking around the messy phone desk, I found a pad of yellow foolscap and a pen that worked. Before I began writing, I ordered Martha and Josh to take baths and was about to add, "and change into your pajamas," when I reflected that might not be the best gear for a potentially life-threatening ceremony. Understanding they weren't about to be sent away after all, they both nodded and silently left the kitchen. Martha had her lower lip thrust out like she'd won. Josh looked terrified.

"Okay," I said, turning my focus back to the telephone receiver. "Go ahead."

~~~~

Twenty minutes later, Nightingale Sweetness raised her head from her hospital bed pillow as Ramirez rushed into the room. He'd still had her cell phone when they'd checked her and Naea into Highland General, so he'd been the one to take her mother's call.

As he relayed it to Sweetness now, she felt her stomach tighten inside her as she imagined what David and his kids had been through. Worse, she could hear her mother's voice through the message Ramirez conveyed and caught the note of panic.

Which wasn't like Angela. She explored the weird and believed in spooky things, but she never panicked.

Sweetness pushed herself up to sitting with a groan, trying to ignore the pounding pain in her bandaged thigh as she swung her legs down over the side of the bed. "Okay...unh...this is what we're going to do," she said, then stopped for a second to grit her teeth and keep enough blood in her head. "You call up one of the local airports here. I think there's one at Livermore, one up near Concord. Book us a charter plane for ASAP tonight, four-seater. Then discharge Naea and me. We're all going."

"But—"

"Just do it!" She swayed a little and touched her forehead. "Please." Ramirez nodded and ran.

~~~~

The summoning, or calling of ghosts, Angela said, had less to do with ritual and paraphernalia then with mindset and intention. Chalking a "magic circle" on the ground to contain the ghosts, however, might be effective as a psychological snare, since the ghost we were calling was effectively seven years old and suggestible. The tagalong ghost might also be suggestible, since he obviously had resorted to Hawaiian magic in the past. Angela described some symbols to put at the north, east, west, and south points of the circle which she said were Polynesian and sometimes used as wards against evil.

The one critical factor in this séance, Angela stressed, was everyone holding hands and keeping them joined. It was a symbol of our unity as a family, something which Birdy's ghost could hold onto and which would help strengthen any individual member of the circle whom Luka might attack.

The idea of forming solid bond with my father had made me almost overrule this, but then I figured there were four of us. I'd hold my kids' hands. I wouldn't have to hold my dad's.

It was almost ten-thirty by the time we'd gathered in the upstairs main bedroom, sitting cross-legged inside a circle chalked onto the cracked gray linoleum. Martha was to my right, Josh to my left. My dad had agreed to join in, "for the bird's sake." His version of cross-legged was more loose and hunched so that his outstretched boots almost touched the flickering candle I'd put in the middle of our circle. I'd left on the small lamp by the double bed behind me as a fail-safe; the night was cold black outside the single dormer window and the air had that thick feel it got when a storm was rising. Dead-eye lay just outside the chalk line. His eyebrows twitched each time one of us shuffled around.

Everyone had joined hands and waited for me to begin, but my mouth was unaccountably dry. It was as if starting this little ritual was a commitment to see it through to the end. Tonight. And since I had no idea how to steer this the way we wanted...

"Okay, Dad," Martha said. She rocked back and forth on her butt. Her hand was hot and twitchy in mine, uncomfortable at our physical contact. The hug from earlier was obviously forgotten.

"Give me a minute," I said.

"Like we haven't heard that before," she muttered.

"Pardon me?"

"Nothing."

"Fine." I took another deep breath. Another. Avoided my dad's rolling eyes.

"Jesus Christ," said Martha.

"Excuse me," I said and squeezed her hand a little too tightly.

"Ow. Fuck."

"Nice mouth your kids have got there, Davie," said my father, as if he too wanted to help distract from what we were here for.

"That's enough," I said. "Everyone."

"Yeah. Of course," Martha said. "For you. You're scared, aren't you, Dad. Admit it."

My father huffed a laugh of agreement.

Josh began whimpering to my left. In the state I was in, I wanted to shake him.

Daddy.

Oh, great. Here we were. "Sh!" I said.

Josh whimpered loudly and Dead-eye lifted his head to whine. "This is fucking stupid," Martha muttered, oblivious.

Go away, said Birdy's voice in my head.

What?

Please.

"Be quiet, Martha!" I said.

She glared at me and I closed my eyes. But I could get nothing now. Birdy had come and gone. Gone. And I had barely even been able to sense her this time. I'd been too distracted, too emotionally torn to even—

"Mom told me you'd do this, you know," said Martha quietly to my right.

"Do what?"

"Be too scared about hurting anyone to actually *do* anything."

"That's what she said?" I said. Then, unable to help myself, "When?"

"All the time."

I was about to say something but bit my tongue. I could hear my father shuffling his feet, his legs probably arthritic from years of labor. Or maybe it was satisfaction at discovering his son was just as he'd pegged him so long ago. Scared. Ineffectual.

The walls creaked a little as the wind that had been building since dinner swept over the house and pushed it so the closed dormer window behind Martha rattled in its frame. Dead-eye whined. I thought I could smell the wet smog from the potash pits to the south.

"Someone farted," Martha said. "Josh?"

Josh whimpered and shook his head. His hand was sweaty and scared in mine. My genes obviously. Whereas Martha, with her hot, twitchy hand, had obviously gotten her mother's. Like gut-punching honesty under stress. How much more was there? Something about Sherry's infidelity maybe. If Sherry had been so sure I was a coward.

"How long we gonna sit?" said my father.

"As long as it takes!" I said.

"Stinks in here," he said and shuffled again.

I was going to snarl something about the potash pits and leaving a window open, when Dead-eye jumped to his feet and padded in a growling circle around us, his hackles fully raised.

"Oh, shit," I whispered.

"Oh, shit," repeated Martha beside me, still not catching on. "Oh, shit. Oh, fuck. Oh, Jesus-fucking-motherfucker."

"Martha!" I squeezed her hand hard, my face flushed hot. Dead-eye was brushing by me like an electric charge.

"Ouch! This is like that table-pounding thing, hunh? You get mean for the *important* things. You can send Mom to a stupid hospital, for instance..."

"Martha, don't," said Josh.

"Listen to him," I said.

"Listen to him. Listen to him. Little wimpy Joshie."

"Don't."

"Let go of me, Dad!" She was shaking her left hand that I was squeezing so hard. The windows were rattling with the growing storm outside. "I don't want to *be* here!"

"Just sit still!" I said.

"No!"

"For Birdy," I said. "For your sister!"

"My sister's *dead!*" she shouted. "Let her *go!*" She shook my hand hard and my father's too now, trying to stand up. My father rocked back and forth with the strain of holding her. His head rolled from side to side.

"Sit DOWN!" I roared, trying to pull her back. I was choking on the stink in the room. I needed to open a window.

"Let me go! Let me go! Ahhhhh!"

She broke into a red-faced, screaming tantrum. Josh began wailing to my left. My father groaned and shook like he was having some kind of attack as he held Martha's right hand. The wind howled and rattled the windows. Jesus *Christ!*

"Go then!" I shouted and flung her hand away from me.

She tumbled backwards. Her screams and Josh's wails both stopped in surprise.

Even the wind stopped for a second.

Then my father grunted hard and I saw his eyes roll back in his head. His hands, still holding Martha's and Josh's, shook wildly. The smell I'd thought was sulfur from outside rolled off *him* now. Pungent, rotting garbage.

Dead-eye stopped circling. He snarled and backed away from his owner.

"Daddy? Daddy?" Josh said, high and quick. His nostrils flared as he stared at his grandpa and tried to draw back his hand from the old man's grip.

"No!" I shouted. "Keep holding on, Josh! Martha, take my hand again! We've got to call Birdy to us for protection. Come on!"

Her face white, Martha scrabbled back inside our chalk circle and grabbed my hand. We began saying Birdy's name over and over. Calling. Beseeching.

But even as we did, my father became more and more agitated. He couldn't seem to tear his hands free from his grandchildren, but the rest of him began doing a strange dance. His head jerked up then down, then back up again, his torso and legs twitched.

"Come on, Birdy," I muttered. "Join us here. Separate. Help us fight Luka. Help us beat him."

"Birdy," Josh cried beside me. "Come on, please."

"Birdy Birdy *Birdy*..." called Martha.

"Come on, honey," I said. "Help us. Come."

Dead-eye barked. The candle in the middle of our foursome began to flicker wildly. Then—a presence! Happier and brighter than Luka's, but...scared?

"Yes!" I cried. "It's okay, honey. Show yourself. Right here. Inside the circle."

My dad kicked his legs like he was trying to kick over the candle, but his eyes were squeezed shut and he missed. A form started to coalesce in the air in our circle. My little girl. Seven years old with white-blond hair, wearing Winnie-the-Pooh pajamas, kneeling with her hands pressed tight to her cheeks, eyes wide in fear.

"You...," she said softly, audibly so that even Martha, silent now and blinking her eyes furiously at what she saw, obviously heard it. "You should all run away," she said.

"We're not running, Birdy," I said. I tried to sound sure. "W-we're safe in this circle. You're safe. It's protection."

Birdy shook her head at me and my heart plummeted. I had never, in all the years from the time she was a baby right to the last moments I saw her on our roof at home, seen that look in her eyes. Fear, yes, anger, even fleeting sorrow, but never despair.

Until now.

Dead-eye's frantic barking caught my attention and I looked to its source. My father, blank-faced, bum-wiggling backwards. His seat smudged, then broke the protective ring I'd drawn.

A shock whipped through my hands, and both Josh and Martha cried out, releasing their grip on their grandpa. Then my dad flung himself backwards like he'd been hit by a truck, thumping onto his head and shoulders and flipping over them to crash face down, arms spread, knees bent up where his work boots hit the chest of drawers I'd kept my clothes in as a child.

He lay still, but Dead-eye continued to growl and the smell still roiled. I looked for Birdy. She'd vanished.

"Dad?" Josh tugged at my hand.

"What?"

"Holy shit," murmured Martha.

I looked back towards the dresser and saw my dad dragging his knees and arms under him, pressing himself up. One boot. The other. Standing.

When he raised his head and looked at us, though, it was no longer my father. The eyes that stared across the six feet of cracked gray linoleum were as black as the night outside. The pupils swallowed everything.

He gave a slow, sly smile and stepped towards us.

27

WE WERE GOING TO DIE.

But instead of my whole life flashing before my eyes, I saw the one day my father believed in me.

I was nine. Tim had convinced my dad to go hiking with me through the mountains. It was when Tim had recently started working in the mine and the old man was happy as spit. That was the reason, I think, that he deigned to give his younger, "waste of skin" son one Saturday afternoon.

I didn't care why. I led him excitedly up through Whistler's Trail northwest of us then cut back towards First Peak. It was a two hour climb, but there was a spot near the top that suddenly opened up in a sloping field. From there you could see the whole river valley; our town and house looked like little white peas. And when we reached it that day, it was *perfect*. The air smelled like sweet moss. Two stellar jays screeched and fought over a blasted jack pine grown out of a rock down to the right.

I turned to my dad. He'd walked right past my spot and kept climbing like he'd forgotten I was there.

Crestfallen, I hesitated then plunked myself down on a rock. I took from my backpack the charcoals, sketchbook, and watercolors my mother had bought me for my ninth birthday. I carefully poured some water into a plastic cup for my paints, set it into the grass beside me, and decided to capture the fighting jays and the blasted jack pine.

Streaks of movement, black wood, washboard clouds...

I entered such a state of flow as I sketched, did a blue-green wash, roughed-in the landscape, that I lost track of everything else. No ghosts came that day, no insects stung. But somewhere in the middle of it, my dad returned to stand at my shoulder unnoticed. He might have been there ten minutes or forty. When I finally looked up with a start, he was standing still as an oak, his heavy mouth slightly open, his eyes fixed on my work.

I moved to pack it all away but he stayed me with a big blunt hand. His eyes moved from my crude painting to the scene it had tried to capture.

Finally he nodded and took his hand away. He didn't say a word all the way back down the mountain.

Later my mother told me that he came to her and asked how long I'd been painting, whether I'd had lessons, and where all the rest of my pictures were. When my mother dug them out of my and Tim's room (I kept them under my bed in an old Sears, Roebuck box), he examined each one of them slowly and finally chose six to take into town and get framed at the glassworks shop.

They hung around our home until the day I left it, the only art, other than a photo of him and his mining crew that some journalist had taken once, that my father ever put on our walls.

He hung the one of the fighting stellar jays on the wall beside my bed. As if he wanted me to remember he'd been there with me.

Now, as he shuffled one foot towards me with Luka's sly smile on his face, I realized with a shock that the grime-coated picture on the wall behind him, over my childhood bed, was that picture.

"Get behind me," I snapped to Martha and Josh.

They did, both scrambling around the metal-framed double bed that had been Tim's growing up.

The thing that had been my father sniggered at us, a sound my father had never made in his life. He was always booming, pressing, driving, puking. He never sniggered or whispered. Yet now he did. "S-s-son," he croaked with difficulty and sniggered again.

"Get back," I said. My eyes shot right and left to find something I could use as a weapon. My brain zinged hot, kicking me for not seeing this possibility or something like it. Hadn't I learned? Hadn't I seen two other possessions already?

The circle.

Oh, sure. That had worked well. And holding hands. I'd blown that one.

Dead-eye was growling and circling his changed master now, his canines fully exposed. But his target turned to him and snapped, "Shut it!" so commandingly that Dead-eye whimpered and dropped back.

"Birdy!" Martha cried. "Help us!"

Josh joined in while my own body shook with adrenaline and I took a clenched fist, karate pose. The memories of Luka in our house suddenly rushed back. This time it was Martha and Josh with me. And this time the monster would *not* pass.

"Back off," I said.

That seemed to amuse my father—it was hard to think of him as anything else—and he crinkled his black-pupil eyes. Straightening up, he gestured at his own chest, as if to say *Come on.*

I hesitated, then catapulted forward. Hitting him in the chest, I drove him back so we crashed against the wooden dresser on the far wall. It thumped the paint, shaking the picture of the battling jays off its hook so it crashed down left of us, shattering between the bed and wall.

But my nose was full of my father—his farm sweat, the rot of Luka's ghost. I fought to keep his larger body jammed against the dresser and wall as I tried to grab his thick arms. As I did, he reared his head back and butted me hard on my nose.

Pain exploded like the front of my skull had cracked open. Wet warmth gushed down over my mouth. Sparks filled my eyes.

My father shoved me backwards and staggered after. I felt, as much as saw, him coming. My hands and shirt front were covered with blood. Everything was hot copper in my nose and mouth. Bubbling wet. Drowning. Martha and Josh screamed. I had to save them, but I could hardly see. My head swam. Vision dimmed. My father lumbered past me. I was going to pass out.

Then Dead-eye threw off his earlier command, lunged for his changed master's leg, and sank his teeth deep. The man yelled and whipped around.

And Martha—I could just see her as my vision started to clear— leapt from the bed to grab an old metal barometer that sat on the windowsill. She ran with it towards her staggering grandfather, swung it hard at his face. It thudded against his cheek and snapped his head back.

He shook it off and grabbed Martha, but I could see now. Through a roar that must have come from my own throat, I jumped at him and battered his hands loose. Then I grabbed his shoulders and kneed him in the crotch like I remembered Tim doing to a schoolyard bully.

The old man's face blanched and he dropped to his knees. But the force of Luka was still inside him, disconnected from his pain. It swept over his face and opened his mouth in a wordless rictus. He got one booted foot under him. The other. Dead-eye rushed him only to get whacked back to the wall beneath the window.

Then George Alden Friesen turned towards me and snarled, his eyes their frightening black, Luka's stench rolling off him.

"Come...on...*wahine*," he said. He thumped his chest again in challenge, then pointed to Josh and Martha, both back on the bed again. "I...kill them like I kill your little girl."

That snapped it. The threat to my kids, the vestigial memory of my drunk dad slapping around my mother—they drove me at my father without a sound, hitting him so hard that I carried his larger body back with me to my childhood bed and collapsed on top of it like lovers.

There my father/Luka fought back, but even with his massive strength it didn't matter. I battered his face with my fists, not sure or not caring whether it was my father or Luka I was hitting. The blood from my smashed nose sprayed across each of us so we were slick with it, tangled and spitting, grunting.

Until one of my full-bodied rights missed my father's face and rolled me sideways. As I scrambled up in the gory bedcovers, the old man did the same. Faster.

A fist to my stomach drove the air out of me and he jumped on top. He went for my throat as I retched. In desperation I rolled. The slickness of the blood let me twist over to my stomach, my right cheek mashed against the wall, eyes down.

I saw the broken picture glass.

Down there, between the wall and the bedframe, the picture of the stellar jays lay ripped between pieces of broken wood and glass like my shattered childhood reaching up to me.

My father was punching me in the back now, trying for my kidneys. I tried to blank out the pain as I whipped my right hand forward and twisted it down between the side of the bed and the wall, almost impaling it on a long shard of glass before managing to reach to the base of that shard and wiggle it free of the frame.

I couldn't bring it up, though. My father must have seen what I was doing; he'd jammed a knee, with all his two-hundred-plus pounds over it, onto my right shoulder. Now his hands grabbed me by the hair, pulling back. My neck!

A running scream and thump from above told me Martha had come to my aid yet again. For a second the pressure on my shoulder and neck increased, then George/Luka yelled and twisted to throw off his attacker.

I half-saw her fly off him as I jerked my right arm up and spun my own body below my father.

My right hand was slick and red, not only from the blood of my face, but from the wounds from the grimy glass shard it clutched.

George/Luka turned back towards me, his face bared, dripping copper gore like we'd been face deep in each other's flesh. "Useless," he hissed, and went for my throat.

For a split second I couldn't move. I was just me again, the man who's biggest accomplishment of his childhood was running away from home. The man who'd been nothing, a drifting poseur, a vagrant almost, until Sherry had found me.

His hands closed around my windpipe. Squeezed.

And I saw how hard I'd worked to become strong, become someone worthy of Sherry and his children, but who was still whispered about behind his back. Still weak.

Couldn't breathe.

Still couldn't save Birdy, Sherry, because love alone wasn't enough. My father taught me that. You could love and fuck up. You could love and destroy everyone close to you.

Everything going red, weak. Dying. Because that was the Friesen way. Like father, like...

"Naagh!" I yelled, and both my hands drove the long shard of glass into my once-father's belly.

Somewhere Martha and Josh screamed. And even as I retched and coughed and felt my enemy's body convulse around the glass, I heard a gasp of terrified disappointment that seemed to come from the air itself.

Then my father was dead. I could feel it clear as a flame snuffed out, and he became just a horrid limp mass pinning me down. With the last of my strength, I pushed him off me and rolled off the bed to the floor.

Across the room, from on top the other bed, Martha stared at me, her mouth and eyes wide. Josh too, but his hand tugged Martha's at the same time, as if of its own volition.

I looked where his eyes kept darting.

In the reflection in the dark window, I thought I saw Birdy, her eyes filled with tears, shrinking away into the night.

28

SWEETNESS'S CELL PHONE WENT OFF as she was limping from the gas station, the only open business she'd found in Morris, seeking directions to the Friesen homestead. She stopped on the dark sidewalk and pulled the phone from her jacket.

"Yes?"

The phone connection crackled. Sweetness swore and looked from the dark mountains surrounding the town to the dim headlights of the rented van where Ramirez waited with Weki Naea. The old man had insisted on new boots, jeans, and jean jacket. They didn't hide the wreck Aznar had made of his face.

The crackling stopped and a voice came through. "Gale?"

Oh, wonderful. Her mother. "What?"

"I..." Her mother broke off and Gale thought for a minute the connection was failing again. Then her mother's voice resumed, more clipped and measured. "Something has happened, Gale. Out where you're going. Something involving David."

Sweetness's attention focused sharp. "Tell me."

"Gudrun and Nanna both called me, as did another medium I use occasionally who lives in Oregon. They felt a dramatic change in the bad ghost, Luka, the one you think has been killing people. Now I know you don't—"

"For God's sake spill it, Mom!"

Another pause, then Angela said, "Luka is happy, dear. In his mind, he's won."

~~~~

Sherry curled on the bed in the "secure" room, not strapped, but not given privileges and not listened to.

And she shivered. Her eyes were closed. She saw everything.

It's...not over, David. It can't be over.

This time, though she felt like she was right there with David and the children, she could not get even Josh's attention.

~~~~

Following the directions of a gas station attendant and a cluster of light in the blackest valley she'd ever driven through, Sweetness drove them to the Friesen property, pulled up behind two cop cars and an ambulance, and got out.

"Stay put, okay?" she heard Ramirez order Naea, but not the old man's response. Then her partner was at her shoulder. "We go inside?"

"In a minute."

Ignoring the rookie deputy who seemed to be the only one left outside to control access, she nodded Ramirez over to the tombstones in the front yard while she surveyed the outside of the house.

"Hey, boss," Ramirez called a second later. He was shining his flashlight on the newest looking stone, over to the side. She walked over and saw it had Luka Keawe's name on it.

She nodded to Ramirez then walked back to the rookie deputy, who now stood outside his vehicle, shifting back and forth like he had to pee.

"There any real bodies buried here?" Sweetness demanded.

He nodded. "Um...a few, yeah. Um, Tim Friesen, George's son; George's wife; two or three dogs, I think..."

"And all these other headstones?"

The rookie shrugged so that his Adam's apple bounced. "George makes 'em. He's...got this thing about ghosts. These are like his lucky charms against them."

Sweetness looked significantly back and Ramirez, who dropped his head and rubbed his little pug nose. "Runs in the family."

"Now we go inside," Sweetness said.

~~~~

Weki Naea leaned forward in the back seat of the minivan to watch the proceedings. His right eye was nearly swollen shut from his beatings and torture; his left eye was blurry. But he did not need to hear to read what was happening.

The tombstones he understood. They were markers of fear, put here by a man who was afraid of the dead. It was *hô ailona*, an omen of turning, a battle ground of spirits. Something big had happened here tonight. And if it involved this man Special Agent Sweetness pursued, David Friesen, husband of Sherry, father of Birdy, the night's outcome might be final.

Groaning in the pain of knowing at last what he was called to do, Weki reached under his rear to where he had pulled been pulling apart the van's seat cover. He turned and knotted his bruised fingers around the three feet of string he had already pulled free. With a hard tug, and another one, he felt the string tear out more. The cheap stitching unraveled beautifully. A final yank snapped it off so he had an arm's length of rust-colored cotton twill. With a chant of reverence, he tied the ends together and slipped the loops over his fingers.

It was like a familiar pair of sandals or shirt. More, it was his way through the darkness of this night.

He began chanting as he had done when he escaped the pursuit of Special Agent Ramirez, and when he had snuck in to interview Sherry Friesen about where he daughter's ghost might be. Still chanting and beginning an elaborate *hei* web that would hide him from human sight, Weki clicked open the van's sliding door and stepped out.

He padded painfully around the left side of the two parked police cars, whose lights still pulsed like angry spirits in the night.

A sound from the house made him freeze beside the fender of the front police car. Voices. A clink of glass shards in a bag.

Gruff voice: "Gotta book him."

Sweetness: "The children said he was being strangled."

"By his daddy?" said another man's voice. Sarcastic. "George just saved his life few hours ago. I know George. Never hurt a fly less he was drunk."

"But managed to smash in his son's nose and leave bruises all over him?"

"I knew Davie as a kid," said Sarcastic. "Probably had it coming."

"David," Sweetness said, "say something."

Children's voices suddenly broke in. "Dad? *Dad?*"

"Come on," said Gruff.

The tired man, obviously David Friesen, said, "Wait."

"What?"

"My kids. Can they... Can they stay with Special Agent Sweetness? Gale?"

Weki had to strain to hear her answer, "Of course."

"Dad," said a girl's voice. "I want to come with you!"

"No!" Friesen snapped. "It's not safe! Do you understand? You saw what happened today!"

"But—"

"Look, Martha, you and Joshie go with Gale here. She'll take you back home. I'll see you as soon as I can. They know it's self-defense but they'll still have to question me. I'll be fine. I love you both, okay? Stick together. Martha? You stick with Josh. Gale...?"

There was a moment's silence and Weki imagined a desperate look passing between Friesen and Agent Sweetness, their feelings deeper than either would admit, both aware how awful the situation was. For it did not seem to Weki that the police "knew" it was self-defense at all. How to explain a ghost possession? Back in Molokai, perhaps, a man could argue ghosts in defense, but even there, he might get nowhere today. Truth was saved for the wise.

Weki's heart almost stopped as he heard the door open on the other side of the car where he stood and the gruff man spoke again. "Get in," Sarcastic said. A shuffling sound was followed by the sound of the door closing.

Gruff called back from near the front of the car. "Kyle, you take these feds through the scene while Ray finishes sketches and photos. You bag any evidence, wait around til the Ogden M.E. gets here, then come back join us at the jail, awright?"

"Ye-Yessir," answered the young deputy from the second car.

Chanting quickly under his breath, Weki faded back and around the tail of the second car and had climbed inside it by the time Sheriff Gruff started up the first. As Gruff rolled David Friesen out of the driveway and off to the police station, Weki chanted concealment under his breath and waited.

~~~~

Sweetness made the kids wait in the living room while she and Ramirez followed the bloody footprints from the downstairs bathroom, with it stash of dripping red clothes in the tub, back up the narrow stairs to a bedroom that reeked of death.

"Nobody opened a window?" Ramirez said as Sweetness led him in.

"They're all stuck," said Deputy Burton.

Sweetness and Ramirez walked the scene slowly, asking questions, putting it together. At one point Sweetness went downstairs to interview David's children again and reassure them everything would be okay.

Around twenty-past-midnight, after the Medical Examiner from Odgen had arrived and pulled the sheet off the body again to do her own examination, Sweetness ushered the kids outside after Ramirez, and Deputies Peaboden and Burton.

To Ramirez's disgust, Weki Naea was gone. Sweetness was surprised to find she didn't particularly care. "He'll turn up," she said.

"Yeah? Where?" Ramirez asked.

"Wherever Keawe, or whatever's channeling him, strikes next."

"And you know where that's gonna be."

Sweetness glanced at Martha, blinking around the driveway and black fields, trees, and mountains beyond like they could explain what was happening to her. Josh had a blanket wrapped around his body and shivered madly even though it was a warm night. Yet he seemed to be listening hard as well. Like there was something about this night that wasn't done yet.

"Maybe," she said.

Ramirez snorted. "At least we're done with Friesen."

Sweetness signaled for Josh and Martha to wait, then motioned Ramirez away from the van. When he joined her, she reached casually up to his upper right arm and squeezed her thumb into a pressure point in the armpit. He went stiff, his face pale.

"Just because you saved my life," she whispered, "you don't get to be an asshole. You say another word about David Friesen where his kids can hear you and I'll drop you, as a man and as a partner. Got it?"

His eyes flicked to the kids and his mouth dropped open like he'd truly not thought. "Uh...yeah."

Sweetness released him. "Let's find a hotel."

~~~~

Sherry panted, her face red, her body trembling and flushed. But her eyes were shut tight, trying hard to will her presence to David, then to Josh, to Martha.

But the strange little connection she'd had with them had snapped so that now she just spun in darkness. All her control was gone. She was helpless. She was Birdy.

Lost.

Afraid.

Angry now too. Very very angry. Because Daddy—*David*—had been bad. Why? She felt confused and awful. Where was Daddy? Where *was* he? Everything had changed. Everything she'd believed. Like Luka said. Everything was different now.

No! Come to me, Birdy. I'm still here.

Daddy was bad. That meant the world...was bad?

No! Birdy. Come to me, Birdy.

It meant she wasn't going to what was right any more. Right?

A foul, terrifying blackness snapped through Sherry's mind, crooning, *That's right, daughter. That's right.*

And Sherry, caught in the white-roomed prison she'd let herself be packed away in, called out desperately with her mind—*David! Whatever I have to do, I'll try to get to you! Don't give up! Don't!*

29

THE CELL WALL WAS COLD AND ROUGH AGAINST MY BACK. The cement floor harder and colder under my butt. They both smelled of disinfectant. I wished t hey'd shut the lights off completely rather than put them on this low, sputtering gloom. I was the only goddamned prisoner. What were they going to miss?

I wasn't going to try to escape, after all. I wasn't even under arrest yet, despite what Sheriff Klatt had said at my dad's house. I was just "held for questioning."

A game.

Like the noises in the other room—mutterings with my name, telephone calls, laughter.

Like the game Luka had played with me. He'd let me think he was just killing people, trying to hurt Birdy by making her watch, but that hadn't been it at all. No. He'd wanted to lure me after him. He'd wanted to threaten my kids, taunt me, scare me, and *pervert* me. Because I was the one Birdy had hung onto, the one she'd needed. And I'd failed her. Oh, Jesus. I'd killed. I'd killed my own father.

I dropped my heavily-bandaged nose down between my gauze-wrapped hands and wept. My whole body shivered like I'd caught pneumonia and my throat filled with so much mucus and blood it was hard to breathe. I coughed, wept more, and finally slept there on the floor.

When I awoke next, my head was cocked against the metal frame of the prison cot. The sputtering light had gone out. I heard no sounds but a muted snoring from the other room. Deputy Kyle Peaboden, I remembered. He said he had to sleep here when they had someone in lockup.

Fighting stabs of pain everywhere, I straightened my neck and sat up, blinking in the dark. My hands clenched and unclenched. They drummed silently on the floor, then on my legs, my chest, my head. Myself. What I'd done.

When I calmed enough to spread my hands out on the cold cement floor, I wondered if I had the guts at last to find a way to end myself. Except I couldn't, of course. Because of Martha and Josh. And Sherry. Because there was always...hope? Wasn't that what Birdy had always been about? Didn't I owe that to her?

But when I closed my eyes I saw the bleakness in hers staring back at me and shot my eyes wide again in pain.

No hope. None.

What had I done? I'd broken the contract. Broken the fundamental contract of family and civilization and there was no going back. Ever. I was...alone. Finally. I'd never get my kids back. Never get my wife or my life back. I was bottom-of-the-blackest-pit alone. Forever.

And the hours dragged on.

Somewhere in that time in the middle of the night, I ended up curled into a fetal position in the middle of my cell floor, blind and despairing as the look my dead daughter had given me. No more analysis. No more recrimination. Just...empty.

Which is when the voice spoke to me.

Hello.

It was just a whisper. It brushed so quietly through my thoughts that at first I thought it was myself.

Then it spoke again.

Hello...David.

Out of my emptiness, all I could manage was a little cry, half sob, half sigh. This seemed to encourage it. Him? Her?

It has been soooo long, said the voice and sighed in a way that made me sure it was female. But not Birdy. No. And yet...the voice seemed familiar. Like a face I'd seen once in a crowd, or some teenage girlfriend's perfume.

When you were just a child, sighed the voice.

And me too, kid, said a second, male, comically sad like an old dog, a companion on early morning walks...walks up the mountain.

"Mathilde," I breathed. "Bert."

It's about time, about time. A third voice.

I pushed myself to sitting looking around me blindly, reaching out to reaffirm I was still in my cell in Morris, Utah. "I'm losing it," I said.

Something, yes. You have lost your fear of us? Mathilde's voice. Her soft presence had been my earliest fantasies. *Or maybe the fear of yourself?*

"No," I said clearly to the dark, half hoping Deputy Peaboden would come in to shut me up. "No, I still fear myself. Or...hate myself, anyway. What I did. What I've become. There's not much left. That's why I'm back to my childhood again. Talking to nothings."

There was silence for a long moment after that, but I didn't feel the ghosts leave. They just hovered silently. Once you're mad, you don't just pop back to sanity.

Bert was the first one to speak to me again. I remembered him as one of the mine blast ghosts. Someone who always understood me somehow after my dad stopped talking to me. Now I wondered why. How awful had his own life been to relate to mine?

Listen, kid. Don't go stupid on us. You don't trust yourself yet, fine. Here's the proof. In about five minutes, there's some foreign guy with long greasy hair gonna come in through this place and get you out of here. Seems to know some stuff. You listen to him, okay?

"Gonna bust me out, hunh?" I dragged my stiff legs under me and pushed myself painfully to my feet, still feeling out around me in the dark. "Well, good. Cause I'm getting bored in here. The room service sucks. Crazy folk deserve better!"

David...

"What, Mathilde?"

Tell him now, now, urged the presence I didn't recognize.

David, you must learn to trust yourself again. It is not only your daughter who needs you. All of us...

"Ghosts?" I said.

Yes. We can feel the change this evil man brings.

"Luka."

It is not just evil to your daughter, but through her, to all of us. She can give him power he must not have, to break the separation of the living and the dead. You must stop him.

"I tried."

You must try again. You must not give up. Whatever it takes.

"Don't I get to see you this time round?"

David. It is urgent.

"What?" I spread my arms wide. "I can't get a clear answer even in my hallucinations?"

Another new voice cut through the dark in real time. Real sound. "I got answers for you, brah," it said.

And the lights came on.

~~~~

For a few seconds I could see nothing at all.

I imagined the voice was Deputy Peaboden, awake at last and in here to shut up my jabbering. Or maybe even that partner of Nightingale Sweetness.

But with my hands cupped over my squinting eyes, I could finally see Bert's foreign guy with long greasy hair come in to bust me out.

What Bert hadn't said was that the guy was Hawaiian, old, dressed like Willie Nelson in denim and cowboy boots. He held his bony hands up in front of him with some kind of elaborate cat's cradle. As my eyes adjusted I saw his face was clean-shaven but covered with bruises and bandages. Even the hands were mottled. He smiled and showed me a row of blackened teeth. I was betting it wasn't from bad oral hygiene.

"You call me Weki," he said at last. "I come get you outa here."

So saying, he collapsed his cat's cradle, produced a small ring of keys he must have fished out of Deputy Peaboden's pocket, and hobbled up to my cell door.

"Wait," I said from the middle of the cell as he slid the key in, turned it, and pulled the door open. "I can't just walk out. There's no point."

Weki Naea smiled again and this time I noticed his lips were cut up too and he had little round marks like punctures under the eyes. What on earth had this man been through? "Your wife, Sherry," he said. "She want you to live."

I jerked to the open cell door. "You know my wife? You saw her?"

Naea held his hand to his lips, nodded. "You come. I tell you."

"I...can't. My children..."

"Listen," he said. "You Martha and you Josh, they gonna be fine you stay away. Luka don't care. He only care about you little girl, you Birdy. You the only one who can stop him. Gotta be soon."

My earlier shivers returned full force. I was in a hurricane of insanity. This man knew my wife, knew about Birdy and Luka, and was telling me... telling me what my hallucinations had said—that I actually could do something.

"If...if I..."

There was a snort from the other room and Naea held up his finger. Then he carefully set down the keys on the floor, and stepped back. As he did so he pulled his cat's cradle taut again and began chanting some kind of song under his breath.

As Martha would have said, O-o-o-okay.

Go with him, David, said Mathilde's voice, pure and strong in my head.

I took a couple of quick breaths and shook my head, but then stepped out of the cell, trying to creep as my father's oversized boots slipped around my feet. We passed Deputy Peaboden and snuck out the front door. Around the side of the Sheriff's office, Naea showed me two bicycles I presumed he'd stolen.

"Quiet way," he said and climbed on. "I got car on the end of town."

Also stolen, presumably.

"What time is it?" I asked as he began wobbling away. My fight with my father had broken my watch and I'd left it in the mess in his bathtub.

"Almost too late."

I nodded, looked up at the cold darkness and set out after him.

STAY WITH ME

30

*I*N WHAT PASSED FOR HIS DREAMS NOW, Luka Keawe relived his last week in the islands.

He floated happily over the sharp coral reefs around Wailea Point, Maui. The clouds were threatening rain overhead, but below the surface it did not matter.

Through his goggles, Luka watched the seaweed and grit swish in and out below and around him. It made a constant chitter this close to shore, like the reef was hungry. It wanted to suck him into the *wana*, the spiky black sea urchins that would stab him and break off in his skin. Or into the coral itself, a living mass of edges that would rip and tear his flesh.

But it would not. Because Luka *lived* this water life. Had grown up with it. Had blood that was saltwater and a heart as strong as the tides. He even studied forbidden *huna* with a Molokai priest now to control the fish and crawling creatures. *You lie down and die*, he could order, and they would.

And this worked on humans also. He could make them overtip when he brought them towels. He could growl and make them leave the poolside. They feared him.

The power!

Still, he thought with a sudden laugh inside, he'd give up all of this to keep the even greater thing he'd found at last. Love.

Oh, yes, brah. Love.

As he thought it, he swooshed himself back with his hands—it made his fingers pulse—and took a quick breath above the water to look for his companion.

There, five feet away, Jennifer Makeula snorkeled in a pink string bikini, all she needed in this warm water. Her long black hair floated back behind the rubber strap of her mask and snorkel like a sheet of satin on the water. She kicked her flippers slowly behind to steady herself in the growing waves. And when Luka ducked his head down to watch her, his eyes could pick out every bump of her nipples and cleft of her *nohea*. She had no extra fat, this girl. She was a gymnast back in Los Angeles, studying to be a veterinarian. Strong and quick and smart. She had white teeth like shells and a silver laugh. When he had first seen her as he passed out the towels last week, his breath had caught in his chest. He had almost tripped over a patron of the hotel. She had seen and giggled. And he'd looked for her each day after that by the pool. He could not speak to her, never once thinking of his usual tricks, his gift of manipulation. But finally she had spoken to him. Then he'd opened to her like a child, even told her tricks he pulled, the *huna* he studied.

She had chosen to walk with him openly at first, not ashamed. Then, when her father had objected, she met with Luka secretly, kissed him, and gave him the hot flower of her girlhood.

Luka's cock stiffened as he remembered. He'd been no virgin of the body, but a virgin to love. And to fall in love with someone so very fine...

She saw him watching her and her eyes dropped to the front of his swim trunks. She grinned around her mouthpiece. It made him stiffen more and his heart squeezed unbearably. Oh, if her parents only knew. If they only saw how he could make Jennifer smile like a rainbow and scream like a monkey in the borrowed rooms of the hotel. Under his fingers, his tongue, his cock.

Someday soon, he would tell them. He would walk up to Mr. Makeula and use all his wiles on him. And the man, like all the other rich men Luka had beguiled this year, would see things his way. Would see that of course his daughter must stay here on Maui with Luka. This was the place for her. This was—

The daydream cut as he finally took in the strain behind her smile. Her eyes were frightened. Her neck, jaw, and mouth were tense.

Luka swam to her and she motioned him up. As they lifted their heads, the air hole of her snorkel dipped into a wave. She got a mouthful of salt water and choked, frantically spat it out and left the snorkel out of her mouth for good.

Luka almost laughed. Jennifer Makeula was by heritage a full Hawaiian, something Luka would never be because of his white mother. Yet Jennifer had been born and raised in California. At twenty-one, this was her first visit to the islands. She had never, before today, even snorkeled a coral reef.

Then he saw she was truly afraid.

"It's getting rough!" she said. She spat more salt water from her mouth.

Luka trod water and lifted up his goggles, his only gear. He looked at the sky. Overcast. Gray. The wind that blew unceasingly on this side of the island was stronger, true. It thudded over his ears. Whitecaps and surfing curls leapt along the shoreline where earlier there had been only gentle chop. It made him bob easily up and down with the swell.

But Jennifer kept rising up and falling back awkwardly as she did panic kicks. He noted she was also letting herself get carried in towards the shore's coral break.

"Farther out!" he called and gestured.

She looked, saw what was happening, and kicked after him like there was a shark on her tail. He caught her as she passed and made her come up again.

"Okay," he said close to her face.

But even as he spoke, the wind seemed to take a breath then let it go in a gush of splattering rain. Ricochets stung their faces and everything around them went hazy with rain. Luka saw Jennifer inching back towards panic.

"Sh-sharks?" she said, giving her jerky little flipper kicks. "Or hitting the reefs? The signs on the beach..."

"No problem, hotness," Luka said, mimicking his father's pidgin because she always found it amusing. "It be too early for the bad *mano*. And under the water, the fish, they don't care. You look."

So saying, he brought down his goggles, adjusted them, took a breath, and went under. The whoosh and patter cut out, but the chittering was louder. And the fish closest them, a large school of blue Rudderfish, *nenue*, with an arm long yellow cornet fish above them, were swept sideways to the coral then just as dramatically swept back.

Completely normal. But something in their movements troubled Luka. He raised his feet behind him, dove down almost fifteen feet to be among them, and suddenly knew.

The fish didn't slide away.

In fact, they seemed hardly aware he was there. As if stunned, they swept in and out with the current. A striped unicorn fish the size of a dinner plate, its spine an iridescent purple, swept by Luka and actually brushed his leg before the unicorn flapped his fins and fluke enough to turn towards Luka's face.

It stared at him, eyes unblinking and black. *Who are you?*

The chittering grew louder around him and Luka whirled in sudden panic to see where Jennifer was. The churn was so bad now he couldn't see her. Looking up, he saw the water roiling high above, a full storm now. What had he been thinking keeping Jennifer out so long? Her instincts this once had been better than his. Not because of reef breaks or sharks, but there were other dangers when the currents moved this fast on the leeward side of the island. Jellyfish, of course, the worst being the dreaded *pololia*, the strangely named Portugese...

Man-o'-war!

A smack of them appeared in his line of sight suddenly, drifting perhaps eight feet below the churning surface. More than just a smack. This was a swarm. Thirty, forty, hundreds...thousands. The longer he looked, desperate for a sight of Jennifer, the more he could see. Their purple air sac bodies, like wrinkly tits with coiled threads drifting below, came towards him in a spongy mass. A uniform mass, not high and low, but all on a plane eight feet down.

This explained why they hadn't been spotted far out by the usual beach trackers. It was almost as if these poisonous lumps of jelly had volition, had *wanted* to sneak into shore and done so by exercising the only movement control they had—vertical. They'd sunk as one to the lower currents, out of sight, to be carried straight towards the Luka and Jennifer.

The last thought snapped him from his horrible awe and he shot for the surface, his lungs desperate and his stomach turning and twisting inside him. If she was still up here, he had to tell her to *stay* up, stay flat on the surface and kick to the side. Because while one sting from a *pololia* was painful and rarely fatal, thirty stings, a hundred, could easily kill.

"Jennifer!" he yelled as he broke the surface, his eyes whipping about.

The waves were whitecaps now, choppy and churning, the rain a steady downpour now. He couldn't see her! And the Man-o'-war, they must be almost under him by now.

He swam towards where she'd been last and was about to duck under to check when he caught sight of her in the waves. She was floating face down, not moving. Dead?

No! Her flippers were still beating their irregular rhythm. Luka's heart, as he breaststroked towards her with his legs up flat near the surface, was thudding hard and fast. The fear she'd shown earlier... What must she be feeling now to look down on this field of death below her! She who had no connection to any of this. She for whom everything must be a threat.

Luka ducked his face for just a second to assess their situation as he neared her. The *pololia* were spread below them as far as he could see, a wobbling purple blanket so complete under this rain-spattered water that they even seemed to have caused a calming of the waves immediately above them.

He lifted his face and confirmed it. He and Jennifer were in an area of calm, like a giant flattening whose edges he could just make out through the downpour.

Reaching forward, he touched Jennifer's arm. She jerked in shock, raising her mask and starting to sink her body vertical.

Luka shook his head furiously and motioned her to keep her feet up. Then he gestured her to follow him and began his methodical, flat-to-the-surface breaststroke towards the nearest edge of the calm, unfortunately further from the beach but it couldn't be helped.

He wanted her just to swim, lift her mask high enough to follow him and kicked for all she was worth. Instead, she struggled to raise her face and imitate his own stroke, awkward with her flippers. She spat out her snorkel and gasped, "Wh-what...?"

"Jellyfish!" he shouted back to her through the rain. "Many many jellyfish! You do not want to drop your feet to touch them! Swim ahead of me to get clear! Fast as you can!" He pointed the direction for her.

She nodded jerkily, but just before putting her snorkel back in, shouted, "You didn't call them all here, did you? Just to impress me!"

Before he could answer that even he did not have such power, she'd cleared her snorkel with a huff of air and set off like the toned little athlete she truly was.

He watched her cut a strong line through the rain-spattered water with a sigh of relief and pride, then set out after her with a strong front crawl.

He considered her words as he cut through the water. *You didn't call them all here, did you?* Because she knew what he studied, had seen his gift for impressing his will on other creatures. His mother, a Russian mail-order bride, had told him he was conceived in a time of pestilence and disease to both animals and people. But she had kept their house safe with old magics until the day the village elders had dragged her out to be flayed alive in a field of taro. They had ceased only when Luka, still barely developed in her womb, had kicked out with such force that the elders saw it and drew back in fear.

"They obeyed you, even then," she'd said to him many years later. "All things, all people will obey you."

Yet why, he thought as he raced over the purple swarm below him, would he call such death to himself?

Others called them, he almost heard his mother whisper. *But not to you.*

With a flicker of horrific premonition then, he looked forward as he swam. Some thirty yards ahead, kicking her flippers and using her muscular gymnast's arms, Jennifer looked to be almost clear of the *pololia*. Another ten seconds maybe and this unthinking strangeness would be behind her, then behind them. And the thrill of escaping death, that would surely be an excitement to—

What was this?

Luka's stroke stuttered and his heart sank at what he saw.

Ahead of him under the water, the far edge of the Man-o'-war swarm was rising up. Jennifer's kick stuttered too, stopped. Then her head jerked, swiveling her entire body one way, then the next. She finally chose to go left, towards the shore, and kicked furiously in that direction.

But a line of Man-o'-war rose up there too. As if it could see her, or feel her. As if it could think. Hunt.

No. Luka began swimming desperately towards Jennifer. But just as lines of *pololia* had risen up to block her escape, now they rose up to block Luka reaching her.

Impossible.

His heart was thudding so hard in his ears now that he thought his head would burst. He could see Jennifer through the forest of stinging tentacles. She was turning every which way, looking for escape, looking for Luka.

Then, just as he considered trying to jump, porpoise-like over the line of *pololia* between him and Jennifer, the entire wobbling bed beneath her rose up as one.

Even through the water and pounding rain above, he could hear her scream.

~~~~

"Daddy read me about jellyfishes," Birdy said to him, angrily making the garden around her wither and blacken. "They don't do that."

He rolled over in her ferns. "They did it. Bad men made them. They were jealous of my power."

With her he never used pidgin. When he had tried, she'd laughed and told him to stop. He never asked how she could see inside his dreams either. He expected this closeness. It was why he had sucked in her last breath when he had killed her. Both his father's lore and his mother's talked of this. The stealing, the joining, of souls.

Yet little Birdy Friesen was too special to be simply absorbed or manipulated. No. She was the one Weki told him he must find, the 'ī ane, the great breath of life, the doorway between the land of the dead and that of the living, Luka's way back to Jennifer. But for Luka to win this power into himself would take one final piece of careful maneuvering. He had separated her from her mother and father. Now he must show no more anger himself but gradually blacken the darkness he had planted in her until it matched his own and he could absorb her or eat her soul. Weki had been unclear on the actual method but assured Luka he would know what to do when the time came.

"How come?" said the little seven-year-old, suddenly in front of him, scowling.

"What?"

"How come you want to see her again. She's dead."

And as if it was *she* controlled *him* then, drawing the memories, the decision, straight from his mind...

~~~~

A resort lifeguard boat that had found them, Luka kicking for shore, dragging Jennifer's unconscious, red-streaked body behind him. The two lifeguards hadn't believed him about the Man-o'-wars but they'd pulled Luka and Jennifer aboard. The rain pounded down as the boat raced them for shore. Luka didn't care.

It had been only ten minutes before the swarm had released Jennifer and sunk down again to different heights so they could drift apart. But for Luka the world had changed completely. There was great horrible magic in it beyond what he had studied. Great *dark* magic, slapping back at him.

"Good job, mate," said the medic as the boat thumped over the shoreline surf. He was blocky, blond and muscular, calmly balancing beside Jennifer's prone body as he jabbed some kind of needle into her thigh.

"Heh?"

"Got all the bits of tentacle off, right? All that water swished over her. I just gave her some eppy. Get her breathing again." And now he had tilted her head back to give her mouth to mouth resuscitation for three or four breaths even as the pilot ran them up onto the beach.

In the uproar that followed, Luka recalled only that Mr. and Mrs. Makeula were there. They had somehow discovered Jennifer missing and tracked her path through questioning. It was clear from their looks they believed Luka was responsible for this.

Luka himself stumbled about numbly on the outside of the crowd, trying to see Jennifer, to see if she was breathing again. The fear stench alone almost pushed him back. The parents and all these emergency people from the resort who tried desperately to revive her until the ambulance came and rushed her away—they all stank of fear.

And the few glimpses Luka caught of Jennifer's body told him why. That perfect tautness, his sexual monkey when he had her on white sheets, was covered with harsh streaks, red and purple lash marks that covered her everywhere but around her eyes, and those were still wide in fear. Glassy. Dead. *Who are you?*

Staggering backwards with a rising moan that the circle around Jennifer ignored, Luka turned and ran.

~~~~

"You were scary," said Birdy, in his mind again as clearly as he was in hers.

"You mean scared." Luka nodded and let the emotional memory overwhelm him, for it was these that held her attention. Like her mother before her, Birdy was drawn to psychic pain. And since Luka had taken her, Birdy was a junky for it, needing more and more.

In this way Luka had been turning her. From their first consciousness after death, he had drawn on their joining to *push* at people, at first getting almost nothing, but finally taking that drunken psychic off the pier at Huntingdon Beach. That had been the turning point. Oh, how the man had screamed. How Birdy had vibrated beside Luka, within him. Then the suicidal woman in the car, the angry short order cook, the depressed ranch owner...

Yes, that last one. Birdy had screamed in the fire with the man, horrified for both him and his horses, even as she tried to push Luka back from her father and sister. And when her father and sister had escaped, she had laughed in such a crazy relief that Luka knew she was becoming his.

The grandfather's house. That had been a work of art. First the roaring threat of a chain saw, the sheer *mayhem*, then the up close and personal attack with the grandfather.

And oh, how the *haole* father had helped him! Killing his own father! Feeling the hate! Yes!

This was why Birdy was so angry. Shaken up. *Shaken*. And in her confusion Luka at last could take control of their path. Their path...

~~~~

Luka's teacher, the legendary Kahuna whom Luka had enslaved with drugs and put up in the Honohono Motel, was not there when Luka came banging and shouting at his door. Nor was he at his usual shack by the beach, soliciting tourists and telling fortunes.

Perhaps he had done a run up to Kihei or even Lahaina to scavenge for more crack money. Perhaps. But there was something about the smell of the place, the way the Honohono owner looked at him as he left. Craftiness, maybe. Revenge?

Circling back to the motel office's back door, Luka slipped in and pulled from his pants the switchblade he always carried there. When the owner shuffled back to use the bathroom, Luka grabbed him and put the switchblade to his throat until the man told him what had happened to Kahuna Weki Naea Kapu.

Sometimes direct ways were best.

Luka left the owner his life and ran for his own motorbike. He revved it up and tore north down the road to Lahaina.

It took an afternoon of searching, images of the lashed body of Jennifer driving him like fire in his veins, before he found the little house Weki's friends had rented. It was a one-bedroom, condo on the edge of town, in a tourist development gone to seed. Luka knocked politely on the door, then kicked it as it was opened. The fallen elder and his three cronies crawled and cowered back against the wall. Kahunas all, sorcerers of Molokai, older even than Weki, they tried chanting at him, weaving their hands in the air as they had no doubt done all morning to summon the *pololia* to murder Jennifer.

Luka stepped forward with his switchblade, grabbed the jaw of the first babbling sorcerer, and slit his throat as cleanly as he had killed pigs for his father growing up. Then he felt the magics of the other three starting to dull his mind, snare his muscles. With a roar and counter chant, Luka threw it off. He stepped to the elder he'd knocked down with the door, grabbed him by the hair, and raised his head.

"You summon the *pololia*?" he said.

"*Hûpô o nâ hûpô,*" the elder croaked.

"No, you are the fool, old one." Luka brought his face down so he could look him in the eye as he slit his throat. And as the man breathed out his life breath, his *ane*, Luka inhaled it.

One of the two remaining sorcerers screamed a curse and tried to flee. Luka caught him, threw him down, and stomped on his knees until he felt the bones splinter. He left the old man moaning there while he calmly took the third man and bled him out, stealing his *ane*. Luka returned to the moaning man.

"*Iliho wahine*," he whispered. The throat slash was brutal, but Luka still managed to score the *ane*.

In the condo's bedroom, Luka found Weki Naea Kapu tied to the bed, his eyes wide and unfocused, his pupils little pin points.

"They gave you bad shit, old man," Luka said. Then he untied him, carried him out past his four dead abductors, and managed to make him sit on the back of the motorcycle. He held the old kahuna's hands around his body, kickstarted the cycle, and roared them back south.

Later, in the old man's room in the Honohono, when Luka had bathed and shaved him, fed him, and coaxed him back to awareness of the present, he told Weki what had happened and what must be done.

The old man blinked stupidly. "No can. Even the Molokai priests, they just stir up dead. They don't bring back."

"But Hiku brought back Kewalu. He stole her spirit from Milu of the underworld. He breathed it back into her body. Even in my mother's religion there is raising from the dead. Jesus. Lazarus."

"*Hehena*," Weki muttered.

"No! Not crazy!" He grabbed the old man's shoulder so hard he felt he could crack the bones as he had the knees of his sorcerer friend. "I took you in, I got you this room, because you got real stuff! I see you cloud a mind! I see you use a *ki'i* to bend a white man's will! You have talked with the *akua noho*! You have called on *uli* for help! The dead come to you! They listen! You will help me—find—a—way!"

And five years later, after much seeking and risk, they had.

~~~~

Luka rolled to his knees in Birdy's garden and waved a hand to make the decaying green under him turn to fine black volcanic sand. Another wave and he heard the surf of trickling waters of his child-hood, smelled the perfumed air from the mountains, the *ker-LOCK whoo-whoo!* and *KOO-dee-dee-dee-dee* of the island birds. In his hand appeared a papaya, round and ripe and sweet.

"Come," he called gently to Birdy as she turned towards him with bruised, surprised eyes. "Come and eat. And I tell you where we going to go next, yeh?"

31

THE DODGE PICKUP WEKI NAEA HAD STOLEN for our escape out of Morris must have been twenty years old. It rattled and squeaked over every bump. I think we lost chunks of rusty tailpipe or struts near Salt Lake City, but the truck held together more once we hit the long silent night of the Salt Lake Desert, with its solitary ghosts wailing quietly over the sands. I pushed it to eighty-five miles an hour out there, rushing like a geriatric dragon under the stars.

We rolled through Reno near six-thirty a.m. as the sun rose balefully behind us and kept going into north-eastern California.

Naea had slept from Salt Lake onwards. After I woke him up for a drive-through Wendy's breakfast, ordered, and got back on the road, I began hitting him again with questions.

"Why Birdy?" It came out nasal because my nose was still packed and taped over. And my questions had to struggle through a morass of emotions. Because this man, this decrepit bag of skin and bones, had been somehow involved in killing my little girl, driving my wife insane, destroying my family.

The realization of it, figuring out he was guilty as he talked of Luka's plan on the ride out of Morris, had almost made me vomit. Then I'd wanted to slam on the brakes, grab his skinny neck and squeeze out the air, snap the bones, mash him into the car seat and punch him over and over and...

But it was too unreal. Everything. Driving this truck. Even the fact of Naea's "magic" and the insanity of his saving me.

And so my hands vibrated on the steering wheel—my whole body thrummed—but I just kept driving. Because he was now my way out, the vessel who could tell me how to finally kill Luka and save Birdy, save my own life, my family.

"Answer me! You say he needs some sort of...what? Conduit? Gateway?...which he thinks can give him total power over other dead souls. Bring himself back. Why her?"

Naea ignored both my anger and the hills whizzing past and sipped his coffee so the skin of his cheeks sagged. Physically he was in even worse shape than me. His left eyes was swollen, and a cauliflower-shaped bruise and three scabbing cuts underlined his right eye. And those puncture marks. Needle marks? More drugs? He hadn't wanted to talk about them.

Three times the old man began to speak but stopped, until I was ready to pull over and follow through on my earlier strangulation plan. Then, as we hit the flatlands again, he squinted out at the brightening desert and spoke.

"You see ghosts when you a little boy, yeh? And again now. You daddy too?"

I nodded, mouth clenched tightly.

He sighed. "It run in families. You woman, you Sherry, she had different kind of power."

I felt a chill run down my neck as the old man vainly smoothed back his long white hair.

"She din't see ghosts," Weki said, "but ghosts see her. They cling to her like...to honey. She so good they want to eat her up. Luka almost think it is her. He hears stories of her, rumors. But when he get to know her, he find she don't know. She can't do nothing with that. Then she mention you daughter one day. Birdy."

My fingers were white on the wheel and I noticed we were somehow up to ninety again, the old truck rattling and shaking under my hands.

I forced myself to breathe and eased my foot back. Sacramento—fifteen miles. Only about ninety miles past there to home.

"Tell me," I said.

"Sherry call her the little saint. No doubt. Never fear. Never tell a lie." I knew he could see me gulping as he spoke because he paused for minute to let me get control again. "So Luka follow Sherry, watch her, watch you house, follow you round. And when he finally get close to little Birdy, he know for sure."

"What?" I said through clenched teeth. *Watch the speed. Watch it.*

"Your daughter get both of you. She see. And all the dead, all the living things, they see her. She be a beacon that love everything, always look, draw all to her, so many."

The old man stopped as if he himself was overwhelmed at all my little girl had been privy to when alive. Me, my heart was thumping so hard, my throat so full of it, that I had trouble keeping us going straight. It explained so much—the constant curiosity, the abstracted look she got so often, the lack of normal playmates. God, she'd had so much going on around her all the time it was a wonder she had ever learned to read or do simple addition. "Self-contained," her grade one teacher had called her, but she'd been just the opposite. She'd been so *open* to everything that attending to the mundane tasks of her school must have been like trying to filter out a whisper in a shouting crowd.

I had a flash too of the time when she was conceived. Sherry and I had been fighting about whether to have any more kids after Martha. All the computer companies were downsizing; I was scared shitless I was going to lose my job. But Sherry heard her biological alarm clock ringing in her ears. "*I'll* work!" she kept saying. "We'll make it!" Making me want to spit and stomp out of the house forever.

Then we both had this dream, the same night, I think. It was like beings of light I now figure were ghosts from my past came to each of us and said *Don't worry. Do it.* Something like that. We were both so freaked we fucked like rabbits. No more arguments.

Birdy was born nine months later.

This Christ-echo that I'd long ago laughed off now slapped me in the face. As we blasted through Sacramento and out the other side, my face felt hot and tingly. I felt like it was floating somewhere above my body and didn't want to come back. Until I felt Weki staring at me.

"What?" I said. "There's something more."

He blinked and tried to shake his head. His bruises looked awful in the morning sun.

"About what Luka's going to do with Birdy? Or to her?"

The old man took a long breath. "I told Luka he need to kill eight people before he can work the big spell. Just a number made up. Eight islands of Hawaii."

I frowned as I stared out at the highway, counting in my head as the white road lines flashed by dimly under us. "He's killed seven? He's got one more to go."

Weki nodded. "One more to feel ready. But it has to be a big one, yeh? He has to turn you little girl right around, make her to be like him so she be willing to break the rule of *Akua*."

"The rule of God," I said. "What? That the dead stay dead?"

He nodded.

"And you think the last big death is going to be...?"

Weki sighed. "He hate his own father. He hate Jennifer's father for stopping her coming to him, then stopping him going to her funeral. He hate the Molokai elders who were like father to me. Luka kill all those mens. Now he hate you."

"Really. He's only tried to kill me three times so far."

Weki shook his head. "No. Not before he make you a bad man, so it seem right to Birdy you die."

A chill ran right down to my tailbone. "You think he's done that. When I killed my father."

"We find out soon enough, I guess."

For a long time after that, I just drove.

~~~~

Where are we going? Sherry felt Birdy ask as if Sherry was inside her, blowing through a whirlwind, a tumbling, crazy cloud.

Where you want to go, Luka answered somehow.

No.

Luka laughed and the whirlwind inside Birdy tumbled faster. *Oh, yes, little gatekeeper. We follow your father. When he stops, we stop.*

The wind became fire, became a blinding scream of pain that seared Sherry's mind until, eyes open but blind, she cried, "Be ready, David! Be! Ready!"

32

FOR THE FIRST TIME IN HER LIFE, Sweetness felt completely out of her depth. She'd driven David's two children back into Morris with her and Ramirez, rented two rooms at the town's run-down hotel, and put the guys in one room, herself and Martha in the other.

Little Joshua Friesen had looked at her with big woebegone eyes when she'd dictated the arrangements, but he'd shuffled after Ramirez without a peep. Martha Friesen, though, had followed Sweetness into the musty room, seen the one double bed and bathroom with no shower, and crossed her arms over stoutly over her developing chest.

"I want my own room," she said.

"Bureau doesn't pay for that," Sweetness said. "I don't think they'd like the fact I've suddenly taken custody of two minors either."

"Until tomorrow. They can't hold my dad without bail. I've watched TV."

"Yeah?" Sweetness turned from her, tiredly took off her jacket and holsters, and made her way to the bathroom. She knew she should sympathetically explain the situation to this girl, but the girl had been there, and she wasn't stupid. She had to realize how things looked. Besides, Sweetness grated over the girl's tone. She saw the pierce marks in the nose and eyebrows, the signs of bleached hair. And she'd shown absolutely no signs that her grandpa's death affected her at all. Her dad's incarceration was probably only awful because it cramped her freedom. No more little princess of the hill.

Then she came out to find Martha still standing exactly where she had been and sobbing soundlessly, her little shoulders shaking, her snotty face collapsed, chin bobbing up and down with each contraction of her diaphragm.

Sweetness stopped, stunned. Then she got the white girl a tissue from the bathroom, had her blow her nose, told her to get ready for bed.

When Martha had silently changed into pink pajamas, brushed her teeth and washed her face, hands, and feet with a blank face, she came back to her bed and sat on the side of it, staring at the floor. Sweetness backed against the wall by the closet and shoved her hands into the pocket of her slacks.

"I lost my father when I seven," she said. "He just walked out on us. I never saw him again."

Martha sat on the far side of her bed, staring at the wall. "And your mom went crazy?"

"Sort of. We struggled for a couple years, five different boyfriends. Then one day she suddenly woke up and hauled me and my little sister onto a bus heading west. She got a job in a casino in Reno, then waitressed in L.A., went back to school, made me study as hard as her."

"Awesome," the white girl said flatly and climbed into bed, faced away from Sweetness. Hours later she cried out in terror, "Daddy! Daddy!" Then nothing. A nightmare.

Like Sweetness's own.

This morning, chewing through greasy meals of bacon and easy-over eggs at a place called Meg's, both children looked like warmed-over corpses with dull eyes, slumped shoulders.

Ramirez seemed oblivious, yattering on about how the black sheep in his family ran a place like Meg's once. It got killed by the interstate. "Yeah, so he turned it into a titty—" He stopped and winked at the kids. "I mean he opened an adult entertainment establishment."

Martha laid down her knife and fork to stare silently out the greasy spoon's front window.

"Ramirez," said Sweetness, "your mouth."

"Yeah? Well, you know it's not exactly like we have keen conversationalists here, all comp—"

Sweetness cut him off with a raised hand and stood quickly. It was Deputy Ray Burton, the sarcastic one who was ready to lynch David on the spot last night. The weasely man went to a table near the counter and made to sit, but stopped when he saw Sweetness approach.

"Hey, gorgeous," he said and flashed his teeth. "Sightseeing the state?"

Sweetness frowned. "You don't remember me?"

"From...?"

"Last night. The Friesen house."

Burton blinked once or twice and squinted a bit like he was looking through a fog. "The... Oh. Yeah. George...got killed. His neighbor too. We're investigating those. You were there?"

"As were those children." Sweetness pointed. "And the man you have locked up in your jail."

Burton squinted at her again. "We don't got nobody locked up. Let Reg Abrams out yesterday morning once he'd sobered up."

"That's it?"

"Yup."

"And you don't remember me."

"No." He shifted about awkwardly. "But, you know, if you say you were there, I guess I should..."

"Where's your jail? And your Sheriff?"

Burton pointed. "Block down the street. On the left. You want—"

"We'll find our way there," Sweetness said. She walked quickly back to their table, paid the bill, and dragged Ramirez and the kids out the door after her.

At the jail, Sheriff Klatt was as fogged at Burton, but hid it better. There was, he pointed out, no record of anyone being arrested at the Friesen residence. And if Sweetness or anyone else had been there, he'd have recorded that as well. Most likely George Friesen was killed during a break-and-enter, though whoever did the crime must have been disappointed by the slim pickings. Since the winter night George had gotten drunk and accidentally locked his wife outside to freeze to death, he'd kind of let things fall apart. Put up a hell of a last fight, though, looked like.

"Uh-hunh," Sweetness said flatly. Then she walked Ramirez out to where the kids waited and made him and the children get into the rental car.

"What the eff?" Ramirez said the second the car doors closed.

"Do you still believe," Sweetness said quietly, "that we're just dealing with drug dealers and a messed-up father?"

"My dad?" piped up Martha from the back. "You think—"

Sweetness shushed her. "Your father's no longer in custody. I'll explain later." Then she turned back to Ramirez, waiting for his response. "Well?"

She could see him thinking hard through everything, eager to spout about David, but honestly trying to assimilate the rest into some sort of coherent whole. He shook his head, failing. "Don't know."

"We'll start with that," Sweetness said. She started the car and put it into gear.

"Wait," said Ramirez. "We're not going to give them a statement?"

"If you really want to,"—Sweetness accented the *really*—"you stick around here and do it. I'm taking these children back to San Francisco now, with or without you."

Ramirez opened his mouth, shut it, and sat back in his seat, eyes forward.

Sweetness skidded the car away from the curb and headed for the airport.

~~~~

Six hours later the four of them, including Ramirez, were driving casually away from the Friesen's Richmond neighborhood. Only Ramirez had approached the house and he'd done so on foot, blending in behind three other men on the sidewalk. What he'd seen were two watch cars stationed a half block on either side of the house. Whether they were Aznar's men, still zoning on Friesen because he might be working with Keawe, or police who'd somehow been alerted by the Utah police, he couldn't tell. He'd turned into one of the front lawns, cut to the rear alley, and jogged back to report.

There was another car near the in-laws' house in Sausalito. No sign of David Friesen at either place.

Worried over what would happen when David *did* show, Sweetness still realized her first duty was to the children. And making a report, of course. Calling the office. Writing a report.

But she was damned if she had any clue what she was going to relate.

"So?" said Ramirez, huddled with Sweetness away from the car and the Friesen children. He'd been restrained ever since leaving Utah, like something had finally clicked about the weirdness of this case. He seemed finally willing to follow Sweetness's lead, though.

"We stall reporting. At least until we reconnect these two with their father."

Ramirez nodded without looking at them. Sweetness knew it signaled his new level of faith, since she was sure his first instinct was call things in, get instruction, turn the kids over to the authorities. He had to understand Sweetness was hoping to reunite them with their father first, then probably let their father walk away free. Whether he thought it was because she'd gone soft on David Friesen, or because she wanted to give him some running room and see what happened, Sweetness wasn't sure. She herself didn't know.

Maybe it was just that she saw two kids who desperately needed their father and, unlike Sweetness, actually had a chance of finding him again.

"Hotel?" Ramirez asked her.

She shook her head. "I've got a better idea."

33

WE MADE A STOP HERE FOR FOOD, there to fill up for gas, a desperate roar down a side street as we realized my house was being watched. I also stopped long enough for a phone call to Rose and Gunther, just long enough to hear a line buzz that could have been a wiretap and Rose's voice insisting no one had called about the children.

Finally, nighttime, I was cruising the pickup through the downtown streets of S.F., when my own personal kahuna suggested we'd have to stop sometime.

Did I mention I felt like a condemned man?

The Morris ghosts and Weki had said I was the only hope to stopping Luka's perversion of Birdy. Weki even had some idea of how to do it. My rediscovered ability to see ghosts again—I'd psychically brushed past a dozen or more on this road trip, most sad, one howling that I was the Antichrist—would help me find Luka and Birdy. Then I just had to use the same Hawaiian chant Luka had used on our rooftop. It would bind Birdy to me, away from him.

But that was only if I could somehow survive another direct encounter with Luka *and* beat him down enough to make Birdy's ghost come close to me. To kill me herself?

Without Martha and Josh there forcing me to be strong, I had no confidence in my ability to do anything.

"You think Luka attack you only when stop?" Weki said.

I looked sideways at him as we rattled down Van Ness for the third time and felt my mouth drop open. Of course. I'd been keeping us moving because I'd unconsciously figured it was safer, but one of Luka's first victims had been driving when he made her drive off the cliffs at Ragged Point.

Looking back to the traffic, I saw everyone had stopped at a light. I stomped on the brakes. Our pickup skidded up within half an inch of the Jaguar's bumper in front of us.

When the light changed, I took the next right to find a cheap hotel.

We parked, checked in using cash because I feared being traced through my credit card, showered, and I lay like a board on one of the two twin beds, waiting for some possessed crazy from outside to fling himself through our door.

They didn't.

I slept.

I woke.

Nothing had happened.

That next day we drove around the city, not talking much. I almost went to Rajiv's home in Oakland, but Weki seemed to sense it and filled me in on Rajiv's death and, coincidentaly the torture Weki himself had gone through. I gripped the steering wheel harder and butted my chin against it. I pulled over for some air. The fact it was human drug scum who'd killed my partner didn't make it any less Luka's fault.

That night we stopped at a place called the Vista Luna, a dive that still somehow managed a view of the Bay...over harbor factories and warehouses.

At two a.m., without turning on the lights, I shook Weki awake demanded he tell me why neither Birdy nor Luka had shown up.

The old man rolled painfully to sitting. His bandages and bruises looked black and white in the shadows. His hair hung forward around his face like a prayer shawl. "Mebbe he want you scared before you *maki*," he mumbled.

"What?"

"Gonna scare you, then kill you," said the old man. "Or mebbe he just be done. Kill someone else. Fade away, poof."

"Or maybe you have no goddamned idea anymore what's going on."

He nodded, shrugged, and rolled back into his bedsheets. A moment later he was snoring.

The next day I roused us both before eight, bought us breakfast at a nearby family place, then drove us to the Oakland Bay Bridge and across. It was time to stop running.

~~~~

Two of the ghosts I'd heard in San Francisco's cheap hotels seemed to be tapped in to things that rippled the fabric of their world. They'd given me timetables, names, and a clear picture in my head of an address.

I pulled up in front of it now.

Dr. Angela MacPhail's Berkeley residence nestled in a newer development of gated townhomes on a hill five minutes north of the campus. The narrow street that wound through them was discretely planted with small Japanese maples and lumpy bushes with yellow flowers that made Weki smile. We parked in Visitor's parking and walked to her door. It had no supplementary garden, just stones and a cement patio beside the short driveway. Urban chic.

Angela didn't look surprised when she answered the door in slacks and a light chenille sweater to find Weki and I standing there.

"Let me guess," I said. "Your psychics told you I was coming."

"Gudrun and Nanna. They're on the deck out back."

"Do the children know?"

She shook her leonine head. "They're upstairs watching television. My daughter and her work partner are out back. I imagine Gudrun and Nanna are filling them in now."

I hesitated for just a second, swallowing hard, then looked into Angela's eyes with my unspoken question. She smiled, stepped backwards, and pointed towards the stairs. As I stepped in and removed my shoes,

Sweetness came rushing in from the back deck. Her physical hardness, the laser beam thrust of her, made me flinch backwards.

But she stopped before reaching me. No attack, no arrest. Just her fine, proud face staring at me with open curiosity and concern. I realized my face was still bruised and my nose still packed and bandaged, though the doctor who'd done it at the jail said nothing was seriously broken. I carefully peeled the tape and gauze off, took a tentative sniff, and winced. Sweetness stepped forward.

As much as I wanted to feel her touch, just for a minute, just for an affirmation of life, I waved her back. First I had some stairs to climb.

Everyone downstairs let me. They watched silently as I ascended in sock feet, fighting to stay calm. The TV sounds guided me to the half-open door to the right of the landing. When I pushed it open, I saw some anime cartoon was playing. Josh and Martha were slumped, watching, like pictures I'd seen of children after their villages were bombed or tornadoes had destroyed their homes. Martha held a delicate-looking guitar on her lap, silent. Both kids' faces were flat, their eyes empty.

Then Josh blinked. He sensed me there. He let out a little sigh and turned. Martha, aware of Josh, at least, turned too.

"Dad?" said Josh, a little stunned.

"Daddy," breathed Martha.

Like they'd talked about this moment in whatever form it would take, they shot each other looks and stood up.

Martha put down the guitar and faced me. "Um...hem...Dad." The pallor of her face grew red. Her young-woman's body shifted back and forth. "Josh and I, we want to say that...we don't blame you for what happened. Not back there,"—she waved a finger in the air, vaguely hunting for the direction of her grandfather's farm—"or before. For Luka...killing Birdy, for Mom, for dragging us out to find Birdy and... the other people who got killed. We, Josh and me, don't think it was your fault."

It was so unexpected that my legs turned to jelly; I almost fell down.

Then Josh squeaked out, "And we love you," and I did stagger a bit.

But I caught myself and held myself up as a torrent of emotions gushed through me—a silly *relief*, a wonder that my children could think of me at all after what they'd been through, and mostly an immense pride that rushed through me, making my scalp prickle.

My arms opened up as if a force far greater than me insisted. "Can we hug now?" I said.

They ran to me and we did.

~~~~

Downstairs, Sweetness watched Ramirez sulk into Angela's kitchen and pour some more corn chips into a bowl. He brought it out to the other five adults crowded into the living room and front hall.

"The guy should be under arrest, and you all look like you're aching to hold a candle and sing," he said.

"What this mean?" asked Nanna, pressing into his arm.

"I believe he means," said Angela, "that we are penitents waiting to see if our deliverer will descend from the mountain whole or broken."

Sweetness rolled her eyes out of habit, then grimaced for real as she saw Ramirez hastily push Nanna away with the chip bowl then scuttle closer to Sweetness herself. Wrong, wrong, wrong, Francisco, she thought. You should stick with Nanna. Go get laid. Take off some of your tension with this case because I sure as hell don't need you adding it to mine. Especially with the reappearance of this elusive father who fights off ghosts, walks out of jail cells leaving mind-wiped law enforcement in his wake, and still gives me the trembles whenever I get too close to him.

Then she heard a small intake of breath from the others and saw the old kahuna, Weki Naea, nod his head in approval. She looked up to see David standing halfway down the stairs with one hand around each of his children. That close together, there was no mistaking the family resemblance, particularly in the deep contentment of their eyes. Family. That's what it was. The look of family.

Sweetness bit her lip and felt Remirez shift forward. Shit, he was going to try something stupid now, like putting David into custody. Sweetness stepped sideways to block his movement with her shoulder.

"Gale," David said. He looked into her eyes so long and deep that she felt her stomach flutter. "And Special Agent Ramirez," he said. "Angela. I want to thank you all sincerely for looking after my children. A bunch of drug dealers seem to have staked out our house right now. I'd like to ask the boon of your extended hospitality."

Out of the corner of her eye, Sweetness saw the psychic sisters trying to parse it out. She felt Ramirez grind his teeth but step back.

Angela, the smiling cat who'd found her cream, stepped regally forward and waved David and his children down the steps to the bottom. When they reached it, she kissed each child on the head and David on the cheek. More physical affection than Sweetness had seen from her in years. She said her house was theirs.

"Over lunch," she added, "perhaps you can tell us exactly what you plan to do about Mr. Luka Keawe, scourge of the spirit world."

34

*T*HE PLAN OF ACTION.

Strictly speaking, I didn't have one. But at least I finally understood what we faced. As we crowded around Angela's dining room table to eat sandwiches of tuna and fresh basil on whole grain bread with mayonnaise, I spelled it out for them. I also told them I believed we would only succeed in separating Luka from Birdy if I and my children remained together. Even more than the words Weki Naea had given me, it was the family unit, as much of it as we could muster, that was going to pull Birdy away from Luka.

Also, contrary to what Weki had suggested the previous night in our hotel room, I said I'd know when and where the next attack would come.

"Because?" Gudrun challenged. Her chin stuck out with two poppy seeds on it. Her lanky blond hair fell down in question marks.

"Josh's sixth sense. And the ghosts who speak to me now."

"The ghosts," Gudrun said sarcastically. She crossed her arms over her chest. Even Nanna, her more cheerful sister looked doubtful. I tried to ignore the sneer of Ramirez, the questioning look of Gale Sweetness.

"You don't believe me," I said.

"Pugh," Gudrun said and threw up her hands. "What is not to believe."

"Gudrun, your tattoo?" I said. "It's of a...crucifix? On your inner left thigh. Your ghost Iakov finds it highly erotic."

Ramirez almost choked on his milk.

It shows great character and devotion to God, Iakov added.

"He says it shows great character and devotion to God."

If only my grandson had not gone back to Russia.

"He wishes he could have set you up with his grandson."

Petya.

"Petya."

Gudrun's eyes were wide, and her pale face turned blotchy red. Ramirez and Weki were both snorting. Angela and my children were covering their mouths discretely. Gale was giving me a smile that seemed to say much more than simple amusement.

Nanna had her eyes wide too, but with delight. She clutched Gudrun's hand and shook it hard. "Then you know," she said to me. "You feel the fear."

"I feel the ghosts' fear," I said, "of what they don't understand. But I don't think Luka understands either. He just *wants* something really bad and he'll do anything to get it."

"Which makes him stupid," Josh said.

I shook my head. "It makes him dangerous. But defeatable. He's not a great magician himself. He's just doing what Kahuna Weki here told him to do. And Kahuna Weki made it up. Right?"

Weki opened his mouth, but I wasn't sure if it was to agree or disagree, because he just closed it and swooped his head towards his plate in body language I didn't understand. Gale was frowning.

"Angela?" I said.

As if she'd been waiting for the chance, our hostess carefully folded her napkin over the crumbs on her plate and smiled around the table. "Upon reflection and discussion at the university, my colleagues and I have decided that the decreasing entropy of David's little girl and Luka—their apparent increase in power, that is—is not inconsistent with our model of persistent personality wave forms. In fact, the more we have discovered about these two ghosts, the less surprising it is that their struggles to communicate or possess the living have intensified their own signatures. Not because there is a net increase in energy, but because their focused concentration has increased the order of their thoughts. They may be consciously willing themselves coherent."

Ramirez stared at her as if she was loony, but Gale looked thoughtful. The kids, not following, stuffed themselves with the last of their sandwiches, then slipped off into the living room where Martha picked up the delicate guitar I'd discovered was Angela's, and began picking out a soft melody.

"What bout Luka's *wahine*, the Jennifer?" Weki Naea said.

I looked, surprised to see him calm but tightly focused on Angela. I'd grudgingly assumed from the way he'd broken me out of jail that he had some kind of power over people, but I'd also assumed he was basically unschooled and superstitious.

Maybe I'd been wrong.

Dr. Angela shrugged at him. "Increasing their own coherence is one thing," she said. "I don't know how he believes he can increase that of another ghost. If this Jennifer never became a ghost, furthermore— and I would assume he'd have found her by now if she'd continued on in that form—there will simply be nothing to increase."

"Nothing to bring back from the dead," I said.

"Of course not."

Weki Naea looked calmly from me to her, then back again. Martha's guitar song in the living room hit a discordant note. Weki's mouth twitched and he scooped the last of his crumbs from his plate.

"Mebbe," he said.

~~~~

Much later, after more discussion of ghosts and our experiences thereof, and multiple retellings of all that had happened with each of us, the psychic sisters were bundled off, as was Ramirez, who was ordered to go find a hotel and draft a preliminary report that Gale would vet tomorrow.

Then she and her mother, myself, the kids, and Weki Naea, had a quiet dinner of ordered-in Chinese, including a bottle of red wine for all the adults but Weki. He no longer drank, he insisted. I sent the kids to bed early because they seemed exhausted. Gale noted they hadn't slept well for the last three nights.

When I'd tucked them both into the second bedroom upstairs, I came back down, topped up my, Gale's, and Angela's glasses with the dregs of the wine, and faced them all.

"So who's ready to deal with Luka showing up here tonight?" I said.

Weki looked very serious. "He not come here, brah."

"Why?"

"It's too calm peaceful, yeh? No one calling him. No one deep sad."

"No one deep sad, hunh?" I drained my glass and looked around at the others, feeling a little flushed though I'd only had about two glasses. I reached to my left and grabbed Gale's hand, big as my own with the edge hard and callused. From karate, I'd finally discovered.

She jerked a little, surprised, but didn't draw it back. I pulled it to my chest and pressed it over my heart with both hands. "You feel that?" I said.

She nodded.

"I'm surprised. I've got my kids back and, yes, it's wonderful. But my wife's insane, I killed my own father, I have no home, nowhere to go..."

Suddenly the feel of her strong black hand on me and the intense look in her eyes as she leaned towards me made it hard to breathe. I sat back and dropped her hand with a gasp and laugh.

"God, I get maudlin on a glass and a half. The kids aren't the only ones who haven't been sleeping." I pushed back my chair and fumbled to my feet. "Gale, Weki, Angela, goodnight. Concrete plans tomorrow."

So saying, I dragged myself upstairs to the pull-out couch of the townhouse's third small bedroom, normally Angela's home office. Weki would sleep downstairs on a couch. My kids were right through the wall by my head. Gale would share her mother's bed just eight steps down the hall and around the corner.

~~~~

Sweetness ignored her mother's knowing looks as they cleaned up. But when Angela started humming "I Don't Know How to Love Him" over the kitchen sink, she snapped.

"He's married, okay?"

"I didn't say anything, dear." Angela smiled wider.

"I just find him fascinating. He seems like such a wimp at times, but the things he's done…"

Angela's smile vanished. She turned and held out the last washed wine glass for Sweetness to dry. "Being gentle and loving isn't weakness, Gale," she said.

"I know that."

"Do you?"

She took the glass and stared at it. She'd found her own father's name listed in the NYC morgue sheets five years ago on one of her periodic searches. She hadn't told her mother. That would have been weak.

"He's still married," she said, and dried the glass.

~~~~

I heard Gale and her mother come upstairs at last. They bumped about for fifteen minutes or so, using the bathroom, talking quietly. Weki meanwhile bumped for a few minutes downstairs and was still.

Finally the two women quieted too. Everything was still. I could almost hear the calm breathing of my children through the wall at my head.

I was exhausted. Totally worn out.

So why couldn't I sleep? Like Weki said, *He not come here, brah. Mebbe.*

I couldn't sleep.

Then I did.

~~~~

The powerhouse that was Birdy Friesen exploded silently through the mist of the townhouse. The only person who heard it was Luka Keawe, also dead. And it was Luka who reined in Birdy's frustration at not being able control or understand what was happening.

Birdy's bright face was pinched and her fists clenched as she tried to descend onto the pull-out couch where her father slept. "I...want... to...touch him," she said, half snarling, half wanting to snuggle under his arm..

"Can't do, little gate," Luka said, with a glint in his eye. "But you can watch."

"Watch...what?"

"This."

~~~~

I jerked in my sleep and shot my eyes open.

There was no one in the room with me. Nothing but a vague bump from somewhere else in the house. Upstairs. Gale or Angela? My eyes drooped again.

I'm not sure if it was the smell or noise that wakened me next. My brain was so worn out it fought to keep me asleep and dreaming. I was shivering in a downtown alleyway beside a rank pile of garbage. Suddenly a wave of heat pressed me back against the wall so it was hard to breathe. The wall squeaked.

And tilted to horizontal under me. The hot weight on top of me drew back as I blinked open my eyes. It rose to a black shadow above my belly, then resolved itself into a woman with her knees on either side of my torso on the pull-out bed, her body taut and dark, her hair ultra-short, her nightshirt just as. No panties.

"Gale?" I whispered.

She held a finger to her lips and folded down to me, kissing me once, long and slow with both lips and tongue before drawing herself upright again.

As I stared, vaguely aware of the blood pounding through my body, my penis stiffening, she reached to the bottom of her nightie and drew it up over her head in one smooth motion.

Her small breasts popped free, nipples pointing stiffly through the air above me. I saw her smile in the dark and fold down again, pressing her heat onto my swollen member, dangling her breasts above my chest. Begging to be touched.

If you did, literally, fuck with her, I'd thought that time she'd stayed over at my house.

My hands twitched up, almost by themselves, to trace the warm curve of her waist first, up over the ribs. Then my fingers curled and formed over her breasts, cupping and squeezing them. The hard pebbles slipped out between my fingers.

The dark. It was so full of her, the heat of her, the quick sighs of her breathing, and a fetid smell too, almost overpowering, but I didn't care. Couldn't. My groin was rising against her instinctively and she rocked back and forth over it, groaning. She was wet, hot, slick. I could feel it through my briefs. My penis felt so huge it was going to rip through my briefs any second and plunge into her, fulfill the heat I now realized was there every time she got close to me.

"Let me...," I panted.

"Yes," her husky voice said, and rolled her long body off me to lie on her back to my right, naked. Waiting.

But something in the awkwardness of that little move, or maybe the calculation with which she did it, triggered a further level of waking. So even as my fingers got the waistband of my briefs, I paused.

"You smell it?" I said.

"Smell what?"

"Garbage."

"Ignore it," she said and reached to help me with my underwear.

I slid my groin back on the sheets out of her reach, but caught her face with my hand. "Kiss me," I ordered. And as my lips swam against her, felt their pliancy, the heat of her tongue, I felt a wave of horror and regret surge up inside me.

I pulled back, almost gagging on the smell and taste I now was sure came from her. Yet not from her. From Luka *in* her.

"Why?" I breathed.

"Oh, David," Gale's lips crooned. "Davie."

Suddenly I knew. I sprang from my bed and whirled around the room, trying to see all the hiders. I tried again with my eyes closed, reaching out in a way I hadn't consciously done since I was fourteen or fifteen years old.

She was there by the window, but I almost didn't recognize her. Birdy's face looked swollen, huge and fiery. Her seven-year-old's body seemed lumpen and distorted, shot through with ugly streaks like purple bruising.

Worst, though, were her eyes. Bloodshot and swollen, they looked at me with the sort of horror I would not have thought Birdy capable of. My heart squeezed so hard I thought it would burst. If I could just reach out. If I could just touch her.

She vanished.

"David."

Struggling to breathe, I turned to see Gale standing naked before me. *Focus!* It was clearly not Gale, for Gale always had a kind of grounded grace that made her movements both frightening and compelling. This woman slouched with a hand on one hip, lower belly sticking out, lips leering.

"You always been so lucky, eh, brah? Birdy keep me from killing you even now. Bet I could do it with this body, yeh?" He dropped Gale's body into a combat stance, then sniggered and drew it upright again. "And you little boy, Josh, help pull me off you so you don't burn. You girl Martha, she swing a mean club at me in you daddy's house. Even this nigger woman, she and she mom. Oh, they trying to help you so much. Yeah, you so protected. I can't get you.

"But you know who not be so protected? Hunh?" He grinned and spread Gale's knees wide, reaching down to hold open her vaginal lips for me as he thrust her hips back and forth.

I stepped forwards, wondering just how strong the body of Gale Sweetness would prove if I tried to restrain it right now. "Let her go."

He stopped and gave me a wider smile than I think Gale's lips had ever done.

"Oh, no, brah. I am not talking bout this hotness here. Uh-unh. I talking about you wife. You Sherry. Oh, yeah. I take her once, you member? Now, like this, mebbe I make everyone take her."

"You son of a—"

Gale's hand streaked up to my mouth and slapped it hard. "Don't talk bout my mother, Davie, or you maki die dead, yeh?" Even as he did it, I could see his expression jerk about on Gale's face, struggling to stay in control of this woman he'd possessed. And I understood why he wasn't trying to make her kill me. She was too strong for him. He finally grinned and waved. "Bye."

I could *feel* it when he slipped out of her body, as if he'd been in me too. It was like having a giant bowel movement and watching a slug come out and slip away.

Gale slumped and I caught her, lowered her back onto the bed. I reached to pull a sheet over her, but she suddenly shook her head. "Not much point in that now."

I met her eyes and saw the shame in them, and the sorrow.

"I guess not," I said, but handed her the short top she'd worn in here anyway.

She fingered it, maybe considering how she now had the proof she needed that ghosts, and Luka in particular, were one hundred percent real. She raised her eyes to meet mine. "I was aware through it all, you know."

I swallowed and said nothing. Waited.

"I'm almost not sorry he made me do it. I've wanted to."

"I know. Me too." I dropped my head to the side ruefully then glanced down at the front of my stained shorts. "Obviously."

"Then..." She rose to her feet and took a hesitant step forward.

For a second I imagined reaching for her again, stroking her smooth dark skin and kissing her lips, but honestly this time, fully awake and alive. Her nipples were still erect. Her strong body seemed to bend its middle towards me, draw mine to her.

"I can't," I said.

She bit her lip but didn't draw back. "If...Sherry doesn't make it?"

"Would my promise on that keep you from helping me save her?"

I sensed her blush. "Of course not."

Still she stood there, her naked chest rising and falling, the hands holding her nightie making no effort to put it on her again. I felt my own body break out in a sweat. My hands actually trembled as I held them at my sides.

"I think," I forced myself to say, "that I really need Special Agent Gale Sweetness right now. You said the White Pines where my wife is cared for is being watched. I'm going to need you and your partner to get me in there."

"Now?"

"The sooner the better."

The softness in her eyes dropped away completely. She nodded, stepped back, and donned her nightie. She looked around for her panties then obviously remembered she hadn't worn them in here.

She put one hand on the room's doorknob. "You realize Luka probably threatened Sherry specifically to make you go there."

I nodded.

"And you said this morning you had no idea how to stop him."

"That was this morning. He just gave me a way tonight. Right here. Through you."

She waited. When I said nothing more, she nodded and turned to go. Paused once more.

"In a few hours we could be dead," she said.

"Or free."

I didn't clarify what I meant by that.

35

STRANGE AS IT WAS TO BE ROUSTING THE HOUSEHOLD at two a.m. to congregate at the dining room table around a sketch I'd made of White Pines, the operation had a sense of inevitability. Even Ramirez, when he joined us, barely grumped at the hour. Gale murmured to me that it was because he hadn't been to bed yet. She'd heard a distinctive Nanna giggle on the other end of the line when she'd phoned.

Ramirez, swiped at the scowl he'd worn since he arrived. "Why can't you just check your wife out?"

"Paperwork and time," I said calmly. "They have to do evaluations, endless forms. She'll be dead before then."

"Yeah, right. This ghost."

I stared at him, then at Gale, who *knew* now that Luka was real and what he was capable of. She dropped her eyes. "Or Luka's old drug dealers," I said. "They've already killed my partner. How long before they move on my wife, trying to get to me or Weki?"

That made Ramirez sit back. "We could get protection."

"By tonight? By morning? When?"

Ramirez turned to Gale. She nodded. "We go in tonight," she said. "With Martha and Josh."

"Wha—?" Ramirez said. "Shit no."

"Yes."

"It's child endangerment. End of story."

"They're safer here, David," said Gale. "My mother will watch them."

"You try to take them and I arrest you this time for sure!"

I waited until they'd calmed down, then calmly reiterated the reasoning that had only been made stronger by Luka's possession of Gale.

It boiled down to three things beyond my love for them: 1) Josh, while not being able to speak with ghosts as clearly as I, was actually more sensitive to their moods and thoughts, Luka's in particular; he could let me know how I was scoring with the mind games I was planning to play; 2) Martha had always had a calming effect on her younger sister; and 3) if we were going to help Birdy be a distinct personality from Luka, then it was critical we gave her a united, appealing family to identify with.

Ramirez couldn't sit still through it. He rose and paced the room, obviously close to bursting.

I threw him a bone. "Apart from any ghosts, the kids will convince my wife to leave quickly, without causing a scene."

The agent's jaw set. He'd already gone over the line by not calling anyone when I'd shown up last night. He was obviously trying to figure just how far he could go and still save himself if things went south.

Then he surprised me.

"Let's say," he said as gruffly as his young face let him, "that this 'ghost' Luka Keawe shows up with your 'ghost' little girl. How you going to keep him from killing people like he's supposedly done every time you're around?"

I stared, then saw Gale waiting for an answer too. I turned to Weki Naea.

"The girl give Luka power," the old man said. "If she not with him, Luka pzzzt."

"You mean he loses coherence," interrupted Angela. "He dissipates. Vanishes."

Weki nodded. "He got no family but her. He got nothing else."

Don't talk bout my mother, Davie, or you maki die dead, Luka had said. But this time I *was* going to talk, and it was Luka who was going to die, permanently.

"So," I said to Gale and Ramirez, "if you can get us all in there with a twenty minute window, either we smuggle Sherry out to safety, or Luka shows up and we finish this thing."

There was a long pause, then both agents shook their heads. Gale was about to explain when Josh stood up on a chair and looked down at all of us. "If you don't let us go,"—he pointed to Gale—"I'm going to tell everyone your secret. And yours." He pointed to Ramirez. "And yours." He pointed to Angela.

"Whoah!" said Ramirez. "You got me scared."

"Still think the bit about Gudrun's tattoo was a fake?" I said. "You know Josh is better at this stuff than I am. Shall we try him out?"

Ramirez opened his mouth. Closed it and cast a sidelong glance at Gale. She was staring hard at me.

"If anything happens," she said, "we'll swear you got in yourself. You'll be responsible."

"I always am" I said. "I'm their father. Now how exactly *do* we get in?"

~~~~

It was almost 4:15, but still moon dark, by the time we approached the rear walls of the White Pines. Despite it being warm out, we were all dressed in long-sleeved dark shirts. In Weki's case, a faded denim blue. We'd seen no one.

The walls were twelve foot high brick, but it was easy enough to find a tree whose branches let us drop onto the top, Josh leading. I and Gale had to help Weki. Ramirez meanwhile showed off by climbing the wall itself by finding small edges for his fingers and toes.

On the other side, there was just enough light for me to lead us through the gardens and circle towards the front of the house. We stopped just short and Ramirez phoned the cops, telling them about the dark Cadillac we could see through the trees. Ray Aznar's troops. Watching. I thought I even saw the tiny spark of a cigarette butt in the car.

Twelve minutes later a cruiser approached quietly, its lights flashing.

The Caddy roared to life, backed up for a wild three-point, and shot past the cruiser, which itself skidded around to follow.

We ran for the front door.

Eight minutes later, the security orderly at the front door snoozed peacefully while we located the security office and I quickly reprogrammed the security cameras to start looping their recorded tape.

All was well, but Weki continued weaving his little cat's cradle (a *hei*, he called it) and mumbling under his breath. Maybe that's what kept the nurses and patients oblivious as the six of us stole upstairs and down that hall to Sherry's room, the second-to-last door on the right. All the rooms were on lockdown tonight—must have had some ruckus the last evening or two—but the doors had windows. Under just the red glow of the emergency exits, the corridor looked like a canal through a sleepy suburb of hell. It was wider than tall, but not much.

I jogged to Sherry's window.

She wasn't there.

I swallowed and looked anxiously up and down the corridor. Gale raised her eyebrows at me. Before I could say anything, though, Martha was hissing.

"Dad!"

She was standing on her tiptoes to look in the metal-screened window of a solid door halfway back down the hall, the opposite side. Josh had his ear pressed up to the door like he could hear something through it. As one, we adults hurried to join them.

36

*I*T WASN'T THE DARK SHE FEARED.

No, as Sherry rocked back and forth on the edge of the wall-bolted bed and waited, she couldn't fear the dark because *everything* was dark. She'd been struck real-world blind and dumb on the day David had killed his father then broken out of prison.

So the dark meant nothing to her.

What scared her was Luka. She knew he was coming because he'd finished with David. That left Sherry as Birdy's last refuge against Luka. And despite Sherry's kicking and screaming enough to be locked up in the "calm down" room, Sherry knew all the padded walls and double-thick doors were no defense at all.

A tapping on her door made her stop rocking. She turned her face and its unseeing eyes towards the door.

"Mom?" she heard faintly.

She stopped breathing. Martha?

Not possible. It had to be one of the other patients. One of the truly crazy ones, somehow escaped from their room and wandering. *Breathe.*

The tapping came again and a second, more timid voice Sherry knew instantly was Josh called out, "Mommy?" Then. "Something's wrong, Dad."

Oh, God. David had come here. And he'd brought the children.

Leaning forward, Sherry pushed herself unsteadily to her feet. She was dressed—cotton sweater, slacks, and slippers because she'd refused to let them force her into pajamas or a nightgown. But her legs creaked from so little recent use. She took a tentative step and heard scratching and clinking at the door. A moment later, a rush of cool air washed over her. Footsteps, an intake of breath, and David was in front of her. She could smell him. His male smell. Clean and strong. His hands went to her shoulders, then smoothed back her hair. "Sherry," he whispered.

"Told you I could do that," said a cocky male voice from the direction of the door. Probably the Mexican federal agent she'd seen through Birdy's eyes once.

"She can't see?" said a husky female voice close by.

Sherry froze. That would be the tall African American federal agent David was infatuated with. When Birdy had passed through David's head once, Sherry had seen the woman through David's eyes—younger, exotic, beautiful. Sherry had almost wished David would go off with her then, take the children, run far away so that Birdy would have to come to Sherry and leave the others alone.

True insanity.

For now, as David walked her gently back to sit on the bed, Sherry realized, in a way that made her entire insides squeeze together, she could not live without him. She loved him. From the first time she'd seen him literally lose his balance and fall for her outside that South of Market eatery. Then it had been for his sensitivity and wild imagination. But since then, she'd unconsciously relied on his determination to do what was right, his ability to adapt and change and shape himself for what he (mistakenly) believed were the needs of their family. She'd grown roots into these traits, into this man. They were the base that had let her stretch back towards work without fear of falling.

But now what did she have to give *him*? Her body was still a close shell around her, so traumatized it would not let her out however much she might think and feel inside. She was blind and dumb. She desperately...*wanted* to move, to apologize to David for all her disappointments in him, but...she could not. She wanted to smile at him and kiss him like the woman she had once been. Wanted...

She managed a single tear. It welled up in her blank eyes and slid down from her left one, hanging for a moment on the underside of her jaw until David reached up and wiped it off.

"It's going to be okay," he said. "Birdy's ghost *is* real. Luka's ghost that you saw following Birdy? He's real too. He's got some kind of hooks into Birdy but it seems like he needs us out of the way before controlling her completely. Do you understand?"

With great effort she managed to blink once.

There was a pause, then, "Do you hate your children?" David asked.

Sherry felt a surge of hope and blinked twice, hoping he would ask if she hated *him*. Or even better, if she loved him.

"Does two plus two equals five?"

She swallowed and blinked twice. No.

"Okay, Sherry. Listen. Me and the kids are here with an Hawaiian witch doctor and some federal agents—don't ask me to explain—who are going to walk us out of here just as soon as they say we're clear. Can you walk?"

One blink.

"Good."

It sounded like he was about to say more, but Josh's voice suddenly squeaked up from just to Sherry's left. "Dad? Luka's coming. Kind of like...hovering."

And from out in the hallway, the brisk sound of the Mexican FBI man. "Shit, people. We got company."

37

IN THE SECOND IT TOOK ME to process the shout from Ramirez, events splattered.

A smell like rotting garbage exploded through the padded room and Sherry flung me to the side so I stumbled and fell off the bed.

She spun, fully-sighted, and grabbed Josh's arm with a grip that made him yelp in pain. Her face whipped back towards me and even in the red dark I could see the malice. It wasn't Sherry any more.

At the same time there was a visceral *WHOOMP!* and crashing sound like a concrete wall somewhere close had been blown open with a bazooka. Ramirez screamed something but I didn't catch it because I was scrambling after Josh. He was biting his mother's arm through her sweater. Luka, possessing her, refused to notice.

Then Martha jumped on Sherry/Luka from behind and jerked back on her long hair. Gunfire from the corridor made me twitch my face back towards the door but I still saw Josh yank free and drop down to grab his mother's legs.

I reached Sherry/Luka and drove her back to the wall; Martha jumped to the side so as not to get caught. The walls were padded but the impact still knocked the breath out of her.

"Son of a *bitch*, is what you are," I said and saw Luka snarl at me from behind Sherry's face. "No mother. Killed your father. Dysfunctional prick." *Get out of her. Go on, get out!*

Before Luka could make her fight back, I yanked her/him off, spun her around, and side-kicked her in back of her knees so she folded and fell face first.

More gunfire from the corridor.

Yelling in Spanish.

Female cries—residents waking. Shouts.

I fell on top of Sherry and grabbed both her wrists. Fighting to ignore who my eyes said this was, I used one of my hands to pin my captive's hands together behind her back. The stench of her wasn't Sherry. With my free arm I wrapped up the struggling legs and jerked them into me so her slippers came off and I had her bowed backwards and helpless.

"Feel...familiar?" I grunted.

I jabbed my mouth down to her ear to whisper lies about Luka's mother so filthy I couldn't let Josh and Martha hear. And bringing it back to him always. How it made him nothing. Made him less than nothing. Stink. Unloved. Excrement.

Bullets thudded into walls, Ramirez and Gale yelled at me, but I didn't hear any of it. I kept whispering foulness into my captive's ear. Pushing him. Feeling his rage grow and his control slip. Harder for him to hold on. I shoved images at him I'd never have considered thirteen months ago.

Then I heard Josh shriek, "Dad!" and I pulled back as I felt the familiar tide of nausea. Then, like with Gale only hours before, it felt like I was vomiting a giant slug.

And Luka was gone.

"Yes!" I cried and released Sherry with shaky hands.

A burst of machine-gun fire tore chunks out of the doorjamb to the corridor.

Suddenly gunfire ripped back and forth like a fireworks. Everyone on the floor seemed awake, screaming and pounding on doors. I hoped the residents were locked in their rooms.

"Get to the right of the opening!" I shouted to Martha and Josh. I grabbed Sherry up and dragged her with me as she sobbed, blind again, and shook her hands back and forth.

"Again! Again! Again!" she cried, at least no longer mute.

"It's not! It's different this time!" I shouted at her. "We're winning. We'll make it!"

The screams that started up over the crack and clatter of bullets made me doubt it. I considered darting forward to grab the open room door and close it, but risked a quick look out first and almost swallowed my tongue. Goddamn it! Some idiot had opened the residents' doors. The disturbed women were running out in their nightgowns and getting shot to shit. Falling in clumps. Blood bubbling all over. Ramirez and Gale had managed to kick in the door opposite us and were taking turns swinging out to fire. Their targets were somewhere in the stairs end of the corridor, now a hazy mess of rubble, smoke, and gunmen. No bazooka blasts, though. The bad guys obviously wanted someone alive at the end of all this.

Where was Weki?

"Yes, *not* again. *Not* again," Sherry whimpered behind me as she clutched and reclutched the back of my sweatshirt. So she'd heard me. Somewhere behind those blank eyes was my wife. My life. We had to make it through. I deserved a chance to save her, to save Birdy, to make things right again.

Don't deserve nothing! screamed a male voice in my head. A ghost. Some ghost stuck to this place.

Unfair! Unfair poopy you! Another.

I shook my head to block them out because they frightened me. I could sense they weren't new ghosts from the mounting body count out there. They were old ghosts, some very old. Something about the gunfire and screaming was charging them up, bringing them *up*. Luka?

"Josh," I called back over my shoulder. "You sense any—?"

I was cut off by a throaty old voice from down the corridor, towards the stairs.

"Hey, Ray! Merco!" it shouted. "Hey, Brah!"

Weki? The guns stopped, which only made it easier to hear the screams and death cries.

When I darted a look, I wanted to tear out there myself. The old fool was standing in the middle of the corridor. Nearly a dozen dead or dying women lay around him. One male orderly writhed there too; he must have come up a back way. Weki held up his two hands with his *hei* all meshed about the fingers. I doubted it could stop a bullet.

"D-Dad, who are the guys shooting at us?" whispered Martha.

I pulled back in and looked at her. I'd forgotten she and Josh weren't up on this whole Weki side of our adventure.

But a voice down the corridor near the stairs answered before I could. It was more heavily accented than Ramirez's, with a coldness to it that told me everything I needed to know about its owner.

"Hey, old man," it called. "My boys told me someone called the cops on them. A little voice said in my head said it might be you, hunh?"

"No!" shouted Ramirez across hall from me. "That would have been me, shithead. You're under arrest, by the way."

"Sure thing, *bacalao*, but I'm talking to my man, Weki now, hokay?"

"No, it's not, *chapero*!" Ramirez yelled back.

Weki stopped it by clearing his throat and saying, "I know where Luka is."

I blinked and frowned back over my shoulder again. Josh's eyes were growing wider, like he saw something bad. "Daddy..."

Then I smelled the stink again and reached back to grab Sherry's wrist. No! But it wasn't coming from her this time. And it wasn't just the stink of rotting garbage either. It had a burning smell, like something exploding over and over.

I ripped my gaze back to the corridor where I saw a light growing in the middle of it just a few feet down the hall between me and Weki. It washed over my face and I felt heat. Growing hotter.

Weki raised his *hei* up high. Across from me I saw Gale squint hard. Ramirez rubbed his eyes and shook his head. Even the moans of the dying quieted.

The light filled the whole corridor now, buzzing, crackling, glaring over the walls and driving off all shadow, so that when I darted my head out to look back towards the blasted rubble end, the entire tableaux was lit like a summer day. Standing forward in the middle was a short man holding a large pistol, clearly the leader. Ray Aznar, I presumed. His acne-scarred face glistened with sweat and dust. His oiled hair shone like a helmet. Around him cowered four others, two of them obviously shot, but all still aiming their guns.

A harsh, grinding sound snapped my eyes back to squint at the center of the light as the sound became a high-pitched whine and a shape formed. Four feet tall. The only one it could possibly be. My youngest child. Birdy.

But, God, she looked like she was in agony. Her long hair and clothes danced and snapped about her like she was a living lightning bolt. She had screwed her eyes shut, tightened her mouth to a slit, trying to hold it all together.

"What is it?" said Sherry behind me, scared into coherence, still clutching my shirt.

"It's Birdy," I said.

"That's not Keawe!" shouted Aznar and waved his gun.

"You wait!" shouted Weki from the other end of the hall, but I had the sense he was calling it to me. A warning.

I didn't need one. I could smell the garbage stink that had snuck in under the burning. A part of me wanted to run to my little daughter. The rest hunted madly with my ghost-sense, trying to pin where Luka was setting down.

It wouldn't be Sherry or my kids or me. We *knew* him now. We'd thrown him out. For the same reason, he wouldn't go after Gale. But Weki? Or Ramirez across from us?

Then Sherry helped what had probably been Luka's plan all along. With a shove that tumbled me sideways into the hall, she bolted past and dove towards the form she must have heard or felt...only to pass right through her.

Sherry tumbled down to the floor against the far wall, stunned, blind, too far along for Gale to reach her, and openly in the line of fire. "Stay here," I ordered Martha and Josh and prepared to run for her.

Aznar's voice stopped me. Or should I say, Luka's voice through Aznar's lips.

THE OTHER SIDE

37

"YOU SEE, KAHUNA?" Luka/Aznar called down the corridor. "The spell works! You thought I was *hûpô o nâ hûpô* to believe you, but the spell works! I got just one more person to kill!"

So saying, the possessed Aznar turned and in quick succession shot three of his men before the fourth recovered from shock enough to fire back. But by then Aznar had dashed sideways. The man missed; Aznar shot him.

He spun back to crow down the hallway. "Eleven dead! You think that enough? No! She not be changing, yeh? Need something more, yeh? Final push?"

He started walking forwards.

Ramirez threw himself out of his doorway to fire at Aznar, but Luka must have felt it coming, because he had Aznar's gun shooting once, twice, thrice before Ramirez could get a bead. Two of the shots hit. Ramirez thudded down with a grunt almost at my feet.

I saw Gale reloading her hefty-looking gun across the hall from me, her face intense.

"Luka!" I yelled.

"Shut it, *mahu!*" roared Aznar and fired at the doorframe, making me jerk back. I saw Birdy's light-form jerk, her eyes open wide and stare at me, then at Aznar. The possessed man was almost to our door now but had his gun aimed at the opening where Gale was hidden. I waved my hands madly at her to stay back.

"Birdy," Luka/Aznar said in a suddenly honied voice. "Little gate. I know you can't move right now. Too tough, yeh?"

My gaze flicked to Birdy and I realized it must be true. She was here. She was still herself, however crackling with energy. But she no longer had control. Nothing but her face had moved since she'd appeared, even with all that Luka had threatened us.

An old female resident who'd been standing, stunned like most of them down near Weki, suddenly howled and ran towards Aznar. He shot her through Birdy's light form but had the gun back on Gale's entrance before the old woman realized she was hit and pitched forward.

"Bastard," Martha whispered behind me.

"Don't, Martha," Josh pleaded.

I held out my hand to block her, but Martha knew she was as trapped as the rest of us. We weren't going anywhere.

"So here's what we do. I know I got at least one bullet left in here, little gate. But I'm going to let you choose who I kill. It be either you mother or you father."

Birdy's eyes went wide and rolled from me to Sherry—Sherry had finally pulled herself up to sitting, huddled blindly against the far wall, her knees drawn up with her arms clutched tightly around her them— and back again. My little girl's strained face quivered and she opened her mouth just enough to squeak out, "No."

"Oh, yes, little gate. Or I will kill both. You know I will. *Choose.*"

I longed to run to her and grab her, shield her from this animal who'd already killed her once and now was brutalizing her again. But I was as helpless now as the first time, because he didn't need to touch her body at all, just her mind, and how could I...?

"M-ma...," Birdy was stuttering. Stopping. Flinging wretched eyes at me. "D-d-d..."

"CHOOSE!" Luka/Aznar roared.

"I...I..." Birdy's lips were trembling, making her whole body shake. She was losing form! Her arms were starting to split open! Just as I'd rocked Luka, he was killing my daughter *again*.

And it came to me. The choice was killing her. One parent lived, one died, because of her. There was a way to take that choice away.

With a snapped, "Stay!" to the children behind me, I shot from my doorway and ran straight at Luka/Aznar, seeing him raise his gun towards, his surprised face, everything, in slow motion.

Kill me, damn it!

And then a double gunshot, Aznar's going wide, tearing my shoulder, as I hit him, and Birdy screamed, wrapping the whole corridor in a crackling explosion of light.

38

So close to the light explosion, and already in motion after shooting Aznar, Sweetness was struck blind and deaf.

She still did a clean drop and roll across the stone floor and came up with her gun trained in Aznar's direction, a two hand grip. She blinked her eyes furiously.

Red to purple to gray with stars, and she could finally see again, the sound muffled. Aznar was down. David was on top of him. Dead?

No, David fumbled himself off him and stared dazedly at the bloody mess that was once the right side of Aznar's face. Whether from the sight or from finding himself still alive, David dropped to his hands and knees to puke soundlessly beside the body.

Then his head jerked up. Whipped around.

But he wasn't looking at Sweetness. He was staring in horror at a black shape sliding past her to her left. The smell of rotting garbage went with it.

"No-o-o!" David cried and he scrambled to his feet.

"Daddy!" Martha or Josh called from somewhere.

Sweetness wanted to call too, but had to clear her head because something was not right. David and his children's cries had been like calls from a deep well. And that shape... As Sweetness squinted to see the black shape David now ran after, she saw it shift and flow like a man of water. A man of water running into the sun. In the middle of the corridor.

David reached it. Ran through it. Vanished into the sun.

Sweetness blinked again and the blazing sun condensed once more to the little girl, David's Birdy.

Sound and physical feeling came back in a rush and Sweetness swallowed hard. She swung her Desert Eagle quickly around the corridor to check for live combatants. None. So she refocused on the weirdness, crouch-walking slowly that way.

The girl floated now, rigid in the air, eyes wide, being held aloft by the gentle fingers of the inky-water man. Yet even in her weightlessness, she seemed to flicker in and out of color and solidity, dipping towards the floor as if she suddenly had mass. How would Dr. Angela explain this one? And the way the all the walls and floor and ceiling around them now seemed to shift, wobble in and out of transparency, a great void of space beyond.

David was there too, swiping his arms through his daughter and the water man, shouting some kind of chant, unfamiliar words. Something Weki Naea had taught him? Not working. Sweetness paused as David roared in frustration and dropped to pound the floor with his fists.

"Let her go, you son of a bitch! Son of a whore! Your mother was a whore, Luka! She never loved you! Your girlfriend, Jennifer? She laughed at you! You think she loved you? You think you were her first? You weren't! You *weren't!*"

Then he was sobbing, "Let her go. Please God, let her go! I'll do anything. Take me instead. Make me your gate!"

And Sherry Friesen was crawling towards him, blinking rapidly like her sight was returning. Why? Was David hurt enough now that she didn't have to do the sympathy play?

Sweetness cut the jealous thought off as the inky water man began to move. Pushing Birdy's floating form ahead of him, he walked through the dead and wounded towards the closed door past the room David had identified earlier as Sherry's. He didn't stop, though. He pushed his ghost prize through it and stepped lightly after her.

Vanished.

"No!" yelled David and sprung to his feet. Brushing his wife off him, he ran to the closed door, tried the knob, and found it unlocked. "God damn security," he said, laughing crazily.

He lunged through it and up a flight of stairs that must have led to the roof.

Martha and Josh had run to their mother, helped her up and were hugging her and sobbing furiously.

Okay, then.

Sweetness double-checked that her gun was cocked and locked, then trotted to the stairs and up after David and the ghosts.

39

*I*T WAS A ROOFTOP AGAIN, I noted as I stumbled out onto the gravel platform that edged the sloping red clay tiles. The bastard liked heights.

Except here I was almost twice as high as our rooftop at home. The steep peak of the roof had to be a good sixty or seventy feet up.

And I didn't give a fuck. I was not going to look down. I was not going to let Luka mess with my mind or my daughter's. Weki's chant hadn't managed to bind Birdy to me. My one surprise weapon gone. But I didn't care. I was *not* going to lose her again. Not this time.

"Luka!" I yelled and saw him.

He was, of course, up on the peak, and appeared to be holding Birdy above his head like some kind of beacon. To see what? Do what?

I didn't care. Swallowing the sour vomit that lingered in my mouth from earlier, I stepped over the edge of the gravel platform onto the tile and began climbing. It was cool and dry and my running shoes slipped minimally on my way up. At the top, though, one of the tiles came loose and chinked and banged down the side, whanking off the edge of the roof and falling for a sickeningly long time before it shattered on the front stones below.

"David!" someone called from below. Gale?

I ignored her. I was straddled across the roof, hands sweaty, heart pounding in my ears. Twenty feet ahead of me, I knew Luka was now a fully independent ghost, Birdy suspended in front of him.

The only difference between a year ago and now, I thought as I forced my feet under me to walk one foot at a time on either side of the peak, was that this time Luka and Birdy were already dead. They couldn't get deader. I could.

Fuck it, I told myself. *Fuck* it.

I was almost there. I raised my head. What I saw made my shaking knees weave inwards so I fell to a straddle.

The night, the universe around us, had changed. Instead of there being stars only above us, I could see them all around us. Orbs. Energy spheres. They floated through the trees, walked the silent back gardens and front drive. Two police cars were racing through the forest towards the White Pines, their lights and sirens going.

Far, far too late.

"Show me," the dark form of Luka demanded and shook Birdy's luminous form like a rag doll before he spun her over in his hands and slapped her.

And I *heard* it. I swear I did. Solid flesh to flesh.

But the next second everything I saw and heard changed, my whole perceptual field, bending and rushing, expanding in impossible ways so that I could see my house in Richmond, downtown San Francisco. I could also see a shoreline of sharp rocks, stretches of sand in moonlight, floating, multicolored fish, a silent resort pool and cabana up the slope.

And downtown Los Angeles.

And New York.

And a rolling green field somewhere.

A rocky summit.

This, I understood, was the way the dead saw. Distance was meaningless.

Or was it only what *Luka* saw? For the sights kept shifting as I watched, darting and stopping, sunshine to night, finding more orbs but coherent forms too, ghosts clinging to the world or lost in it, not knowing how to leave.

The shifts grew faster, jerkier, and I felt Luka's frustration as he blasted the field wider and wider to somehow encompass it all, the whole world at once. His power through Birdy became a giant wail of demand that wrenched at the fabric of things as if to rip it apart.

Unwillingly, I became part of him, felt the little boy lost, motherless. I wandered on the sands outside Lahaina and, in Luka's remembered mind, brewed bloody revenge. Summoned birds to me. Insects. People. Until I saw a vision of beauty in a pink bikini that smiled with teeth like rounded white shells and a silver laugh.

I held up the vision and swept it through the world before me, looking for its match, demanding it to appear, making orbs flicker to coherence and coherent ghosts wail with physical pain as I rushed past. The stumbling pain of living again.

Pain.

Physical pain.

Luka's gut-wrenching pain of loss and need drove my mind free of his and I dropped forward flat on the roof peak with my eyes squeezed shut. I clenched my fingers on the tiles. Felt the sharpness and drew in a hard breath of air. It drove me forward, crawling inch by inch, until I was right there. In the same space as him. I could *feel* his filth and terrible bleak anger like an icy whirlwind around my head.

"She's...not...out there," I said into it.

"Aghhh!" Luka roared and the force of him slammed down on me, like his foot on my back, driving me into the tile.

"There's...no one there to bring back," I said.

"*Kokahele ia paka!*"

"No one. It's all for nothing. You're alone."

"No!"

The pressure on my back increased so I could hardly breathe, but I forced my face up and saw he still held Birdy, her face towards him in that terrible, silent scream. But Luka was breaking apart too. Chunks of blackness flying off him, features losing shape even as he roared at me. "Jennifer-r-r!"

With a desperate effort, I forced my hands into the tile, my knees, my toes, and I pushed. The force on my back increased and my shot shoulder burned but they could not drive me down. Not this time.

Not. This. Time.

Then my feet were under me and my arms wrapped around Luka's disintegrating form. Crusts of sewage and rot, humming in and out of solidity, like it was becoming part of me. I gulped it. I swallowed it as I clawed my way up him, trying to rip him apart faster. Because if I could only take him apart *now*, if I could wrest Birdy from him before she—

A whoomf around my head, and my body exploded in pain, thrown staggering backwards across the peak of the roof. My feet stumbled, slipped, I fell. My hands shot out and grabbed either side of the peak as my body dropped and skidded down one side.

"Get up!" Luka screamed at me.

I scrabbled to comply. With my feet under me, I saw his lips stretched so far back on his angular face he was a spitting black skull—not alive, but not dead either. Something else. Something brighter and more terrible. Siphoning off the light that was once my daughter. Feeding on her pain.

As she, face stretched in terror, grew darker, pale, heavy.

Save me, Daddy!

"Give her...to me," I said.

"*Give* her?" the Luka-thing shrieked.

"There's...nothing for you...here. Nothing. No one. Give her back to me. Please."

His teeth chattered at me. Knots popped out along his neck. His legs seemed to grow and shrink—six feet, two, four. Arms stretched to the vistas of the world then snapped back to himself, still holding Birdy. Still holding her.

"I not only make the dead living with this puppet!" he screamed and shook her. "I make the living *dead*!"

So saying, he clutched the front of Birdy's now-dingy teddy bear jeans and tee-shirt, hoisted her over his head, and, as his body started to crumble, threw her at me!

Even as she left his hands I could see his form starting to break up, come apart. Then Birdy hit with a thud. I clutched at her physical body, stumbled backwards, and she dissolved into me. In shock, I slipped sideways, cracked my head on the tiles, and tumbled.

40

D ADDY!" I think someone screamed from somewhere far away. And I think a strong hand grabbed me, my body whipping in a rolling arc.

As my world tumbled into blackness.

~~~~

And I was floating in a great void. Cold. Before me was Birdy, my blond haired angel. She was no longer in agony, but her face was so sad and gray, her eyes wet, her small mouth turned down, that my own eyes welled up too.

I held out my arms, but she shook her head.

"It's no good, Daddy."

"What, darling."

"Everything."

I cocked my head, momentarily stunned into silence. Was that the final perversion, then? To teach my little optimist that the world was shit? Because she'd seen both sides, hadn't she—the love and the pit?

She should know.

And that was the end Luka had given me—making living things... dead.

Only...one little thing.

Birdy hadn't seen all sides. She'd seen childhood and she'd seen loss. Like I had, a long time ago. But I'd been lucky enough to grow up, to survive long enough to find Sherry, to find my children. I'd learned you *could* find good after bad. If you were open to it. If you looked hard enough for it. If you cared.

But how did you communicate that to a child? To a hurt, vulnerable child?

Somehow willing my feet to find purchase, to *make* a ground under both of us, I knelt down, held my arms open wide towards her and spoke firmly.

"Come here, Birdy."

"Why?" She sucked her lips in like Martha and Sherry did.

"Because I need to tell you something."

She hesitated, but finally stepped forward into my arms. I wrapped them around her and buried my face into her hair. "Just this, darling. Only this. Me and Mommy? We love you completely. We have always loved you. We will always love you."

Once more I felt her melt into me, as if she needed to know for sure.

A moment later the warmth of her joy spread through me and I felt my chest swell as if my heart had decided to start beating again.

~~~~

"David!" a sharp, husky female voice demanded. "David! You did it! Weki says he's gone now! Truly gone!"

More voices. Clanking sounds. My body lifted onto something. Moving fast. Medical babble about atropine, bagging me, anaesthetic.

~~~~

Daddy. I couldn't see her but felt the hope in her voice.

What, darling?

I love you too, she said, fading for what I knew was the last time.

And Mommy, Martha, Joshie. Tell them for me.

~~~~

I half-woke up in the ambulance and saw Sherry's face weaving back and forth above me. Seeing me.

"Sh," she said. "Sh."

"Remind me," I murmured, swimming down. "Something to tell you."

41

THREE WEEKS LATER, when the coffin of Francisco Ramirez was lowered and the dirt was being shoveled on, I stepped over briefly to the FBI crowd and pulled Gale to one side.

"I never thanked you properly," I said.

She looked at me and quirked up one side of those beautiful scarred lips. "For what? Saving your ass from Aznar, from Luka on the roof, or from all the confused S.O.B.s who wanted to pin every unexplained crime in the last decade on your head?"

"Yeah, those. But more for the earlier stuff. Sticking with me when everyone else thought I was crazy."

"I thought you were crazy."

I shook my head at her. "Thank you anyway."

I turned back to where my kids waited, Sherry still needing hospital time, and took five steps before Sweetness called out, "Hey!"

I turned. "What?"

"You know there's still a shitload of stuff that's going to come out of that night in White Pines."

"Yeah."

"Okay." I turned to go and she called me one last time.

I waited.

"You take care of your wife and kids, okay?"

This time she left first, turning and walking quickly to join her colleagues. Her mother hadn't shown up.

I got back to Josh and Martha, asked Martha to wait for a bit by herself, and walked Josh with me to a more secluded part of the cemetery. There I looked around carefully to make sure no one else was watching. No one to see me except my son.

"What, Dad?"

"Pick a grave, Josh."

He pointed to a small, square headstone that looked like a scaled-down version of one my father might have carved.

"Okay," I said. "I've got no idea what they did with Luka's real body and I don't want to know, but this is now officially his grave. Join me in a tribute to him."

I unzipped my fly, and with Josh staring, agog, I stepped up to the mound in front of the selected tombstone, pulled out my penis, and peed a long yellow stream all over the grass and flowers there.

~~~~

Sixteen months after that, after my dad's funeral, after the White Pines charges and lawsuits were all settled out of court by the Bureau, after Martha and Josh had made it through another year of school with trauma counseling thrown in, and October winds were blowing leaves like tornadoes along the streets of downtown San Francisco, the kids drove Sherry home from the hospital.

To our new home, that is.

I'd found a place on the outskirts of Sausalito, of all places, shouting distance from Rose and Gunther. It was less pretentious than our last place, old and a bit rambling. This wasn't from lack of money, because Rajiv's wife somehow "lost" the agreement I'd signed that sold Rajiv my half of the company. Instead, she got her life insurance and had me to manage the sale of the business (more valuable with me attached) for a sum that would keep both her and me quite comfortable for years. Not to mention the fact that I was staying on as adviser. A part of me really enjoyed the clean logic of the work.

No, the reason for the new house aesthetic had more to do with the studio in the back with its plentiful light.

"You're going to show me what?" Sherry laughed as we walked her to the front door blindfolded. "I've seen so many pictures of this place..."

"Front step," I said and waited as she stepped up nervously. God, she looked beautiful. The autumn light made her red hair crackle like fire; the gray in it now made it shot through with character. I remembered why I had loved her so fiercely once, and was pretty sure I would again.

I creaked open the front door—have to oil that—and led her in, stopped her in the entryway/living room, and removed her blindfold.

"It's beautiful!" she said as she took in the room.

"Not that, Mom," Martha sighed, and turned her to look at the wall beside the front door.

I held my breath.

The painting, maybe my eighteenth or nineteenth one in the mad rush of rediscovery I'd gone through, hung in a simple gold-rubbed, wooden frame. It was of Birdy. I hadn't followed any photographs we had exactly, merely used them as double-checks to my memory. I'd debated putting in a subtle light from above because that had, after all, been how she'd gone out. I also knew it would give Sherry's religious beliefs a bit of confirmation.

In the end I left it out. I wanted it to be just Birdy, how she was. I hoped it was enough.

Sherry's eyes shone and she grabbed Martha's sleeve to dab them before her daughter grabbed it back, saying, "Mom!"

Still sniffing, Sherry laughed, and squeezed my arm long and hard enough so I could feel her true reaction. "Yes," she said. "Now can I see the rest of the house?"

~~~~